VEI

A big semi-truck ▭ ▭ ▭ ▭ ▭ stopped, the driver's side door opening and a figure pulling out what looked like an old M72 LAW, shouldering the tube before he was even out of the cab.

David hauled the wheel over, almost rolling the vehicle, as the guy in the cab fired the LAW. The rocket slammed past us, missing the rear of the Land Rover by inches, exploding against the low wall alongside the road. I caught a glimpse of the truck's cab filling with smoke as shattered glass cascaded to the pavement.

Unfortunately, this had been better planned than we'd expected. Two SUVs swerved across the road to block the lane right in front of us. We were boxed in.

The traffic around us scattered like quail, as the SUV doors opened and several men piled out, one of them putting an MG4 in the "V" of the door and opening fire.

Muzzle flash strobed in the gap, and our windshield starred and clouded as bullets rained against the front of the Land Rover, hitting with a thunderous chorus of brutal *thud*s and *bang*s. "Get down!" I reached back to shove Gorman as low as possible even as David ducked below the steering wheel and stomped on the gas.

They weren't expecting us to charge them. The machinegun fire slackened suddenly, and David yelled, "Hold onto your nuts!" Then we hit.

POWER

VACUUM

MAELSTROM RISING BOOK 8

Peter Nealen

Prologue

New Russian Military Exercises in Serbia

Recent reports indicate that what appears to be an entire Russian airborne battalion from the 7th Guards Air Assault Division has entered Serbia and is conducting joint exercises with the Serbian Army near the Hungarian border. So far, there have been no border crossings, but there are reports of live fire near the border. Hungarian Defense Forces are on high alert.

Serbian relations with the West soured considerably following the Fourth Balkan War, in which Western forces intervened in the dispute between Serbia and Kosovo for the second time. The aftermath of that war saw Serbia drawn far more firmly into Russia's orbit.

With Russian forces pushing along the borders of Slovakia and Poland, ostensibly to create a "security buffer zone" between Russian-occupied territory and the war that erupted in Slovakia last year, this new movement presents a matter of some grave concern.

Chinese Naval Forces Shift Focus

Following reports of violence on and around the Spratly Islands in the South China Sea, including the reported—though vehemently denied by PLAN spokesperson Bai Guanting—

sinking of several PLAN destroyers and severe damage done to the PLAN aircraft carrier *Shandong*, it appears that the People's Liberation Army Navy has, for the most part, withdrawn from the South China Sea, leaving the bulk of the Spratly Islands to the Philippines.

Beijing insists that this is and will remain only a temporary redeployment of forces, due to growing Japanese naval activity in the Senkaku Islands and off the coast of Taiwan. Bai Guanting did allow that there had been an uptick in what he called terrorist and pirate activity in the South China Sea, aimed at legitimate Chinese security operations. However, he insisted that the terrorists were being dealt with and that there is no correlation between that activity and the redeployment north, closer to the mainland Chinese coast.

Increased Chinese Presence in Kashmir and Pakistan

While a series of bombings and growing violence between not only Pakistan and India, but also Pakistani authorities, the Pakistani Taliban, and Lashkhar e Taiba has been cited as the reason for the increased security presence of PLA soldiers in Pakistan, some analysts believe that China is making a move to completely control lines of communication through Central Asia, particularly after the recent withdrawal of PLAN forces from the Spratly Islands.

It does appear that most of the Chinese security forces in Pakistan and Kashmir are concentrated along railroad and ground transportation routes, as well as protecting the new oil pipeline coming from Karachi, as well as mineral routes out of Afghanistan. There are even reports of PLA Special Forces infiltrating into Afghanistan, ostensibly to advise local security forces of the Islamic Emirate of Afghanistan, though many analysts suspect they are moving in to strike at any threats to Chinese mining interests in that country.

While many deny its plausibility, especially given the ruggedness of the country in between, it appears that the

2

People's Republic of China is actively working to secure a new logistical route for strategic materials, separate from the Straits of Malacca and the South China Sea. Time will tell.

New Wave of Terror and Infrastructure Attacks Rock East Coast

Power went down across large swathes of New Jersey, Pennsylvania, West Virginia, and Ohio, as a cyber attack struck the RFC in conjunction with multiple bombing and arson attacks on major substations. Shortly thereafter, drone strikes on Capitol Hill in Washington DC killed three and temporarily forced lawmakers to take cover in a secure area. No one has taken responsibility for the attack, though Representative Claire Wolverton immediately called a press conference to call for further sanctions and the mobilization of the National Guard to quash the "right-wing terrorist militia" known as "The Triarii." Senator Trent Corwin, however, pointed out that it was Triarii counter-drone teams that kept the attack from being much worse.

Unrest, instability, supply chain and energy grid disruptions, as well as out-and-out terrorism continue to be facts of life for much of the United States, now a year after the cyber attacks that crippled nearly sixty percent of the power grid in the Lower 48. The worst part of this chaos, however, appears to be an ever-widening rift between states, as more and more Americans blame each other for the disruption and the violence.

Balkanization Continues to Harden in the Lower 48 States

While it could be argued that the United States has been in a cold civil war for the better part of a decade, it has always been a relatively low-intensity conflict, largely carried out on a social and political level—even if that "social level" included riots and mass demonstrations. For the most part, while there has been plenty of *political* warfare between various states and the federal government, it always stayed mostly within the realm of rhetoric and legal wrangling, if occasionally spilling over into the realm of economics, as state governments attempted to place boycotts on other states with different politics.

All of that has changed over the last two to three years. Not only has political violence intensified—and there is no mistaking the fact that, despite known foreign activity behind many of the terrorist incidents since the cyber attack last year, much of it has been fed by domestic organizations for political purposes—but the divisions between states have become far sharper.

With the non-governmental organization known as "The Triarii" taking on more and more local and interstate security tasks, and the country appearing to fall into "Triarii States" and "Federal States," this divide can only get worse.

Months after the Fall of Brussels, Europe still has no Peace

While it appeared that the war between the US and the European Defense Council ended with the capture or death of the permanent members of the Council itself, stability has not followed the fall of the EDC.

Crime is rampant throughout the former EDC countries, particularly Germany and France. An uneasy truce has been declared along the line running from Toulouse to Marseilles, while the Nouveau Gallia group refuses to stand down. Rumors abound of a separatist movement in Bavaria, while the crime wave throughout the rest of Germany hits new heights.

US Army spokesperson Major Jane Kinsey refused to consider parallels to Iraq from 2004 to 2007, insisting that the Army is working closely with the *Bundeswehr* and *Bundespolizei* to ensure stability and peace in the region, and that while the European Defense Council might be no more, the German government is still intact and working toward a new Europe, despite those rare opportunists who would try to use the chaos to further their own goals. While Major Kinsey did not specifically name Russia, the implications, given the growing Russian advances in Poland and eastern Slovakia, are unavoidable.

Chapter 1

I hate PSD work.

One of the benefits of being in the Grex Luporum teams is that we can be mobile and unpredictable, moving quickly and often invisibly through the AO to get the mission done. When the mission is to act as a Personal Security Detachment, escorting a public figure, though, especially one who might end up becoming the next Prime Minister of Germany, it gets harder to stay unpredictable.

Which was why I wasn't all that surprised when the lead vehicle blew up just short of the bridge over the Ochtum.

The armored Land Rover disappeared into a boiling black cloud that slammed out of the trees on the side of the road, the heavy *thud* of the detonation traveling through the ground toward us. I caught a glimpse of the vehicle a moment later, slewed halfway around with its back wheels against the median, the armored glass starred and a few hundred frag holes punched into the doors, as I keyed my radio.

"Contact, right." The Land Rover that had been hit cracked its doors, the Germans who formed the bulk of Wenzeslaus Gorman's official PSD sticking their MP7s out through the "V" and covering down on the flank the IED had hit them from. "Shift left, get off the X." I felt for Meyer and Shultz, but the skinny, balding man with the wire-framed glasses in the back of my vehicle was the mission.

David Reyes was driving our vehicle, and he didn't hesitate or ask questions. We all knew what needed to happen. As soon as Brian Hartrick had told us we'd be doing this, we'd practiced these sorts of scenarios until we could react to contact in our sleep.

After years of low-level warfare, and over a year of much more high-intensity warfare in Europe, we almost hadn't even needed to practice anymore.

Bouncing up and over the curb, he sped past the stricken Land Rover, the weight of additional armor bogging our own vehicle down somewhat on the damp grass and earth in the median. We dropped into the opposite lanes with a jarring series of impacts, the other three vehicles in the motorcade following, as Meyer and Schultz covered us. So far, they hadn't opened fire, which suggested that the attack was just the one IED.

I didn't necessarily buy it, especially given some of what had been going on in Germany over the last three months since the New European Council had been gutted on the day of its own inauguration ceremony.

We roared into oncoming traffic, but fortunately the explosion had halted that, as nobody in their right mind wants to drive into an IED kill zone. Most of the Germans are still mostly in their right mind, never mind the influx of Middle Easterners and Balkan Islamists, most of whom were pretty close to batshit crazy in my experience. Even the ones that *didn't* want to kill all the infidels. That meant we had a barrier of stopped vehicles in front of us, but we didn't need to worry so much about a head-on collision.

David still had to get onto the brick sidewalk to the side of the road, since there wasn't exactly a lot of room to maneuver, with both oncoming lanes taken up by traffic. We raced past two big BMW semi-trucks, then had to squeeze past a trio of sedans and smart cars to avoid hitting the light pole in the middle of the sidewalk.

Horns honked at us, but no more explosions rocked the midday bustle of Bremen, and I couldn't hear any small arms fire, either. Maybe it had just been the one IED.

For his part, Gorman was calm. This wasn't the first attempt on his life. It seemed that espousing common sense and a more decentralized Europe didn't make a man particularly popular among some of the more violent groups running around since the fall of the EDC.

Not least, the remnant of the European Defense Corps itself. They were still lurking around Chemnitz, still a threat, but one that nobody wanted to deal with. Least of all the US Army, which was currently busily repeating every mistake we'd made for the last thirty years as they tried to hold down the violence in Germany and France in the aftermath of the war.

Some of them were even still insisting that the war was over. The wreckage and rising smoke behind us suggested otherwise.

People yelled and more vehicles honked their horns as we kept moving along the sidewalk, pedestrians jumping out of the way. I twisted in my seat to check behind us, seeing the follow vehicles still all behind us and staying close. Probably too close, given the IED threat.

David found a gap at the intersection and stomped on the gas as he pulled the wheel over, getting us back on the southbound lanes as we passed a massive IKEA and headed out of the commercial section of town, making for the overpass that arced over the autobahn. The other vehicles followed, even as Gorman got on the phone. From the sounds of it, he was talking to Meyers and Schultz, making sure they were okay and could get clear.

That said good things about the man. Despite my general distrust of politicos, I had to admit that what I'd seen of Wenzeslaus Gorman over the last week had somewhat impressed me.

I started to tense up as we got closer to the overpass. It was a choke point, and while we were now almost half a mile away from the kill zone, and no follow up attack had hit us yet, that did not mean I was going to relax. We'd been through too much since everything had gone sideways in Slovakia the year before.

David was driving fast, probably right at the edge of where he could keep the heavy Land Rover under control. Up-armored SUVs tend to have an even higher center of gravity than most, and if you maneuver too quickly, you can lose it fast. David was a hell of a driver though, which was part of why he was driving and I was riding shotgun. Sure, I was the team leader, which meant I had to keep track of everything and run comms, but Tony was my assistant team leader since Scott had gone down on the back stairway of the European Defense Council building, and he wouldn't let Jordan drive the trail vehicle. He'd shoved his way behind the wheel himself as soon as we'd gotten ready to move out.

Scott's death still stung, months later. Along with Dwight's, and Phil's, and a lot of other people's.

We roared over the autobahn and kept going south. We'd planned on hitting the autobahn itself and heading east, toward Wildeshausen, where Gorman had his next meeting with several industrialists, but with the IED strike behind us, that plan was out the window. We kept going south, toward Brinkum.

"We've got a drone overhead." Jordan was keeping an eye out. I craned my neck to try to see, but the reduced interior space on the inside of the Land Rover thanks to the armor package, never mind the distortion brought on by the thickness of the laminated armored glass, meant I couldn't see much. It was a partly cloudy day, and the sun was shining brightly on us at the moment.

"Roger." I switched channels for a moment. "This is Deacon. I need some counter-drone coverage over Brinkum, time now."

"Deacon, this is Smiley." Don Charron was one of our recent recruits, having hit his end of service in the Army, which hadn't instituted a Stop/Loss for some unknown reason. Instead of heading home—which had been a bit of an issue with the airspace problems during the war—he'd joined up with us, and now he was holding down the Northern Germany TOC. "We've got a counter-drone swarm on the way, but it's going to be at least fifteen minutes."

"Roger." Nothing to be done about it. The logistics and the time and distance were what they were. We'd already known we'd be on the outside of what drone coverage we could manage before we'd left Hanover that morning. I switched back to the team net. Unfortunately, the vehicle didn't have a built-in radio—a major oversight, from my point of view—so we had to rely on our personal rigs, and the armor made those spotty.

We sped past Brinkum without incident, but that drone was still shadowing us. I got a glimpse of it as we went around the curve to the south of town. It didn't appear to be armed, or one of the warhead-bearing kamikazes we still had nightmares about after the battle for Nitra. But it didn't need to be. All it needed to do was tell the bad guys where we were.

"Is it still there?" Gorman had heard enough that he knew we were being followed.

"It's still there, sir. We've got countermeasures coming." I didn't look back at him, but kept my eyes forward, watching the road and our surroundings. The good news was, we were on a highway, and unless they had IEDs set in all over the place, just in case, we'd be difficult to ambush.

Didn't mean it was impossible, especially not with that damned drone up there.

"Should we take shelter until the drone is eliminated?" Gorman might be surprisingly common sensical for a pol, but he still wasn't a shooter, and he didn't understand a lot of this stuff.

"No, sir. That drone's probably sending a live feed to whoever's controlling it, so stopping and sheltering in place will only give them a stationary target." As the team leader, I was stuck doing most of the talking. David had to concentrate on the road, anyway.

We were moving fast, weaving through the traffic, which was still pretty thin for the time of day. At least, it seemed that way to me, but some things still hadn't stabilized in the New Germany. Or the New France, for that matter. That IED back there hadn't been a unique occurrence. A lot of people were still being very cautious on a day-to-day basis.

We almost made it. But the highway opened up a bit at the intersection with Delmenhorster Street, and that was where they hit us.

A big semi-truck pulled out into the intersection and stopped, the driver's side door opening and a figure pulling out what looked like an old M72 LAW, shouldering the tube before he was even out of the cab.

David hauled the wheel over, almost rolling the vehicle, as the guy in the cab fired the LAW. The rocket slammed past us, missing the rear of the Land Rover by inches, exploding against the low wall alongside the road. I caught a glimpse of the truck's cab filling with smoke as shattered glass cascaded to the pavement.

Unfortunately, this had been better planned than we'd expected. Two SUVs swerved across the road to block the lane right in front of us. We were boxed in.

The traffic around us scattered like quail, as the SUV doors opened and several men piled out, one of them putting an MG4 in the "V" of the door and opening fire.

Muzzle flash strobed in the gap, and our windshield starred and clouded as bullets rained against the front of the Land Rover, hitting with a thunderous chorus of brutal *thud*s and *bang*s. "Get down!" I reached back to shove Gorman as low as possible even as David ducked below the steering wheel and stomped on the gas.

They weren't expecting us to charge them. The machinegun fire slackened suddenly, and David yelled, "Hold onto your nuts!" Then we hit.

The impact rocked us, and I felt Gorman bounce off the seat behind me. I had braced myself, so I didn't hit the dash too hard. David kept the gas pedal down, but while the Land Rover with its ten thousand pounds of extra steel and composite outweighed the two civilian SUVs, we still hadn't been moving quite fast enough to shove them out of the way. We were stuck.

I'd already pulled the cover off my Wilson Combat SBR Tactical, and now I snatched it out of the gap between my seat and the center console. The need to stay somewhat low-profile— we were all in civilian clothes, for one thing, instead of our Triarii greens with the crossed-rifle patches—had precluded bringing our full-length LaRue OBRs on this op. So, while I would have preferred the full-power 7.62 NATO, the .300 Blackout was going to have to do the trick.

More bullets smacked into the laminate windshield, and I thought I heard an alarming *crack*. The armor wasn't going to hold up much longer. "On three!" I had my weapon in one hand, my other on the door handle.

"One!" David was just as ready, his own SBR tucked under his left arm, the muzzle pointed at the ceiling.

"Two!" I already had the door unlatched. Gorman was down on the floor in the back, doing what he was supposed to do. A different sort of principal might be freaking out right then, demanding to know what was going on, but again, this wasn't the first time someone had tried to kill Wenzeslaus Gorman.

"Three!" We threw our doors open at the same time, immediately dropping our weapons as we pushed out, fingers tightening on triggers before our muzzles had even come level.

As my vision cleared the smashed and clouded armored windshield, I spotted one of the shooters. Dressed in dark clothing and a black balaclava, he looked a little banged up, almost as if he'd been knocked down when we'd hit the crumpled Volkswagen Tiguan. He wasn't moving all that well as he tried to bring his MP5 up to shoot me.

He was far too slow. I Mozambiqued him from about ten feet away, my first two shots hitting so close together that they sounded like a single report, just before I blew a smoking hole between his eyes, knocking him over backward and out of sight.

The SBR Tactical was suppressed, but we were running the supersonic .300 Blackout rounds. There wasn't currently a lot of need for the subsonic, and the supersonic hit harder. The suppressors just meant we didn't need earpro.

I stepped out, using the vehicle as cover, even as David's rifle *crack*ed off to my left, and more fire poured into the SUVs from my right, as the rest of the motorcade set up and broke seal to lay down cover fire. I spotted the Tiguan's driver, looking a little dazed, as he tried to bring a G36 out to shoot at me through the cracked windshield. I shot him in the face, my first rounds going high and punching into his forehead as the glass diverted my rounds. Red spattered on the cracked and starred window glass.

Then I was rolling out as more bullets smashed into the attackers' SUV, a hail of 7.62 fire punching holes in metal and plastic and shattering more glass. Jordan must have hauled Tony's Mk 48 out of the back of the trail vehicle. We might have been rolling with lower profile weapons for the most part, but Tony hadn't been willing to cover a couple hundred miles of still-unsecure German territory without a belt fed.

Yanking the rear door open, I grabbed Gorman. "We've got to go!" Chris and Greg had pulled up in the next vehicle, and they already had the doors open, Greg yelling at us to get in.

Keeping Gorman's head down, I hustled him around the back of the smashed-up Land Rover. The front was riddled with bullet impacts, the hood and bumper crumpled from the collision with not just the Tiguan, but the older BMW next to it. The up-armored vehicles only had armor around the passenger compartment, not the engine.

Greg was shooting over his own open door at the SUVs. The man who'd fired the LAW at us lay on his face in the road under the semi's cab, red spreading slowly out onto the asphalt, a gaping exit wound in the back of his head.

David crossed to the second vehicle with us, still slamming rounds at the bullet-riddled SUVs. More glass cascaded onto the road, and a car alarm was whooping, as I piled into the back of Chris's and Greg's vehicle, dragging Gorman with me. David piled in a second later, slamming the door and yelling, "Go, go, go!"

Chris already had the vehicle in reverse as Greg slammed his own door shut rather than risk having it swing closed on his leg. He pulled back and started a J-turn to get us going back north.

Just as he got us turned around and heading back the way we'd come, though, as the other three vehicles in the motorcade started to turn to follow, three more big trucks came down the pike, turning to block the road only a hundred yards away, men piling out of the back to spread out around them, taking cover behind the vehicles and their trailers. The first shots *snap*ped past us, though they were shooting high, and hadn't struck the vehicle yet.

We were cut off.

Chapter 2

Almost cut off. Chris stomped on the brake and slewed the wheel over, throwing Gorman and David against me as I was crushed against the inside of the door. A moment later, he stomped on the gas again, struggling slightly against the sluggish weight of the armored vehicle, roaring up Am Pumpwerk, around the back of the "Autohaus" at the intersection. The other vehicles followed, chased by bullets and at least one rocket, which skipped off the pavement, as the idiot shooting it apparently tried to compensate for recoil that wasn't there.

We didn't get far, though. A black UAZ Hunter roared out into the middle of the road in front of us, the doors flying wide and an HK21 sticking out through the "V" of the door on the right. The machinegun opened up with a ripping, staccato thunder.

The gunner wasn't very good, fortunately, and rounds sailed over our vehicle with a snarling crackle, but this wasn't going to end well. We *might* be able to push past that Hunter, but then a moment later, two more shooters with LAWs came around the back.

We weren't going to dodge those rockets, even if they flinched.

"Get out, get out, get out!" David and I kicked our doors open before the vehicle had even stopped moving, and I dragged Gorman out with me as I dove for the side of the road. Chris wasn't far behind, dragging his go bag and his own SBR with him.

A moment later, one of the LAW rockets hit with *boom*, the vehicle rocking as smoke and frag blasted from the grill. A faint flash blasted through the interior, as the High Explosive Anti-Tank round blew a plume of superheated plasma through metal, plastic, and ceramic. It was followed a moment later by a second blast as the other LAW hit. The Land Rover started to burn.

I was already hauling Gorman through the bushes next to the road and toward the "Autohaus." Momentarily letting my weapon hang on its sling, I keyed my radio. "Smiley, Deacon. We have troops in contact, motorcade disabled, at…" I looked up at the building, but there was no sign.

"This is the T&R Ihr Autohaus, on the intersection of Hauptstraße 3 and Am Pumpwerk." Gorman was clearly scared, but he was keeping his head.

I passed the information along. Since the war had started, GPS had been entirely too unreliable for anything more than about a grid square level of accuracy. Which wasn't going to help us when we were waiting for our QRF. "We are strongpointing in the Autohaus. Be advised, the enemy has anti-tank rockets and at least one drone."

"Good copy, Deacon. QRF is spooling up as we speak. Fifteen minutes." Smiley had proved himself over the last couple of months and easily a dozen incidents, though so far, we hadn't seen anything this serious since Strasbourg.

The Autohaus was a car dealership, and while there was a lot of glass in the front—much of it probably already shattered by concussion and gunfire—the back was mostly solid brick, with only a couple of doors, all metal and windowless. I hauled Gorman toward one of the back doors, passing the double line of cars parked close together in the back. Between the cars, the big outbuilding at the end of the row of bushes, and the couple of houses and outbuildings beyond that, we had some cover and concealment for a few seconds, giving us some breathing room.

I tried the door, but it was locked. That didn't last long. Reuben showed up with Tony and Jordan, dragging the trail vehicle's breacher kit, while the rest of Gorman's German PSD laid down 4.6mm fire past the vehicles, trying to keep the attackers suppressed while we found a way into the building.

Gorman straightened and knocked on the door, unwilling to just have us break it down right away. The gunfire continued to echo off the surrounding buildings, but it had slackened somewhat, as the attackers tried to maneuver, and Bachmann, Forney, and Häusler kept laying down cover fire.

I could appreciate Gorman's sentiment, but when you're under fire is hardly the time for sentiment. We could pay for the broken door later.

At any rate, nobody answered the door, to my complete lack of surprise. "Reuben, break it open."

My big secondary medic, whom the late Phil Kerr had called "the biggest Mexican I've ever seen," much to Reuben's displeasure—he'd insist he was "Texican," not "Mexican"—already had the Halligan tool in his hands, his SBR Tactical dangling from its sling in front of him, and he slammed the duckbill into the crack between the door and the jamb, throwing all his weight on the shaft as he wrenched on the door.

The door was metal-sheathed, and I could see this being harder than it looked, but again, Reuben was a *big* dude, and he was putting a lot of force on the Halligan, not only with just his weight. Pushing hard against the ground with his legs—and I'd seen what Reuben could squat—he strained, the veins popping on his neck as the door *crack*ed, then the latch tore through the metal jamb with a hellish shriek.

We were in.

I went in first, David on my heels, weapons level and clearing the corners. The door opened onto a short hallway, with what appeared to be offices on one side and utility rooms on the other. I half expected some of the attackers to be coming in the front, but for the moment, we had the back to ourselves.

I held on the hallway leading toward the showroom in the front while David and Chris stacked on the utility room door. I might have been able to hear noise from the front, gunfire and smashing glass, possibly shouts, but my hearing was so brutalized by years of gunfire, explosives, and helicopters that I couldn't be sure what was coming from in front and what was coming from the back, behind me, through the open door.

Chris reached around David and threw the door open. The two of them flowed in quickly, and I heard no gunshots. Stepping forward, I cleared the door as Greg, Reuben, Jordan, and Tony hustled Gorman inside behind me.

We needed to clear the building, but leaving Gorman outside where the bullets were flying was not going to be a good idea. I held on the hallway for a moment, until Jordan squeezed my elbow and said, "With you." Then I was moving, sidestepping to the door to the offices—there was a narrow window above the door handle, through which I could see the desks and computers—threw the door open, and went in.

Half a dozen people were huddled under the desks, peering over the tops and past the computers as we made entry, SBRs leveled, clearing our corners quickly before we moved to one wall, carefully checking the dead space beneath and behind each desk, scanning each worker, checking hands and demeanors, just in case someone there either decided to try to play hero, or else was on the bad guys' side.

Whoever the hell the bad guys were. The list of suspects in post-EDC Germany was pretty long.

"Everyone stay down!" Jordan had not been what I might have considered the team's go-to public relations man. Being the sole black man on the team, and also, due to his skin color, something of a rarity in some of the places we'd been lately, he'd been carrying a chip on his shoulder the size of an Abrams tank since long before I'd met him. I knew him well enough that I knew it wasn't entirely unjustified—the man had been recruited into the Triarii after his mother had been beaten to death by Fourth Reich neo-Nazis, after all—but it had been a constant thorn in my side, within the team as well as out. But he was mellowing a bit, and at the moment his tone was even and almost friendly. "We don't want to hurt anyone. We'll do what we can to keep you safe. But you have to stay down on the floor and stay in this room."

We hit the last of the offices. There was another door leading out into another hallway, and we stacked on it momentarily, as Jordan looked back over the frightened faces huddled behind or under the desks. "Lock this door, and *stay where you are*."

I led the way out into the hallway, and immediately found myself in a gunfight.

Even as I came out through the door, half a dozen men in dark clothing and balaclavas burst into the showroom. They were carrying a mix of MP5s, G3s, and what looked an awful lot like a G36. The man in the lead, the one with the G36 lookalike, sprayed bullets across the receptionist's desk as he ran through the doorway.

Their own noise and violence distracted them just long enough to give me a chance to start shooting before any of them had a shot at me. I dumped the guy with the G36-ish thing, hammering three rounds into him as fast as I could squeeze the trigger, the red dot tracking slightly up the side of his torso with the recoil. My suppressed .300 Blackout was downright hushed after the rattle of unsuppressed 5.56 fire. But there was no missing the spatter as my third round went into the side of his jaw and blew out a chunk of flesh, bone, and fluids, splashing them into the next man's eyes.

That guy didn't get time to wipe the gore out of his vision, as Jordan shot him a split second later, blowing his brains out even as he tried to shove the falling body off himself. The dead man had momentarily pinned him against the doorjamb, and Jordan's bullet shattered the glass behind him as his skull got ventilated.

I dragged my muzzle across the group while they desperately tried to get out of the doorway, riding the reset to dump the mag into them as fast as I could. Six to two is not good odds, no matter whether the two got the drop on the six or not, and I had to even things out as fast as possible.

One went down hard, a pair of holes punched in his chest, spitting blood as his heart and lungs got pulped by two 220-grain bullets. Another took a round to the shoulder as he moved, shoving his way past the dying man and deeper into the showroom. He staggered as the impact turned him partway around, and I followed up but missed as a burst of 5.56 fire blew brick and plaster into my face. I ducked back into the hallway as Jordan threw himself behind the receptionist's desk.

The bad guys were scrambling for cover behind anything that might get between them and a bullet, from the stacked wheels along the big glass picture windows to the lime-green Porsche parked in the center of the open floor. They'd left three dead men in the doorway, but that still left three of them in front of us, along with however many more were out front, not to mention those closing in from the back parking lot.

Somebody really wanted Gorman dead.

I was covered by the corner from the guy who'd dived behind the stacked wheels, but the two behind the Porsche had me. I threw myself flat on my side, rolling over my SBR to bring the red dot to bear underneath the car, at least as best I could.

The Porsche was awfully low to the ground, which didn't give me much of a window or much of a target. I dumped about six rounds beneath the vehicle, though I'm pretty sure at least one or two ricocheted off the concrete floor and into the undercarriage instead of into the bodies on the other side.

At least one went home, though, as the man collapsed with a scream, apparently getting in his buddy's way, since the fire from the other side of the sports car suddenly stopped.

If I'd had a frag, I might have ended it right there. But I didn't have one, since carrying frag grenades on PSD missions tended to be frowned upon. I still would have taken a couple anyway, except that we had some delicate relationships to think about, and if we *used* the damn things, we'd have the Army all over us.

So, I had to move. Scrambling to my feet, I used the momentary pause in fire—aided by Jordan's bullets sending shattered glass cascading over the shooters on the other side of the car from behind the receptionist's desk—to hook around the corner and go after the one who'd taken cover behind the stack of wheels.

I almost got my head taken off, as the guy fired a long burst at me as soon as he spotted movement, 9mm rounds ripping past my ear and into the wall behind and above me. He wasn't controlling the recoil all that well, which is the only reason I survived, and he was drilling holes in the ceiling when I shot him four times in the chest, throat, and face. He crashed back against the glass and the low brick wall at its base, leaving a red smear on the plaster as he slid to the floor.

Then I was up and moving on the front of the car, even as Jordan got up and headed for the back. He held just off the corner as I went around the grill, not even pausing as I shot the man with the G3—maybe it was an HK33, since everybody seemed to be shooting 9mm or 5.56—twice in the chest and twice in the head, turning my muzzle on the second man with an MP5 and splashing blood, brains, and hair against the brightly-painted side of the car.

Being almost entirely certain that they were dead, I still stepped back around the car, ducking down to a knee behind the front driver's side wheel while I scanned the parking lot and the road beyond for more bad guys.

I might have seen movement, but right at the moment, the road was pretty clear. The civvies had scrambled for cover as soon as the shooting had started, and nobody else wanted a piece. I was sure there was a *Bundespolizei* unit in Bremen, but for whatever reason, they weren't getting involved. They'd have been here by now if they were.

I had my suspicions about that. The *Bundespolizei were* criminally understrength, but I suspected that while they might not be that eager to go running into a firefight with only a handful of dudes and a couple of G-Wagens, there was also a political angle there. They'd deny it, of course, but it wouldn't matter to us if we were dead, nevertheless.

A lot of the establishment in Berlin and Paris still weren't happy that the EDC was gone. They'd take full advantage of the power vacuum for their own benefit, of course, all the while mouthing platitudes about the Council having gone too far, but the truth was that they all tended to agree with the EDC's goals and ideals, what there were of them. Guys like Gorman and the rest of the *Verteidiger in Bayern*, or Nouveau Gallia, or any number of more "conservative," "nationalist" movements throughout Europe were persona non grata at best.

There was no way the authorities in Bremen, or anywhere else in Germany outside of Bavaria—well, a chunk of Bavaria—or a couple other minor cities were going to risk their cops to rescue the likes of Wenzeslaus Gorman. The man advocated for cleaning up the jihadi enclaves, lower taxes, and a Germany that was effectively economically independent—even from the Americans, which perhaps made our presence a little problematic, but who cared—and to them, that made him the next best thing to the return of Heinrich Himmler.

Not that they'd say that. Repeating those names was frowned upon, somewhat more in Germany than in the US. The implications could be made, though.

It was ironic, given the fights we'd already had with the Fourth Reich, which had a considerable presence in what used to be East Germany, and Gorman *hated* those bastards.

"Golf Lima Ten, this is Tango India Five Six." Tyler Bradshaw led the infantry section that had been our trail unit since we'd inserted into Slovakia on a rescue mission, over a year and several lifetimes ago. Now he was our QRF. "We are five mikes out. Three trucks and an M1200."

"Roger. Be advised, bad guys have LAW rockets and IEDs. Advance carefully. We are currently strongpointed in the

T&R auto dealership." I wasn't going to bother with the German over the radio. "Principal is secure, and we are holding position."

"Good copy." Bradshaw wasn't a particularly talkative man in person. He was even less so over the radio.

A renewed storm of gunfire sounded outside, around the back of the building. They couldn't have that many shooters left, but a couple could still cause us trouble, especially if they hauled out any more LAWs.

More movement, in the bushes across the road. I tracked in on it, but had no target.

Anyone in that field was probably going to have a bad day. There'd been quite a few cows out there, and while they would have run from the gunfire, if there was a bull in the mix, he was not going to be happy.

I fell back from the window, moving deeper into the shadows. The staff must have turned the lights off as soon as the shooting started, which was smart. If the bad guys had started shooting at movement, it would have been harder to see any movement inside the showroom with the lights off.

"Looks like they've bugged out." Jordan should have known better than to say something like that. I was too busy watching my sector to give him the stink-eye for taunting Murphy, but a moment later the *thud* of another explosion was followed by the crackle of 5.56 and 4.6mm fire from the back of the building.

"You had to say it." I shifted across the room, falling back toward the hallway, while Jordan covered the front. Nobody was stirring around the semis that were still jackknifed across the road, even though there was more gunfire echoing from what sounded like the far side. Maybe Bradshaw had overestimated how long it was going to take them to reach us.

The deep-throated *thumpthumpthump* of a heavy machinegun answered that question, especially when several rounds smashed right through the trailers partway across the road.

Bradshaw had arrived.

If only that meant it was over.

Chapter 3

The attackers cleared out pretty quick, once Bradshaw and his section got on the ground. We didn't have the time to clear the trucks out of the road, let alone clean up the corpses. We hadn't lost anyone—Gorman was on the phone with Meyer and Schultz, and he assured us that those guys were fine—but we'd made the bad guys pay one hell of a butcher's bill. And the bodies were all over the road, several residential yards, some farmer's field, and the doorway of a car dealership.

We'd let Gorman handle the remuneration for damages. He had enough money. We sure didn't, and our entire responsibility was keeping him alive. If that meant a lot of dead bad guys and property damage, that was what it meant.

Not that I didn't expect that we were going to get a lot of static over this incident. While we'd developed a decent working relationship with General Reeves, through the retaking of Gdansk and the assault on the French nuclear arsenal—after the EDC started rattling that particular saber particularly hard—and we'd gotten along well with most of the US military that we'd worked alongside since. The Force Recon guys we'd worked with during the assault on Brussels, especially, we'd gotten pretty tight with. But most of the senior commanders *really* didn't like us.

There were a couple reasons for that. The regular mil has never really liked contractors, and to them, that was all we were.

Dirty pirate contractors. Add in the political dimension of the fact that the Triarii had been set up as a parallel security apparatus in an increasingly dis-United States, and that just made our contributions even more odious to those who'd hitched their careers to the political train that was the American officer corps.

We weren't much more popular with a lot of the locals, either.

Don't get me wrong. We had our allies. We wouldn't have been working close protection for Herr Gorman if we hadn't. In fact, a lot of the regular Germans we'd met since the invasion had been friendly, even thankful. There weren't many who thought the EDC or the government in Berlin that had fully signed on with their agenda had had the interests of regular Germans in mind. It was, by all reports, much the same in France.

But the elites were still in charge. We'd taken out the EDC, in a classic American "Cut the head off the snake" op, but all the little bureaucrats and enablers were still there.

Once Bradshaw got his boys out on the perimeter, Tony got the team, Gorman, and Gorman's PSD hustling onto the trucks while I moved over to join Bradshaw where he was standing over the body next to the first truck, the discarded LAW tube lying on the pavement nearby.

Bradshaw was a little bit older than me, though he looked younger. Lean, dark-haired, and clean shaven, he'd been a platoon sergeant in the 173rd Airborne before he'd joined the Triarii. Me, I'd been a regular 0331 Marine grunt, with a stubborn streak a mile wide, who'd managed to bull his way through Grex Luporum Assessment and Selection despite not having the Recon/SOF experience that I was supposed to. I had a lot more gray in my otherwise red hair and beard than I'd had then, but Bradshaw and I had the same lines around our eyes and probably the same thousand-yard stare.

"That looks like it was an unpleasant surprise." Bradshaw nodded toward the fallen LAW tube as we shook hands. I might have been in civvies, fighting from a go bag with an SBR, but he was in full Triarii greens, helmet and plate carrier on, his M5E1 slung across his chest.

"That's an understatement." I nudged the tube with my boot. "They had a couple more up there." I nodded toward the back street where we'd *almost* broken contact.

Bradshaw frowned, looking down at the body, then bent down, rolled it over, and pulled the balaclava off. The man staring sightlessly at the sky was dark haired and dark eyed, clean shaven but with his jaw almost blue from the thickness of his beard, his eyebrows noticeably thicker than mine or Bradshaw's. "Doesn't look all that German, does he?"

I tilted my head. He might have been *slightly* darker than you might expect an ethnic German to be, but he still looked pretty Caucasian. "I don't know. Hard to say, these days." Gorman himself looked like he wasn't exactly "Aryan."

Bradshaw straightened. "Still, with those Turkish OKK dudes being part of the hit in Strasbourg, I've gotta wonder. Guy looks like he might be Turkish, or maybe Lebanese. Plenty of Turkish *and* Lebanese gangs in Germany these days, never mind the Kosovars, the Syrians, Iraqis, and Afghans."

I glanced down at the body, then back up at the trucks. "I'll leave it to the forensics guys. There are enough bad guys running around Germany these days that I can't keep track." I snorted and spat off the side of the road. "We wouldn't get the go-ahead to follow up, anyway. Got to keep on keeping on with babysitting duty."

That came out more bitter than I'd intended.

Bradshaw clapped me on the shoulder. "I think Gutierrez is just trying to give you boys a break, since you're short-handed. You'll get back in it." He glanced around at the bullet-riddled and smashed vehicles and the bodies on the ground. "Hell, looks like you already have."

I shrugged. "Not quite the same."

Yeah, my team and I had been through hell. We'd lost three of our number in less than a year. We'd seen combat of an intensity that most of our generation had only read about in books or seen in movies. We'd been hunted across Slovakia and barely held Poland, before going deep behind enemy lines multiple times, once to try to head off a nuclear holocaust.

Yet we were bored when it got quiet.

If I'd known what was coming, I might have tried harder to enjoy the quiet. Not that today had been any such thing.

Tony waved at me. Everybody was loaded up. I shook Bradshaw's hand again. "Sorry to leave you with the mess, brother, but we've got to get Gorman out of here."

Bradshaw waved it off. "That's why we're here, man. See you back in Hanover." I waved back and trotted toward the truck.

The up-armored Unimog wasn't anything near as slick as the Land Rovers we'd been driving, but it would get us where we needed to go, and unlike the Land Rovers, it had an up-gun, an actual M2 Browning .50 cal, mounted in a turret at the front of the rear compartment. The truck was a recent build, and not one shipped in from the States, either. The up-armored vehicle market in Europe was *booming*, the last few months.

I didn't recognize the driver. He was one of ours, in greens and geared up, but he wasn't one of Bradshaw's boys. We'd gotten a trickle of reinforcements over the last couple of months, but it sounded like the organization was plenty busy at home and in the Pacific, so we were stretched a little thin. Oscar Gutierrez, the overall Triarii commander in Europe, was shuffling around what assets he had.

"Hanover, sir?" The kid sounded like he'd just stepped off the parade ground. I'd had no idea we were getting Triarii that young. Every one of my team had been a veteran, most of us either in our late thirties or early forties.

"Yeah." I settled in next to the window leading from the cab into the rear compartment, which the kid had slid open. The up-gunner stood between me and Gorman, while Tony and Jordan sat on the outside, closest to the tailgate. "Let's be a little circumspect in how we get there, too." I didn't want to run right into another ambush.

"Roger that." He'd already swung the vehicle around to face back north, and putting the Unimog in gear, he started up the highway, leaving the shot-up semis behind. I didn't have a great view through the thick, armored windows on the outside of the passenger compartment, but I could still see that we were getting a lot of looks, most of them wearing that sort of ambivalent stoicism that you get used to after a while in an insurgency environment. Not friendly, not hostile. The looks of people who can't afford to visibly take sides, not when there are heavy machineguns, drones, and bombs in play.

It wasn't calculated to make me comfortable, riding around in big, up-armored vehicles. In my experience, the bigger the vehicle, no matter how much armor it had, the bigger a target it made. The mission precluded the kind of low profile I would have preferred, though.

I just had to keep my head on a swivel and hope that the kid behind the wheel, or the gunner and right-seater, noticed anything wrong before stuff blew up.

***

As it turned out, we ran into an ambush anyway, just of a different nature.

We hadn't gotten far before the driver, whose name was Killian, ironically—apparently no relation to the Army platoon sergeant we'd crossed half of Slovakia with; I asked—was slowing down, braking smoothly as the gunner swiveled to bring the .50 to bear to our front. I leaned toward the open window, peering out over Killian's shoulder through the windshield.

"Oh, hell." The roadblock had the entire highway shut off, both directions, with blue-painted *Bundespolizei* Sonderwagens and ENOKs covering all angles. The *Bundespolizei* had armed up since the war started, and while the Sonderwagens had water cannons mounted, they also had MG5s in the turrets. They weren't pointed at the sky, either.

"What do you want to do?" Plummer, the right seater, looked like he was about fifty, though he was a hard sort of fifty. He might be only about my age, but he'd been out in the weather a lot. His voice was a gravelly rasp that might have been put on, except that he hadn't changed his tone since we'd started moving.

I glanced at Gorman, who was looking over Plummer's shoulder. "I think we'd better get out and talk. Don't want to get into a firefight with the *Bundespolizei*." I levered myself out of my seat and started toward the back, stepping between boots and knees, keeping my SBR pointed at the floor. I wasn't looking forward to this, but it was my job.

Gorman got up and started to follow me. "I should come, as well."

Tony reached out and halted him. "Let Matt go first. Just in case this gets stupid."

Gorman looked down at him. Tony was a big guy, bigger even than Reuben, and imposing in his quiet way. He wasn't jacked, he was just big. The outer softness of his features was deceptive, though. He was strong as an ox, and if he was determined to stop you, you'd have to shoot him to put him down. Gorman wasn't armed, and he wouldn't have a hope in hell if Tony decided to wrap him up.

"I might be able to keep it from 'getting stupid,' as you say." Gorman's voice was calm, though his jaw was tight as he spoke. Someone had just tried to kill or kidnap him, and he was feeling it. "These are not random terrorists like the ones you just fought. They are *Bundespolizei*."

"We still just got through a firefight, and the *Bundespolizei* might be a little trigger-happy after that." *Even though they stayed well away until it was all clear*. I didn't say that last part, but I sure thought it real loud. The fact was, I didn't trust them, especially *because* they had to have known that Gorman had been the target, and they'd sat on their hands. They were *not* his friends. "Just let me get out first and get a feel for the situation, Herr Gorman. If you can do some good out there, I'll have them send you out."

He wasn't happy about it, but he nodded. As much as I hate PSD work of any kind, working with Gorman was somewhat refreshing as such things go, since he actually *listened* to his security guys, instead of simply assuming that he knew better than the mere knuckle-dragging gunfighters trying to keep his hide intact.

I dropped off the tailgate and headed around to the front of the vehicle. I felt exposed as hell, out there in the middle of the road, with just my go bag and rifle, despite the fact that Herter was up on the .50, a Ma Deuce that was probably three times as old as he was, covering me. He had the muzzle a little high, so he wasn't pointing it directly at the roadblock. The threat was implied, though, especially since he'd disconnected the T&E, or traversing and elevation mechanism, so he could easily free-gun the weapon right into the middle of them.

My eyes narrowed slightly as I came around the front of the Unimog and scanned the roadblock. Yes, the bulk of the men and women in blue were *Bundespolizei*, but there were two big Mercedes vans behind the ENOKs, disgorging about twenty men in gray, wearing black plate carriers and sunglasses. They all appeared to be Chinese, and while none were carrying long guns, they all had pistols on their hips. I was sure the long guns were in the van.

One World Holistic Security Concepts had arrived. Joy.

So far, OWHSC and the Triarii had generally avoided each other. Given what we knew about Chinese involvement in the chaos Stateside, not to mention the fact that my team had found Chinese advisors with the EDC during a raid on their headquarters, we suspected that OWHSC were all PLA, and that they weren't in Europe for the humanitarian reasons. Sure, they had "humanitarian" all over their publicity materials, but nothing from the People's Republic of China came without strings attached.

We'd been thoroughly briefed on the attempted takeover of the major ports on the West Coast after the cyber attack that had borked the power grid, supply chains, and most of our comms. There was no way the Triarii were going to get buffaloed by the latest Chinese Communist front organization.

Unfortunately, I couldn't say as much for the Germans.

One of the men in gray, with a pistol belt but no plate carrier, was talking with a short-haired woman in a pantsuit, off to one side of the roadblock. That had the distinct look of a command conference. And from the looks of the woman, never mind the Chinese officer—I wasn't even playing their games in my head—this was not going to go well.

Maybe I should get Gorman out now.

I stepped around to the front of the Unimog and stopped, my hands on my rifle's buttstock. The fact that I was armed, and had a M2 .50 cal looming above my head, was clearly making the *Bundespolizei* nervous. When I glanced at the gray-clad OWHSC personnel, though, they didn't seem bothered.

I waited. A couple of those MG5s were pointed a little too close to directly at me, and if they were going to get that nervous, I didn't want to trigger a jumpy gunner.

After a moment, the woman in the suit finished talking to the Chinese commander and stepped away, as he folded his arms and stared at me from behind mirrored aviator glasses. I ignored him, though I was keeping an eye on his boys, all of whom were still hanging out close to the vans. Probably so they were close to their weapons.

The woman walked up onto the road and met with a tall man in blue, his face covered by a black balaclava, an MP7 slung across his chest. They spoke quietly for a few moments, then advanced toward where I waited, the man waving to a good half dozen other *Bundespolizei* to come with them.

I must have been really intimidating.

They stopped a few yards in front of me, where they probably hoped they were under the arc of the .50. Bad news for them if Herter opened up. Provided he could control the weapon freehand, he could drop that muzzle to engage up to a yard in front of the Unimog's hood. I'd get rocked by the muzzle blast even if he opened fire on anyone farther out, but if this went pear shaped in the next few seconds, I'd probably be dead, anyway.

"What's the deal?" I decided to open the ball. The tall guy didn't seem to be feeling all that comfortable with this situation, and the woman was standing about six feet behind him and the two *Bundespolizei* to either side of him. "We're escorting Wenzeslaus Gorman, and we have all the necessary paperwork." There had been a ton of that, too, and we'd all had to sign a bunch of stuff we had no intention of honoring. I had the thick packet of papers in my go bag. The EDC might be out of power, but the bureaucracy was as strong as ever, and they were not fans of ours.

I'll be honest. As what might be termed a "traditional Catholic," I took my word seriously. Signing my name to forms full of rules I had every intention of violating bugged me. A part of me was deeply regretting signing any of those papers in the first place. Hartrick had made it clear that I didn't really have a choice. This was the mission, and he couched it as essentially the same thing as camouflage and misdirection. We were still at war, regardless of all the wishful thinking flying around.

The tall man stepped forward, obviously keeping an eye on the heavy machinegun above my head, and held out his hand. I dipped into my go bag carefully, even as several sets of hands clenched on PDWs and eyes got real sharp all of a sudden, and drew out the papers, handing them across to him.

"Y'all are awfully jumpy." I kept my tone casual, allowing myself a little bit more of a drawl than I usually use. "We're authorized under the cease fire agreement to carry weapons to protect our client and our persons. Maybe you should be more concerned about the terrorists who just tried to kill us with bombs, antitank rockets, and machineguns."

The tall man ignored what I'd said as he flipped through the stack of forms—it was ridiculous, how much paperwork we had to carry with us—then turned to the woman, speaking low, in German. My German wasn't that great, but I could get by. I could understand enough to know he was telling her that we had all the right forms.

She clearly didn't like it. She had that sour expression that told me all I needed to know. She didn't like the fact that we had weapons, she didn't like the fact we were Americans—quite obviously, despite the lack of insignia—and she didn't like the fact that we were escorting Wenzeslaus Gorman.

Stepping forward, she stared at me from next to the tall guy, her arms folded, her lips pressed tightly together. "Your permits and licenses were intended to allow you to deter violence, not increase it." She stared up at the Unimog behind me, though I imagined she was trying to burn through the steel to see Gorman. "Tell your employer that he and his paid assassins are no longer welcome in Bremen. Your presence is too much of a security risk."

I eyed the Chinese commander type behind her. He was still standing there, his head held high, staring at me from behind those mirrored shades. He knew what he'd put in motion. Though to be honest, I doubted that this chick had needed much of a push.

For that matter, I didn't think the security risk was the real reason they didn't want Gorman reentering Bremen. I suspected that the firefight to the south had simply been a convenient excuse to deny access to someone who was a powerful rallying point for those who were fed up with the worsening security, foundering economy, and sneering disgust with their own culture and history—including the parts that weren't the Second World War—that had characterized the EDC and their enablers.

Gorman apparently thought the same thing. He was already out of the truck, spitting a rapid-fire stream of German at the woman, too fast for me to follow. My German was okay, but not nearly that good.

I stepped out in front of him as he ranted and raved. The *Bundespolizei*—at least most of them—still looked a little uncertain, especially given the heavy machinegun overhead, which was still pointed up and away, but the OWHSC guys were watching carefully, and two of them had stepped back inside the vans.

Grabbing Gorman's arm, I kept my voice low. "I know it's bullshit, but another firefight is not in our best interests right now. It's not in your best interest, and it's not in your constituents' best interest, either. This is the time to deescalate and come at this from another angle."

He stopped talking, staring daggers at the woman, who was returning the glare, her nose slightly up in the air. Finally, though, he slowed down, looking around at the situation as a whole, taking in not only the *Bundespolizei* but the OWHSC operators behind them.

Gorman wasn't a babe in the woods. He'd been an Afghan War veteran and a foreign security contractor. He knew a threat when he saw one, which was probably why he'd been so easy to work with as a principal.

He turned his stare back on the woman. "You will not be able to silence the people of this country forever, no matter how violent your pets get." He turned on his heel and stalked back toward the truck, while the woman turned white as a sheet.

I didn't think that was fear.

Winning the peace was promising to be a lot harder than winning the war.

Provided the war was actually over, which I didn't believe for a heartbeat. Keeping my eye on the shooters in blue and black, while Herter leaned on the .50, I followed Gorman toward the back. We were going to have to find a different route back to Hanover.

Chapter 4

"How is it that you always end up right in the middle of it when things get interesting?" Brian Hartrick looked pissed, but he always looked pissed. I'd had to learn that the hard way during my first couple of years on the Grex Luporum teams, when he'd been my team leader. He was leaning on the table in our little team room, just off Gorman's campaign headquarters in an old, brick building that looked like it could have been built when the Kaiser was a lance corporal.

"I guess we're just lucky that way." We'd only been back for an hour; Hartrick must have moved fast. His headquarters was still in Gdansk, especially given how much the Russians were pushing in the east. We still had a working relationship with the Poles, that Gutierrez wasn't willing to give up—especially given how fragile our relationships with the Germans, the French, and the Army were—so we had to juggle our slim resources. "What's up?"

He shoved a tablet across the table at me. "Bradshaw got some interesting stuff off your attackers. He shot it to me over HF, just to make sure we got the info as fast as possible."

While I started scrolling through the photos of dead men, pocket litter, and weapons, he kept talking. "Most of the weapons came from a *Bundeswehr* warehouse that was raided shortly after the attacks in Strasbourg. One, however, was a bit of a giveaway. It seems that *Binbaşı* Ahmet Sadik didn't want to give up his MPT-76."

I'd just reached the photo of the rifle that I'd first thought had looked like a G36. It was a lot closer to an M4 or HK416, now that I got a better look at it, except for the weird carrying handle affixed to the top rail and the even weirder flare that ran from the front rail down to the bottom of the mag well. "Turkish?"

"Standard Turkish infantry rifle. One of their first truly homebuilt weapons, at least in a while. We identified Sadik's corpse from pictures of his Airborne School class." Hartrick managed to look even more pissed than usual. "Yeah, he's OKK, and we taught him to jump. Or, rather, he *was* OKK."

"What about the rest of them?" I kept scrolling through the photos. The other attackers mostly appeared to be some variation of Middle Eastern or Caucasian, though a couple were definitely blond.

"Most of those that we've been able to identify, thanks to a contact with the *Bundespolizei*, are known members of Turkish or Lebanese gangs in the area. The blonds, though, are another matter."

I stopped scrolling on one of those. The picture wasn't pretty. The man had been shot in the face, and while an effort had been made to shut his eyes, one was noticeably bulged from the pressure of the bullet's passage through his sinus cavity, just beneath it, and the lids wouldn't close all the way. Rivulets of blood had dried on his cheek. "EDC?"

"We believe so. Unlike the others, they were sterile. No pocket litter, no phones, nothing. The list of suspects is pretty long, but that tends to narrow it down a bit."

I looked up at him. "So, how does this amount to 'things getting interesting?'" I put the tablet down on the table. "We've known that the Turks are pushing the jihadi movements in Europe since Strasbourg."

"The potential link to the EDC remnant, for one thing." Hartrick folded his beefy arms across his barrel chest. He was clean-shaven, unlike most of the rest of us, and balding slightly, but he was still built like an ox. "But this wasn't the only attack, either." He pointed to the tablet. "Keep going."

I picked it back up and scrolled farther. I felt my eyebrows rise.

Bombings in Hamburg and Berlin. Two anti-EDC politicians kidnapped, one still missing, the other found tied up, tortured, and shot in the head. Arson. Riots coming out of majority-Muslim neighborhoods in Dusseldorf and Berlin. Counter-riots killing and burning, going into such neighborhoods in Wiesbaden, Mainz, and Stuttgart. The chaos was stepping up. Things were getting sporty.

"You think this is a concerted push?" We'd seen things like that before. Hartrick had seen it in the military, mostly in Iraq, Afghanistan, and Kosovo, but I'd seen it, too, mainly in the States. Widespread chaos was rarely random. It was usually facilitated by someone who looked to get something out of it, whether it was money, power, or both. Not necessarily where the chaos was happening, either.

"It sure as hell looks like it." Hartrick frowned. "We don't know by who, yet. The Turks would be the obvious players, since they appear to be widening the Islamic enclaves, with the corresponding control or influence over the insurgents they helped."

"But you don't think it's just the Turks." That wasn't a question. I didn't think so, either.

"No, I don't, and neither does Gutierrez. Neither does Reeves, for that matter." That was an interesting observation. Hartrick and Gutierrez had butted heads with Reeves a lot during that first couple months in Poland, pretty much right up until the fight to retake Gdansk. Reeves had come around, most notably after reinforcements had arrived from the States, and he'd gotten sort of shoved aside by the officers who outranked him but didn't have his experience or knowledge of the situation on the ground.

Welcome to our world.

41

"While the Turks are definitely involved, and the first wave appears to mostly be jihadis from the enclaves, there's a lot going on behind the scenes, too. The 2nd, 3rd, and 4th EDC Divisions are still sitting still near Chemnitz, though they shot down an overflight bird a couple days ago. It's almost guaranteed that they've got people in the mix. Both the Federal and several state governments in Germany are stonewalling a lot of the efforts that the Army's been making to fix things. And those ChiCom bastards with 'One World Holistic Security Concepts' are fucking everywhere." He couldn't keep the sarcastic sneer out of his voice as he said the Chinese proxy company's name. "Now, that's where you boys come in. We needed somebody to cover Gorman, but he's heading back down to Bayreuth for the time being, and I need another Grex Luporum team."

He pointed at the tablet. "What's not on there is the data from Sadik's cell phone. Yeah, he had one on him." He nodded as I turned a somewhat incredulous stare on him. That seemed like a hell of a security violation if you were going to be running an ambush on a legit local politician with a bunch of terrorists. At least the presumed EDC operatives had been sterilized. "Bradshaw's on his way here with the phone. He'll drop it off on the way, when he picks up Gorman to continue on to Bayreuth. We'll rip it and use whatever info we get off it to find your next target."

I couldn't complain. Like I said, while Gorman was a good dude for a politician—damning with faint praise, I know—I really hate PSD work. I'd rather be on the hunt.

"Ripping the phone is going to take some time, though, so before you get going, I need you to pick a couple of replacements." He raised an eyebrow as my face went still. "I know, they can't replace your guys, but you're down to seven men. That's not where a Grex Luporum team is supposed to operate for long. I let it go because you've been through hell and you needed a break, and you could work close protection for

Gorman with that many. But if you're going back into it, I want you at full strength."

He turned toward the door. "Doesn't have to happen today. Like I said, the phone rip's probably going to take all night. But you need to be ready to step by dark tomorrow, and I want Grex Luporum Team X back at ten gunfighters by then."

***

"We don't need any fucking replacements!" I hadn't seen Jordan this irate in a while.

"Really? You wouldn't have replaced Phil in a heartbeat?" Tony wasn't having it. He leaned against the wall, working a dip in his lip. Dip had run awfully low over the last few months, but he'd gotten some in, now that the war was supposedly over and flights were running into Europe again. It was still expensive as hell, given the instability and other myriad problems back in the States, but he had his fix.

"That's different. And no, as much of an asshole as Phil was, I *wouldn't* have replaced him immediately." That was a surprising admission. Jordan and Phil had never gotten along, and Jordan hadn't exactly been all broken up when the smaller man had been killed in a cruise missile strike to the hospital where he was recovering from wounds.

Jordan looked around at the team. Chris, spare of frame and hatchet-faced, surprisingly quiet for the team's sole former SEAL, also a pastor with some splinter church back home. David, short, skinny, and aggressive, the bullied kid from the *barrio* who'd become a Ranger and then a Triarius. Greg, another former Ranger who'd nearly had his face blown off by an IED, and was the friendliest of us by a mile. Reuben, the big, quiet Texican who took no shit and had displayed little patience for Jordan's racial sensitivities, however well-earned they might have been. Tony, even more massive than Reuben, and so given to quiet that he'd gotten the callsign "Chatty," yet he'd been my first pick as ATL after Scott had gone down.

The gaps left from Dwight's, Phil's, and Scott's deaths were still palpable.

"This team has been through so much shit that there's no way that a replacement is going to be able to fit in, especially not just before a mission. They're not going to be dialed in, they're not going to communicate as clearly and succinctly as we can." Jordan took a deep breath. I watched him carefully. He was getting more passionate about this than I'd expected. I wondered if maybe there was more actual emotion behind his objection than he'd admit.

We were all kind of like that. Can't show weakness.

"If we were getting replacements just before we took on the Gorman detail, then maybe. But just before going fully operational again? I don't think it's a good idea."

"I can see your point." And I could. While I might have suspected that there was a degree of not wanting to see anyone take our dead teammates' places—and even Phil, who really *had* been a pain in the ass more often than not, had had a place there that it seemed somewhat irreverent to try to fill—he was right that a new guy might well be out of sync at a time that we had to shoot, move, and communicate as a well-oiled machine. "I also see Brian's point. This is supposed to be a ten-man team. Being down three puts us behind the power curve."

Looking around at the rest of the team, I saw either stony-faced impassivity, which more than likely masked an agreement with Jordan's objections, or an uncertain ambivalence. Greg actually looked the most uncomfortable. He would be the one who mourned our lost teammates most keenly, while also being the guy who'd welcome the newbies with open arms. He was caught between a rock and a hard place.

"How long before we go wheels up?" Tony asked.

I let out a half-snort, half resigned chuckle. "Tomorrow night."

A chorus of curses went around the room. "Yeah, well, this is why we trained the six-hour planning cycle, boys. Tyler should be here with the phone that needs to get ripped for the targeting intel in a couple hours, and then as soon as we've got a target package, we start getting prepped. Reality of the war." I

44

sighed. "Look, I don't know why we're only getting these guys now. I agree that it would have been better before we went on Gorman's PSD. But it is what it is, so we've got to roll with the punches." I laughed a little, though there wasn't much humor in the sound. I wasn't feeling all that cheery, myself. "It could be a lot worse. We're being asked to take on three newbies, not E&E across Slovakia again."

Rueben gave a little sardonic snort at that. David and Chris both had to give slightly ambivalent shrugs, conceding the point. Tony was as impassive as ever.

Jordan… Jordan was the potential sticking point. The man was stubborn as hell. But he sighed. "No, you're right." His shoulders slumped a little. "Just seems like we never get a break, doesn't it?"

"It's war, brother. Breaks went out the window a long time ago."

"When are the new guys coming over?" Tony had put the argument aside already, and now he was thinking about the practical realities and necessities.

I checked my watch. "Brian said he'd send 'em over at 1900." From what he'd said, they'd been ready the day before, but I needed time to brief the team.

That was in only about half an hour. We had that long to get used to the idea of going into the next mission with three FNGs.

***

I should have known that Brian Hartrick wouldn't saddle me with three actual FNGs. I already knew two of the guys who walked into our team area with their packs over their shoulders. Jim Sullivan and Steve Bealer had been in my Assessment and Selection course.

Jim was tall, barrel-chested, blond, with a small blond goatee turning to gray. He almost matched Tony for size. He'd been a Pathfinder in the Army, then gone to Special Forces for a while before getting out. He was big, bluff, and often loud, but

45

he'd give you the shirt off his back and he'd never stop once he got going.

Steve was about David's size, with a nose that had been broken several times, dark hair, and a perpetual scowl. It wasn't that he was always angry, though being another former Marine, he probably was. Like Brian Hartrick, it was just the way he looked. He was almost as quiet as Tony, at least as far as I remembered.

The third man, Lucas Edwards, I'd heard of, but never met. Older than just about any of us, he was grizzled and wiry, with a couple weeks' worth of salt and pepper stubble on his jaw. Edwards had been all over. He'd been a Marine grunt, then a Ranger, then done some work with OGA for a few years. There were rumors that he'd been down some darker roads between his time with Ground Branch and the Triarii, but so far as I'd heard, they were all just rumors. Always coming from somebody who knew somebody who'd heard the story.

I shook hands with Jim and Steve first. "Damn, Matt." Jim's voice boomed in the small room. "Team leader already!" He started going around the room, his big hand stuck out. Several of the others knew him, too, especially Greg, who shook his hand with the brotherly half-hug. "Damn, some of you guys are a sight for sore eyes. I've been kicking around the support side for the last six months."

"What happened?" Reuben shook his hand firmly. "Last I heard, you were on Team VII with Cole Youngman. Thought you guys were busy as hell."

"We were." Jim laughed. "That's what happened. I caught a bullet in New Orleans and got stove up just before you guys opened the ball over here. I ran out and hitched a ride with the headquarters element when they headed over the Atlantic just before Poland blew up, but like I said, I was still down for the count and so I was sitting on a radio or coordinating logistics for the last few months." He turned to me and took a deep breath. "I'm all good now, though. I won't let you guys down."

46

Steve and Chris shared a quick bro-hug after he shook my hand. They'd been on a team together early on, before Chris had come over to Team X. "Good to see you guys again." He looked over at Jordan. "Jordan." There was a certain coolness there.

Jordan returned his nod impassively. "Steve."

My eyes narrowed slightly. Jordan was playing it cool, but he wasn't *quite* as impassive as he was trying to be. There was some discomfort there. I'd almost call it nervousness, if I could imagine Jordan being *nervous*.

Steve was watching him with what I could only describe as a heavy-lidded look of amusement. "So, I guess you guys haven't sampled the local night life lately?"

Jordan stabbed a knife hand at him. "Don't you fucking start." If he hadn't been black, the man would have been turning beet red.

Steve shrugged. "I mean, I don't imagine there are a lot of gay bars you can accidentally go into while drunk off your ass in Poland. Germany, though…"

"That is *not* how that happened, and you damned well know it." Jordan glared around at the rest of the team, but if there's one thing you learn from many years in team rooms, its that if you let the rest of the team know that something bugs you, it's inviting everyone to pick at it like a bad scab.

"That sounds like story time." Reuben leaned back against the wall and folded his arms.

"It wasn't what Steve will make it out to be." Jordan seemed to have realized his tactical error, and was backtracking to avoid the incessant ribbing that this was going to end in. He was testy enough at the best of times. "We were in Vegas, with two chicks we'd picked up somewhere along the line on a *long* bar crawl along the strip, and it turned out that they were a lot weirder pervs than we'd thought." He glared at Steve as if daring him to contradict him. "Nothing happened, but those two tried real hard to make something happen, just so they could watch."

47

All eyes turned to Steve. He shrugged. "*Technically,* that's exactly what happened. Technically."

I could see the steam starting to come out of Jordan's ears, and decided I needed to head this off. We didn't have a whole lot of time. "Story time can come later. We've got no time to dawdle." I turned to Lucas. "Welcome aboard. Though I can't say what kind of an impression that little show just gave you."

Lucas just smiled slightly. His handshake was like a vise. "Believe me, I've seen worse. If there *hadn't* been some bullshitting, I'd have gotten worried." His voice was a gravelly rasp, even more so than Plummer's had been. "When it comes to a team who's killed more people than cancer since this started, I'm not going to look a gift horse in the mouth."

"What's the mission?" Jim seemed to want to get past the awkward silence, as Jordan was still glaring daggers at Steve, who was just grinning smugly. Fortunately, the ribbing didn't seem to have made Jordan actually lose his temper. He was just annoyed and chagrined. "We didn't get much of a brief, just that we were going to hit the ground running."

"Still waiting on that." Even as I said it, there was a knock at the door. Hartrick didn't wait for any of us to answer it, but just walked in, a tablet in his hands. "And, that looks like our target package."

"It is." Hartrick looked around at the team. "Hope you got all the socializing done, 'cause this is gonna be a bitch."

***

He wasn't kidding. As near as we'd been able to ascertain from the phone rip, Sadik had been using a local jihadi facilitator in Lüdenscheid to coordinate his operations. The guy wasn't an imam or anything. Avdullah Bajrami was a thug, with connections to not only the Albanian mob, but also to the various Western Caliphate groups *and* AQOE. If there was anybody who could lead us to the ringleaders or the contacts for the ringleaders, it was Bajrami. *If* we could take him alive.

That was a big "if." Lüdenscheid had been sketchy ten years ago. It was a straight-up no-go zone now. And Bajrami wasn't known for being a moderate. The man might have no problem working with the more secular Albanian gangsters—some of them were probably his kin, since he was a Kosovar—but he was a die-hard Islamist fanatic. There were plenty of videos floating around of him claiming that he'd die before submitting to the *kufar*, and we had no reason not to take him seriously.

Still, we had to give it a shot. If he didn't know where the Turkish OKK cells were working out of, or who they were talking to, then someone else in his organization might. Or else the computers, phones, or pocket litter we might take off the target site might have something we could use.

Finding the target site was going to be interesting. We had the IMEI number for Bajrami's phone, and he hadn't budged out of the tenement housing north of the commercial part of town, judging by the trace that was already running, thanks to some friends in OGA. They were probably going to get into a lot of trouble if anyone found out they were funneling us information, but then, so would a lot of people who were quietly on our side. At any rate, that tenement housing was going to be a nightmare to get in and out of. As soon as the first shot was fired, we were going to be blown, and then it was going to turn into *Black Hawk Down*. Without the relief column coming to get us.

Fortunately, we had our ways, and we weren't constrained by some of the same factors that the regulars were. We could be sneakier, and we didn't really have any blind spots about using every factor in the area to our advantage.

So, we were up until after midnight working on planning, contingencies, and contingencies for contingencies. To be honest, there was only so much *planning* we could really do, given the information we had. We could prepare, though, mentally and logistically, for all sorts of things to go wrong, and the bulk of the planning phase was spent thinking up ways the situation could go pear-shaped.

There were a lot of those scenarios.

49

Finally, though, I called it quits for the night. If we were going to insert the following evening, we needed to get some rest. There was still a lot to do in the morning.

I didn't crash right away, though. I headed outside, pulled out one of our team phones, and dialed Klara.

It was late, and I wouldn't have blamed her if she hadn't answered. But while she sounded a little sleepy, she picked up after the first couple of rings. "Cześć."

"It's me." I hadn't realized how tired I sounded until just then.

"Mateusz!" Her voice brightened, and there was a warmth and affection in it that I hadn't heard in far too long. "Are you all right?"

"I'm as good as can be expected." There were too many things I couldn't tell her, not over the phone. She probably wouldn't have wanted to hear them, anyway. "It might still be a while until I can get back." I hadn't gotten more than a couple days in Poland to see her since the Strasbourg fiasco. "I just wanted to hear your voice, make sure you're okay."

"We are all okay." She hesitated, and I started to frown. "There was an alert the other day. The Russians flew over the city. They are awfully close, now." She sighed. "I worry about you, but almost everyone else here is more worried about the Russians than the Germans."

"Can't say as I blame them. The Russians are a lot more of an immediate threat right now." I knew enough about the nature of this war to know that immediate threats didn't always translate to most serious threats, but that doesn't take away the fact that the EDC was on the ropes, the Council itself captured, and their client nations in disarray, while the Russians were pushing into eastern Poland, Slovakia, and threatening Hungary. "Have you done what I said you should? Are your parents ready to get out if things get hot?"

Klara had needed to think for a moment the first time I'd used that phrase. Her English was excellent, but it wasn't her first language. This time, though, she knew exactly what I was saying. "Yes, we have bags packed, and a route out of the city, just like you said." She paused a moment. "Can we come to join you?"

"I don't know." And I didn't. We were probably going to be pretty mobile for the foreseeable future, and secure areas were few and far between in post-EDC Gray Zone Europe. "I think your first plan to go to Wrocław is probably more workable at the moment." I thought for a second on how to word this. "I wish you could come here, but I'm still working. It's still pretty dangerous."

There was a bit of amusement in her voice when she answered, "Gdansk during the fighting was dangerous, too, Mateusz." She insisted on using the Polish version of my name, and I couldn't object. Something about the way she said it…

"I know. But I'd be a lot more focused if I knew you were safe."

"And I would be happier if we were closer." She sighed again. "But I don't want you to be too worried about us."

There was a lot I wanted to say. More that I didn't know how to say, not really. Not well. "I should let you get to sleep. It's late, and we both need some rest." I couldn't tell her exactly why I needed it, but she could put two and two together easily enough.

"Be safe, Mateusz." There might have been a faint choke in her voice. "Come back to me. I love you."

"I love you, too, Klara."

There was nothing else to say.

It took a while to get to sleep.

Chapter 5

"Damn, this place was obviously a nice town, once." Jim was driving, looking around at the slum that the northern part of Lüdenscheid had turned into. Most of the buildings were still fairly modern, but the decay was obvious. Graffiti had been scrawled or sprayed on a lot of walls, much of it in Albanian or Turkish. Some windows were broken, others covered in steel bars. There was more trash on the streets than you usually saw in Germany. Despite the chaos, the demographic shifts, and the economic troubles, most Germans were still fastidious people. You only saw this kind of decay in places where gangs had taken over, or ethnic enclaves had been set up.

Most of the southern part of the city was still fairly well kept up, classic German architecture blending with more modern buildings of concrete and glass, with plenty of trees and green spaces in between, the whole city nestled within the rolling, forested hills of North Rhine-Westphalia. It was only when we started getting into the lower-income parts of the north that we started to see the warning signs.

We were already getting looks from the knots of young men hanging out on street corners as we got closer and closer to the area where we suspected Bajrami was hiding out. I turned around in my seat to look in the back seat of the little Audi A7, where Chris was trying to replicate Scott's technological wizardry with the cell phone spoofer.

Actually, the little device in the box on the seat next to him didn't spoof the phones, not really. It mimicked a cell tower, meaning that when we got close enough, any nearby cell phones would lock onto it, giving us a list of nearby cell numbers. It was essentially a Stingray, the same device that a lot of police departments used to a lot of people's outrage. Since we had Bajrami's cell number, it wasn't that hard to pick it out when it pinged on the imitation cell tower.

The hard part was narrowing down exactly where the cell phone was located. It wasn't like the movies, where a blinking red dot showed up on a grayscale map of the area, showing us exactly where the phone was. That would be nice, but it just wasn't practical unless we could trigger a GPS beacon on the phone, and Bajrami—or his group—were too canny for that. They probably had their locators turned off. If we'd had some of the more advanced gear, we might have managed to turn it on, but we were having to do this the old-fashioned way.

"Old fashioned." This wouldn't have been doable even fifteen years ago. Not with the kind of tech we could have gotten our hands on.

"Anything?"

Chris didn't take his eyes off the laptop in front of him, a USB cable running to the glorified Stingray beside him. "Not yet. Wait." He peered at the screen, his eyes flicking up to the post-it note stuck to the frame. That thing was probably a security risk if we got rolled up, but so was the Stingray, never mind the laptop, the combat gear, and the weapons at our feet. "Got him."

"Pull over as soon as you can." I looked back forward as Jim pulled the sedan over to the side of the road, right in front of a cemetery. Unfortunately, that might not have been the best spot to pull over.

About half a dozen men in dark clothing were hanging out on the corner just ahead of us, at the end of one of the big tenements. Several were bearded, though more were clean-shaven than I would have expected from potential jihadis.

They'd been getting cleverer over the last few years, better able to blend into their surroundings. And that was the committed ones, not even counting those who were just violent thugs with an excuse.

If these were Kosovars, or even Turks, they could be both. I'd heard some horror stories about the Turkish and Lebanese gangs in parts of Germany.

Even as we stopped, I checked the rear-view mirror again. At almost the same moment, Jim cursed. "I think we picked up a tail."

"Maybe." It's hard to tell if you're being followed on the road in a city. You usually need several turns and abrupt changes in speed and direction to make absolutely sure that someone's tailing you. That wasn't the kind of tradecraft you learned in the mil, but it was stuff that we'd had to learn on the Grex Luporum teams, given some of our operations in contested areas of major cities Stateside, during the borderline anarchy that had come before things had gotten *really* bad. We'd learned to be ghosts in the city and figure out when we'd been detected. "Just play it cool for now." I saw the vehicle he was talking about, an older Mercedes van, slowing down a little as it came closer. The windows were tinted, and I couldn't see enough of the driver's compartment through the mirror. But the fact that they'd slowed down wasn't comforting.

Still, until we *knew* we were made, we had a mission to accomplish. I looked down at the little burner phone I'd gotten through a contact with the *Verteidiger in Bayern*. Making friends with locals who could procure such things helped, since we didn't want anyone in the German government finding out about US passports being used to buy SIM cards. *That* little tidbit of information would probably be in every bad guy's inbox in hours.

They probably had their own Stingrays, or some equivalent, after all. It wasn't a high-tech vs. low-tech war anymore.

I texted Jordan. *We've got a hit. We're about two hundred yards north of Fox 125.* We'd numbered just about every intersection in the city beforehand. Well, the ops guys back in Hanover had. It meant we had a quick set of reference points without needing to read off grids and hunt for them on the map. With GPS being less than reliable, the more shortcuts we could take, the better.

Good copy. We'll come in from the west. The range on the Stingray was variable, based on other sources of electronic noise, obstructions like buildings and terrain, and atmospheric conditions. Having two of the units out there, we could start to home in on Bajrami's phone more quickly, triangulating his position down to the building, at least. With the tech we had, it wasn't going to get much more precise than that.

That was, of course, provided we could get close enough.

The van rolled slowly past us, and I had to admit that Jim's instinct had probably been right. While the deep tint of the windows kept me from seeing the man's face in the passenger seat, I could still tell he was watching us closely as the van went by, then accelerated away, slowing again as it neared the corner where the young men were still watching us.

I didn't like this.

"Matt…" Jim didn't like it either.

"Just stay cool and be ready to get out of here." The Audi wasn't armored, which was at one and the same time an advantage and a handicap. If we took fire, the thin-skinned sedan wouldn't stop bullets. But it was harder to pick it out from any other civilian vehicle—armored SUVs and sedans are actually pretty obvious, once you see them—and it was a *lot* more agile. Jim could flip that sucker around right there in the road and get us moving in a heartbeat.

We might be made. I tapped out the message quickly.

Roger. Lot of activity out here, too. Looks like they've got lookouts posted all around the neighborhood.

That stood to reason. Most organized criminal outfits had their bases of operation surrounded by rings of lookouts and early warning systems. There were probably tech backups to the thugs on the street corners, too. I didn't see any drones—for probably the same reason we weren't using them the way we had to find Specialist England in Slovakia: they'd be too easily spotted in this kind of environment, and the *Polizei* hadn't cleared out of Lüdenscheid entirely—but that didn't mean they didn't have cameras and RF sniffers all over the neighborhood. Especially if the Turkish OKK was backing them.

Not to mention the EDC remnant, and whoever was backing *them.*

Boy, this kind of warfare gets complicated.

Even as I silently prayed that we wouldn't get into a fight before we could locate Bajrami, the van pulled over next to the guys on the corner and stopped. The group started to move toward us as the van doors opened and three more got out.

Those guys looked like trouble. Two of them were big, beefy dudes, one of them with a shaved head, the other standing almost a head taller than the other two, wearing a kufi hat and sporting a spade of a beard with no mustache. The third one, though, was skinny and pale, with dark hair, a unibrow, and a wicked scar running across his cheek. That one was more dangerous than the other two. I could tell.

He was on the phone, standing at the rear of the van, staring at us. The others took a few steps to the edge of the road and waited on him, all eyes on our vehicle.

"Jim, get us out of here." We only had so many routes into the tenements, but we'd have to find a different way to try to get a stronger signal from Bajrami's cell. This way was a no go. At least for now, in this vehicle.

Unfortunately, the neighborhood's layout meant we had only one way out of this spot without going through, right past those guys who were currently mean-mugging us on the street. There was a narrow road that ran through the cemetery toward the southeast, but the gate was currently shut and padlocked. We'd have to flip a U-turn and go out the way we'd come.

That quickly proved to be more easily said than done. Scarface over there wasn't just talking to somebody back on the block. Two black SUVs came tearing up the street behind us even as Jim twisted the wheel over and brought the Audi around. He stomped on the gas, and we raced past the two vehicles even as they screeched to a halt and started to turn to follow.

"Oh, shit." Jim was watching them in the rear-view mirror. "This ain't good."

"No, it's not, but we're still okay." I had to stay calm and think this through. "Head south, get us into a more populated part of town." There was no guarantee, at that point, that an audience would deter the jihadis, but we'd seen enough *Polizei* presence beforehand to suspect that not *all* of the city was completely dominated by the gangs.

We were moving pretty fast as we raced past the REWE supermarket and onto the Rahmedestraße. There was a decent amount of traffic, and even as Jim wove through the tight gaps between other vehicles, putting some of that traffic between us and the two SUVs and the van now in pursuit, the light up ahead turned red. He cursed as he braked. We had some vehicles between us and the bad guys, but we were now boxed in with nowhere to go until that light changed.

Chris had shut the laptop and had his hand on his SBR, turned halfway around in his seat to watch the bad guys behind us through the rear window. "They're impatient, aren't they?"

I ducked my head to look out the rear-view mirror, and saw the two beefy guys coming up fast between cars, momentarily getting tangled up with two men from the lead SUV as the doors opened. Both of those guys had masks over their faces, but the two from the van clearly didn't give a damn if they were IDed, which wasn't comforting.

I flipped the cover off my own SBR and brought it up into my lap, careful to keep it below the window. The woman in the car next to us seemed utterly oblivious to the fact that anything was going on besides the usual traffic. She wasn't paying any attention at all, until she glanced at her own rear-view mirror, started, and turned around to look at the men in dark clothing walking rapidly toward us. All of them had hands hidden inside jackets that were hardly necessary at this point of late summer in Germany, which was a warning sign all on its own. It meant they were armed.

Not that there'd been any doubt before.

The light changed, faster than they'd anticipated, and as soon as the lane next to us started to turn, Jim had us flying. He split the lane between cars in front of us, almost clipping off a couple of mirrors, and then blasted through the intersection before we had a clear left turn. We avoided a collision by a hair's breadth, and horns honked angrily behind us, but a moment later we were speeding south on Heedfelder Street, our pursuers stuck trying to get back in their vehicles and struggle through the traffic, much of it in disarray thanks to Jim's recklessness. We were opening the gap.

Not far enough, though. "They're still on us!" Chris was still watching our six, and he'd spotted one of the SUVs weaving through traffic behind us only seconds after we'd cleared the intersection. They were not giving up.

I wondered a little at that. What was going on that was so important that Bajrami and his organization would be willing to risk this kind of open pursuit in broad daylight, outside of their enclave? Maybe they'd just gotten that brazen. The cartels down in Mexico and parts of the American Southwest had sure hit that point a while ago. But I still had to wonder. What kind of a nerve had we hit?

It was possible that they'd detected the Stingray. It wasn't a solely passive instrument. It could be, but its usefulness was limited that way. And if they had the tech to do it, they might have figured out what we were doing, seeing outsiders on their turf while a Stingray was pinging phones.

Regardless, I didn't want to get into a firefight in the middle of Lüdenscheid in broad daylight. We needed to lose these guys.

That might be more easily said than done. We hadn't had time to set up the kind of secondary and tertiary plans in Lüdenscheid that I might have wanted to. We had no contingency vehicles staged.

We're being pursued, heading south on Heedfelder Street. Going to need some cover and a pickup. We need to ditch this vehicle. That was going to pinch our efforts going forward, but the vic was burned, anyway. We wouldn't be able to use it without getting made immediately.

Copy. Head for the Stern Center, Fox 32. We can pick you up in the parking garage. Tony was already moving.

"Fox Thirty-Two." In an ideal situation, I wouldn't have needed to tell Jim more than that, but we'd hardly had time to memorize the city. I had the map in my lap, next to my rifle, and had to start navigating for him while he concentrated on driving. "Keep going straight." We could actually take a pretty straight-line course for the parking garage, but I didn't think just going directly there was going to be a good idea. We needed to open that gap, and the best way to do that was to throw some confusion and obstacles in front of our pursuers.

"Turn right here. Now." We were almost passing the intersection as I called it out, but Jim rolled with it, twisting us so hard to the right while barely touching the brake that I could have sworn we almost went up on two wheels. "Keep right, ignore the next intersection, then bang a right on the next one."

Jim backed up my faith in putting him right into an operational slot and not just making him Slack Man Number Two. He didn't ask questions, didn't hesitate, didn't even slow down. He kept pushing, took the turn at almost the same speed, accelerated down the short residential street, braked fast but smooth, then took the next left turn, heading toward Kölner Street.

"They still back there?" I couldn't see much in the rear-view mirror, especially with the way Jim was driving.

"Can't see 'em at the moment, but I don't think we've quite lost 'em yet." Chris was holding on for dear life, especially since I didn't think he'd put his seatbelt on. He was still watching out the back window, though.

We went screaming through two more intersections, barely managing to avoid a collision each time, then we were closing in on the Stern Center and the parking garage.

I hadn't seen any sign of our pursuers for the last couple of turns. Jim was driving like a wild man, eliciting a lot of honking and I thought I could hear those whooping European sirens already. But those bastards hadn't looked like the type to give up.

Jim slowed to a more sedate pace as we rolled into the parking garage, taking the parking ticket just to get the arm up. A moment later, we were deep into the shadows of the garage, which looked pretty full. I got back on my phone, even though there wasn't a lot of signal available under all the concrete and steel of the building next to us. Fortunately, I had it plugged into an adapter that pushed the signal out via radio when there wasn't enough 5G signal available. *In the garage.*

The reply came back quickly. *Level Three, blue van, in the empty spot near the south side.* Tony wasn't talkative at the best of times, but he knew how to be succinct while also being thorough. This wasn't a time to be vague.

I passed it along to Jim as I got ready to move, throwing the cloth back over my SBR and pulling my go bag into my lap. We had to be ready to move fast, and do it as surreptitiously as possible.

There was the van. The doors were all closed, but as Jim pulled into the parking spot right next to it, the side door slid open, Tony sitting right inside, his own SBR under a shirt on his lap. I had no doubt that the Mk 48 was under the seat.

Chris threw the door open, clambered out over the Stingray, then quickly dragged the gear out and passed it into the van. Jim was already shutting off the Audi's engine, pulling the keys, and grabbing his own gear.

I was already out, my go bag slung around my body, my weapon in my hands, though still covered in the jacket I'd been using to make sure it didn't look *too* much like a firearm to the casual observer. I was watching the entrance, ready to drop the jacket and start shooting, as Jim slammed the door and hustled around the trunk. I heard the van creak behind me as he piled in.

"Everybody's in, Matt. Let's go." Tony's voice was as deadpan as ever.

I turned and almost vaulted into the van, as Tony shifted to the other side to give me an opening. I slammed the door while Reuben started us moving.

We saw no sign of the SUVs as we rolled out of the parking garage, though two *Polizei* cars, blue and white, their blue lights flashing and sirens whooping, went tearing inside as we left.

Reuben didn't rush, didn't speed. He just turned off to the right and kept going, driving as sedately as any of the locals. Looking over my shoulder, I thought I saw one of the SUVs pulled over on the side of the street behind us, just across from the Deutsche Bank.

They didn't follow, though.

It looked like we'd made a clean break.

I just hoped and prayed that we'd gotten what we needed.

Chapter 6

It turned out that we'd provided the perfect diversion for Jordan and David. While we'd been running the rabbit, they'd managed to get in close enough that they figured they had Bajrami's building pinpointed.

"Getting in there's gonna be a bitch, though." Jordan had a printout of the photo map on the table in our makeshift safehouse at the south end of town. The house was fairly old, but well kept up, owned by a sympathizer who was also family with one of our contacts. One of the *Verteidiger* contacts, anyway. It was a little sketchy, given the separation and the lack of vetting we'd managed to do, but the fragile truce that had been in place since Strasbourg was circling the drain, and we needed some results, so we were cutting corners.

I didn't think that was necessarily a good idea. Taking a few more terrorists off the board wasn't going to stop the chaos. It sure as hell wasn't going to eliminate the bigger players who were bankrolling all this crap, pushing the instability for their own ends. Whether they were Russian, Chinese, European, or American—and I was sure that all of the above were involved, at a high enough level—they were the big threats.

I figured we could afford to take our time with this, but something was making Gutierrez jumpy, and he'd tagged this target set as time sensitive. So, we were rushing things a little, and relying on a somewhat nebulous network of German patriots who might or might not have direct connections with proven allies. Sure, we'd dealt with some truly sketchy contacts during the early phases of infiltration into Germany and France, but it felt like this was a little more seat-of-our-pants, given the overall situation.

"There are lookouts everywhere, and from what we could see, they've got materials for barricades stashed on every street. There are old, busted-up vehicles, but we saw stacks of tires and old pallets, too. Things go kinetic in there, and it's gonna get ugly, fast." Jordan was using a map pen to mark points of interest around the H-shaped building that was our target. "They can have every route in and out blocked in a matter of minutes."

I scratched my chin through my beard. "Either we're going to have to be stealthy as hell, or we're going to need one hell of a diversion."

"That might be doable. The diversion, I mean." David was studying the map, his eyes narrowed. When he looked up at me, there was some uncertainty in his expression, as if he didn't know how I was going to react to what I had in mind. "I can pass for some kind of Middle Easterner."

"What exactly do you have in mind?" The fact that he wasn't just coming out and saying it made me a little nervous. While he'd never joined a gang, David had grown up in the *barrio*, and he still claimed that he'd joined the Rangers after reading too many *Punisher* comics, which had given him the idea of going to combat to learn the skills to clean up his neighborhood when he came back. He'd always had a bit of a ruthless streak, and while that came in handy at times, there were lines we couldn't cross.

"We've got some explosives. I can put together an IED and set it off somewhere in the south. That should get the *Polizei* coming after me, and then I run like hell toward the target neighborhood. If enough *Polizei* chase me into their territory, the bad guys'll come out of the woodwork and blockade the street, at least, while the rest of the team moves in from the 'safe' direction."

I looked around the rest of the team. Jordan and Lucas both seemed to think it was a good idea. Greg looked worried. Tony was as stoic as ever. Reuben, Chris, Jim, and Steve were ambivalent. "If we start murdering *Polizei* for a diversion, this could end up going south in a hurry." I didn't need to add that I wasn't going to sign off on randomly murking people for any reason. That was a given with this team, though Lucas might not have understood that yet. But the second and third order effects had to be considered, too.

"I'm not planning on killing any of the cops," David assured us. "I'll time the detonation so that it doesn't do anything but break some glass, let myself be seen, then run for it. If I have to lob a brick or two, I can do that, too." He squinted down at the map. "I should probably plan on that. Set the bomb off here, *making sure nobody's close enough to get seriously hurt*." He emphasized every word to make sure I understood that he wasn't going off the reservation. He pointed to the REWE parking lot. "I'll be across the street, and when the cops show, I start throwing shit and run."

"And if it's not enough? If they decide that going into that neighborhood's not worth it?" I was thinking through the possibilities, and given what we'd seen of the situation on the ground in Lüdenscheid, I thought it was unlikely that the *Polizei* would have the will to go in and clear out that nest of jihadis and gangsters. That place was the definition of a "no-go zone."

He screwed his face up in an almost pained expression. "I don't know if you're going to like Plan B."

"What is it?" I probably wasn't, but I had to hear it.

"I jack a *Polizei* vehicle and make a run at the neighborhood. Make 'em believe the cops are coming for them."

I thought it over. Lucas was nodding. "It might work, but it might also get you filled full of lead. Those little matchbox cars they drive around ain't exactly bulletproof."

"That's a risk we're all taking. We didn't bring any up-armors here." Lucas seemed to think that the plan was pretty solid.

"Yeah, but David's talking about running the rabbit and drawing fire." I'd thought Jordan had been all the way on board with David's plan, but apparently, he had his own reservations. "We've been relying on stealth. He's about to go slap Superman in the nuts and run."

I thought about it, as the rest of the team waited. Ultimately, it was my call. I had to decide whether to let David stick his neck out there or try to find another way in.

Jordan was right. They had photos, too. Those guys had gotten in close to try to pinpoint Bajrami's location, and they'd seen the stockpiles of trash and debris that would cut off just about every street coming in and out. And nothing in Lüdenscheid was laid out in a grid, either. Every street twisted and wound its way around and over the low hills, surrounding the tight circle of the original town, which dated back to the 9th century. Despite the open ground around the tenements, there were really only two ways in, if you drove, unless you wanted to offroad it. And it looked like they had defenses in place in those directions, too.

The best bet would be to fly in aboard an S70 to the roof of the building, and then clear from the top down. There were two problems with that. The first being the sheer amount of noise a helicopter insertion involves. We didn't know what kind of reaction this hunt might elicit from Berlin. Or the Army, for that matter. We had a Letter of Marque and Reprisal directed at the EDC, but a lot of the Army's senior commanders in Europe clearly didn't think that was operative unless they wanted it to be, and they would immediately accuse us of going outside our purview by going after terrorists instead of the EDC itself.

Hell, a lot of them figured the EDC was over, and so we had no business in Europe anymore at all. A part of me couldn't disagree, knowing the kind of work that was still going on back home, never mind in the Pacific, but as long as the Chinese were active here, and the EDC was still out there, still controlling territory, I figured we had good reason to keep pushing.

"I think we need to slow down and run some more recon. We've confirmed that Bajrami's phone is there, but we haven't actually gotten eyes on *him*." I kept my eyes on the map, thinking over possible approaches. "Getting one of us into that neighborhood in daylight's going to be next to impossible. Going in tonight to make the hit is probably going to be a non-starter, too, since they've been alerted already. That little chase might have drawn enough of them off that Jordan and David got in close enough to confirm the phone, but they're going to be extra alert for the next day or so."

Lucas was nodding. "If we're going to take a couple more days to look around, how tight are our ROEs when it comes to local infrastructure?"

"What have you got in mind?"

***

Two nights later, we sat in the van, waiting in the parking lot behind the *Polnische Spezialitäten Lukullus* deli.

For the moment, we were all still in civilian clothes, with lightweight body armor, chest rigs, helmets, NVGs, and rifles at our feet. We'd brought the OBRs out for this job. The SBRs were good for low-vis sort of stuff, but we all wanted the range and power of full-sized rifles for this. They were just out of sight and covered with jackets until it was time to move.

The assault team only consisted of the Alpha element—we actually had full Alpha and Bravo Elements again, now that the team was back up to full strength—with David, Chris, Greg, and Steve sitting in the van with me. The Bravo element was handling the diversionary part of the evening's festivities.

Nobody had much to say. We were set back under a sheltered overhang, most of the orange sodium light outside attenuated by the trees. It was late; though the sun had set at 1933, we wanted it good and dark, so the bad guys would be either going to sleep or stoned out of their minds when we moved in.

When you're outnumbered, there's no such thing as a fair fight.

It got less fair a moment later, as all the lights in the northern half of Lüdenscheid went out.

The hit could have gone down the night before. Things had gone generally back to normal quickly, more quickly than we'd expected. But we'd decided to hold off until tonight, since there was supposed to be full cloud cover and no moon.

The bad guys probably had night vision—too many of the bad guys in *Africa* had had NVGs—but any advantage is a useful one under these circumstances.

Without a word, body armor and chest rigs were donned, helmets strapped on and NVGs lowered. The PS-31s needed some ambient light to work, and the fact that Lucas hadn't been able to knock out the power to the entire city meant that we were going to have some contrast to deal with from the lights in the south as we worked our way in from the north.

But the bad guys should mostly be looking the wrong direction.

The explosion lit up the night for a moment, the heavy, earthshaking *thud* reaching us a couple seconds later. Seconds after that, the rattle of full-auto 7.62 fire echoed through the neighborhood.

That was our cue. Ducking around the closed deli, we dashed across the street and into the bushes and trees on the northern edge of the tenements where Bajrami had dug in like a tick.

It was go time.

The bushes provided some concealment, especially in the near pitch black with the lights out. I could hear yelling and somewhere a baby was crying. Probably more than one. This wasn't just a jihadi fortress, after all. There were families here.

We were going to have to watch our fire. Not that I was too worried. I trusted most of my guys not to just start murdering people. I didn't know what Jim and Steve might have been through since I'd seen them last, and there were those rumors about Lucas, but Lucas was on the diversionary team, hitting transformers nearby, and Jim was driving for the distraction team.

Moving quickly but quietly through the bushes and trees, we got close to the first building, steering clear of the covered parking lot between it and the three longer tenements immediately to the east. All it would take would be for somebody to figure out that a vehicle's headlights might make up for the lack of electricity, and we'd be made.

We needed to get a lot deeper inside before that happened.

The machinegun fire continued, though it was quickly being answered by a growing barrage of small arms fire. Despite the strict gun laws in Germany, these guys were armed to the teeth.

But right at the moment, they were all looking the wrong direction.

Several of them came running out of the building we paralleled, rifles and submachineguns in hand, racing toward the fight. I hoped our guys didn't try to hold their ground for long. They were supposed to shoot and scoot, breaking contact just slowly enough that the enemy tried to pursue. They'd demonstrated that they'd chase the rabbit once. Now we needed them to do it again.

And it looked like they were. Nobody looked around as they rushed toward the fight, somebody on a bullhorn yelling in either Albanian or Turkish. I didn't know either language well enough to tell them apart. It wasn't Arabic, though.

More gunfire thundered through the night. So far, it didn't sound like they'd hauled any heavy machineguns out, but the diversionary team needed to move fast.

So did we. We weren't exactly geared up the same as the bad guys, but the darkness would help with that. Especially since I hadn't seen any NVGs yet. These guys were thugs and terrorists, not frontline fighters. From what I could see, they'd grabbed whatever weapons were close at hand and run out to fight. Full credit for balls and aggressiveness, but if Tony and the others had been intent on racking up a body count, these savages would have gotten cut to pieces.

I wouldn't put it past Tony to reap a few extras, if they were going to be this Active Stupid. If they wanted to be *shahid*, we'd oblige them.

Reaching the corner of the building, we paused. The street passing between that tenement and our target building presented a danger area that we were going to have to get past, and we'd be exposed to anyone on rear guard as we crossed. Sure, things were probably going to get nasty as soon as we got inside that building, but close quarters was a different animal. We were going to be out in the open, exposed for hundreds of yards in multiple directions.

David popped the corner and I moved, keeping my muzzle and eyes somewhat toward the other side. That didn't last long, though, as three more local fighters came running out of the door just to my right.

They didn't notice me at first, I don't think. They were focused on where they thought the fight was. In fact, they all got about three paces in front of me before a voice yelled from the doorway.

David shot that one immediately, the *crack* of the suppressed shot almost drowned out by another burst of gunfire to the south. But the damage was done. The three ahead of me stopped suddenly in the middle of the street, turning around and suddenly noticing that the man behind them wasn't quite dressed or armed the same.

Too late. I already had my offset red dot on the first man's chest, glowing white in my PS-31s. His HK33 was still pointed at the ground when I shot him through the heart. He staggered, then dropped. I was already past him, putting a hammer pair into the next man as I kept moving. David and I shot the last man at almost the same time, even as he brought up the submachinegun he was carrying. Some strangely analytical part of my mind thought that it looked like some weird hybrid of an Uzi and an MP5. My bullet went high, smashing through his collarbone and knocking him halfway around, then David shot him through the skull.

Then we were past and running for the target building. A voice called out from behind us, but nobody seemed to have figured out quite what had just happened yet. There was too much noise, too much confusion.

I considered trying to return to the slow and sneaky approach as I rounded the car parked out on the street in front of the building, but quickly discarded the idea as another figure carrying a rifle came out of the front door, looking for the source of the commotion. He must have been sheltered enough from the diversionary noise to have heard our suppressed 7.62 fire.

Instead of trying to hug the wall and slow things down, I shot him dead while I hooked around the car and headed straight for the door. Glass cracked behind him as the bullet passed straight through his torso, and he staggered back against the entryway, leaving a dark smear on the wall as he slid down toward the ground.

Then we were sprinting toward that door, guns up and looking for targets.

Chapter 7

The hit was already going to suck. We might have had the building nailed down, but that wasn't the same thing as knowing which apartment Bajrami was in. Which meant we were going to have to clear the entire building, apartment to apartment, floor to floor, with five men.

It was doable. It was just going to be rough.

Getting out was going to suck, too, but that was why we had Bravo out there. And, if worse came to worst, we *did* have air support and a full infantry section standing by to come pull us out. We'd all rather avoid that, because the long-term repercussions would make it difficult to impossible to continue up the chain.

Chris had the ram, a glorified fence post driver full of concrete, and as we flooded into the foyer, guns up to cover the nearby doors, the elevators, the stairs at the back, and the entry door, he let his rifle hang and brought it around, lining up on the first door on the left.

He didn't have time to use it, though, as shouts echoed down the stairs and two men suddenly came hustling down the stairs and burst out into the foyer, hastily dressed in dark jeans and black shirts, one carrying a G3, the other a submachinegun that looked almost like a Tec-9 with a vertical foregrip. The one with the submachinegun skidded to a halt at the sight of five men, all wearing civilian clothes under plate carriers, with helmets and dual-tube NVGs, the tubes currently folded up out of the way, one of them getting ready to swing a big, heavy pipe at an apartment door. The guy with the rifle collided with him a second later.

They hesitated. We didn't.

Six shots echoed through the foyer, smashing the two men off their feet. I shot the one with the G3 first, punching a bullet through his right lung at almost the same time somebody else shot him in the face. His head snapped back, spattering red droplets against the white tile of the staircase behind him, and he crashed onto his back. The man with the sub gun took four rounds to the guts, chest, and head, and went spinning backward to fall on his face on the bottom step. Red quickly stained the tiles, running down onto the floor in front of the elevators.

Shouts erupted from upstairs. A radio crackled with demands in a language I couldn't make out. Footsteps clattered on the stairs, and a voice was raised, the sound echoing down the enclosed staircase.

I made a decision before Chris could swing the ram. "Up the stairs." Clearing stairwells is an absolute nightmare, but from what I was hearing, I had a sudden hunch that our target was up there. If we could push high and secure him without having to go through every apartment in the building, so much the better. The longer we were on the X, the more likely it got that this was all going to go to hell in a handbasket.

So, I drove toward the steps, gun up as I stepped around behind Steve to avoid cutting off his field of fire. If anyone was going to take the lead risk on this, it was going to be me.

I popped the corner with Greg right at my elbow, two suppressed OBRs pointing up the steps in a split second. So far, so good. The noise from upstairs hadn't calmed down, and it sounded like someone was coming down the steps, but the first landing was still clear.

Pushing to the outer edge of the stairs, I started up, pivoting as I climbed to keep the landing and the next flight above covered.

A good thing, too. Another man in white trousers and a dark jacket came pelting down the stairs with an old G36 in his hands, the stock folded, and almost ran into me. He tried to stop as he hit the landing and realized that the armed and armored man was moving *up*, not down, and began to pull the weapon up with a yell that I cut off with a hammer pair to his sternum, my suppressor barely three inches away from his chest. The blast blew a massive hole in his jacket, and blood spattered from the single, ragged hole as the bullets smashed out through his back and punched pits in the steps behind him. His knees buckled and he dropped. He would have fallen against me if I hadn't sidestepped, transitioning my aim to the next man behind him, at the top of the steps.

Greg had ducked toward the inside of the staircase, though, and double-tapped that guy before my trigger broke. The man in sweatpants and a camouflage vest fell down the stairs on his face, the shotgun he'd been carrying clattering down in front of him.

Then the guy behind him stuck the muzzle of a submachinegun over the rail and sprayed the stairs with bullets.

I heard Greg grunt, but he was still behind me, and stopping to try to treat him was only going to get us both killed. Rather than shrinking back from the bullets, I threw myself up the steps, one boot almost slipping on the smooth tile as I missed the grip tape, pivoting to hammer six shots at the guy, almost without aiming.

My first two missed entirely, one of them smacking off the railing with a *bang*. The third hit him in the hand, and he ceased fire as the bullet blew off two of his fingers and he reared back, his scream of pain turning into a gurgle of agony as my last three walked up his side.

We pushed up to the next landing as another explosion of shouts came from the next floor up.

Greg was still with me, though he was limping. I kept my muzzle on the hallway just outside the stairwell, while David pushed around to cover the next flight up. "Greg, you good?"

"I'm good. Took a round to the calf, but I think it went right through." He was gritting his teeth against the pain, and that could get to be a problem later, but if he was still on his feet and still in the fight then we'd keep pushing.

Not like we had much of a choice at that point. We were about as committed as committed gets.

We were on the second floor of three. Was Bajrami on the second floor, or the third? If it were me, I'd go topside, but I wasn't an Albanian jihadist.

There was a lot of noise, and it echoed strangely through the stairwell. It took a second to decide where it was coming from.

Screw it. I prayed silently that I wasn't about to get us trapped on the third floor, but it was usually preferable to fight up than down. I dropped the hallway as Greg took it up, and headed up the stairs.

The bad guys had stopped coming down, though from the shouts and other noises, it didn't sound like we'd emptied the building of the remaining fighters. They were just holing up while probably yelling for all the other bad guys who were currently chasing Tony, Reuben, Jim, and Jordan to come help them. After all, when everybody you sent downstairs got shot, that's got to be a little unnerving.

I paused just at the top of the stairs, outside the hallway. Steve gave my tricep a squeeze, and we went through the opening together.

My end of the hallway was empty. Steve's wasn't.

I heard him start shooting even as I cleared my end and pivoted, ducking behind the slight bit of cover offered by an alcove just across from the elevators. I got a glimpse of a body on the floor as Steve pushed toward the door on the right, slamming round after round into the doorway to suppress whoever was in there.

I had a slightly better angle, but all I could see at that point was the splintered and bullet-pocked door frame. Whoever was in there had retreated farther back into the apartment.

Great. We were going to have to go in there after them.

Steve had stopped shooting, since he had no target. In the sudden quiet, aside from more muffled yelling coming from inside that open door, I heard a door open behind me.

I pivoted, knowing I was dead, but Greg was already on it, and he let out a quiet curse as he lowered his weapon. I got a brief look at a small girl's face as she was suddenly pulled back inside and the door slammed shut.

Steve was advancing on the open door, his rifle leveled, Chris on his heels while David held on the staircase. I joined the two of them as Steve held just long enough to get a squeeze from Chris before he started moving.

There'd been a time when we would have stormed in, possibly behind a flashbang, taken our chances, and tried to kill anyone in the room faster than they could kill us. There were still times when that was the only way to go. But we weren't trying to rescue a hostage here, and the concrete and tile walls were better for stopping bullets than 2x4s and drywall. So, instead of charging in, Steve started to ease out, pieing off the doorway as he went, leaning over to expose as little of his body as possible as he cleared as much of the entryway as he could from outside.

He fired twice, the suppressor coughing loudly in the hallway. Wild, full-auto gunfire spat fragments off the doorframe and the ceiling, and Steve dropped to the floor, but not because he was hit. Going into a side prone, he rolled out just far enough to drop the shooter with a single shot.

Then I was going in past him. We were at a point where stopping long enough for Steve to get up off the floor would only buy the enemy time. I had to push the fight. Speed, surprise, violence of action.

The geometries weren't great. The entryway was a narrow hall that opened up on a bathroom to the right, another hall on the left, and the living area straight ahead. Steve had the living area covered, for the moment, but I had to go in along the wall with a view into the bathroom, but zero on the hallway to my left.

The bathroom was dark, and there was no movement visible inside. I still didn't want to turn my back on it. I couldn't see all of the interior, and there was probably still room for a shooter to be hiding just inside the door.

I could hear voices down the hallway beside me. What I could see of the living room was only barely furnished, though the floor was cluttered with boxes, crates, trash, and wires. They'd been working on something.

Steve had rolled out of the way, and Greg pushed up the right-hand wall to come even with me. He fired twice, the suppressed shots still painfully loud in the enclosed space, dropping someone still in the living room or kitchen. Then he leaned out slightly to get a good look down the hallway beside me, we exchanged a nod, then he went right, and I went left.

The hallway was short, with a door on the left and another at the far end, just before it hooked right in an L-shape, going around the living area and kitchen, probably toward a third bedroom.

The door directly in front of me was shut, but the closer one was open. Immediate threat. I didn't trust that closed door, and knowing jihadis as I did, I didn't trust that someone wasn't just going to spray a long burst right through the door, the Devil take any friendlies who might have stepped out, but as soon as Chris gave my tricep a squeeze, I started toward that door.

I halted just short of it, still trying to keep an eye on the corner and the far door. No one was shooting behind me anymore, so Greg must have cleared the bathroom without trouble, and presumably, someone was currently covered down on the kitchen and living room.

If I had the layout figured right, then we'd already cleared half the apartment. Maybe we'd find Bajrami. Maybe he was lying dead in the living room. We'd find out once we had the whole place secured.

The walls were still concrete, so I *could* pie off the room. Instead, I went in fast, quickly clearing the immediate front of the doorway before I hooked around to check the corner, then swept back until my muzzle halted just in front of Chris.

The room was deserted. A mattress lay against the outer wall, and more weapons and what looked an awful lot like bricks of plastic explosives, along with several pressure cookers, were lined up against the doors to the closet.

We rolled out. The room was clear, and we could worry about the weapons and explosives later.

Maybe if we killed enough of the bad guys, we could get the *Polizei* to actually do their job.

Gunfire slammed down the hallway. I stopped short of the door, leaning against the wall to get as much of a view down the hall as I could, in time to see movement at the corner. What might have been a body lay on the floor, just outside the next room.

Steve and David pushed past the door, and I flowed out after them, glancing right just long enough to see Greg posted up on the entryway, covering our backs.

The door to that next room was open, and there were two bodies in the hall, one right at the corner, the other lying on its face in the doorway. I could see a bed behind, in the darkened room, but that was it.

That put us in a three-way intersection, which isn't ideal under the best of circumstances.

It got even less so when Steve popped the corner and suddenly reared back, bumping into David and creating a momentary traffic jam in the hallway, just before a long, thunderous burst of machinegun fire tore into the concrete on the outside of the corner.

"Barricade." That one word was enough to make my blood run cold. Bajrami had been ready for a raid, and we'd just stumbled on his redoubt.

I'd been much too young for Fallujah, but some of my senior NCOs in the Marine Corps had fought there. While the Marine Corps as an institution might not have really taken some of the lessons of Iraq to heart, some of those senior NCOs had, and when I'd come over to the Triarii, I'd had to study some of those fights. This was straight out of Operation Phantom Fury, except that we couldn't call in an Abrams to drop the house.

Charging a barricaded machinegun in a hallway is suicide. We don't train for suicide tactics.

"Chris, with me." Chris still had the ram. I had an idea.

We backtracked down the hall while Steve and David held on the corner and the still-uncleared room. Passing Greg, we moved quickly into the living area, guns up and scanning, just in case.

Three bodies lay on the floor in contorted attitudes of violent death. One lay flat on his back, the G36 still across his chest, staring sightlessly at the ceiling. The other two were crumpled around the bullet holes that had killed them.

More crates were stacked around the room, along with about half a dozen rifles and submachineguns, another LAW, a lot of ammunition, an open crate of grenades, several laptops, a pile of takeout food, and several maps. I ignored most of it except for the grenades.

"Use the ram and give me a hole." I pointed at the wall roughly where I figured the last room would be, hopefully behind the barricade, while I bent over the crate of frags. They were M67s, but with Turkish markings.

Chris didn't hesitate, but brought the ram around and started going to town on the wall above the stove. I'd been hoping that the interior walls might be a little thinner, and I was gratified to see that they were. It only took about three swings before he had a hole punched through the wall and into the adjoining room.

I'd already slung my rifle and had a frag in my hand, with two more on the stovetop. As Chris swung out of the way and a yell sounded from inside the room, followed by a burst of gunfire through the plaster between rooms, I ducked beneath the bullets as they punched holes through the wall, pulled the pin, let the spoon fly, counted two, and chucked the grenade through the little gap as hard as I could.

Screams of terror were momentarily silenced by the heavy, resounding *thud* as the grenade went off, black smoke and dust boiling out of the narrow hole in the wall. I already had the pin pulled on the next frag, and it followed the first. I had a sudden moment of terror of my own, as I wondered if Bajrami didn't have women and kids in that last room with him. Some of those screams had sounded awfully high-pitched.

Please, God, don't let me have just fragged a bunch of kids.

More gunfire sounded from around the corner, but it sounded like suppressed 7.62 rifle fire, not machineguns. Then everything went silent. "Clear!" David's voice was slightly muffled through the hole in the wall, but I could hear it well enough.

Getting to my feet, I headed out of the living room and down the hallway. I needed to account for Bajrami, but I also wanted to make sure I hadn't just "collateral damaged" a family. There was a hollow, empty feeling in my guts as I hustled around the corner, to find the FN Minimi still propped against the half-wall of sandbags in front of the door, a bloodied corpse slumped over it. Smoke still drifted out of the doorway behind the barricade, and another slumped form lay on the floor amid more boxes, an MP7 lying not far from an outstretched, bloodied hand.

A quick survey showed no other bodies. I breathed a sigh of relief. The women and kids were somewhere else.

"Check the bodies. Find Bajrami." I started back toward the living room and the laptops and maps.

Fortunately, no one had thought to lock the computers once the shooting had started, and the whole fight had been quick enough that they hadn't had time to go to sleep yet. I was able to quickly go in and adjust the power settings so that they wouldn't, so we shouldn't have to crack any passwords. I was sure that some of Gutierrez's pet nerds could do it, but the less time we wasted, the better.

It didn't take long to get the laptops, the maps, and several notepads full of Turkish, Arabic, and Albanian writing into a handy backpack, that was probably initially intended to be used to deliver one of the pressure cooker IEDs they'd been preparing in the other room.

"Found Bajrami." Chris was in the doorway. "He was on the machinegun. No joy on taking him alive, I'm afraid." He sounded genuinely disappointed, but while he was a quieter man, Chris had always been one of the more even-keeled and Christian of the team, even if he and I didn't see eye to eye on a lot of theology.

I nodded. "It was always a possibility." I hefted the backpack. "Hopefully this makes up for it." Looking around the apartment, I checked my watch. We'd been on site for about five minutes. It felt like a lot longer than that, but the more time we spent in one place, the more likely we were going to get pinned. "We need to destroy as much of this crap as we can, but we've got no time to do it."

"One of these IEDs is already set to go." David stuck his head in from the hallway. "Wouldn't take much to arrange a tragic bombmaking accident."

"Do it. Just try not to blow us up in the process." To say that I had little faith in jihadi terrorists' initiation systems would be putting it mildly. "And try to set it up so not too much of the blast goes into the adjoining apartments." The previous close call still had me feeling a little shaky. I did *not* want to be responsible for a bunch of women and kids getting turned to pink mist if I could avoid it.

"No promises." Clearly, David had the same opinion of the bombmaker's skills as I did.

It took a minute to get the pressure cooker set up in the living room, with as much of the explosives and weapons stacked around it as we could haul in while Greg stayed posted on the front door, and then David pulled the igniter and made sure it was burning. "We've got maybe five minutes. Maybe two."

"Let's go." Frankly, I was surprised reinforcements hadn't already tried to storm the apartment. Maybe the jihadis were more spread out in these tenements than we'd thought.

Or maybe they'd all run out to dogpile on the Bravo Element without taking the time to grab comms, and any yelling that Bajrami might have done to get them back before he died had gone unnoticed.

We hurried out of the apartment, leaving the door shut behind us, flowing down the stairs as fast as we could without dropping security. Three more men came running up from the second floor, but Greg killed them in a heartbeat, dragging his muzzle across as he pulled the trigger as fast as it could reset, the gunfire blending together into a thunderous crackle in the stairwell. We ran over the bodies, muzzles tracking toward the opening and the elevators, and kept going.

No sooner had we burst out of the front door than a van pulled up out front and the side door slid open, half a dozen dark-clad shooters immediately piling out into the street. We were in the entryway with no cover, no concealment at all.

Chapter 8

I'd just stepped out the door, and there was nothing for it. Snapping my rifle up, I opened fire as soon as my dot was in the dark rectangle of the van's door. There was no time for more precise aiming than that, and with no cover, in the open, despite the darkness, the only way we were going to survive the next few seconds would be through speed and aggression.

Steve opened fire next to me, even as a voice shouted stridently through a bullhorn somewhere off to our right. I shifted my aim and shot the driver through the window before he could get his door open and bring a weapon to bear. I could just make out another silhouette behind him, but then that guy was out and crouched behind the van.

I kept moving, angling toward the front of the vehicle. We needed to clear these guys out and make tracks, before the rest of the neighborhood dogpiled on us.

The fact that we hadn't gotten dogpiled already, along with the rattling bursts of gunfire off to the south, suggested that Tony and the Bravo Element were doing their thing, and doing it well. Sirens whooped farther away, but from what we knew, it was unlikely that the *Polizei* were going to intervene anytime soon.

I cleared the bumper at the same moment that the right-seater, spattered with what had to be the driver's blood, leaned out behind an MP5. All I had to do was shift my dot a couple inches higher. I blew his brains all over the pavement, and then we were moving on the van.

Nobody had needed to be told what to do, even Steve. We'd been through enough sketchy situations where we didn't have any support that the obvious solution, as nasty as it might be, had just presented itself.

I moved quickly to the driver's side, pulled the door open, and hauled the dead man out, letting him fall to the street with a limp, final *thump*. David and Chris were already at the back, doing the same with the bodies in the rear, while Greg limped over to us and took up rear security, Steve watching the other direction.

The guy on the bullhorn was getting louder and more hysterical. He *probably* couldn't see what had just happened—it sounded like the voice was coming around the corner from somewhere to the southeast, and with all the power out, any CCTV cameras in the neighborhood shouldn't work anymore—but he knew things were going sideways. The racket was getting more intense: people yelling, more gunfire popping off throughout the neighborhood, kids crying somewhere.

Then the apartment blew up.

The flash and the rolling *boom* were almost simultaneous, and the shockwave rolled across the van as I got behind the wheel and slammed the door. The vehicle actually rocked a little with the wave of overpressure as the fireball in the third story apartment blew out every window for a couple blocks around. A plume of smoke billowed into the night sky as what was left of the apartment's interior burned. Frag and shattered glass rattled on the van's roof.

Steve hauled the side door shut and slapped me on the shoulder. "All in! Go!"

I threw the van into gear and headed out, hoping that it looked enough like one of theirs, the handful of bullet holes in the side notwithstanding, to get us out of there.

Greg was already on the radio. After all, I was busy driving, and he *was* the team's primary comm guy. "Chatty,

Strawberry. We're clear. Break contact and get back to the RV point."

Another long, crackling burst of gunfire sounded through the night, and then we were roaring up Breitenfeld, past the boarded-up, graffiti-marred Markuskirche and into the dark.

***

I didn't take us back to the safehouse. That would have been a bad idea, especially in a shot-up, blood-spattered van that might or might not be associated with the jihadis. We didn't have enough contacts with the local *Polizei* to know for sure how closely they were tracking the bad guys in the north of Lüdenscheid, and if they had a BOLO out for that van, we could find ourselves in a whole lot of trouble, real fast. Sure, we were technically part of the "peacekeeping" force, but after what we'd seen with the *Bundespolizei* reaction outside Bremen, I didn't trust the local cops not to be infiltrated, or just anti-American enough to try to throw us in the clink for carrying weapons.

The local Army commander, Lt. Colonel Beck, was supposed to be one of the good ones, but just how willing the Army would be to step in to back us up had been an open question since before the offensive, back in the spring.

So, I headed north, getting through the darkened residential neighborhood outside the Islamist-dominated tenements, past the back of the Mercedes-Benz dealership, and turned onto a dirt road that led into a patch of woods just south of a local farmer's field, killing the headlights as soon as I made the turn. Pushing about two hundred yards down the road on NVGs, I then turned and drove about fifty yards into the forest itself before parking and killing the engine. "End of the line. Everybody out." I suited actions to words, kicking the door open and bailing out, taking the keys with me. The rest of the Alpha Element was already out, and I started toward the east, keying my radio as I went. "Chatty, Deacon. We're clear, the vehicle's ditched. What's your status?"

I knew I might not get a reply right away. If they hadn't broken contact cleanly, it might be a while.

If Tony was dead, he wouldn't have heard me at all. I tried not to think about that eventuality. If Tony had gone down, as long as any of the others were still alive and kicking, they'd step up.

"This is Chatty. We appear to be clear. Linking up with Boozer in five. Do you need a pickup?"

"Affirmative. We'll meet you by Echo Four Four." We'd pinpointed that spot as a pre-planned extract site, just in case this very thing happened.

"Ten mikes." Tony was moving.

I looked around at the rest of the Alpha Element. "Greg, you good to cover some territory?" I kept my voice low, even though it was unlikely that anyone could hear us over the continuing sporadic gunfire, screaming, yelling on bullhorns, and the whoop of *Polizei* sirens down by the tenements.

"I'm good. Got it wrapped up while we were on the way. Wasn't near as bad as it felt like at first." Greg's voice was a little tight with pain, but he was still trying to put that cheerful face on it.

"Okay. David, you've got point. Keep us in the dark."

***

It took a little more than the ten minutes that Tony had called for. Keeping away from houses—which meant a risky crossing through an open field, weapons held down at our sides so that if anyone looked out their window wouldn't immediately identify men with rifles—meant we couldn't take a straight shot at the rendezvous point, so we had about half a mile to cover.

Still, we managed to avoid any further contact, though it really sounded like Lüdenscheid was going to hell in a handbasket the entire time.

Tony was there with another van, blacked out, parked on the side of the road next to the entrance to the Sport Club Lüdenscheid. A quick exchange of IR flashes on our PS-31s confirmed that we were in the right place, and we were friendlies. Then we were crowding into an already crowded van.

"No target?" Tony was in the right seat, Jordan driving.

"He was there. He's now an ex-Bajrami." I pulled the door shut and banged on the roof. "Let's go."

"So, he's finally a good terrorist?" Jordan pulled us away from the curb and started back the way we'd gone on our initial escape, back toward that Mercedes dealership.

"Finally." I pulled the pack off my back. "We did get some intel, hopefully." I just hoped that we got back to the safehouse before the laptop batteries died.

"Well, hang onto it." Tony turned back to the front. "Because from the sounds of things, it might take some doing to get back."

I didn't need to ask. A line of tracers stitched into the sky, and the southern skyline, dark as it was, was backlit by flashing blue lights.

We'd unleashed a shitstorm, there was no doubt of that.

I prayed for those German cops, whether they were our adversaries or not, as we wove our way out of town and into the country roads, slowly working our way back toward southern Lüdenscheid. Even more fervently, I prayed for the civvies who were in harm's way, even as I reflected on the fact that they'd allowed those vipers to slither right into the middle of their city.

It's a complicated thing, modern war. And there are no good solutions to any of it. Every development since the 1960s has made sure of that.

***

It was close to 0400 by the time we made it back to the safehouse. Fires were burning in the north of town, and the *Polizei* were in a running firefight with the jihadis on several blocks outside the enclave in the tenements. In other places, it appeared that violent mobs were rampaging toward the center of town. We'd stirred up a hornet's nest, all right.

I had mixed feelings about that. A lot of people were suffering who had nothing to do with our mission. On the other hand, we'd all seen what happened when those who could do something refused for fear of the mob. It didn't make things any better.

89

Maybe the Germans would step up, especially now that things had changed.

All the weapons and gear were back in duffel bags when we pulled up to the safehouse, and we piled out and hustled inside. The lights were still on down here, so we could still be seen if anyone was looking, but it looked a lot like the locals were keeping their heads down for the moment.

Once we were inside, security was set, and weapons were hastily cleaned, Tony and I set a rest rotation, then sat down with the laptops and the maps.

We got the laptops plugged in just in time. Changing the power settings had kept them from going to sleep or shutting down, keeping them logged in the entire time, but it had been close. Both had their batteries almost drained by the time we got them plugged into the wall and charging.

Most of the contents were in Turkish and Arabic, but fortunately there are plenty of translation programs out there. The translations could still be iffy at times, but in this case, they did the trick.

"This is useful, but I don't know that it's going to get us any higher up the kill chain." I leaned back and rubbed my eyes. It was almost 0600, and I hadn't slept in over twenty-four hours. I was getting along in years for that kind of sleep deprivation. "They've definitely got plenty of targets in mind, including gutting the local *Polizei*."

Tony nodded, looking just as tired as I felt. "Same here. Though this list of Persons of Interest is pretty interesting. Almost all of them are anti-Islamists, but they just so happen to all be anti-EDC, too. And get this, the email program where some of them came in is still up." He pointed to the screen. "The emails are *fairly* sterile, but I bet the nerds back in Bavaria could dig up an IP address."

"Provided it wasn't masked behind a VPN." I stifled a yawn. "If the targeters were smart, they'd have used at least one."

Tony shrugged. "Maybe. Worth a shot though." He waved at both computers. "This isn't getting us any closer otherwise. Dead end."

"Maybe." I thought about it, but realized that I was getting too foggy for serious intel analysis, not that I was an analyst. "Maybe the eggheads can figure something out from the target list." Sometimes that provided clues, especially in an environment where so many groups had so many conflicting agendas. The Turks, and the jihadis they appeared to be sponsoring, wouldn't be interested in the reinstallation of the European Defense Council, but the EDC would be interested in making life without them as unstable and violent as possible. Which might mean they could be feeding the jihadis target sets, money, and weapons.

War was increasingly becoming a matter not so much of alliances and armies as it was converging methods and interests among a plethora of state and non-state actors. Sometimes all it took was paying someone *not* to act, while another faction—who might be hostile to your goals in the long term—ran amok.

"We'll head out in the morning." I looked at my watch and sighed. It was *already* morning. "After we've gotten at least a couple hours sleep each. Getting out of here might be interesting."

I had no idea.

***

By noon, the riots had calmed down a little. That might have only been because the rioters had gotten tired and gone home. But a lot of other people were converging on Lüdenscheid.

The roadblock set up on the traffic circle ahead, right on the Herscheider Landstraße 199, had a single blue-and-white *Polizei* car off to one side. The other vehicles were all dark, unmarked SUVs, herringboned across the four ways in and out of the traffic circle, surrounded by men in gray, all wearing black plate carriers and helmets and carrying QBZ-03s.

The *Polizei* were short-staffed, so they'd brought in One World Holistic Security Concepts to back them up.

Or whoever was pulling their strings had brought in OWHSC to run the show, under guise of "assisting" the *Polizei*.

We had no illusions about how friendly the OWHSC operators were going to be.

"Well, this doesn't look good." Chris was behind the wheel of our backup vehicle. I'd considered going back for the SUV we'd used on insert, but that hadn't seemed like a good idea, especially not with fires still raging in northern Lüdenscheid.

"No, it doesn't." I didn't want to get into a firefight with these guys. Not yet, anyway. And certainly not on their terms. "Pull in here." There was a steakhouse just off the road, and it was easy enough to get into the parking lot. I pulled out the map.

"We need to head back north." I traced the route on the map, to the next entrance onto the autobahn. Again, by all accounts we shouldn't be messed with, but I was not exactly in a trusting mood after Bremen.

"Might be another roadblock there." Chris wasn't arguing as he pulled out of the parking lot and headed along the side streets back toward the Landstraße. He was just pointing out facts.

"Might be." I was already looking for another route out, off the autobahn. It would be slower, but we might be able to move quietly, without too many questions.

Maybe I was being paranoid. We *did* still have our Letter of Marque, and we *were* moving against known terrorists. We had good reason to suspect that our enemies had the post-war authorities compromised or infiltrated, though. And with what we knew from events Stateside and in the Pacific, we couldn't trust the Chinese as far as I could throw one of those vehicles.

I had a feeling that we were going to have to deal with OWHSC before too long.

We didn't take a direct route, but wove through the roads between neighborhoods before finally heading up through a fairly commercial part of town, a tree-lined hill to one side, various stores and industrial buildings to the left. So far, so good. Traffic was slim to nonexistent—it looked like most of the locals were keeping their heads down after the events of the night before—so we were making good time.

I was relieved to see that while there was a blue-and-white *Polizei* car at the next entrance to the autobahn, it didn't have the OWHSC backup. Two M5 Powell infantry fighting vehicles were parked on the side of the road, and the kids carrying M37A1s were in full OCP cammies and more armor than I wanted to think about wearing.

Granted, I wasn't *that* relieved. In Slovakia, we'd referred to the Army as "Green," meaning allied but not necessarily friendly, instead of "Blue." That had changed during the fighting for Poland and the subsequent assault on the EDC itself. Now, given some of the political statements made by senior US Army commanders on the ground, we had reclassified our countrymen in uniform as "Green."

Chris slowed as we got closer. I glanced back at the rear seats, but all the gear and weapons were bagged—even though the bags were still slightly open so that we could get to the rifles fast.

Mine was actually behind me. So was Chris's. There wasn't room to keep the OBRs well-concealed in the front. I wasn't happy about that, especially since we'd probably be the first ones to get shot if this went sideways. This wasn't exactly an up-armored vehicle.

Two of the soldiers, both young men who looked about twelve to my jaded eyes, stepped forward, hands on their M37A1s, one of them raising a gloved palm to instruct us to stop. I nodded to Chris, though I really didn't need to. He knew what would happen if we tried to run a checkpoint with those two 30mms up there pointed at us.

The soldier who'd signaled us to stop came up to the driver's side window, and Chris obligingly lowered it. "Mein Herren…" The kid clearly wasn't that comfortable speaking German, which put him in the same boat with most soldiers and Marines in foreign lands. At least it was German. I'd had to try to speak several local dialects in Africa.

"We're Americans, son, you can speak English." I leaned over the center console, which coincidentally put my hand a lot closer to my rifle, which was right behind it. Not that getting it out and engaging from that position was going to be easy. Hopefully, it wouldn't be necessary.

The specialist, whose nametape read "Taber," blinked. He hadn't been expecting Americans, let alone Americans in plainclothes. "Uh…" He looked back at the nearest M5. "Can you stay here?" Stepping back, he raised his voice. "Sar'nt?"

One of the other soldiers turned, looking annoyed, then saw our vehicles and frowned. Picking up his rifle from where it had been sitting on the front glacis, he started toward us.

The young specialist met him just off the front of our bumper, and the staff sergeant's frown deepened as the specialist spoke quickly and quietly. He came to Chris's window and looked around the inside of the vehicle.

I knew what he saw, and I could see the gears turning. Five men, all a little older, all still in good shape, in the middle of a city that had just seen a big flareup in violence. He was putting two and two together.

The question was, what would he do with the answer he came up with?

He leaned in a little closer, eyeing us carefully. "Gentlemen. I apologize for the holdup, but there's a bit of a security situation in Lüdenscheid, as I'm sure you're aware."

"We noticed a bit of a commotion, yes." I kept my tone dry. It was hard to miss. I could still smell the tang of smoke on the air.

He glanced toward the city, then back down at us. His voice got quiet. "You guys OGA?" *Other Government Agency.*

"Something like that." I wasn't sure that identifying ourselves as Triarii was going to be a good idea.

He picked up on something in my tone, though. His eyebrows went up a little. "Wait. Triarii?"

"That depends." *On whether you're going to try to arrest us as "extremist terrorists."*

He nodded with a faint snort. "Should have figured. Fuckin' OGA guys wouldn't have been this polite." He glanced over his shoulder. "My brother's with you guys, somewhere down in Texas. Told me a few things, last I talked to him." He straightened. "Head on through." He gave us a crooked grin. "If my CO asks, I'll tell him you were OGA. No offense."

"None taken." A few of our guys had worked for the Agency. Some had some good stuff to say, others not so much. Most had both. "Thanks, Staff Sergeant." I'd probably just given away my pedigree as a Marine, saying that, not that it mattered that much. Marines say the whole rank. To the Army, everyone above the rank of Sergeant is just, "Sar'nt."

He waved, and Chris rolled through the checkpoint, with Tony right behind us. We'd made it out.

Time would tell if we'd accomplished anything aside from getting half of Lüdenscheid burned to the ground.

Chapter 9

Getting back to Bavaria was not exactly a straight-line course.

If we'd been concerned about the Army, there were other factors in play in post-EDC Germany that were every bit as worrisome. There simply weren't enough US Army units to keep the peace everywhere in Germany and France, so a lot of other militaries and security forces had been brought in. The Spanish held a small section of the western part of the country, but the majority seemed to be "vetted" *Bundespolizei*. Unfortunately, the *Bundespolizei* were also too thin on the ground to cover everything, so there were a lot of OWHSC operators backing them up.

Tensions were too high to bring in Russian peacekeepers, but I didn't doubt that *somebody*, somewhere, was considering it and trying to figure out how to make it happen.

Between the Islamist enclaves that were flexing their muscles anew, those US Army units that we knew were commanded by officers who bought the "domestic terrorist organization" propaganda about the Triarii, and the *really* sketchy relationship between the *Bundespolizei* and the Chinese, we had to go far out of our way to avoid getting stopped, rolled up, or ambushed. What should have been about a five-hour drive was going to turn into the better part of a whole day.

And that was presuming everything went according to plan, which of course it wouldn't. Never does.

"Where'd these clowns come from?" Chris slowed as we spotted the roadblock up ahead. We had just passed Remagen, though on the opposite shore of the Rhine, and were heading down the road toward Bad Hönningen. This was supposed to be a fairly quiet sector. We hadn't seen much in the way of patrols or checkpoints, not even around Remagen itself.

Yet here they were, three US Army JLTVs, their CROWS turrets trained outboard, parked behind a serpentine of collapsible yellow steel barriers that had been strung out across the road. The soldiers stood to either side of the obstacle, though there wasn't much room for them between the river on one side and the steep, tree-lined slope looming overhead on the other.

"Maybe somebody pulled a hit or a bombing around here." It didn't seem all that likely in this part of Germany, but it was possible. Maybe I was being a little overly optimistic.

In an echo of the stop just outside of Lüdenscheid, a pair of rifle-toting soldiers stepped out into the middle of the road and signaled us to halt. Chris's mouth thinned in some frustration, but he braked. What else were we going to do?

Once again, the specialist came to the driver's side. "Papieren, bitte, Meine Herren." The young man's German was almost flawless. I doubted he understood the irony of using that turn of phrase in that language.

"What papers, son?" So far as I knew, nobody had yet gotten their thumbs out enough to come up with any kind of universal ID to be used in these circumstances. The paperwork we'd had to carry for the PSD work with Gorman was just for that: PSD work. As Triarii, running our own ops, we hadn't needed anything much. Everyone was still scrambling to catch up with the logistical and administrative headaches of trying to rebuild not one but *two* countries after a war. Presuming that the war was over at all, which it clearly wasn't.

The kid seemed genuinely surprised to hear English in an American accent. "Uh... I need to see some ID, sir. Passports?"

Fortunately, we still carried ours, though we hadn't exactly used them since flying into Hungary the year before. But something was still screwy here. "What's the deal? We hadn't heard there were any Army units holding down the fort around here."

"Security threat, sir." The kid looked at our passports, frowning, then walked away.

"What the fuck?" David was looking over my shoulder. "What the hell's going on?"

"I don't know." I was getting a bad feeling about this. What "security threat?" Why here? We were about as close to the middle of nowhere as you could get in Germany. Something didn't add up.

As I reached for the comms, I realized that we were also in a bad spot for them. That cliff overhead was going to block a significant portion of not only cell signals—which were still pretty spotty—but also radio. I wondered if that wasn't deliberate, too.

I had to give it a shot, though. We had been building a mesh network throughout the country as fast as we could, and I had to hope that there was a repeater *somewhere* nearby. "Happy, this is Deacon. We're getting stopped at what appears to be an Army checkpoint just north of Bad Hönningen. We might need some interference here." I didn't have any guarantee that Hartrick would be listening to the radio right then, but hopefully *somebody* in the TOC would be, and would pass the message.

"Deacon, this is Tango Charlie Radio Watch. Good copy. Stand by."

That was about the best I could hope for, as the specialist climbed up to the cab of the hindmost JLTV and appeared to talk to somebody inside.

"I don't like this." Steve was looking over my shoulder.

"There's nothing to like." Least of all the fact that two of the CROWS turrets, one mounted with an M240, the other with a .50 cal, were pointed at our vehicle. Yes, the US Army was still using the venerable M2, since no one had yet produced a better design for a .50 caliber machinegun.

The specialist got down from the side of the JLTV and another figure followed. The body armor was so extensive, with every attachment possible, from shoulder armor, to side plates, to a neck protector that almost reached the bottom of the helmet, that it was only when the two of them got closer to the vehicle that I saw that the 1st lieutenant was female. *Oh, boy.*

I could have been overreacting. There were a handful of good female officers out there. Just like there were a handful of good male officers. They were few and far between, though, and even in the New Military, a lot of the women were still carrying around massive chips on their shoulders.

Especially if they had shiny crap on their collars.

The specialist hung back as the lieutenant came to the window. She wasn't carrying a rifle, but she had her hand on her M17, which also was not a good sign. "What is your business here, gentlemen?"

"We're passing through." I wasn't giving her any more than I absolutely needed to. There was a look in her eye I didn't like, and the brusque tone of her voice suggested that she wasn't interested in any actual reasons. She was asking for formality's sake, and if she could find any indicator that confirmed her suspicions—whatever they were—she was going to use it to detain us.

Good luck with that, sister. Though that might have just been bravado talking. Those machineguns could shred both our vehicles, and we didn't currently have any weapons that could touch the JLTVs' armor.

"That's not an answer. I'm going to ask only one more time. What are you doing here?"

"That's exactly an answer, and it's the precise answer to your question. We are passing through." I was disliking this woman more with every passing second. "We're Americans, and you've got the proof right there. Why is this a problem?"

She didn't even look down at the passports in her hand. "I'm going to need to see some more in the way of authorization for you to be here."

"What authorization?" This was getting ridiculous, and while I had some flashbacks to issues we'd had with other self-important bureaucrats elsewhere, both before I'd joined the Triarii and after, I couldn't help but suspect that there was something else going on here, something that could turn this entire situation really ugly, really fast. "We haven't heard of any extra authorizations we needed to move around the country."

She didn't answer right away. My eyes narrowed as I watched her. There was something else going on here, that was for sure. I wasn't sure what, but this "authorization" bit was a smokescreen.

We'd rolled right into an ambush, and hadn't quite realized it.

She stepped back from the side of the truck, her hand still on her pistol. This was getting ugly, all right. Faster than I'd expected it to. "Step out of the vehicle, please."

"What is going on?" I'd noticed that in stepping away, she'd also cleared the CROWS turrets' fields of fire.

"Step out of the vehicle now!" Her face had turned slightly white.

I glanced at the specialist behind her. He looked as surprised as we were, and he was looking from us to his CO, confusion and more than a little alarm written across his face. So, he didn't know what was going on any more than we did.

This was bad. "Stay in the vic. Get Brian on the horn as fast as you can." I slowly opened my door and swung my legs out. My OBR was in its duffel, but I had a PR-15 holstered under my shirt. Not that it would do me much good right at the moment.

101

"Sir!" The lieutenant seemed to have forgotten for a moment that she demanded we get out. "Keep your hands where I can see them!"

"What is this all about, Lieutenant?" I planted my hands on the hood with a little more vigor than was probably necessary. I was getting pissed. I could guess, but I wanted to hear it from the horse's mouth, so to speak.

The fact that the lieutenant had a bit of a buck-toothed horse face had nothing to do with that turn of phrase. Really.

"I don't have to explain anything to you. Now, get everyone out of the vehicles." She stepped back another pace. "Specialist Krohn, search the vehicles."

"Hold on just a second." Tony wasn't usually a particularly loud individual, but he sure let himself be heard. I half expected to see his Mk 48 in his hands, but he was empty handed, standing outside the trail vehicle. "I think you *do* need to explain why you're detaining Americans without probable cause, Lieutenant. Did you snatch up the Special Forces guys who were traveling through here a week ago?" We'd been in contact with one of the 10th Group ODAs, just in case.

"That's different. They were Army personnel. We got word that illegal mercenaries would be coming into our AO to conduct attacks on local activists. You seem to fit the description, and your resistance is confirming my suspicions." She was still slightly pale, but had lifted her chin defiantly, as if daring me to tell her otherwise.

"Holy hell, lieutenant. 'Illegal mercenaries?'" I barked a laugh. "Is that your excuse? You want a look at our Letter of Marque from the *United States Congress*? Because I can show it to you." I snorted. "'Activists.' Sure. I'm guessing they're 'austere religious scholars,' huh? Well, you can tell your boys and girls to stand down. We've been authorized full freedom of movement throughout Germany. And France, for that matter."

"You guys are Triarii?" Specialist Krohn blurted out, getting himself a venomous look from his CO.

"That's right." I turned a cold-eyed stare on the lieutenant. "We've been 'authorized' since this war kicked off, long before you stirred your stumps out of the States. So, you can stand down and let us pass, or you can answer to your own CO."

The truth was, I didn't know how much I was bluffing. This was *supposed* to have been a fairly clear AO, meaning we shouldn't have had difficulty getting through. This little roadblock and the lieutenant's accusations had been unexpected. If there was somebody high up trying to get us off the board...

"Hey, Matt?" David's voice was slightly muffled from inside the vehicle. "Brian says somebody should be clearing this up momentarily. He's already on the horn."

"Thanks, Dave." I didn't take my eyes off the lieutenant, who was getting angrier by the second. She wasn't backing down.

"You have passports that might or might not be accurate, but no other paperwork. I'm not going to ask again. Get out of the vehicles. They will be searched. If we find any contraband, you will be detained." She really wasn't backing down.

"Not going to happen." There was only so far I was willing to let the regular Army interfere with our ops. I didn't want this to turn into a firefight, but I wasn't going to lose our intel, either. Not to mention our weapons. "You're out of line, Lieutenant."

"Lieutenant?" One of the JLTV doors had opened, and one of the soldiers stuck her head out. "There's a call for you from the COC."

She stared at me for a long moment. "Better go answer that, Lieutenant."

Turning to Specialist Krohn, she snapped, "Keep them covered. If any of them moves wrong, shoot them."

I watched her with narrowed eyes as she stalked back to the JLTV, then turned my stare on the specialist. He gulped and looked away. "You got any idea what's going on here, son?" I asked.

103

"No, sir. I mean, no, I don't." He must have gotten yelled at for using terms like "sir" or "ma'am." "I think the lieutenant got an intel report in the recent update that, well..." He just kind of trailed off and looked uncomfortable.

No wonder. Ten hardened killers, all much older than he was, were watching him like hawks. And with only two of us out of the vehicles, he had to wonder what kind of weapons were in hand that he couldn't see.

Plenty. A breakout drill from this position would get messy, but it would be doable. The vehicles, and most of the soldiers, were all kind of clumped on the inland side of the road. There was dead space along the riverbank. The wild card was those machineguns. Could we move fast enough to avoid getting turned into dog treats?

We waited. The tension in the air seemed to get thicker with every passing second, even though the lieutenant—who seemed to be the sole driving force behind this little farce—was out of sight inside the JLTV. These kids weren't just uncomfortable, though. They were palpably nervous.

There were stories about the Triarii, that I didn't doubt. Some of them might even be true. Most of them, however, were straight up bullshit made up out of whole cloth to paint us as fascist terrorists, an arm of the Fourth Reich. Which was funny, given how many of those losers we'd put in the dirt.

The consequence of some of those stories, however, seemed to be a reputation for being merciless death-dealers, a rep that I didn't think was part of the initial plan. Those in the military and the press who'd set out to put a stigma on PMCs back in the early 2000s had tried to make contractors out as money-grubbing assholes, willing to shoot at anything that moved but ultimately unreliable when the metal met the meat. It had had its effect, too. But when you were trying to get people to reject and possibly fight the Triarii, building a legend of stone-cold, relentless killers could work against you.

Finally, the JLTV door opened, and the lieutenant got down, stiffly. Even from a distance, I could tell she was *not* happy. When she reached us, she'd composed herself somewhat, but her face was set and there was what I could only describe as fury in her eyes, a flush in her cheeks that wasn't anything flattering. "I don't know what kind of connections you people have bought, but I now have orders to let you pass." She jerked her hand at Specialist Krohn, as if she was pissed at *him* for the orders she'd just gotten. "Give them back their passports. Presuming they're really theirs."

Krohn stepped forward and proffered the passports, and Chris took them from him. The kid looked more scared of his CO than he did of us at that point. I pitied him. The lieutenant seemed like the type to take her frustrations out on her unit.

She stared at me. She probably thought she was being intimidating, but given some of the things I've seen and the people who've tried to kill me, she was about as intimidating as a chihuahua. "You might have gotten off this time, but more people are waking up to just what you people are." There was an intense bitterness in her voice. "Your time is almost up, along with everyone who supports you."

"You're not the first one to think that, Lieutenant." I turned back to the cab. "Just remember the sort of people *you're* siding with." I stopped and met her gaze just before I got back in the vehicle. "Our organization exists because people like you put your fucking politics ahead of your duties and responsibilities to the American people. Think about that."

Before she could respond, though I knew there was a response coming, as she turned white as a sheet and opened her mouth to scream at me, I got in the vehicle and slammed the door. The soldiers were already pulling the barrier plan aside to let us through. "Get us the hell out of here."

Chapter 10

"What the hell was that all about?" We'd gotten to the other side of Bad Hönningen before Chris broached the subject. "I thought we were on the same team?"

"The warning signs were all there even before the offensive back in the spring." I was still watching the countryside as we went. "I'll have to talk to Brian when we get back, see what's up, but I suspect that higher command has decided to start pushing us off the board. We're politically inconvenient at best, outright enemies at worst." I grimaced as I watched the rolling hills, fields, and stands of trees go by. "This ain't gonna get any easier."

"Especially not if the Chinese have somebody's ear." Steve was leaning back in his seat, his eyes closed. "Word we've been getting is that our boys have done some serious damage in the Pacific. If the ChiComs get wind that it might be us…"

"They'll be all over that I/O campaign." Information Operations were a sphere that a lot of Americans were definitely behind the eight ball on, but the Chinese were pretty good at. At least, they were good at it as long as their target audience was gullible enough. What I'd seen of Chinese propaganda tended to make me think that they were far too used to a captive audience that was afraid to call bullshit on the official line. They were ham-fisted to the point of hilarity at times.

"You think that might be part of what's going on?" Chris didn't take his eyes off the road as he asked the question.

"With the 'One World Holistic' PLA in everybody's back pocket here?" I laughed without humor. "It's unavoidable."

"Weird how they showed up so fast." Greg might occasionally seem somewhat naïve, given his perpetual cheerfulness, but he wasn't. The sarcasm in that statement was palpable.

"Given what we found in Trollenhagen? I'd guess their advance elements have been here the whole time." We'd gotten briefings about Chinese activity in the West and Southwest back home. Forensics pointed to strong indicators that Unit 61398, the PLA's cyber warfare division, had played a large part in the cyber attack that brought down sixty percent of the CONUS power grid. Between that and our encounter with Chinese 'PMC' personnel advising the EDC 1st Division, I was starting to suspect that Beijing had been behind this entire shit-show. Not that the EDC had likely needed that much of a push, judging by the attitudes we'd seen in Slovakia, but Beijing had been right there, ready to offer every bit of assistance they could. And when the EDC had gone down, Beijing was still ready to take full advantage of the opportunity.

I wasn't forming this opinion in a vacuum, either. I'd seen things in Africa. So had Jordan. That was why he had such a hate-on for Communists.

"Great. So, we did all that only for the ChiComs to take over because we're a day late and a dollar short, again." David sounded every bit as bitter as that lieutenant back there had when she'd been told she wouldn't be allowed to detain Americans who were on her own side. Ostensibly, anyway.

"War ain't over yet, brother."

***

It almost ended for us sooner than we'd expected or looked, for though.

Mainz was a hotbed of unrest, especially since nobody seemed to be able to keep the power on for any length of time.

The city had escaped most of the violence during the offensive, having been far from any of the major targets, and the offensive having been audaciously small as it was. No, the chaos had started *after* the EDC was no longer calling the shots.

That had to be deliberate, too.

At any rate, we'd planned to steer well around the city. Unfortunately, we got a call that we needed to go in.

"I know you guys have some intel to bring in, but we've got a situation." Hartrick didn't sound especially apologetic. "Mainz just blew up; I mean worse than it has already. Two bombings, followed by riots. Half the city's burning. It looks a lot like a push to take control, too. The *Polizei* and several other government buildings have been the primary targets.

"One of our allies in the German government is in the middle of it, and he appears to be a deliberate target. He's being hunted, and he needs extract quickly. It looks like the riots aren't just trying to take control of the city away from the *Polizei*. They're also being used to cover for kidnappings and assassinations elsewhere. Two local community leaders who have been speaking out against the violence coming out of the Muslim enclave in Mainz have already been killed. Herr Giehl is another one, and says he has information for us. He's already ducked one attempt, and he's heading southeast through Bretzenheim. He needs an escort and extract."

It was a frag-O, not a request. The tone of Hartrick's voice made that clear, not that we were going to say no.

"Have we got a rendezvous?" I was already pulling the map out and looking for Bretzenheim. There. It was a suburb of Mainz, stretching roughly from the center down to the southwest.

"He's heading for the Aldi Süd supermarket." I frowned, but Hartrick obliged with the ten-digit grid a moment later. "Meet him there and get him out. If you can avoid an engagement, do it. The *Polizei* in Mainz are already touchy, and we've been rebuffed on offers of assistance twice already. There's a convoy of OWHSC personnel on the way from

Frankfurt, so step carefully." He paused for a moment, as if considering whether or not to tell us the next part. "Be advised, it sounds like OWHSC has put a bug in several German government officials' ears that the Triarii are a terrorist organization, a rogue contracting company. Do not expect cooperation from any unvetted *Polizei* personnel."

"Copy." I was already plotting our route, and only listening with half an ear at that point. "Fits what happened with that roadblock."

"Agreed. Just watch your step, get Giehl out, and get back here. Things are changing, fast. You're going to have to move like your asses are on fire, because the *Polizei* who are getting in bed with OWHSC are going to look for any reason to arrest you."

One more reason to treat Germany as non-permissive. This was starting to feel like we hadn't won in Brussels at all.

Of course, I'd always known we hadn't. The days of decapitation strikes ending a war were long in the past, if they'd ever really existed at all.

"Roger all. We're moving." I gave Chris the general route, then got on the radio to Tony to fill him in.

We were just outside of Bingen am Rhine. We'd be on the ground in about twenty minutes, if things didn't go completely haywire.

***

Smoke billowed above Mainz as we moved in. Things were getting serious.

Still, the outskirts of Bretzenheim were pretty quiet. That was probably why Giehl was heading this way.

Aldi Süd was easy to find, set on a corner and with half the roof covered in solar panels. The parking lot was pretty empty at the moment, which stood to reason when half the city was on fire. The people living nearby were just trying to keep their heads down.

We pulled in, setting up next to the building for cover, otherwise able to cover down on the major approaches to the north. Reuben was watching the south, just in case, mainly because Tony hadn't been willing to relinquish the Mk 48.

The roar of the mobs, the rattle of sporadic gunfire, and the whoop of distant sirens reached us easily. The tang of smoke was on the air, biting at the back of my throat. I set in next to a tree and pulled out my phone. Hartrick had given us Giehl's number. I hoped he was in a position to pick up.

The phone rang for a long time, then went to voicemail, Giehl's greeting going on for far too long. While he was still rambling on in German, talking fast enough that I was only catching about one word in three, the phone buzzed against my ear. Pulling it away, I saw it was Giehl.

"You are the rescue force?" He sounded scared and out of breath.

"That's us. We're in position, at the Aldi Süd supermarket. Are you safe?"

"Not yet. They are still following me." There was a pause, and I suddenly got the impression that Giehl was on foot. "They shot my driver. If I hadn't run, they would have shot me, too. I cannot..." He was suddenly cut off, and I could have sworn he was sprinting. I could hear shouts in the background, and what sounded like gunfire. "Help me!"

"I need to know where you are." This was getting bad, fast. Intercepting a man on foot in a large urban area, before he got hunted down and killed, when the bad guys had a lot better idea of where he was than we did...

"I can see... the Hans-Albert... Decker... in front of me." He was running all out, all right. And it didn't sound like he had much left in the tank.

I swore, digging out the map. I hoped it was close.

It was. In fact, it was just down the street, less than a hundred fifty yards. "We're coming to you. Look for men in civilian clothes and body armor, with rifles." I realized that probably described his pursuers, too, but there was only so much we could do, particularly over the phone, with a principal who was panicking and running for his life. At least we had a photo, so we could recognize him.

"Our boy's on foot and the bad guys are in pursuit." I turned back to the rest of the team. "Bravo stays with the vehicles, Alpha, on me."

The area was still relatively quiet, so we could move fast. I sprinted across the street, David with me, while Greg, Steve, and Chris kept to the left. That way we could cross-cover as we moved.

I didn't keep my rifle up in the high ready as we walked quickly up the street. That gets counterproductive if you're trying to move quickly. I was patrolling at that point, not in immediate risk of contact. I still pivoted to check each opening between buildings as I passed, able to snap my muzzle up as soon as need be if a threat presented itself.

I saw some movement, but it usually turned out to be a face peering out a window, quickly withdrawn as soon as they saw weapons. Nobody shot at us.

It only took a couple minutes to get to the back parking lot of the Hans-Albert Decker auto repair shop. I turned in with David, while Greg, Steve, and Chris kept going, moving to take the north side of the shop. Despite the number of vehicles parked in the lot and in the bays, the place looked deserted at first glance, until I saw the mechanics and what were probably a few of the customers hunkered down in the most sheltered spot behind the bays they could find.

I didn't bother to try to reassure them. As long as they stayed out of the way, they weren't a threat to us, and we weren't a threat to them.

As I threaded my way carefully between the parked vehicles behind the shop, a figure came running in off of the street beyond, turning into the parking lot while looking over his shoulder. Slim and sandy-haired, Giehl was younger than I'd expected from looking at his photo, but he was clearly not in the greatest of shape. Either that, or he'd run across half the city already. He was gasping and stumbling, clearly all in.

"Herr Giehl!" The look he shot me at hearing his name barked was wide-eyed and nearly panicked. He skidded to a stop, clearly thinking he'd just been cut off, but then my description seemed to sink in through the haze of fatigue and fear. Men in civilian clothes with plate carriers and rifles, coming from the south. "Come to me!" Hearing English would probably help, too.

He glanced over his shoulder one more time as he started to jog toward us, then his eyes widened and he tried to throw himself behind a car.

Two men in civilian clothes, over-the-shoulder bags by their sides, came around the corner and spotted Giehl. The one with longish hair lifted a radio out of his bag, while the one with the short, salt-and-pepper hair pulled some kind of 9mm AR pistol out of his own, bringing it up as he closed in on Giehl, before he noticed David and I closing in on him.

The calculation didn't take long. He just wasn't very good at math.

I was a lot faster than he was, and my 7.62 rifle was a lot closer to his centerline than his 9mm was to mine. I blew a bloody hole through his A-zone a split second before he could even get his own weapon pointed almost at the car right in front of me. My follow-up shot was already on the way as his fingers went slack around the weapon, his eyes glazing as a red stain spread across his chest and his knees buckled. He was already falling as my second shot blasted his collarbone to fragments.

The second man's eyes went wide, and he tried to shove the radio back into the bag and reach for his own weapon. David shot him through the temple a split-second later, while I was still tracking in on him with my own red dot. He went over backward, crumpling to the pavement in a heartbeat.

David was moving, right off to my left as I stepped around the car, my rifle still up and trained on the first man, but my eyes already scanning the corner beyond as more gunfire echoed from the far side of the shop. Greg and the others were getting stuck in. "Grab Giehl." I moved on the two shooters we'd dropped as David shifted course, stepping around behind me and moving toward our package while I closed on the corpses, putting myself between Giehl and the bad guys.

I popped the corner quickly and found myself facing another man with another one of the 9mm ARs. He got off the first shot, but he was high, and I heard and felt the bullet pass over my head just before I slammed a 7.62 round through his chest from thirty yards away. He fell sideways onto the pavement.

"Strawberry, Deacon. We have the package, moving back to the vics." I bent and retrieved the two ARs from the dead men at my feet, slinging the second man's bag over my shoulder, with radio, weapon, and everything else before grabbing the first man's sub gun, throwing the one-point sling over my head and shoving both behind my back. David had Giehl on his feet, instructing him to keep a hand on his shoulder as he moved, his weapon up and held in both hands, ready to move.

"Let's go." The crackle of suppressed rifle fire and answering 9mm fire had slackened to the north, but there was clearly a full team after Giehl, and we didn't know what kind of backup they might have. David didn't hesitate or dawdle, but quickly started toward the street, retracing our steps.

I moved up next to him as we got closer, though not without pausing behind the minivan at the end of the parking lot to check our six. The bodies lay where they'd fallen, the people inside the shop were still holding in place, trying to go unnoticed, and no one else had followed the three we'd shot yet. Then I moved up ahead of David, popping the corner to the north to cover as he turned back toward the Bravo element and our vehicles, taking his hand off the forearm of his OBR long enough to key his own radio. "Chatty, Peanut, coming to you."

I held on the corner as David and Giehl ran across the street and toward the Aldi Süd parking lot. A final hammer pair of suppressed 7.62 shots sounded on the far side of the shop, and then Chris and Steve came out onto the street. I dipped my muzzle as they crossed my line of sight, then signaled as Greg came out last, turning once as he came out onto the sidewalk to check behind them. Then the three of them pushed across the street and started to collapse back toward the parking lot and the vehicles.

"Last man!" Greg shouted the words over his shoulder as they ran past me, then he stopped and got down on a knee behind a tree, his own rifle trained back down the street. "Turn and go!"

I sprinted across the street, angling to pass right behind him, and clapped him on the shoulder as I went by. "Last man."

Then we were collapsing on the vehicles, both Tony and I yelling, "Everybody in!" as we suited actions to words and piled into our SUVs.

Moments later, we were pulling out of the parking lot and putting Mainz in our rear view, while Giehl shook and sweated in the back seat.

Chapter 11

The TV was on in the living room, showing a nearly continuous loop of the smoke and fires in Mainz. The city was burning, and things seemed to be getting steadily worse. According to the news, if I was reading the German right with the sound down, most of the *Polizei* were now besieged around Alstadt, the center of the city, while the mobs rampaged through the rest.

I wasn't paying too much attention to the TV. Giehl was, though. He was sitting on the couch, staring at it like a man in the middle of a nightmare.

This wasn't a safehouse, not really. While most of the "regular" Triarii forces were farther south in Bavaria, those that weren't still working the outer states, the Grex Luporum teams had been given a local headquarters in this farm just outside Bayreuth. It was a nice place, and while the central farmhouse was just being kept for living quarters and the occasional meeting, one of the barns had been hastily converted to house three team rooms. We were settling in in Bavaria.

Which boded somewhat ill for the foreseeable future in Germany. We were pulling back to Bavaria more and more, as the rest of Germany, both American occupied and otherwise, turned less and less permissive.

Hartrick came in from the secure room in the back, where most of our meetings were held. It wasn't quite a SCIF—

that would have taken some serious construction that there hadn't been time for—but we could use it without too much worry about eavesdroppers, whether they were German, American, or Russian. Or Chinese.

He glanced around at us. I was sitting by the window, while Tony played solitaire at the little dining table against the inside wall. Giehl looked up expectantly from the couch, but Hartrick looked at me and jerked his head. "Matt. In here."

I got up to follow. Giehl watched us both, unblinking. He'd settled down a bit from his near panic in Mainz, but he was still quiet, still apparently unsure as to who he'd sided with, or just whether or not it had been a good idea.

I suspected that whatever he was worried about, being with us was still far better than being hunted down and shot in the back of the head.

Hartrick led the way into the secure room, and I secured the door behind me. He picked one of the 9mm ARs off the map table and tossed it to me. "Seen one of these before?"

"SAR 109T, isn't it?" I only knew that because of some of the intel reports we'd been getting after it turned out that Turkish OKK had been involved in the attacks in Strasbourg.

"Yep. You'd think the OKK would be a little more subtle than coming in with their issue weapons." He snorted as he leaned on the table.

"I don't know." I set the weapon down. "I haven't seen any of *our* guys, either Triarii or Green Beanies, carrying local when they go loud. Our SBRs and OBRs ain't exactly common around here."

Hartrick grimaced. The man always looked annoyed by something, even when he wasn't. "You might have a point. Anyway, it's a pretty good indicator that the guys after your boy were Turks. Question is, what does he have that got the Turks after him?"

I frowned. "I thought he was just an anti-Islamist pol. That should put him on their target deck all by itself, shouldn't it? Especially if he's picked up any kind of following."

"Oh, he's got a following, all right. But when he initially contacted us, he said that he's got information. Less than an hour later, he's screaming for help and an OKK hit squad is on his heels." He stared at the SAR 109T on the tabletop. "And the same day, Mainz goes up in flames. I don't think any of that's a coincidence."

"Probably not." I stared at the map, covered in red pins marking where flare-ups had already happened. Most of them were major metropolitan areas, and most of them were, very noticeably, outside of either the EDC remnant's territory in the southern half of what had once been East Germany, or several noticeable enclaves clustered around Bonn and Berlin. "I'm seeing a pattern here."

"So am I. And at this point, I'm expecting Giehl will only confirm it, rather than tell us anything particularly new, though I can hope." He nodded toward the door. "The intel you guys brought back told us something's moving, but a lot of it was sterilized to the point we can't get any targeting data out of it. Target lists from rando email addresses. Data on targets, same thing. Whoever was feeding Bajrami his intel, they were careful to cover their tracks."

"I was afraid of that." I sighed. "So, we didn't do much more than take one scumbag out of circulation."

"Afraid so." Hartrick shrugged. "It be that way, sometimes."

"Should I bring Giehl in, then, or are we waiting on somebody else?" I hadn't seen Gutierrez yet, but he might be back in Gdansk. We still had a few GROM guys in Germany—one of the teams was on the farm with us—but most of the Polish forces were back in the east, now, watching the Russians.

"Bring him in. Things are so scattered and so fucked that we're it for right now." He waved a hand disgustedly. "I don't even have a proper analyst down here yet. Easton and Albert were supposed to get here yesterday. But if Giehl's got time-sensitive info, we need it now."

I nodded and stuck my head out into the hall. "Tony. Bring our guest in."

Giehl looked around keenly as he walked into our secure room, Tony looming right behind him. We'd all shed our gear, though our rifles were still close at hand, just in case. This was an insurgency environment, we all knew it, and that meant that there were no "safe" areas. We were targets wherever we went, and we could either act accordingly, or end up kidnapped or dead.

Not that that was a new mindset for any Triarii who'd been working for the last few years, even before the war had really kicked off.

Hartrick had flipped bedsheets over anything sensitive in the room, both the maps on the walls and several rosters and mission planning schedules. It wasn't quite the same as sterilizing everything, but it would do for a short time.

"Herr Giehl." Hartrick was standing by the table, his arms cross across his broad chest. "You said you have some important information for us."

"Yes." His voice was kind of soft, though his English was quite clear, with only the barest hint of an accent. He reached into his pocket and came out with an 8GB flash drive. "This is what they were trying to kill me for."

"What's on it?" Hartrick didn't move to take it. He was a hell of a poker player. I'd known him for too long as his subordinate to ever agree to play against him. He never gave anything away, and whether he thought the contents of that drive were worth a moment of his time, not to mention the effort it had taken to get him out of Mainz, was completely hidden.

Giehl put the drive down on the table in front of him. "Emails between General Metzger, who is the current Supreme Commander of the European Defense Corps, several politicians in Berlin and Paris, senior officers in the *Bundespolizei* and *Bundeswehr*, and the chief operations officer of One World Holistic Security Concepts." He looked down at it, his shoulders slumping a little bit. "They have been working in the background to stir up the violence while hamstringing the security forces that were 'disloyal' to the Council. They are even supplying the jihadis."

"How and where?" Hartrick wasn't feeling particularly chatty.

"Shipments of weapons and ammunition coming into Antwerp, Hamburg, Le Havre, and Caen, supposedly for One World Holistic Security Concepts, are being deliberately diverted and left for Islamist militias to retrieve." He waved at the drive. "It's in there. Someone named Leung was sending Ernst Janz times and coordinates, and Janz was assuring him that he would pass the word along to some of his 'friends.'"

"Who's Ernst Janz?" Hartrick was frowning, with that look he got when he was pretty sure he knew the answer but just wanted to be sure.

"He is a politician based out of Hesse. He was a junior staffer under Angela Merkel, if that tells you anything." From the tone of Giehl's voice, it told him plenty, none of it good. "He is a very wealthy man and a committed Marxist. Also something of a playboy, without any apparent self-realization of the hypocrisy of it."

"Oh, we've had enough experience with 'committed Marxists' that none of that surprises us anymore," Tony drawled from where he was leaning against the doorframe. "Kinda par for the course."

"Is he a player?" Hartrick asked. "Or does he just want to be a player?"

"You can read the emails yourself." Giehl was getting kind of defensive, but I could sort of understand. He'd just been through probably the worst hell of his life, chased by men with intent to kill him, and we were questioning whether he'd brought viable intel or not.

Not that we'd do anything differently. Intel has to be vetted, and you can't go chasing off after every rumor that some earnest informant whispers in your ear. I know, the mil did that for decades, patting itself on the back for operations that furthered nothing, but we didn't have the luxury.

"And we will. But I'm assuming you read them already, which is why you brought them to us. I'm also assuming that you figure you can't trust too many people on your own side of the line, because otherwise why wouldn't you have taken it to someone in the *Bundespolizei* who *isn't* on the list of email contacts?" Hartrick sounded downright bored. He had an infuriating talent for that.

Giehl visibly struggled with his own impatience. "Yes, I read them. And yes, Janz is a player. I knew that fighting him in the *Bundestag* for years. He can be a very charming man, but he has no conscience. He has been gathering power and influence to himself since he first gained a seat. There was talk that he was due to be one of the next delegates on the European Defense Council before it was brought down, though he was always careful to criticize it when he felt he needed to. Those criticisms were always in one direction, though—the Council wasn't doing *enough* to counteract those who stood in the way of the New Europe.

"He made no secret of the fact that he thought the Chinese system was best, too. He was far from the first German politician to make friends with Beijing, but he has been one of the most vocal recently. He also became one of the richest men in Hesse as a result.

"The man has connections everywhere, far more than you might expect of someone still in his early forties. All of them either on the far left or otherwise hostile to any sort of traditional European identity. He has friends among the jihadis, as well as the DDSB, but he was already insulating himself before the assault on Brussels. He changed his tune suddenly, about a week before the assault." Giehl had no way of knowing that we'd been on that assault. "Suddenly he was all for peaceful solutions and talking with the disaffected. Yet nothing really changed. If you follow the entire string—and that drive is almost full, so that should tell you how many emails there are—Janz

122

was already being groomed to be the EDC's man in Berlin even before the Council fell. Metzger saw the writing on the wall. Or else someone who was giving Metzger his marching orders did."

"So, Janz is pulling the strings?" Hartrick still hadn't lifted a finger to touch the drive itself. "Or is he just the coordinator that the real string-pullers are going through?"

"I think he's the coordinator. I suspect he is being used, but he is far too arrogant to realize it." I was getting the impression that Giehl really didn't like Janz, and when I traded a glance with Hartrick, I could see that he was thinking the same thing. We'd both seen personal vendettas presented as viable target packages before.

"So, who's using him?" Those were the real targets.

Giehl sighed. "It's all in there. You might have decapitated the EDC, but almost everyone in the national governments that you Americans propped up as the answer believed in the same things. They believe in central control, and they don't want anyone believing strongly in anything but what they get told by their government and their mouthpieces. They don't like you, they don't like the Slavs in the east, and they think they can get rid of you and get back to their technocratic experiment, no matter how many of their own people have to die in the process. They don't actually like their own people, after all."

"How do they intend to do this?" Hartrick asked.

Giehl sighed. "They do not lay out the entire plan in the emails. I am not welcome in their circles. I can see the shadows of the plan, but no more than that." He pointed toward the living room, indicating the TV by implication. "Mainz is only the beginning. If they have been moving weapons to the jihadis for months, then they intend to create enough chaos and havoc that your Army is overwhelmed."

"I wonder how they intend to put that genie back in the bottle?" I was eyeing the map that we'd left uncovered, with its growing forest of red pins.

123

"That part is easily explained." Giehl sounded particularly bitter. "They've already offered several Turkish, Lebanese, and Iraqi imams swathes of Bavaria and southern France, along with enclaves in most major cities. Those negotiations have been going on for some time." He snorted. "For only four percent of the population, they are offering the Muslims an awful lot of territory."

"And it still won't be enough." Hartrick was a student of history, despite his generally anti-intellectual façade. He'd been in Kosovo, too.

"No, it won't." Giehl straightened. "They are putting their own necks in the noose, and they are inviting a war they cannot win. If it were just them, then I might be willing to leave them to their fate. But I am a German and a patriot. There are hundreds of thousands of Germans—and Frenchmen—who will die in what is to come, if we cannot stop this."

Hartrick glanced at me with a raised eyebrow. I shrugged slightly. It was more than what we'd had to go on, and if those emails that Giehl was talking about really did point us at some targets, so much the better. If things didn't completely blow up too soon, we could take our time, follow up on the leads as quietly as we could. We weren't stuck with the Army's ROEs, having to go everywhere in full gear and in gigantic up-armored JLTVs, Strykers, or M5 Powells. We weren't always the most convincing Germans, but it was better than trying to blend in in Africa.

"Thank you, Herr Giehl." Hartrick nodded to him. "We'll look it all over. You'll be safe here for a while." That was for certain values of the word "safe," but it was still better than being stuck in the middle of riots in Mainz.

Tony ushered him out, and Hartrick and I got to work.

***

Two hours later, we'd barely scratched the surface, but the picture was already getting clearer.

Hartrick leaned back in his chair and dragged both hands over his face. "Holy fuck."

124

I had to agree. "If anything, I'm starting to suspect that Giehl was understating the case. This Janz guy is a friggin' capo."

"Most people who are really interested in power are." This was a conversation that Hartrick and I had had before, but right then we both needed to process what we'd read. Janz was dirty, all right, presuming that these were all genuine. Greg had looked the files over—as team comm guy, he was a lot better at the tech stuff than any of the rest of us—and was reasonably certain that they were. Most were screenshots from an encrypted email program, and Greg was pretty sure none of them had been altered. While software that could do that sort of thing was getting awfully advanced, there were still artifacts that were left behind, and Greg hadn't spotted any of them. "And apparently Janz is *really* interested in power."

We had emails between several EDC officers, prominent French and German politicians, more than a few Chinese businessmen, politicians, and military officers, including one we were pretty sure was MSS, a good dozen known jihadis—not the hard-core, public fanatics, but the "moderate" types who poured honeyed words about the poor, downtrodden Muslims in the right ears on one side, and funneled money and information to the mass-murderers on the other—and with several individuals we hadn't identified yet, but I was pretty sure were organized crime. Some of the phrases were off, as if they were code for something. Maybe weapons and terror attacks. Maybe drugs and prostitutes. Maybe worse.

"What do you think?" I waved at the screen. "Even the little we've seen suggests that he's every bit as hands-on as Giehl suggested he is. About half what I've read talks about face-to-face meetings. He *might* get us closer to an actionable target." I looked at the latest screenshot again. "Presuming there really *is* something big in the offing, maybe we could get out in front of it and at least disrupt things a bit."

"That's what I'm thinking." He leaned forward, putting his elbows on the table. "A lot of this is awfully vague, but there's enough here that I'm fairly sure you're right, and Janz is an actionable target." He reached for one of the phones next to the laptop. "Let me make some calls. You're going to need some local backup for this."

Chapter 12

Finding Ernst Janz's estate in Kronberg, just north of Frankfurt, wasn't all that hard. While rolling blackouts were hitting half the rest of the country again, through a combination of supply problems and deliberate sabotage, the two-story, stark, boxy, and obviously very expensive house was lit up like a Christmas tree, and loud techno music thumped across the fields to where we waited in the trees.

"Man, I thought that Eurotrash techno thing was a cliché." Greg was watching carefully over my shoulder. The party that had spilled out onto the lawn behind the house looked like it was fueled by a lot of money, drugs, greed, and some serious daddy issues.

I was watching through my scope. There was enough light that I could see the whole sordid mess without needing NVGs. Clearly, most of Janz's friends—if they were really friends at all, and not just desperate and greedy hangers-on— were some pretty depraved folks.

I wondered how many of them were the sort of jihadis who would openly condemn this stuff while they peddled it on the side and indulged whenever they could get away with it.

"Well, you can't expect Janz to listen to something *good*, can you? It's either going to be classical, which is probably boring when you're baked out of your mind, or country, which is too American, or metal, which is too unprogressive for a peace-loving hipster like him, who pals around with jihadi terrorists and mobsters." I was deliberately leaving a couple of genres out, and Greg rose to the bait.

"Come on man, what about blues? Or jazz? Or R&B? Ska? You know, happy music?" Greg knew he was taking the bait, but we'd been waiting for over an hour, and as long as we kept the noise down...

I didn't take my eye from the scope. "Those aren't *good.* They're crooner music. I hesitate to call them 'music.' Notice I didn't include rap, either."

"It's just because they're happy, isn't it?" Greg's whisper was still obnoxiously cheerful. "You could use a little more happiness in your life, Matt."

That made me think about Klara, and I shut that down in a hurry. That was a distraction I didn't need to indulge in right at the moment. Particularly not with some of what was going on in front of us.

So, I just grunted and checked my watch. Falk was supposed to be in position soon.

There'd been no way to pull this off without some kind of top cover. The Army was iffy, at best, and the local commander, Colonel Greggson, was not our friend. It turned out, however, that one of the local *Bundespolizei Erster Polizeihauptkommissar*s, a man named Falk, was one of a handful of law enforcement and military officers who had been involved in Vogt's attempted coup but had evaded the purge that had followed. He'd done his utmost to cover for the *Verteidiger in Bayern*, and had worked with us and the Army on a few things. He was ready to back us up, especially since Hartrick had sent him some of the emails from Giehl's drive, specifically some of those we hadn't been sure about. Falk had recognized a couple of the contacts, and he'd proved our suspicions right.

Ernst Janz was in bed with some very, very bad people, people the *Bundespolizei* wanted behind bars.

Of course, Janz was guaranteed to have some serious lawyer-fu at his beck and call, and Falk was deliberately compartmentalizing this op, since Janz also had friends with OWHSC and among the senior officers in the *Bundespolizei*. This was the kind of guy that you'd probably be better off hauling away to a barn somewhere, wringing him dry, then shooting him in the head and burying him in the woods, because then he wouldn't be able to wiggle out and come after you.

I dismissed that line of thought. That way lay a dark and ultimately destructive road.

I still had to get through this war with my soul intact.

The radio squawked in my ear. "In position." Falk's English wasn't nearly as good as Giehl's had been, but it was a sight better than my German. "We can see a lot of lights and hear a lot of noise from here."

Keeping my voice to a low murmur that would just barely travel over the radio, I keyed my radio. "Affirmative. There's a party going on. Looks like a lot of guests and a lot of illegal substances." I might have added that last part in the hopes that Falk had enough guys with him that it might have triggered a clean sweep. I had little doubt that most of the other people I was watching—or trying not to watch too closely—on that lawn were dirty.

But either Falk didn't have the men, or he was jittery enough about going after someone like Janz that he wasn't going to rise to the bait. "Acknowledged. We will wait for things to quiet down."

I supposed I couldn't blame him. Especially given the armed security I'd already identified, stationed at the corners of the property and patrolling outside the splash of lights from the house. If we went in there hard and fast, this could easily turn into a firefight, which could just as easily turn into a bloodbath with all the drunk, high, or otherwise stupid rich people floating around, along with their "entertainment" for the night.

A bloodbath here would have far-reaching consequences, not only for Falk, but for the entire war. Information and narrative mattered every bit as much as warheads on foreheads, and we'd do no one any good if we got a whole bunch of people killed who could be used as a weapon against us later.

Welcome to Ground Level Strategic Decision Making.

So, we stayed put, watching and waiting. It got boring fast. The party might be a grand old time to those people, but from the outside looking in, it all kind of looked desperate and sad. The music sucked, half of them—at least—were too chemically blasted out of their minds to even know where they were, and the rest all seemed to be too focused on what they could get out of whatever conversation they were having to be enjoying themselves.

I was just as glad to be out there in the weeds, waiting.

***

The party went on far too long. Midnight came and went, and they were still going at it, despite the fact that more and more of the guests were passed out on the lawn or the furniture on the back porch.

Finally, about two or three in the morning, things started to wind down. I saw obvious security personnel start to assist—or outright carry—their principals back into the house, and through the narrow window I had on the glassed-in passageway between the main house and the addition to the west, I could see a few being carried or assisted to vehicles parked out front.

The wind-down took at least another hour. Sunrise was going to come all too soon, and I found I was getting a little antsy. I did *not* want to still be on the X when it got light.

It was almost 0430 when the last of the lights went out, aside from a handful of security lights on the corners of the main building. The security presence thinned out but didn't go away. I could still see at least six, either out on the grounds or inside, visible as faint, dark figures through the big picture windows.

There was nothing for it, though. We were running out of darkness.

Falk knew it, too. "All clear here." The last of the vehicles had moved away. From where I lay, I could see the interior lights going out, the inside of the house going dark as the inebriated Janz and his guests went to bed.

I keyed my radio twice to acknowledge that I'd heard. "It's go time."

Janz's security was some of the best that money could buy in Germany. I suspected that few of the guards were German. Most of them were probably Ukrainians who'd fled after the coup. Most of those were probably veterans of the fighting in Donbass before everything had unraveled there. That meant they were some dangerous dudes.

Unfortunately for them, that meant we weren't giving them half a chance.

Ordinarily, even our suppressed OBRs would have made one hell of a *crack*, but we'd loaded up with 200-grain subsonic rounds. That had required some experimentation to figure out the holds, though they were still pretty close to point of aim, point of impact up close.

We didn't wait to get up close. I lined up on my prey— we'd divvied up our targets hours before—and flipped my rifle to "semi." "I have control, I have control, I have control. Five, four, three, two, one." A series of faint, hissing *thump*s sounded through the trees, and the nearest security guys dropped. My target's head jerked back as the bullet punched through his cheekbone, just beneath his NVGs, and he collapsed.

Like ghosts, we rose from the forest floor, weapons held ready. We were all in greens, though sterilized, without the Triarii patches that had stood us in good stead in Poland. Green balaclavas had been added, too, just to make sure nobody IDed us.

It was becoming that kind of war.

We glided through the shadows, spreading out as we swept toward the outer edge of the estate.

With the outer cordon down, getting over or around the low hedge was easy. Then we were closing on the house, moving fast, guns up and ready. I would have hoped that Falk might have cut the power, but if those security lights were on solar backup, then he might not be able to. We still tried to keep out of the light as much as possible as we closed on the house itself.

Almost the entire wall of the dining room was a sliding glass door. David tested it. Unlocked. It slid open smoothly and we flowed inside.

The bottom floor was empty. We stayed on NVGs, showing no lights as we moved through the darkened, stark, modern house. The place looked like it had come out of a 70s science fiction movie. It was probably usually even more sterile than it appeared at the moment, but the hired help hadn't showed up to clean up the mess from the party yet.

Including the hooker passed out on the couch. We bypassed her, though every muzzle swiveled to cover her as we went, just in case. She was still as death, though, so we probably didn't have anything to worry about.

A part of me wanted to check just to make sure she was still breathing, but we had a mission to accomplish.

Tony took the Bravo element left, gliding silently through the hallway between the main building and the extension, while I took Alpha right, continuing to clear the main house.

With David at my elbow, I moved through the dining room, the living room beyond it, and into the entryway. The floor was stone or concrete, the walls stark white where they weren't almost entirely built of glass. If anyone was outside looking in, they'd know something was up. There were too many dark figures moving through the house with no lights on. And we hadn't had the front covered to eliminate the security out there. That was supposed to be Falk's job.

Whatever he'd done, or planned to do, he'd been slightly too slow.

I heard the radio crackle before I saw movement. Two figures were moving toward the front door, just visible through the glass wall of the living room. Both were dressed in khakis and tactical vests, with suppressed MP9s slung in front of them.

One had his weapon in his hands, while the other had one hand on the pistol grip, the other holding a radio up to his face.

They'd lost contact with the security in the back, and now they were coming to investigate.

Tough luck for them.

The door creaked open, and I heard either Russian or Ukrainian as the guy with the radio tried once again to make contact with the guys in the back. I checked out front, but while I couldn't see anyone else, I knew they were there. The estimates we'd gotten from Falk said that Janz had at least eighteen or twenty security guards on site. We'd eliminated a third of them, quietly, but it looked like the night's killing might not be over.

We might fade into the shadows and hope they didn't conduct a thorough search, but there was no time, and as soon as they confirmed that their buddies were dead, the game was up, anyway. They were armed, and that made it about as fair a fight as it was going to get.

They came through the door and as soon as they came within sight through the door from the entry hallway, I opened fire.

David and I shot the first man at the same time. The muted *thump*s of our weapons were still pretty loud inside the hard-surfaced box of glass, concrete, and stone that was the house's living room. The man stumbled as the first shot clipped his plate and plunged into his chest, then his head snapped back and he dropped as David shifted aim and shot him through the skull.

I should have shot the guy with the radio first, because he immediately sounded the alarm, just before both of us shifted aim and spattered his brains against the white wall behind them.

The radio went nuts. We were made.

Chapter 13

I considered the next course of action for about two seconds. "Bronze, this is Golf Lima Ten. Shots fired. Move in." Falk hadn't understood the callsign "Bronze" when we'd given it to him, and there hadn't been time to explain Mad Max.

We were moving, the pace suddenly a lot faster than it had been a moment ago. We'd just lost the element of surprise, so speed and violence of action were going to have to take the place of stealth.

The rest of the ground floor sweep went fast, especially given how open the floor plan was. We didn't stop or pause, simply gliding through the rooms and the open hallways between, weapons shifting to check corners and dead space, even as two black vans came screaming up to the front, spotlights pinning the remaining security men as they moved toward the doors, a voice in German on a megaphone demanding that they get down on the ground and keep their hands visible.

I didn't know how well that was going to work, if Janz was as dirty as he appeared to be. If he figured he was above the law, he might have instructed his security to go ahead and fight, even against the *Polizei*.

As we hit the stairwell heading for the second floor, gunfire rattled from out front, confirming that the bad guys weren't going to just go ahead and lie down.

We hustled up the steps, weapons still up and ready, David twisting to cover the open landing above and behind me as I led the way up.

I heard him take a shot just as another dark figure loomed in front of me. I identified the MP9 a split second before I hammered a pair of 200-grain bullets into the man's chest before shifting upward to put a third through his brain pan as he staggered and grunted. His front plate had stopped my initial shots, but the hits had knocked the wind out of him, buying me a split second for that follow up.

Janz must have been expecting trouble if his security were all wearing plates.

I came up off the stairs and pivoted, sweeping the rest of the open central loft with my muzzle. Another body was slumped in the door leading to the western room. I was right next to the door to the east room, which we were pretty sure was Janz's bedroom.

That was our target, unless he was screwing around elsewhere.

Without slowing down, I flowed through the open door, Chris right on my heels while David, Greg, and Steve pushed on the western room.

We split on the way through the opening. The bedroom was huge, filling half that wing of the house. The bed itself was central, the covers currently rumpled and tossed to one side.

I took that in out of the corner of my eye, as a man in khakis with an MP9 shut a small door in what looked like a large closet in the corner and turned to point his weapon at me.

Ordinarily, we didn't wear plates, but given the nature of the objective, we'd made an exception for tonight. It was a good thing, too, because that dude was *fast*, and his aim was dead on. I felt the hammer blow of the 9mm round in my chest, just before my own trigger broke, my red dot just crossing his chest.

My first shot was off, having been knocked slightly aside by the shock of getting shot, and I blew a hole through his collarbone and trap, just above his plate carrier. He was knocked back against the wall, a dark smear of blood spattered on the white, then David and I shot him at almost the same moment, our bullets crossing through his skull, leaving even more of a bloody mess on the plaster behind him.

He collapsed and we closed on the closet he'd been defending, guns up and ready.

It wasn't a closet. The heavy door had an electronic lock on it. I'd seen just that sort of thing before. Janz had a safe room, and his security had gotten him into it while we were moving up the stairs.

I had to hand it to the guys lying in puddles of their own blood out in the hallway. They'd bought their principal time. Now we were running out of it.

Figuring that Janz probably wasn't going anywhere for a few more minutes, we finished our sweep, which just led into the bathroom. That was huge, a lavish, luxurious space almost the size of a bedroom itself, with a rain room shower *and* a jet tub. Janz clearly enjoyed his money.

Working our way back out into the bedroom, I heard Chris call, "Clear!" from the other room. The upper floor was cleared, which meant unless Tony and the Bravo element had run into trouble in the extension, we held the entire house. I could hear Falk's *Polizei* moving around downstairs, and the front of the building was lit up by spotlights from the cops' vans.

"Bronze, Golf Lima Ten. We've got a safe room up here."

Falk didn't answer right away. I suspected that was because he was swearing a blue streak in German. I didn't actually know a lot of German curses—which is a little weird, given my profession and background; Marines use profanity as *punctuation*—but I could kind of imagine. "Acknowledged. I am coming up."

He didn't waste time. "Friendly!" I didn't know Falk's background, but he knew enough to deconflict before coming up the steps. I moved to the doorway.

"It's clear up here. Come ahead." I waved to him as he mounted the steps.

Falk was a bit of an older man, slightly pudgy, with a pointed nose. Currently completely dressed in black fatigues, black body armor, and a high cut black helmet, he had a G36K in his hands, the muzzle pointed at the floor as he came up, two more of his SWAT cops behind him. They both wore balaclavas, but Falk apparently didn't give a damn if he was identified or not.

In this environment, that was either brave, stupid, or both.

My money was on both.

I ushered him into the bedroom, while David, Chris, and Steve kept an eye on his compatriots. It wasn't that we didn't trust *them*. We just couldn't afford to trust *anybody* who wasn't Triarii at that stage in the game.

"Looks like a hardened steel door with an electronic lock." I pointed at the barrier that stood between us and our target. "We didn't bring a Broco torch this time." We'd sure thought about it, but time and availability had been against us.

Falk eyed the door, his eyes narrowed. "We don't have a torch." The corner of his mouth lifted in a sardonic, slightly evil grin. "We do have explosives, though."

I raised an eyebrow. Explosive breaching, given what I could see of the size of the safe room, would probably turn Janz into a red smear on the back wall. "I don't know if that's such a good idea."

"Oh, we will see." Falk clearly had something in mind, and he turned to one of his guys and rattled off quick instructions in German. The *Polizei* cop nodded sharply and hurried back down the stairs.

Falk turned to me, then motioned to a couple of black buttons on the ceiling. "He can see us. Those are probably on battery backup. He can probably hear us, too. Can't you, Herr Janz?"

138

There was no reply. Janz was probably shitting himself right then. The door still didn't open, though.

A few minutes later, the cop who'd gone downstairs came back with two blocks of C4, what looked like about eight feet of shock tube, and an initiation system. My eyebrows climbed higher. That was a lot of boom for a breaching charge. I looked at Falk, wondering if he was really trying to *capture* Janz, or if he was plenty happy with just turning him into mush.

Trouble was, our mission kind of depended on getting him alive.

But Falk seemed unperturbed, and just motioned to me to wait and see. At least, I thought that was what his placating handwave was trying to communicate.

His two *Polizei* started setting up the charges. Falk looked up at the cameras. "I think you see what is happening here, Herr Janz." I'm sure he spoke English for my benefit. "These men would rather you were taken alive. I could not, personally, care less. You see, I have my own instructions, from Fynn Leitzke." He looked up at the cameras with an expression I can only describe as "darkly amused." "I know what part you had to play in that, Herr Janz. Guess how much I care about your life."

We waited. If Janz had a speaker to the outside, he wasn't using it. Not yet. The *Polizei* kept setting up the charges. If Janz was watching, he had to be getting nervous.

"There was a raid on a major organized crime syndicate, a couple of years ago." Falk's voice was conversational, his eyes still fixed on the cameras. "It turned out later that Herr Janz had a financial stake in one of the syndicate's shell companies. He publicized the raid—ostensibly to celebrate the *Bundespolizei*—while the force was still en route. Five men died, including Fynn Leitzke's younger brother." He glanced over at me. "Fynn Leitzke is now the second-highest ranking officer in the *Bundespolizei*."

I wondered a little at that, given our recent interactions with the German Federal Police. Maybe the vendetta was enough to get the *Bundespolizei* to look the other way when working with us, just this once. Or maybe there were simply many factions at work, rather like other governmental agencies on both sides of the Atlantic that I could name.

If it got us our target without having to fight our way out of an ambush, I'd take it.

The C4 had been taped up on the door, right against the jamb, and the cops were adding the shock tube. I wanted to be well outside the building when that charge went off. But I was starting to get Falk's game as he watched the cameras.

It paid off, too. After a moment, the door opened with a loud *click*, and a voice called out from inside, sounding thin and scared. "Ich komme raus! Nicht schießen!"

To my utter lack of surprise, Janz pushed the two scantily-dressed young ladies who'd been apparently sharing his bed out in front of him. The two black-clad *Bundespolizei* pulled them aside and quickly handcuffed them. Neither was searched. There wasn't exactly anywhere they could secret a weapon at the moment.

Janz was in his boxers, and Falk himself hauled the politician out, kicked him in the back of the knee, and handcuffed him. He looked up at me. "How long have we been on target?"

I checked my watch. "About thirteen minutes." Which was a hell of a long time, in my book. Especially given the circumstances."

"We should go, then." He dragged Janz to his feet, then looked at me. "I think that I can get you permission to sit in on the interrogation, at least for a while." He glanced at Janz, then apparently thought better of saying more where the man could hear. "Two of you can come in our vehicle. The rest may follow."

I nodded. It was probably about the best I could hope for.

I won't say I was trying not to think about the possible threats involved in going into a *Bundespolizei* station as a

Triarius. I was thinking about them real hard as we headed downstairs, the other two German cops dragging the girls with them. They wouldn't be left behind for more of Janz's apparatus to find out who had been there and where we'd gone.

I called in the rest of the team as we hit the ground floor, consolidating on the entryway. I quickly gave instructions, picking Lucas to come with us. Stories be damned, I knew that man could slay some bodies, and if we needed to shoot our way out, he'd be a hell of an asset. I glanced at Falk. "It'll take a couple minutes to bring our vehicles around."

He nodded. "We will hold just outside the Taunusgymnasium until they can link up."

I glanced at Tony, who nodded. He knew the place. And we'd be on comms the entire time. I knew that a simple call of "Wildfire" would tell Tony everything he needed to know, if things got weird.

If things got weird, Falk was going to be the first one to die, too, and I think he knew it.

With Falk steering Janz by pushing an arm up between his cuffed hands and gripping his shoulder, we headed out onto the front lawn, watching for Janz's security's QRF, then piled into the dark police vans and headed out.

Chapter 14

The interrogation room looked like every other police interrogation room I'd ever seen, either in real life or on screen. Windowless, the walls bare, white painted cinder block, except for a two-way mirror on one wall, the only furniture was a metal table and two metal chairs, one of them bolted to the floor. Ernst Janz, now wearing a bit more clothing, was handcuffed to the chair that was fastened to the floor. The other chair was currently empty.

Falk joined me in the observation room. "The interrogator will be here shortly." He leaned against the wall on the other side of the mirror.

I took my eyes away from Janz to study our liaison. He was watching Janz, and while he was making an effort to stay impassive, I could see the contempt in his eyes.

He felt me watching him and turned his gaze to meet mine. "You are wondering why I'm working with you."

"It crossed my mind. The *Bundespolizei* hasn't exactly broadcast its love for Americans very much." No reason to bring up the "T-word" without needing to.

He sighed, watching Janz again. "We are in a strange time. I admit that I am not alone in thinking that you Americans have, once again, tried to solve a problem in the most ham-fisted and brutal way, and now we are left trying to pick up the pieces. You did it in Afghanistan, you did it in Iraq, you did it in a dozen other places, and now it has come here." He met my eyes again. "I am a German patriot, as are most of my fellows, on *both* sides of the disputes going through the security apparatus. I think that the EDC was no longer serving the needs of the German people, but I also do not think that the Americans have our best interests in mind, either." He raised an eyebrow. "Though I gather that your people are not entirely agreed on anything."

"We're not." I left it at that. "Like you said, strange times."

He nodded, turning back to the mirror as the door to the interrogation room opened and a slight, blond woman walked in, sitting down at the table with her back to us.

"Herr Janz." Her voice was cold and businesslike. "We have much to discuss."

She was speaking German, but her voice was clear, and she was speaking slowly enough that I could follow. I probably wouldn't be able to have a clear conversation with her, but that wasn't why I was there.

"I have nothing to say to you without my lawyer present." Janz had gotten some of his equilibrium back since being yanked out of his house just before sunrise. There was a sneer on his face as he stared at the *Bundespolizei* interrogator. At least, I assumed she was *Bundespolizei*. "In fact, if you people knew what was good for you, you'd let me go now." He tilted his head and just about leered at her. She *was* quite attractive, though she didn't hold a candle to Klara. "I'd be willing to let this be forgiven, though someone will have to pay for the damage to my house."

The interrogator wasn't fazed. "I think you misunderstand your position here, Herr Janz." She put a tablet on the table and swiveled it around to face him. "We have evidence of your involvement in several very serious crimes."

Janz slumped in his chair, looking like he'd fold his arms if the handcuffs would allow him to. "I want my lawyer."

The interrogator *did* cross her arms as she leaned back in her chair. "You misunderstand your position, Herr Janz." She pointed to the tablet, which he'd barely glanced at. "There is information there pointing to your involvement with an active terrorist plot, and this is a state of emergency." She leaned forward on the table. "You are in a position that no lawyer is going to save you from."

Janz, however, didn't seem convinced. He stayed slumped back in his chair, still wearing that arrogant smirk, as the interrogator started asking questions.

***

The next three hours felt like three days. I kind of stopped listening to the interrogator's questions, as they were becoming increasingly repetitive, to the point that I hardly needed to translate the German in my head anymore. Janz's lack of answers was getting even more repetitive.

I was getting steadily more nervous the longer this went on. I knew that interrogations were messy things, rarely going according to plan. It took an astounding degree of luck to get a subject who folded immediately and sang like a canary. And striking the balance between putting enough pressure on the subject to get them to talk and pressing them so hard that they'll tell you whatever they think you want to hear, just to make it stop, takes a professional, the likes of which I knew I wasn't.

But I was pretty sure that Falk, and the other *Bundespolizei* working with him, weren't entirely in the best of graces with the rest of the German government, and in fact, I wasn't convinced that everyone in the building was on their side, either. Word about who we had in the tank was going to get out, and I had zero doubt that Janz had friends in high places that would move quickly to back him up.

The blond interrogator left after about two and a half hours. They left him sitting there for about half an hour, then another interrogator came in and started right in on the same questions.

By the end of that third hour, however, Janz was starting to look a little nervous. He was still refusing to answer the questions, but the fact that his lawyer hadn't showed yet seemed to have him rattled a bit. He fidgeted, and his curt non-answers were getting sharper and more agitated.

Falk had hardly moved except to drink coffee and chain smoke the entire time. He *was* watching the time, perhaps even more keenly than I was. Probably for the same reasons. I had my suspicions that the bad guys had people in his unit. He probably knew exactly who they were, too.

Finally, Falk looked up at me. The interrogator was still firing the same questions at Janz, and making the same amount of progress, but Falk seemed to have reached a decision.

I could see in his eyes and the stiffness of his stance that he wasn't happy about it, but he'd made up his mind. "Come with me."

I was still in civilian clothes, still wearing my plate carrier, scarred by the 9mm strike to the front plate as it was, and while I'd left my rifle with the rest of the team out in the parking lot, I still had my pistol, a Polish PR-15 9mm, on my hip. I was also still wearing my balaclava, despite the fact I'd taken my helmet off, because I really didn't need any of the *Bundespolizei* adding me to a facial recognition database.

I was probably already on one, just not in Europe. Unless the data had already been piped over by some bastard politician who wanted the Triarii out of the way. Gotta love globalization.

Falk led the way out into the hallway, quickly turning in toward the interrogation room and leading the way in. I followed. I was still armed, and I still had my radio, so I'd follow Falk's play. For now.

Falk let me shut the door, though it would have swung shut with a *bang* even if I hadn't lifted a hand. The pneumatic cylinder on the door was stiff as hell.

Unlike the movies, the interrogation room was well-lit, a pair of fluorescent lights overhead glaring off the white of the walls, floor, and ceiling. So, there were no shadows for me to lurk in, but I still stood next to the door, still geared up and armed, my face hidden, my arms folded over my scarred plate carrier.

I didn't know if Janz had the presence of mind to identify that bullet impact. He'd been a little rattled when we'd pulled him out, and he might or might not have registered the fact that I'd gotten hit before David and I had killed his last security goon. Even if he had, he might not make the connection.

Maybe if he did, that would work to our advantage. *If* that was what Falk's had in mind.

Falk moved to the end of the table and put his fists down on the tabletop, thrusting his face toward Janz.

"You are wasting my time, Herr Janz. This is not a simple criminal investigation that you can just walk away from while your lawyers take care of it." He stabbed a finger at the tablet in front of the interrogator. "You are directly implicated in terror attacks on German citizens. And as has already been pointed out, this is a state of emergency, and the rules are not what they once were." He straightened, and then sighed and looked at me.

I thought I saw the tack he was taking. Maybe not quite what I would have done, especially since I suspected that the law wasn't nearly as loose in Germany as he was suggesting, uneven enforcement for political reasons notwithstanding. But it was his play.

"Now I am out of time. You could have done this the easy way, and simply told us what we needed to know. Now, I have to hand you over." He stepped back and turned to me. "He's all yours. For what it's worth." He switched to English there at the end, as if to make it clear that Janz was about to get handed over to the Americans.

After all, the Brits had enough problems of their own that they'd sat this out, despite the opportunity to beat on Frenchmen *and* Germans. Americans were the only ones involved who spoke English.

Whatever had been fueling Janz's resistance, apparently the idea of being handed over to Americans, particularly an

American who wasn't in Army cammies, dressed like a civilian except for the combat gear and the balaclava, got to him. Maybe it was the stories about waterboarding, maybe the anti-American propaganda about the way we slaughtered entire villages and tortured people indiscriminately had really gotten into his head. Whatever the reason, he suddenly *really* didn't want to go away with the man in jeans, a black shirt, and a coyote brown plate carrier and green balaclava.

"Wait, wait, wait." Janz was moving in his chair for the first time in the last hour, apparently trying to get away from me. "We can work something out."

"I told you, I am out of time." Falk tilted his head as he studied Janz for a moment. "Unless you have something to tell me?"

It was transparent as hell, and I couldn't help but think that it wasn't going to work. There was no way it *could* work.

But I guess Janz was just too scared of ending up in an American black site, where his connections and his lawyers and his money couldn't help him. Maybe all the bullshit propaganda about the murderous, loose-cannon Americans would actually act to our advantage, for once.

"You can't give me to them." He looked up at Falk, almost pleading. "I didn't do anything!"

Falk looked down at the interrogator, who was watching Janz. I suddenly began to suspect that this wasn't quite as ad hoc a strategy as I'd thought.

The interrogator flipped the tablet's display from the emails to several photos. I couldn't make out a lot of detail, but they were pretty clearly the aftermath of a bombing. It had been a hell of a bombing, too, even from my limited angle on the screen. There was a lot of smoke and a lot of red.

Janz blanched. He looked away.

"That was where an IED struck Agnes Wirt's car." The interrogator stabbed a finger at the tablet. "It just so happened to be right in front of a school while the children were getting out for the day." He flipped through the pictures, one scene of up-close carnage after another. "Do I really need to move back to the email where you were telling Ahmad El Hajj how much you wanted Agnes Wirt out of the way?"

Janz seemed to slump, though he was still leaning away from me. He wasn't quite folding yet, though. "That was just venting." He looked up, and something had just changed. He thought he'd found a way out. "Of course I have friends in the Islamic communities. They are marginalized and oppressed in this new, nationalistic environment. An environment I'd thought we'd gotten away from, until people like *you* sided with the Americans."

"Is that your reason for funneling money to El Hajj, Zaid Hussein, and Devrim Uzun?" Falk demanded.

"They are activists, spokesmen for their local populations..." But the interrogator didn't let him finish.

"Zaid Hussein is a known leader of the Western Caliphate, and I do not believe that a man in your position would not know that." The dark-haired man, who looked like he probably had a good bit of Arab blood in him, himself, half stood up and leaned across the table. "Half of those contacts in your emails are wanted criminals or terrorists." That didn't technically include Uzun, which was a name I remembered from one of our intel briefs, but there was a reason the interrogator had mentioned him, anyway. Devrim Uzun was a *Binbaşı*, an O-3 or captain, in the Turkish OKK.

A knock came at the door. Falk turned and answered. I couldn't make out the low, brief conversation in German, but the look I got from him as he shut the door told me we were about out of time. Janz's friends must have come through for him.

"If you can give me more information, I might be able to buy you some time." Falk looked at me again, then leaned in and lowered his voice. I could still hear, but he was apparently still using me as the boogeyman, and Janz probably assumed the stupid, hyper-violent American couldn't understand German, anyway. I hadn't said a word since we'd come in here. "If you are willing to cooperate, to help us find any of those three men, I can keep you under *Bundespolizei* protection, and keep you out of American hands."

Janz looked at me. I did what I could to look like a murderous, hyper-violent Ugly American while only showing my eyes.

"Uzun has always been the main contact with the others. He introduced me to El Hajj. He has an apartment in Aachen. I always met with him in the Aposto Aachen, even though it was not halal. I never saw him get out of a cab, he always walked. He said something about living nearby." He glanced at me again, then looked up at the two *Bundespolizei*. "But I don't believe he had anything to do with this."

I didn't believe him for a second. Insincerity dripped from every syllable, and given what we'd seen of the man's connections, he was trying to save his skin, and didn't actually believe a word he was saying. He was *probably* telling the truth about his meetings with Uzun, because he thought it wouldn't get us anything.

We'd see.

Just then, another knock came at the door. Falk answered, listened to the whispered message, then looked at the interrogator. "Take down every bit of his statement you can. I will be back momentarily." Taking me by the arm, he ushered me out into the hallway.

I could hear the commotion near the front of the police station even as Falk steered me toward the back. "Janz has powerful friends. And several of them just arrived to demand his release." He was moving quickly toward the back. "Your team has already been warned off. They will meet you in the back."

"You'd better come too." I knew that Falk was likely going to face some fairly serious repercussions for helping us.

"No. That would mean leaving my subordinates to deal with the consequences of my actions. I cannot do that." He pointed toward the rear door. I hoped there wasn't a cordon back there, but if this was a political pissing match, they might have simply figured they had enough pull to force the issue without

150

resorting to violence. That was most likely, if this was coming from within the *Bundespolizei*.

I hustled out the back door, though not without shaking Falk's hand. "We'll do what we can with the intel he did give up."

He nodded. "Aachen. If you can find that restaurant and expand your surveillance from there, maybe you can find something." He paused. I could tell that it stung to ask American "mercenaries" to help him out. "Stop these murderers."

Then he went back inside the face the music, while I moved quickly to the van and climbed in, the sliding door slamming shut behind me as Jordan pulled away from the police station.

Chapter 15

The Aposto Aachen was not what I would have called the best starting place for a manhunt.

The Italian restaurant was right smack dab in what I would have called downtown Aachen. Which was a pretty big city. With a population of almost two hundred fifty thousand people, it was the twenty-eighth largest city in Germany. That meant that downtown was pretty damned crowded, and without any solid intel on a set meeting, we couldn't be sure that Uzun was even going to go near the restaurant anytime soon.

"This is bullshit." Jordan was sitting across from me in Day Du, a sushi restaurant across the street and around the corner from the target building, but with enough of a view of that side of the street that we could watch people coming and going without worrying too much about being observed doing it. There were CCTV cameras all over Aachen, so we still had to be careful, but you'd be surprised how fast you can disappear into the crowd, especially if you wear a hat and sunglasses and are careful not to look straight at any of the cameras. Facial recognition software's made leaps and bounds, but it has its limits, like all such tools. It would never take the place of a Mark One Eyeball.

"I know. I friggin' hate sushi. There had to be a better place to set up." I picked at the plate of chicken and rice in front of me. It was fine, tasty enough, and fortunately cheaper than the sushi.

Jordan looked over at me like I'd just announced that the sky was green. "I meant…"

"I know what you meant." I didn't wave or act in any other way like I was doing anything but talking over our food. Jordan *did* like sushi, and he'd already devoured half a platter. "And I agree. The restaurant was always a long shot. *However*, it's a starting point, and it always was." I scooped up some more chicken and rice with my chopsticks and took a bite. "Did you see the patrols on the street?"

"The OWHSC guys? Hard to miss." There'd been a time when Jordan would have been hard to miss, but most of metropolitan Germany was multiethnic enough that a black man didn't stick out that much. "They're everywhere."

"Means we're going to have to step carefully." I didn't know for sure that the Chinese would be targeting us, but I suspected, from the updates we had been getting sporadically from the Pacific, that Americans were going to be on the general Chinese and Chinese minion shit list shortly, if we weren't already. Not that we weren't already in majority-Islamic neighborhoods.

The people who ran those neighborhoods weren't the kind we'd worked with in Africa when I'd been a Marine. Not all of those people had been trustworthy, but most of them had still just wanted to live in peace. I'm not saying that some of the people in the Lebanese, Turkish, Syrian, Iraqi, or Kosovar neighborhoods weren't just trying to do the same. I'm sure a lot of them were. But the gangs, the Western Caliphate, and various other jihadi organizations were the ones who ran things in there.

I was classing the Turkish OKK as a jihadi organization after Strasbourg.

"How long are we going to sit here?" Jordan forked another roll of sushi into his mouth after dipping it in whatever sauce he was using.

"Until we're done with our meal." I wasn't expecting Uzun to show up, but if this was going to be the epicenter of our search, there was a possibility that we might pick up on someone else who might lead us to him. We weren't just looking for Uzun himself, after all. Our intel guys back in Bayreuth had worked up what we knew about not only Uzun but several of his associates. Which meant we had photos of not only El Hajj, Hussein, and Uzun, but half a dozen other known Kosovar and Turkish operatives in central Germany. If we spotted any of them, we'd have a potential lead.

Of course, the odds of spotting one of them strolling down the Kapuzingergraben in the middle of the day were next to astronomical. We were going to have to find a way to penetrate into the jihadi-dominated neighborhoods.

That was going to be more difficult, since we could expect that the jihadis would have their own extensive early warning network set up. They might have been at an advantage due to the political unacceptability of messing with the "immigrants," no matter how many mass murders came out of their neighborhoods, but in our experience so far, that hadn't led to complacency. They had more lookouts than the cartels in Mexico and the Southwest.

I was thinking about that as I finished my chicken and rice, keeping an eye on the street. I wasn't just watching Aposto Aachen, either. I'd scanned it to begin with, but knowing that it was unlikely to be a common meeting point, I'd expanded my scans to the rest of the street.

Downtown wasn't a great place to start, but it was a start. There were a lot of people out and about, which might seem strange, given the war and the subsequent increases in crime and violence. But people still cling to a sense of normalcy even in the midst of hardships and threats of sudden violence and chaos, and they *will* try to go about their lives whenever they're not in immediate danger.

Sure, there are those who cling to the emergency for their own neurotic ends, but they're a minority.

The crowds would disperse quickly if something clacked off. I could see it in the mannerisms and the expressions. These people were doing what they could to act normal, but they were looking over their shoulders. There had been a drone strike in Aachen just a few days before, at least three kidnappings in the last month, and an IED had gone off a week before, attempting—unsuccessfully, fortunately—to drop a major intersection on top of a railroad underpass. All was not well in Aachen, and you could see it in the crowd's demeanor.

That was going to make infiltration more difficult. When everybody's keyed up, the bad guys will be keyed up, too, and they're going to be on the lookout.

Fortunately, there was more than one way to narrow things down.

My chopsticks still in one hand, I pulled out my phone and set it on the table before powering it up.

It was a burner, purchased only a week before, through a cutout. It was still a smartphone, which was much more common these days, and was kinda necessary for what I was planning on doing with it. It didn't have a SIM card, but with the Wi-Fi in the sushi restaurant, I didn't need one. That was kinda the whole point.

I'd use this for about a week, then wipe it down and toss it in some public trash can, replacing it with another one. Wasteful as hell, but necessary for security's sake. The lack of a SIM card not only kept my passport from being matched up to the phone's activity, but it also kept me from pinging on anyone's electronic surveillance when the phone was powered off.

Greg had gone over the phones extensively once we'd gotten them, installing several commercially available apps and a few that our Triarii code geeks had come up with. The VPN from hell was the first one I turned on, increasing the security of what I was doing. Then I started up a social media search application.

Now, I could search for particular accounts, or particular keywords, but that wasn't really what I was looking for. Somebody could post something about a target from half a world away. No, I wanted posts from local sources, preferably with photos.

I kept eating, almost absent-mindedly, while Jordan kept watching the outside. This was all part of the plan.

Scrolling through social media posts localized to a large city is a grinding, disheartening chore. After half an hour, I was ready to quit regardless of the fact that we'd planned to only keep the phones up for about that amount of time. Most of it was mundane and boring, a lot of it was vicious and disgusting, and the vast majority of it was completely useless.

But that's intel collection. Most of the information you get and pass on up the chain isn't particularly useful. You hope that there's a nugget in the landslide of crap, somewhere.

And there it was.

Most organizations, be they commercial, criminal, or ideological, use social media a lot. It's a major—if not the primary—attack vector for information operations and outright propaganda. The jihadis are no exception. And in a city that is a battleground for their ideology, they will be posting a lot.

They were, and while it had taken me a while to find the right accounts, I'd picked them up. Scrolling through them was worse than the mundane, boringly self-absorbed stuff that accounts for the bulk of social media. Most people who complain about the characterization of Islamist terrorists have never been around them, never seen any of their propaganda, and don't actually understand just how cruel, bloodthirsty, and psychotic some of these people are.

A lot of them don't bother to try to hide it. They revel in it.

Sifting through the constant barrage of hatred, insincere assertions of victimization, and celebration of death was rough. But finally, I had what I needed.

Powering the phone off, I shoved it in my pocket and finished the last bits of chicken and rice. They were getting cold. "Let's go."

***

I hadn't found a social media post with Uzun taking a selfie with his ten-digit grid and itinerary for the next week, down to the minute. That would have been nice, but that's just not the way intel works.

What I *had* found was a propaganda video. It hadn't had Uzun in it, or any of his immediate circle of known associates. Fawzi Amari *was* a known associate, he was just more of a client. A Tunisian "refugee" who was wanted for terror attacks in France, Spain, and Italy, he had been a driving force in the jihadi riot in Strasbourg. The fact that the OKK had been instrumental in that riot was a connection in and of itself, but there were photos of meetings between Amari and Uzun himself, both before and after. Uzun wasn't *publicly* known to be OKK. We only knew that because of contacts we had in the intelligence community. To the public in Europe, he was an activist, pushing the "marginalization" of Islamic communities in Germany and France as hard as he could.

So, if we found Amari, there was a good chance we'd find a thread that would lead to Uzun. And thanks to that video, we had all we needed to find Amari.

If he'd been smart, Amari would have had the camera facing a blank wall, probably with Western Caliphate flags and all sorts of other jihadi propaganda on it. Instead, he'd left an angle to the window, with a clear view of a building mostly covered with green glass, next to what looked an awful lot like an industrial smokestack. That had made it easy.

Of course, the fact that Amari hadn't disabled his location services before he'd posted helped, too.

"Still quiet." Lucas was shuffling along the Schillerstraße, convincingly dressed as a homeless vagrant, though he had his own PR-15 in his waistband. It was a risk, letting him go in there like that. The *Polizei* seemed to be generally leaving the homeless alone, but the OWHSC operators tended to treat them pretty roughly, and we weren't confident that the gang or militia patrols closer to the jihadi centers of gravity would do much better. He could defend himself, but if Lucas had to pull, we were going to have to go in there fast to get him out before he got dogpiled and shot to doll rags.

I was sitting with Chris and David in a Peugeot just down the street, my go bag at my feet with my SBR Tactical in it, listening to the radio in a small, Bluetooth earpiece. I couldn't talk to Lucas—well, I could, but it might draw more attention to him if he was talking to himself more than he needed to. His history, and what I'd seen of his performance since he'd joined the team, told me that if there was something that needed to be reported, he'd report it.

Naturally, as soon as I thought that, he had something to report. "Crows coming out." A "crow" was radio shorthand for a bad guy. "Getting into a van."

I nodded to Chris, who put our ancient car into gear and eased us up to the corner. We had been sitting on the side of the Weberstraße, out of sight but close enough that we could support Lucas if he got in trouble. He wasn't in trouble yet, but if Amari or his buddies were moving, he might be shortly.

Chris got us up to the intersection, but there was no room to park the vehicle there. We were going to have to move through, which might be necessary anyway so as to avoid the appearance that we were sitting there watching the target building.

As we passed, I saw the blue van pull away from the building. That was pretty identifiable, and I was confident that we could probably pick it up again farther down the line, provided it didn't get too far ahead. I waved at Chris to keep going straight. We'd circle around and pick it up again.

It might be nothing.

It might lead us to our target.

Chapter 16

As it turned out, the van didn't lead us to our target. Nor did any other leads we picked up over the next three days.

We still kept up surveillance on Amari, though I kept dropping into random cafes and restaurants to use their Wi-Fi to look for any more useful indicators. I was getting really tired of the social media open-source intel collection, but it had been mighty useful before. It's not as great as having someone on the inside bugged or otherwise talking to you, but you'd be surprised what you can find out just by scrolling through social media.

Uzun was keeping his head down, though. I didn't know if he'd figured out that with Janz getting picked up, he was on *somebody*'s target deck, or if he just had something else in mind. But there had been no sign of him in Aachen. At least, not that anyone was talking about, even indirectly.

I was starting to consider just wrapping Amari up and seeing where an interrogation would lead, when things started moving.

Suddenly, all the jihadi accounts were hinting at something big. Something that "the Faithful" would rejoice over. And that was when Uzun showed back up on the radar.

It was nothing solid, at first. There were just indicators. "Friends from the east" seemed to be a common phrase, and I took it to mean outsiders bringing support. Russians seemed unlikely, though I wouldn't have put it past them to help jihadists out as long as it was in somebody else's backyard. Saudis or Iranians were also possibilities, but they were awfully busy tearing each other's guts out at the moment, and the Turks seemed to have the most interest in central Europe.

We didn't know for sure, but half the team scattered across the city, stepping up surveillance on the targets we'd identified. We were watching Uzun's potential contacts and anyone else who might be in touch with whoever was pushing whatever new nightmare was in store.

"Contact. On Amari's place." Jordan was playing tourist, and so far, he had been generally unmolested, though he'd gotten some nasty looks when passing by OWHSC checkpoints. "Time now."

With five of the ten of us on singleton surveillance ops, we didn't have quite the assault force available that I would have wanted, but if we had targets in the AO, we needed to move now, especially if things were moving the way the traffic was suggesting they were going to. We were already in the vehicle, so it was a fairly simple matter to drive to the rendezvous with Jordan.

The rendezvous was in the parking lot of the nearby *Edeka center Vieler*, a supermarket about a hundred fifty yards from the target building. We pulled into a parking space back under the trees and Jordan worked his way through the parked vehicles and got in, acting as nonchalant as if he'd just come out of the store and gone to his own car.

"Five dudes pulled up in an SUV, got out, and went up, meeting Amari at the door." Jordan had already started talking as Jim handed him his plate carrier and SBR. "One was definitely Uzun. Another looked maybe Caucasian, maybe Turkish. The other three were definitely Caucasian. German or French, I suspect."

"EDC?" It was a distinct possibility.

"That'd be my guess." He ducked his head through the plate carrier, wrapped the cummerbunds around himself, then started to shoulder back into his light jacket. Anyone paying attention would notice the increase in bulk, but Jordan had been doing his best to avoid attention already, so hopefully no one had given him a close enough look to tell the difference. "Looked like they were all business. Not sure how long they'll be there."

"Then we'll move now." I keyed my radio. "All stations, begin to collapse on Target One. We might need you to run interference. We're moving in, time now."

If it had been the middle of the night, we would have moved in on foot. But it was mid-afternoon. This was going to get hairy.

Greg was driving, and he pulled the van right up into the only empty parking space on the curb in front of the building. He didn't speed in and screech to a stop. He drove normally and sedately, and we all got out casually, shouldering our go bags as if they were perfectly normal civilian backpacks, and headed up to the door.

Fortunately, we didn't need anyone to buzz us in. We'd had enough time over the last three days to figure out which apartment was Amari's. Granted, that had been easy enough to figure out from the angle of the buildings in the background on his video. That should make this go more quickly.

Provided everyone in the building didn't come after us as soon as we moved.

The entryway looked a lot like the tenement in Lüdenscheid where we'd killed Bajrami. As we walked in, a door opened on the narrow hallway, and a woman and two kids came out. The woman was wearing a hijab, and she stared at us for a moment before hustling her kids out of the front door.

I traded a glance with Reuben. We might be made, especially if she had a phone. That look she'd given us had told me that she knew we didn't belong there.

Just meant we had to move fast.

If I'd had the whole team on the ground, I would have posted somebody on the elevators. But with only five of us, the rest on foot or riding scooters elsewhere in the city, we all took the stairs up toward the target.

Nobody needed verbal instructions. We paused on the landing just below the third floor, unzipping go bags and pulling our weapons out. Everyone already had his gear on, as streamlined as possible to fit under cover shirts. Those weren't *quite* as low-profile as I might have wished, but sometimes beggars can't be choosers.

Then, with Reuben in the lead, me right behind him, and Greg, Jim, and Jordan covering behind us, we headed up.

Despite being spotted on the way in, we were going to stay soft as long as possible. Our surveillance guys had reported an OWHSC patrol only a few blocks away. If we went loud too soon, we might find ourselves getting squeezed between jihadis on one side and Chinese "contractors" on the other.

The hallway at the top of the stairs was quiet and dark. Reuben and I split to cover both ends anyway. There was a camera at the top of the steps, but it appeared to have been smashed at some earlier time.

The jihadis must not want the *Polizei* potentially keeping tabs on their movements.

I was half expecting to get peeked on from behind one of the doors on the hallway, but they were all shut, and the only sound on that floor was the loud jihadi rap thumping and wailing from the apartment at the northeast end.

That didn't seem to be in keeping with what we knew about Uzun, but maybe it was just supposed to stymie any audio surveillance.

We moved quickly to the door, weapons up. To my utter lack of surprise, the door was locked. Of course this couldn't be easy.

All the same, we didn't have the ram, and I didn't want to be kicking the door half a dozen times trying to get in. Fortunately, we'd come prepared.

Jordan stepped up, slinging his SBR to his back and pulling out his bump key. He'd gotten pretty good with it, despite—or maybe because of—all the jokes that David should still be able to beat him every time. He didn't disappoint this time, quickly getting the door unlocked with a minimum of noise. The music helped.

However, somebody had to know that the door had just opened, and I guessed that they weren't expecting anyone anytime soon, either.

That was why Jordan shoved the door open but didn't enter right away. It saved his life.

A burst of suppressed gunfire tore through the open doorway and blasted plaster off the far wall. The bad guys must have heard the lock open and had figured someone was coming right in.

Instead, Jordan dropped to a knee and leaned out just far enough to spot the first shooter. His SBR rapped twice, and then I stepped up next to him, adding my own muzzle to his.

The wall was thick enough to keep us somewhat protected for the moment. Any heavy, rifle caliber gunfire was going to tear through it eventually, but fortunately the building was old and made of brick.

Leaning out over Jordan's head, I spotted movement, identified a weapon, and put a round through the optic and into the side of the man's head.

I hadn't killed him; the bullet raked across his cheekbone, snapping his head partway around with a spray of blood. Before I could get a follow-up shot off, a flashbang sailed through the doorway.

I squeezed my eyes shut just before the bang went off. It was a nine-banger, too, and the flashes and concussions seemed to go on forever while I staggered back from the door, dragging Jordan with me. The hallway had dissolved into brilliant flashes, smoke, and deafening noise, and I knew, even as I moved with my rifle tucked under my elbow, that the bad guys were coming out after that banger, and they weren't going to be half-blind and battered by the concussions that were hammering at my inner ear.

I wasn't the only one pulling. I felt a hand under my arm, and then I was being hauled back, fast, toward the end of the hall. Or maybe the stairs. A moment later, my back foot found itself out over empty space, and I got shoved against the wall. My head ached and my ears were ringing like church bells, but when I opened my eyes, at least I could see. I hadn't taken the full brunt of the flashbang.

We were back in the stairwell. Reuben had seen the banger come out, grabbed Jordan and me, and hauled us back to cover while Chris and Greg had headed there at a sprint. But we couldn't just sit this out in the stairway.

Jim was already barricaded on the corner at the top of the stairs. My hearing was so battered that I couldn't really hear the *snap* of his .300 Blackout past the roaring and ringing in my ears. I could see the casings spiraling away from the ejection port as he fired down the hall.

Then he ducked back behind the wall. At least, that was what I thought he'd done, until he came tumbling past us down to the landing below, almost wiping Jordan out in the process.

More bullets smacked plaster into our faces. The bad guys were advancing on us fast.

I was afraid Jim had taken a round and was dead or seriously wounded, but right then wasn't the time to check. We were all going to be dead in the next few seconds if we didn't act now.

Greg threw himself out into the hallway, running the rabbit for the rest of us. Fortunately, he moved sideways, almost leaping across the darkened hall, despite the hole in his leg that still hadn't completely healed, presenting his plates to the enemy. He took at least one round that I saw before Jordan and I popped the corner.

I got two shots off at the three advancing, armored figures before one of them fired back at me, forcing me back behind cover. I felt a savage blow alongside my helmet as I moved, and knew I'd taken a hit. Jordan fired twice more then ducked back himself, as a bullet smashed through the corner next to his head with a shower of plaster and fragments of brick.

Greg was blasting away, swearing a blue streak. I saw him get hit twice more, though I'm sure his plates saved his life.

The fire coming at us dwindled as Greg sprayed down the hallway. His bolt locked back on an empty mag as Jordan, Chris, and I surged up out of the stairwell.

A body lay in the hallway. What might have been a boot stuck out of the bullet-riddled, shattered doorway.

Chris lobbed a flashbang from his go bag into the doorway. We followed it, almost close enough to eat half the blast. My hearing was screwed for the rest of the day, anyway.

I came through, immediately coming face to face with a man in civilian clothes and black body armor, practically running into his muzzle. He'd eaten the bang, though he was turning back toward me as I came out of the cloud of smoke filling the doorway, his short-barrel HK433 already almost pointed at my centerline.

I bashed the weapon aside with my own barrel, shoving forward into him, all too painfully aware that I was leaving the corner off to my right flank exposed, but I had an immediate threat right here. He let go of the forearm of his own weapon and grabbed for mine, and while I tried to withdraw it and shoot him, I couldn't step back far enough, since Chris was moving in behind me to clear that corner.

We were clinched, and he was trying as desperately to keep my weapon out of action as I was trying to get it lined up on his vitals. He threw an elbow at me, and I took it on my shoulder, then wrenched the rifle down as I shoved inside his arm, trying to simultaneously stomp his knee in the wrong direction.

My first attempt missed, my second, as I drove him over the couch in the living room, connected. Unfortunately, his foot was coming up off the floor at the same time, and I didn't get as much force into the blow as I'd hoped. The two of us went over the back of the couch with a crash, as suppressed gunfire thumped and snapped around us. I couldn't spare a moment to see who was winning. My world had just compressed down to this tiny, desperate struggle.

He tried to turn the fall into a clumsy throw, but I hooked my foot on the top of the couch—completely unintentionally—and then tucked and dropped an elbow on his throat as I landed on top of him. That took some of the fight out of him, and I rolled to my left, the rest of the way off the couch, dragging his HK 433 with me.

There was a risk in that. I wasn't really thinking consciously about it at the time, but I was still trying to keep that muzzle away from my guts. He was doing the same thing, one hand clamped on my SBR Tactical's forearm, keeping the suppressor away from his face.

He pivoted his weight on his back and tried to kick me off. I twisted, taking his shin in a glancing blow to my side that smacked against my rifle, jarring it almost all the way out of my hand. I was about to lose control and then he was going to get loose and kill me.

Throwing my weight backward, I got a boot up between us and stomped on his groin. He felt that, and while he didn't give up—this guy was clearly too well trained for that—he still shuddered, going slack with pain for just a second.

That was all I needed. Letting go of my SBR, I snatched my PR-15 out of my holster and pumped two rounds into him just below his plate carrier, then threw myself backward as he lost his grip on my rifle and put a third round into his head.

For a second that I couldn't afford, I lay there on my back, panting, my pistol still pointed at his young, slightly shocked looking face, a puckered, smoking hole dripping blood in the center of his forehead, gore painting the couch cushions behind him. His eyes were staring at me, unseeing, the pain of the gut shots wiped away by the surprise of the bullet that had ended his life.

He was German. This guy was no Turk, no Kosovar.

168

Then I remembered what else was happening and rolled to my knees, ignoring the pain, my pistol up and scanning for threats.

"Clear." From the tone of his voice, Jordan had called that out already. I just hadn't heard it.

I hauled myself painfully to my feet, holstering my pistol and bringing my rifle back up. "Status?"

"Everybody's alive, but Jim's going to need medical treatment soon." Greg had hauled Jim inside and was throwing a dressing on the bullet holes in his leg and shoulder. Greg himself was bleeding from his shoulder, but he apparently figured it was superficial.

"Deacon, Chatty." Tony's voice was tinny and scratchy, but that might have been my hearing after the bangers and gunfire.

"Chatty, this is Deacon. We're on target. Gruff's been hit. We're going to need extract soon."

"Roger. Be advised, you've got about five minutes to clear the target and get down here." Tony wasn't overly excited, but he wasn't pretending everything was fine, either. "*Polizei* and OWHSC are on their way, and we can see more shooters coming out of adjacent buildings.

"We're going to be in one hell of a firefight in the next few minutes. If you don't get out of that building before then, you might not get out at all."

Chapter 17

The apartment was a wreck. Bodies were sprawled on the floor, blood spattered on the whitewashed walls and pooling against the furniture. Bullet holes had blasted plaster off the walls and shattered a framed photo hanging on one of them. Upholstery stuffing lay on the floor, some of it soaking up the crimson puddles.

There was also a lot of incriminating stuff in there, if we could trust the *Polizei* to be interested. Or even to look past the fact that we'd come in shooting.

We *did* have that option, officially. Whether the Germans would honor it, let alone the Chinese who seemed to be increasingly taking over their security, was another question.

Maps spread on the kitchen table had just about every American FOB in Germany, France, and Poland pinpointed. Hell, that looked like a patrol and logistics convoy schedule for the main MSRs between Hamburg, Berlin, Frankfurt, and Stuttgart. *How the hell did they get* that? I had my suspicions, and they weren't good.

"Grab everything you can. Phones, those two laptops, that map." I looked around as I grabbed two phones off the table, then bent to go through the pockets of one of the dead men. I looked up at where Greg was finishing tying off a bandage. "Jim, can you walk?"

"I can fucking run if the situation calls for it." He winced as he hauled himself to his feet with Greg's help. He was looking a little pale, and blood soaked his side and his leg. But he was on his feet, and he had a hand on his weapon. "I might not be much good for much else for a while afterward, but I'll gut it out until we're out of here. I just need to stop getting shot."

I nodded, giving up on the search. The dead man, also Caucasian, dark haired and bearded, was completely sterile. No wallet, no phone, no identification. I still had my suspicions. "Photos of everything and especially everyone."

Jordan was carrying the camera, and fortunately it hadn't been damaged or destroyed. As I looked around, I saw that every one of us was bleeding, somewhere. I didn't feel anything yet, though I had my share of lumps from that fight on the floor. I was sure it was only a matter of time and adrenaline.

"Deacon, Chatty. Out front with the vehicle. We need to go *now*." Tony was still calm, but there was a tight, intense urgency in his tone.

"Grab it and go! We are out of time!" Tony hadn't said just what he was looking at, but if he was that insistent, then it wasn't good.

Greg and Jim were already at the door, and they flowed out—or limped out, in Jim's case—to clear the hallway. Chris, Jordan, and I moved in after them, guns up and scanning for any movement.

We cleared our way down the stairs, our pace picking up a bit as we heard gunfire outside.

Coming out into the foyer, we ran into an absolute cluster.

Gunfire rattled out on the street, but Chris and I had barely reached the bottom of the steps before a back door opened and three men with FAMAS rifles stormed in.

They were all in civilian clothes, but there was no mistaking them for anything but jihadis. One even had an ISIS beard, covering his jaw and chin but with his mustache shaved off.

Chris shot the first one through the head from about six feet away. His feet flew out from under him and he crashed backward into his fellows, bringing all three of them down in a heap.

Jordan and I shot the other two dead in the next second. They were down, but they still had weapons and they were still a threat. Leaving them conscious and breathing behind us was a good way to get shot in the back.

With Jordan and I holding on the stairs and the back door, Chris, Greg, and Jim hustled out the front and toward the van where Tony, Lucas, and Steve were trading fire with someone down the street.

"Turn and go!" Jordan pivoted and headed for the front door, slapping me on the shoulder to make sure I knew he was moving, and then we were both sprinting for the van.

A bullet *snap*ped past my head, answered by a long burst of suppressed .300 Blackout. Tony was on a knee beside the passenger door of the van, returning fire at the dozen or so shooters that were trying to leapfrog up the street toward us. One of them stumbled and fell sideways into the street as glass shattered, and car alarms whooped over the sound of gunfire.

I launched myself into the back of the van behind Jordan. "All in!" Bracing myself, I stood up in the back, firing over the top of the passenger side door as Tony piled in and slammed it.

"Everybody's up! Go, go, go!" Lucas was behind the wheel, and I almost fell out as he stomped on the gas, accelerating *toward* the shooters. Jordan grabbed my belt and hauled me back inside just before Chris slammed the sliding door shut.

Lucas was getting more power out of that van than I would have expected. He barreled through the rough skirmish line of jihadi shooters in an eyeblink, hitting one of them a glancing blow with the front bumper and sending him spinning to bounce off a parked car before collapsing into the street.

Then he wrenched the wheel around, practically lifting the vehicle onto two wheels as we went around the corner. He barreled straight into three more jihadis, armed with a mix-and-match assortment of submachineguns, at least two of which were probably homemade, denting the hell out of the front of the van as he sent two of them flying and ran right over the third, the van bouncing over the body with a sickening, final *thumpthump*.

A moment later, we were speeding away, racing over the train tracks and toward friendlier territory.

***

"Friendlier" did not mean "Friendly."

We hadn't made it a mile before OWHSC locked down all the major thoroughfares through Aachen. We were now looking at a checkpoint about six cars ahead of us, covered by two CS/VN3 armored cars. To make matters worse, we were blocked in. Two more cars had turned in behind us.

"Well, looks like we get to test just how hostile OWHSC is willing to get." Lucas seemed perfectly relaxed, his SBR Tactical next to his leg, his go bag open at his feet. He was ready to go or fight, either or.

The rest of us were a little banged up. Tony had gotten trimmed, a bullet tearing through his shirt sleeve and scoring a bloody trough along his shoulder. I was sporting a couple of similar wounds, Greg had one alongside his neck that we were going to have to keep an eye on, and he was currently resetting the dressings on the holes in Jim's leg and side. There was a lot of blood on the inside of the van, not to mention the weapons. We'd mostly shed our gear, but we were still too close to the fight to just pack everything up.

I was already on the radio. "Tango Charlie, this is Golf Lima Ten. Could use some interference at a checkpoint on the intersection of Boxgraben and Krakaustraße."

"Stand by." I didn't recognize the voice. "Are you stopped now?"

"We're in line." It wasn't moving fast, either, as the gray-clad Chinese PMC operators questioned the driver and

174

passengers in the lead vehicle carefully, men with QBZ-03s standing alert and ready to either side. "Probably another fifteen minutes." I looked over my shoulder, but the jihadis weren't coming after us at the moment.

Or at least, they weren't actively in pursuit. I could see a figure in dark clothing on the other side of the street, a couple blocks back, watching us closely, a phone to his ear.

If I needed any more indicators that the jihadis were probably in bed with OWHSC in some way or another, I got them as one of the men in gray up at the checkpoint answered his phone and looked right at us. He grabbed three of the shooters next to one of the CS/VN3s and started along the side of the street toward us.

"We've got company coming." Glancing back behind us, I saw the man with the phone pocket it and turn away. My eyes narrowed. I knew a tip-off when I saw it. Which meant that the guy on the street had the Chinese PMC officer's phone number. Or at least *a* number that could be forwarded to him.

"Tango Charlie, Golf Lima Ten. Might need that interference sooner rather than later." I didn't know how this was going to work, but I had to trust our guys.

Or be ready to get into a firefight with OWHSC in the middle of Aachen. Seven on four, I was confident we could probably win it, until the gunner in that armored vehicle up there decided to kinetically convert our van into a sieve.

"Hold what you've got, Golf Lima Ten. The cavalry's on the way." I didn't know who was on radio watch in the regional Triarii command post, but he'd clearly practiced being calm and reassuring.

Which was great, but I wanted a bit more information than that. "Who is it, and how far out are they?"

There was a pause, while the Chinese PMC operators got closer. They weren't hurrying, but they weren't casually sauntering up to us, either. Their weapons were still held in the low ready, and they were scanning their surroundings while watching us closely.

"We have our liaison with BCT 7 en route, ETA five minutes."

I wasn't sure exactly who that was. Gutierrez would have picked someone who knew their stuff. Not knowing who I was dealing with bugged me, though. Most Triarii, especially those who had been brought over to Europe, were dyed-in-the-wool pros at what they did. That was a requirement that Colonel Santiago had made ironclad when he'd started the organization. But there's always that ten percent who slip through the cracks. They're inevitable and unavoidable. That was why I really kinda wanted to know who was coming.

Then we were out of time.

"Identification, please." The Chinese officer was at Lucas's window, the shooters spread out with one to the front, the other two on our flank in an L-shape. They weren't relaxed, either. They knew what they were dealing with, and they were clearly ready for a fight.

They also knew we were Americans. He'd spoken English, not German.

Lucas wasn't cowed, though, despite the fact that the man right in front of the front bumper had his rifle within a few inches of pointed at his face. Lucas had probably been in a lot hairier situations.

Rolling down his window, he held up the placard that said, in English, German, and French, that we were, in essence, not to be trifled with according to the terms of the cease fire. That had been a bitter pill to swallow for several of the Army commanders, but our role in bringing down the EDC had been undeniable, and we hadn't done anything that they could point to as a violation of the Law of Land Warfare to try to get us banned.

I was sure somebody was working on it, but they hadn't succeeded yet.

Unfortunately, the OWHSC officer didn't seem impressed. "Identification. Everyone in the vehicle."

"Not happening, bud." Lucas kept holding up the placard. "Just keep walking. Nothing to see here."

One of the gunmen on our flank said something sharp in Mandarin. The officer stepped back, and the rifles came up. "Everyone out of the vehicle. Now!"

Each gunman was suddenly covered by two SBRs. We'd have to shoot through the glass, but they were outgunned, and from the looks on a couple of their faces, they knew it. The one kid I was watching looked like he was about to puke. "Like I said, not going to happen." Lucas hadn't moved a muscle toward his own weapon. "You're in violation of cease fire terms, my friend. That makes you the bad guy here. We've already got support on the way, and drones have your vehicles pinpointed." That was utter bullshit, but I wasn't going to be That Guy and correct him. We *could* have had drone coverage, as thin as the supply was, but given the atmospherics in Aachen, we'd been trying to maintain a low profile until the hit. Even though the days of the "flying lawnmower" were largely past, drones were neither invisible nor silent, and their presence would have made the bad guys suspicious.

The Chinese officer wasn't sure what to do. He was suddenly outgunned, and far enough away that he couldn't just back up and yell at the gunner on his vehicle to open fire. We were, for the moment, at an impasse.

He also wasn't sure if Lucas was bluffing or not.

"Gents, we've got more company." I spared a glance away from my target to see more of the men in gray and armed with QBZ-03s advancing up the other side of the street. And there was too much traffic for our support to get there in anything like a timely manner.

At least, that was what I thought.

The roar of a helicopter rattled windows, as a Triarii S70 thundered overhead. Whoever our liaison was, he'd pulled out the stops.

The helo circled overhead, the side doors open, the door gunners plainly visible along with what looked very much like a

Triarii infantry section in greens behind them. "Attention down there! Everyone needs to stand down! Put your weapons down, now!" The loudspeaker was even louder than the rotors, and the van's windows vibrated with the sound. But that wasn't our liaison.

He showed up on a motorcycle, about the same time that the helo made its third circle. The OWHSC commander had told his men to lower their weapons and step back, and we'd returned the courtesy. He was still watching us, his face hard. It was clear that he figured we were the enemy.

We probably were. If he was PLA, which I was about seventy-five percent sure he was, then we most definitely were his enemy. They'd tried to take over a chunk of the American West Coast with this same "humanitarian" bullshit.

Tom Harris slewed the bike to a stop between parked cars, put down the kickstand, and got off. Tall and rangy, he was in smartly turned-out greens, in decided contrast to our battered, torn, bloodied civvies.

I had suddenly decidedly mixed feelings. I knew Tom, and we'd never really gotten along. He wasn't a bad guy, we just had conflicting personalities. He was a one-upper, for one thing. Anything you said, he knew more about, anything you'd done, he'd done, too, only more intensely.

But he was a people person, there was no doubt about that. I just found him annoying.

"I need to see your authorization papers under the terms of the Strasbourg cease fire." Tom had all but ignored us, and walked right up to the OWHSC officer, or supervisor, or whatever he was. He presented a smaller, pocket-sized version of our placard. "I'm also going to need an explanation as to why you're harassing sanctioned counter-terrorist forces."

The man looked up at the helicopter, then stared daggers at Tom, before barking an order in Mandarin to the gunmen to either side, who immediately began to fall back toward the checkpoint. It was clear that it wasn't Tom's legal authority that

178

had prompted the disengagement, but the threat of gunfire from above.

Tom just waved at us, got back on his motorcycle, and headed out. There wasn't much else he could do at that point.

The checkpoint collapsed a few minutes later, and traffic resumed. We headed out of the city, the helicopter flying overhead the entire way, just in case anyone got froggy.

Chapter 18

The safehouse was actually less a safehouse and more a hostel in Idstein, just north of Wiesbaden, where the Army had retaken the old base that had been turned over to the Bundeswehr—who had then turned it over to the EDC—five years before. There didn't seem to be the same amount of military traffic that the town had gotten used to, back in the day, but clearly there were at least a few Germans in Idstein who liked Americans.

It was weird. I'd encountered two types of Germans: those who hated us and those who loved us. There didn't seem to be much in between. I'd started to understand some of the stories from World War II, when the GIs who had fought through from Normandy had generally detested the French and Italians, but had loved the German people, themselves. They'd killed German soldiers in job lots, but the interactions they'd generally had with the people out in the countryside had been far friendlier. We were running into similar sets of attitudes.

The older woman who owned the hostel was warm and friendly, and hadn't objected in the slightest when we'd effectively closed down her business and moved operations in. Of course, the amount we were paying her—not a small part of it confiscated from various EDC and terrorist cells we'd raided since the war had "ended"—probably helped. *And* we were still paying her for food.

The end result was that we had the entire, fairly large house to ourselves. Which was a good thing, given what we were looking at.

"This is bad."

"That's putting it mildly." I stared at the emails on the screen in front of me, unlocked by the wiry, hard-muscled IT genius sitting in front of the other laptop we'd seized. Carl Worther was a triathlete, a veteran of warfare on three different continents, and could make a computer sit up and beg. The man was the opposite of your mental image of an IT nerd, but if there was one man in country who I trusted to get every bit of information out that someone might want hidden, it was Carl.

What I was looking at were the pieces of a plan that made the strikes on American forces in Slovakia, almost a year before, look tame. The bad guys had been mapping out the hastily-erected FOBs and former Army bases since Strasbourg, observing and timing the logistics convoys and even the security patrols. It was starting to look like the only American units they *didn't* have dialed in were Triarii.

And from some of what I was reading, that was a matter of some concern to the bad guys. Rather tellingly, the reassurances that we were going to be dealt with were coming from emails that Carl had tentatively identified as Chinese or EDC in origin.

"We need to get this back to Bavaria." Chris was reading over my shoulder. "Though... Should we send it to the Army in Wiesbaden, first?"

"You trust the Army to do anything about this? Especially coming from us?" David laughed bitterly. "They'll either spit in our faces or thank us fake-sincerely and then sit on it."

"I'm working on it." Carl didn't look up from the computer. He waved at the laptop in front of me. "Most of what was on that just got dumped to Gutierrez's HQ, just about every Army inbox in country, *and* Wikileaks. And a few other open-source sites that I could name." He did glance up then, with a wry sort of grin. "Trust me, this *is* getting out."

"Somebody's going to have an aneurism." I was already looking for indicators we could use for targeting. "Sources and methods, you know."

"Who gives a shit? *They* know they got hit, and they have to know that we took everything already. If they change their plans, well, that just buys us time, doesn't it?" He turned back to the computer in front of him. "Keeping this under our hat just to avoid letting secrets out wouldn't do anybody a *damned* bit of good. We don't have the assets to go after every attack vector all at once, which is what we'd have to do, if I'm reading this right."

From what I'd gleaned from the emails I'd seen so far, he was right. This was all being coordinated to go down over the course of a couple of days at most. This wasn't a pinprick, death-of-a-thousand-cuts insurgency. This was an all-the-marbles offensive, aimed at crippling the American presence in Germany, at the very least.

That alone was troubling enough. We'd smashed the EDC—or so the commanders assured everyone—only to face threats that weren't nearly so easily identified. It was an outcome that most of us, who'd been fighting irregular wars our entire careers, could easily have predicted.

The amount of coordination and support, however, was new. There was no way, even with Turkish support, that the jihadis were going to be this all together. It wasn't their way. We'd all seen it over the years, from Afghanistan to Iraq to Africa to Kosovo. They were usually too busy fighting each other in between fighting us. Somebody had exerted a *lot* of pressure to get them all in line.

Not to mention the sheer tonnage of munitions that would be needed to pull off coordinated strikes all around the country at about the same time. For most insurgencies, it takes a long time to put that much boom together. From what I could see, it sounded like they had everything they wanted or needed.

That told me that someone else was funneling in stacks of weapons and explosives for these bastards. The list of suspects was pretty short, though when we really started digging, I suspected that we were going to find that they were burrowed into the "friendly" governments a lot deeper than anyone wanted to think.

I was under no illusions that OWHSC had risen to the role it was currently in just because of one or two naïve idiots in Berlin who were desperate for some help on the security front.

I was staring at a worse problem than we'd faced even before we'd gone into France after their nuclear arsenal. We'd "won" in Brussels, only to quite potentially lose the war.

Presuming it wasn't already lost, and we weren't just sitting there waiting for the axe to fall.

I reached across the table and grabbed one of our new toys. Carl called it a "T-Phone." It was a cell phone, but it was tied specifically into our radio mesh network and entirely encrypted. It could do everything a smart phone could, without actually carrying a SIM card or showing up at all on the local cell network. Much harder to trace and much harder to listen in on.

Brian Hartrick was right at the top of the phone's contacts. He answered almost right away, too.

"Talk to me." He sounded harried, which was no surprise if he was looking at what I was.

"You seeing Carl's infodump?" I was pretty sure I knew the answer.

"Looking at it right now." I could almost see him drag a hand over his face. "Holy fuck."

"Where do you want us?" There was no question in my mind what our response needed to be. It was entirely possible that Carl's theory that getting the information out there might head some of it off, but I wasn't confident that that would be enough. The bad guys weren't going to give up altogether. They'd reschedule, adjust, but all blasting their plans across the internet was going to do was slow them down.

If that.

So, the only possible option was to start rolling up the killchain that the emails presented us. Going after the action cells first was probably the best bet, as badly as I wanted to hit the decision makers and put them in the dirt.

"Where to fucking start?" He was distracted, apparently still looking at the nightmare we'd unearthed. "Where are you?"

"Idstein." I could read the situation already. Right outside of Wiesbaden, that put us in position to head off any attacks aimed at the infantry and cav units stationed there.

"Okay. Let me take a look here." There was a pause, and I'll admit that I got ahead of him, looking through what I could find around the Wiesbaden/Frankfurt area. We'd already operated near here—we were less than ten miles from Janz's house—which presented some difficulties if we had to go into Frankfurt itself. We hadn't heard from Falk, and reporting said that there were far more OWHSC goons in the city now than there had been, and that it had become somewhat non-permissive for Americans. Even the Army was careful where they went in Frankfurt these days.

Hartrick apparently remembered all that. "Damn. You guys might be compromised there. Let me see."

There was another long pause. I wasn't sitting there idle, though. Scanning the information in front of me, I was looking for a target. One that we could hit within the time window.

Because there *was* a time window. Even as Carl was putting their plans and preparations out on the internet for anyone to see, they would be moving and adjusting. Given the fact that it looked like the first attacks were supposed to launch in just over a week, they'd *probably*, *hopefully* push to the right. But they might just move the schedule up, instead.

Which meant we were going to have to move fast.

"Mainz." There were three FOBs in or around the city, which was still wracked by regular riots and urban warfare. All of them were on the target deck, and we had enough emails that I was pretty sure Carl, at least, could put together a pretty

185

extensive targeting package. And it was on the far side of Frankfurt from where we'd last popped up, so it was unlikely that we'd hit anyone's radar, not that we'd made it easy for the *Bundespolizei* to identify us. Even Falk hadn't seen faces. "We'll need drone support and possibly air cover, if yesterday was any indication."

"I'll get you what I can. You'd better get moving."

I hung up and turned to Carl, who just held up a hand to indicate he was already working on it. We had to get down to planning. Time was flying.

Chapter 19

Unfortunately, intercepting a terrorist attack is more easily said than done.

We moved into Mainz in three VW Atlas pickups, all low-profile, though Tony and Reuben still had our Mk 48s under the seats in the back, ready to go. In the interests of staying as invisible as possible until it was go time, we didn't caravan in, either. Each vehicle had a different route, entering the city from a different direction and at a different time. If anyone was watching—and given the implied connections between the bad guys and whoever was pulling the *Bundespolizei*'s strings, we had to assume someone was *always* watching—hopefully they wouldn't put the pieces together until it was too late.

We didn't have a safehouse in Mainz. The city had been non-permissive ever since we'd pulled Giehl out, and there simply hadn't been time to get anyone in to run prep for this. This was a time-sensitive target, and worse, we didn't know just *how* time sensitive it really was.

While I'd generally agreed with Carl's rationale for dumping the attack plans on the internet, if only to try to force the Army's hand, we were now having to deal with unintended consequences.

Someday, I was going to get an op where I had all the time I needed to really get sneaky, do all the prep and reconnaissance we wanted, get in, and get out, without everything blowing up in our faces because we'd had to adapt on the fly.

Someday.

At this point, though, we were driving through Mainz, Greg in the back working to keep the drone with the ersatz Scorpion overhead, trying to avoid the riots that were burning down whatever they could closer to the river.

From the emails, we'd gathered that one "Abu Murad" was the main coordinator for the Mainz cells, and was going to launch the attacks on the Mainz garrison. The FOBs were all hastily-erected compounds encircled by T-walls and concertina wire. Two had been set up in farmers' fields to the west and south, while the third had been built in the old Willy-Brandt Platz, where the Army had maintained the old Lee Barracks before handing the land back over to the German government. As far as we knew, they had most of a grunt company crammed in there, but they'd been unwilling to use the nature preserve that would have been a more natural spot for a FOB.

I figured that was the most likely first target, since they had zero standoff and probably the strictest ROEs. And if I knew that, just by looking at their position, then I suspected the bad guys would, too.

If I'd had more time and more assets, I might have just tried to set in overwatch on the FOBs. All indicators pointed to no such flexibility, though. We needed to find Abu Murad and put him down.

We *thought* we had a neighborhood and a cell phone number. That had taken Carl's cyber magic to find, but we were fairly sure. Maybe sixty percent. If we had enough time, we could find him, just like we'd found Amari and Uzun.

But I was afraid that just hitting Abu Murad—whoever he was, really—wasn't going to do the trick. We were close enough to zero hour that his cell had probably already briefed, rehearsed, and staged any materiel they needed. They were just waiting for the "go" order.

If we took down Abu Murad—especially if we did it quietly—they might never get that go order. But if they had planned contingencies, they might just go ahead with it regardless of orders or the lack thereof. More and more, irregular combatants ran on timelines and initiative-based tactics, rather than centralized decision making and command. I found it extremely unlikely that this cell out of all of the terrorists and guerrillas we'd gone up against would have been the ones to rely on one commander to steer them.

It was possible, but unlikely.

This is what makes counter-terrorism ops difficult. You might get a line on a bad guy, but where there's one, there are often more, and finding even five people in an entire city is like finding a needle in a haystack.

I was musing on all of this as I scanned the tree-shrouded houses and apartment buildings as we worked our way up from the south. Greg interrupted my increasingly gloomy musings as we went through the intersection with Berliner Street.

"Got him. I think." I looked over my shoulder to see him squinting at the screen.

"Is it him? Or a similar number?" I had a bad feeling about this entire op, and I realized it was leaking into my analysis.

Greg didn't answer right away. "Lost it. We need to go back." He looked up at me for a second. "It was the right number. I'm sure of that."

I nodded and turned back to the front, as Chris turned off the main drag and started looking for a way back, though the street immediately took us deeper into a shadowed, residential neighborhood, lined with smaller houses or cottages, looking nothing like the kind of neighborhood we'd found jihadis in so far.

"There it is again." Greg leaned forward, tapping keys to adjust the drone's course. "Signal strength looks like it's..." He frowned and tilted his head slightly. "Looks almost like he's somewhere to the southwest."

"What's down there? All the riots are up north." Chris leaned over the wheel, looking for some way out of the cul de sac that we'd driven into.

"Maybe that's why he's down there." I was looking at the map. The Academy of Sciences and Literature was down that way, along with a lot of student housing. Was Abu Murad recruiting among college students?

It sure wouldn't be the first time. They tended to be stupid enough and eager enough to burn everything down.

"Or maybe… Nah." Greg shook his head.

"What?" I twisted around to stare at him when he didn't answer. "What, Greg?"

He was frowning at the screen. When he spoke, his voice was pretty low. "Or maybe Carl made a mistake and we're following a spoofed number?"

I didn't have an answer to that, at least not an answer that was any more useful than an angry growl. I turned back forward as Chris gave up, pulled over to the side of the street, and pulled a five-point turn to get us turned around. I watched the houses, noticing that there wasn't anyone out on the street at the moment. I did see a curtain move, but when I focused on it, I saw it had just been pulled more tightly over the window to hide anyone inside.

The residents of Mainz were nervous, and with good reason.

I was sure that the longer this all went on, the more used to it they'd get. I'd seen it in Africa, where a massacre could be happening two blocks over, and people are going about their lives as if nothing was happening. They were numb to it, as long as it was far enough away from them at the moment. The Germans weren't to that point yet. The chaos and the violence were still too fresh, too new. Aside from those who were willing to fight, most of the Germans were trying to hide.

I wondered, briefly and bitterly, how many of them had cheered on the invasion of Poland, or the crushing of the Slovak Nationalists, thinking that those knuckle-dragging regressives

190

had it coming. And now they were running and hiding when the same terror they'd invited on the Poles and the Slovaks to maintain their elites' grasp on power—not even theirs, but that of snooty, rich oligarchs who didn't give a damn about them—had come to visit their own backyard.

I knew there were a lot of them who thought about Americans that way. After all, we'd intervened militarily all over the world, and rarely done an effective job of it. A lot of death and a lot of chaos had happened without the end result really being worth it. The *intended* end might have been, but over and over again we'd been clumsy, hesitant, and too focused on the process to realize that the process wasn't working. Up until we'd given up.

Was the same thing happening now? Only faster?

I was pretty sure it was. Which made the question of how long the Triarii were going to stick with it that much more urgent.

I'd hate to abandon the Poles. I was engaged to marry a Polish woman, for crying out loud. But the handful of us couldn't end the war all by ourselves.

At least, not under these circumstances. If this all went all the way south, and Option Zulu ended up on the table…

Even then, it wouldn't be a peace, but a cease fire, as Germany ceased to be a coherent country. Provided the plan worked the way we'd figured it.

We kept circling for another hour. Chris had to divert twice when it started to look like we were getting more attention than we wanted, even as the smoke drifted down from the fires burning closer to the river. Greg was swearing quietly in the back, trying to nail down the target phone.

The longer this went on, the tighter the circle got, until we were looking at the middle of student housing. "I don't think it's spoofed." Greg was staring at the blip on his digital map. "I think it's the right phone." He finally looked up at me, and there was something uncharacteristically bleak in his ordinarily cheerful expression. "It's not moving. Not at all. I think it's the

191

right phone, and he dumped it. We'll probably find it in a public trash can."

I met his gaze, making the same calculations he was. That might just mean that Abu Murad had cut away. More likely, it meant it was go time, and he'd dropped the phone that he no longer needed.

Not long after, while we wordlessly continued our search, coordinating with the other two trucks via T-phone text messages, the reality of the situation became obvious, as a rolling *boom* echoed across the city.

All eyes turned west, just for a moment. A massive, roiling mushroom cloud was rising above FOB Williamson. Plumes of smoke were rising from the direction of FOB Lewis-Cant in the south, as well.

We were too late. The attacks had already started.

There wasn't a lot of hesitation. None, really. We knew what had to happen now. Covers came off weapons, as Chris turned us toward the FOB. I was already turning the radio to the shared net we'd worked out with the Army.

"Crash Five Two, this is Golf Lima Ten." Ordinarily, I might launch right into the offer of assistance, but given some of the issues we'd had getting comms with the Army, I figured it was just as well to make sure we were actually talking before I wasted my breath on dead air.

There was no reply. "Crash Five Two, Golf Lima Ten."

Nothing.

My T-phone buzzed. I looked down at it, knowing I was dropping security to do so, in a city that had just gotten way more non-permissive than it had been a few minutes before. It was Hartrick.

"Send it."

"Are you in contact at the moment?" Typically terse, Hartrick's voice brooked no delay in answering.

"Negative. We just observed strikes on FOB Williamson and FOB Lewis-Cant. We are moving to render assistance." Something in Hartrick's voice had my nerves suddenly on-edge.

The continued silence from the Williamson COC was making things worse. Chris glanced at me, slowing down slightly. He sensed it, too.

"Are you on comms with them?"

I glanced at Chris, frowning. He wore the same expression, even though he couldn't hear all of the conversation with Hartrick. "Negative. We're still trying."

"Then get out. Make for Hof." Once again, the order brooked no question, no delay. Something was wrong, and we had to move fast.

"Stand by." I backed out of the call and quickly sent a text to the other two trucks. *Disengage. RV at southern ORP. Time now.* Then bringing the phone back to my ear, I said, "We're disengaging now. What's going on?"

"I'll explain more when you get to Hof. Sending out an all-hands blast over the T-phone network now. It's not everywhere, but if the Army's not talking to you, then you have to expect them to react as if anyone with a weapon as hostile. Get clear, avoid contact, and regroup at Hof. We've got problems." He hung up without any further ado.

A moment later, as we jumped on the autobahn and headed for the bridge over the Rhine, the phone buzzed again, this time with the all-hands message Hartrick had mentioned.

Widespread attacks on American assets and forces country-wide. Several German government outlets are openly suggesting that the Triarii are behind them, using the info-dump as a smokescreen in an attempt to justify continued American occupation. Unknown number of local commanders are going along with it. Avoid contact with regular Army units until deconfliction can be expedited. Avoid all contact with Bundespolizei *or OWHSC forces. Regroup at rear area bases in Bavaria. All sections/teams acknowledge receipt of message.*

I quickly tapped out a *GL X, Rgr*, then turned my attention back to the road. "Looks like Carl's idea backfired. They moved the timeline up, and now the Germans, the Chinese, and some of our own people are blaming us." I stared at the open autobahn in front of us. "We'll need to avoid all checkpoints on the way to Hof. That means backroads." I was already hauling the map out. "Keep your eyes out, and up. I don't want to get a Hellfire dropped on our heads if we can help it."

Chapter 20

"I swear to you, this *is* getting worked out."

"I should fucking hope so." Hartrick was in grand form, his arms crossed and his perpetual scowl deeper than ever as I walked into the GP Medium tent that had been set up as our field TOC just outside Hof. The Army officer facing him and the towering grizzly bear of a man who was Major Tierce, still alive and still commanding the 10th Special Forces Group's contingent in Europe, didn't seem cowed, but she wasn't comfortable, either. "We've shed a lot of blood to pull the Army's asses out of the fire, only to have the guns turned on us when the fucking ChiComs say so."

"It's not like that." The woman in cammies and full battle rattle, her helmet under her arm, turned to look over her shoulder as Tony and I walked into the tent. We were both back in our greens and geared up, my OBR hanging from its sling. Tony still had his SBR Tactical on him, just because the Mk 48 was a little bulky to be carrying around the TOC.

"Really? It sure fucking sounds like it's 'like that.'" Hartrick was a on a tear. "One section detained, two others taken under fire by Army gate guards. And all the excuses parroting a statement made by a German politician we all already *know* is dirty, with a PLA—I'm sorry, *One World Holistic Security Concepts*—Colonel standing right behind him." He stared daggers at the woman. "Show me where I'm wrong."

"The current emergency has led some commanders to take action based on what little information they have." She wasn't rattled, at least. But if she was Civil Affairs or Public Relations, then she was probably trained to deal with angry local leaders.

None of whom held a candle to Hartrick when he was *really* pissed. And he was downright livid at the moment. I knew him well enough to see that clearly. This was not what I would call a safe room to be in.

I glanced at Tierce. His face was stony, but I could see the frustration in his eyes. One of the rare breed of officers I'd respected from the get-go, Tierce had been on our side from the moment we'd first set foot in Poland. He'd recognized what was happening, even when his superiors had refused, and had done whatever he could to head off the inevitable. He'd had his hands tied more often than not, but he'd been a stand-up guy. And from the looks of things, he was still holding his ground. But he wouldn't publicly take sides against another Army officer. He couldn't.

"*Incomplete information?!*" Hartrick's angry bark was almost an explosion. "Is that the excuse for suddenly turning on *Americans*, when the enemy is clearly jihadis and EDC remnant special forces?"

"The Triarii's irregular legal status…" She got that much out before Hartrick took two steps back, snatched a piece of paper off the table behind him, and slammed it down with a *crack* on the table between him and the liaison officer.

"*That* is a copy of a Letter of Marque and Reprisal, issued entirely legally by the *United States Congress*, as outlined in the Constitution." He straightened and folded his arms again. "So, tell me, *what* 'irregular legal status' are we talking about? Exactly?"

The officer—a captain, I saw, as I stepped around to the side of the table, just kind of standing off out of the way, instead of getting right in the middle of things—didn't back up, though there was definitely a bit of flight-or-fight in her eyes as she glanced over at us. She was already on the defensive; I didn't think it would do any of us any good to get her back up even more. Especially if she was actually trying to extend an olive branch. I could fully understand Brian's fury; I felt more than a little of it myself, just from the fragmented reports we'd gotten on the way down to Bavaria after leaving Mainz behind, the smoke blackening the sky in our rear-view mirrors. It sure sounded like the majority of the US Army's senior commanders in-theater were taking the more politically palatable option of turning on the Triarii, blaming us for warning them but failing to stop all the attacks, instead of facing the bitter reality of the insurgency they weren't ready to fight, in no small part because they'd allowed the enemy into the authorities they'd tried to stand up. Or else, they hadn't ferreted the enemy out of those authorities.

You'd have thought, after Korea, Vietnam, Bosnia, Kosovo, Afghanistan, Iraq, Syria, Libya, Kosovo again, and all sorts of little interventions across Africa, that we would have learned by now.

"Your organization might have been granted a Letter of Marque due to the nature of the emergency, but there are a lot of people, a lot of senior officers, who are aware of your activities CONUS, and are understandably wary." She was trying to sound placating, but it wasn't working. I could only watch. I'd seen somebody try to calm Hartrick down with tone of voice before, and it always had the opposite effect. "There are those in the government who believe that you've acted outside the law, and that makes you suspect in many eyes." She held up her hands. "Like I said, it *is* being dealt with. EUCOM is working up a general directive as we speak. *I* don't believe that you and your guys were behind any of this, or that you leaked the intel to cover your own power play." She rolled her eyes. "Seriously, what would you hope to gain? It makes no sense. You don't have the structure in place to take power, you don't have the numbers, and you don't have the support of the population."

The fact was that her indictment of the idea that we'd try to take over Europe via terror attacks came close enough to hitting every problem with the plan that had been followed since just after Vogt's failed coup that it was painful. That wasn't lost on me, either, nor was the fact that we currently *did* have a lot more local support than I suspected either the Army had, or suspected that we did.

How much did American intelligence, outside our own house, know about the *Verteidiger in Bayern*? Or any of the other groups we'd been quietly consulting with, trying to create a grassroots security network in order to head off just this kind of thing?

That we'd been too slow didn't invalidate the necessity of the effort.

"It's getting sorted out," she continued. "You'll have full freedom of movement within a couple more days, I promise. We just have to make sure that the word is fully disseminated that you are *not* a threat, and had nothing to do with the attacks." She glanced at me and Tony, and for a second, I wondered about her sincerity in assuring us that she didn't believe the Triarii had had anything to do with them. She wasn't happy about being here, facing Hartrick's wrath—who would be? —but I also got the impression that she wasn't happy just being here, being liaison between the Army and *us*.

Maybe I was being paranoid. Hard not to be, after all these years.

She didn't seem to have much more to say, and neither did Hartrick. The awkward silence stretched for a moment, then she saluted Tierce, turned on her heel, and left the tent.

Hartrick was feeling extra professional that day. He waited until she was probably out of earshot before letting go with a blistering flood of profanity.

"Did you really expect anything else?" Tierce just sounded tired. He looked it, too. He and his boys must have been running themselves ragged, for the same reasons we were. "Hell, I've got to keep my mouth shut about working with you guys

198

half the time, or I'll either get shut out, or probably have a quiet word stuck in somebody's ear that will end my career as soon as I get back Stateside. Maybe even before. No offense, but that's not a hill I'm willing to die on, yet."

Hartrick let out a long, angry breath. "None taken." He looked up at me and Tony. "Hold tight for a few minutes, boys. I've got a whole brief, but Tucker's still en route."

That was a bit of a relief. At least Tucker's team hadn't gotten snatched. "What about Burkhart?"

"Already been through, moving into Hof." He scowled, more than usual. "We've got a developing situation there."

"Sounded like it." But Hartrick turned his attention back to the laptops and maps on the tables, as unwilling as ever to repeat himself if he could help it. He was like that.

"Major." I turned to Tierce.

"Matt." We shook hands. The big SF officer had a grip like a vise. We still didn't know each other *well*, but I was pretty sure he was a mustang, having been an NCO before he went to the Dark Side, so that tended to make me respect him a little more. "Rough day."

"You're telling me." I still had images of the smoke rising above those FOBs around Mainz dancing behind my eyelids whenever I closed my eyes for more than a blink. It reminded me of Keystone. It was all far too much like Keystone.

The horror of picking through what had been an American base, blasted to ruins and littered with the dead, was something I still saw in my nightmares, most of a year and a lot of death and destruction later.

The tent flap flew open, and Shane Tucker came through, geared up and armed. "What the fuck is going on?"

Hartrick looked up with an arched eyebrow. Shane wasn't fazed, but threw himself into a camp chair in front of one of the tables, his rifle clattering against the frame. He looked down, frowned, and checked it, as if he was worried that he might have just thrown the zero off, but he hadn't hit it that hard.

"Well, the intel dump that Matt and his team pulled out of Uzun's safehouse turned out to be pretty spot on, except our strategy of throwing it out there to get the targets ready and hopefully deter the bad guys backfired." Hartrick leaned on the table with a map of Germany and France, covered in red pins on it. The plastic and metal table creaked under his weight. "They moved things up, and there were more moving parts in the works than we knew about. We got a couple of the jihadi cells, but the DDSB has come out of the woodwork in a big way.

"They *were* disrupted enough that only about half the planned attacks—that we know of—actually went down. It got pretty gruesome in some places. Most of the attacks were IEDs and rockets, though several patrols got ambushed, too. A battalion headquarters got hit in Hamburg. That was a professional hit. Three, maybe four gunmen got inside security in the middle of the night. Killed just about everybody. Shot the TOC to shit, killed the BC, the XO, the OpsO, and a bunch of other people. Waltzed right out, too. Whoever the hell they were, they knew their shit."

I frowned. That didn't sound like jihadis. They'd certainly try something like that, but the getting out part didn't jive. They'd be more likely to hold the TOC to the end, or just clack off and try to kill even more people, along with themselves. Even the Kosovars weren't *that* good. Unless the Army's standards for security had dropped to that abysmal a level. I didn't think so, though, not after Poland, the assault through Germany, and the subsequent low-level unrest and warfare.

"Any ID on them?" Tucker had picked up something about that story, too.

Hartrick shook his head. "There wasn't any CCTV coverage, and the survivors just said they were dressed in dark clothing and body armor, had their faces covered, and they were carrying submachineguns. Nobody had much more than that. The gunfire and grenades seemed to be about all anyone could remember."

Tucker looked over at Tony and me. "That doesn't sound like a bunch of rando terrorists to me. What do you guys think? Spetsnaz, maybe?"

I squinted at the map. "I suppose it's possible. The Russians sure want Western Europe in as much turmoil as they can get. I don't know, though. There are plenty of suspects who are closer. The EDC, for one."

"The Chinese for another." Tony rubbed a thumb along his jaw. "That sounds a lot like some of the potential commando raids that the North Koreans might run in the event of a new invasion of the South. And we know that the Chinese have done a lot more cross-training with the Norks than they'll admit."

I nodded. It made some sense, especially if you suspected—as I did—that OWHSC was really just a front for the PLA. If they were really in Europe to conduct a power play, then they would have brought special operations forces, as well. Each Army under the PLA Ground Forces had its own Special Warfare Brigade, so they had plenty of people.

And Tony was right. There was no telling for sure without more solid information, but something about the description of that raid sounded very North Korean or Chinese to me.

The Russians probably would have blown half the place up getting out.

"Where does that leave us?" I asked.

"Nowhere good." Hartrick started to point to more red pins on the map. "That info op that blamed us for the whole thing wasn't just a matter of throwing whatever at the wall and hoping it sticks. Several sections have already dropped off the map, at least one well within American-patrolled territory. It does, however, look like the majority were targeted by the *Bundespolizei* and OWHSC. And they moved fast enough that they had to have planned it in advance."

Tucker nodded. "Not that surprising. We're simultaneously a threat and a convenient scapegoat."

"Which sections?" I had a sudden bad feeling.

201

Hartrick's lips thinned. "I'm afraid Bradshaw's is one of them."

"Fuck." I'd been trying not to cuss so much, but that one slipped out. Tyler Bradshaw and I had become brothers, through first the nightmare E&E through Slovakia, then the fighting for Poland. He wasn't Grex Luporum, but I wasn't so stuck up that I thought our mission made us necessarily inherently better than the regular infantry dudes. If anything, the current war and the demands on our limited manpower had eliminated much of the distinction between our branches of the Triarii. They'd been running many of the same missions we had, with slightly less top-of-the-line equipment but more men.

Tyler Bradshaw was a hell of a fighter and a good man. And if he had gone down in this treachery, I was ready to burn Berlin to the ground. Not to mention the rest of his section, who had been our backup on more than one raid, and were all good dudes, too.

They'd taken more losses in this war than we had. If they were all dead...

I know war's not fair. *Life's* not fair. But it really hits you, sometimes, that nagging question in the dark hours of the morning.

Why is that guy dead and I'm still alive?

"Where were they when they went dark?" I was already up and looking at the map, already starting to think ahead to the rescue mission.

Hartrick didn't answer right away. And when I looked up, he was watching me carefully. Grimly. I started to get mad. "Brian..."

"The last POSREP we have on them was just outside Weimar." He didn't move. "There's been a sizeable *Bundespolizei* and OWHSC buildup there in the last month or two."

"Weimar." I started searching the map, but then Hartrick's hand closed around my upper arm.

"You're not going after them, Matt. Not yet. I need you here."

I stared up at him. "We are not leaving Tyler and his boys in their hands."

"The *Bundespolizei* are still too civilized to let the ChiComs run wild." He didn't let go. "They'll be uncomfortable, but for the moment, we can rest assured that they won't be shot out of hand. The bad guys want a show trial, they want scapegoats to justify the rest of this. We have time."

He stabbed a finger at Hof on the map. "At least, *they* have time. Hof has exactly none, which is why I'm going to need you to put your personal vendetta on the back burner and get the mission done. *Then* we can go after Bradshaw and the rest."

I held his gaze for a moment, but Hartrick was as unyielding as ever. I glanced at Tierce, then, and saw the flicker in Hartrick's eyes and the warning tightening of his grip on my arm that told me that I needed to stand down.

Brian Hartrick was entirely capable of kicking my ass to *make* me stand down if it came to it. He didn't want to, especially not in front of Tierce, but that was part of the whole point. I shouldn't be pushing this in front of the Special Forces major, either.

I nodded slightly and straightened, gritting my teeth as I forced the rage and the dread to the back of my mind. "What's going on?"

Hartrick let go of my arm as I straightened up. "Most of the rest of the attacks around the country were largely aimed at Triarii, the Army, the *Bundeswehr*, some of the *Bundespolizei*—rather suspiciously, none of the units that were extensively backed by OWHSC—and a few politicians and local militias. Except here."

He grabbed a tablet off the table behind him and set it on the map table, tapping through a couple of windows before bringing up a video.

It was CCTV footage, showing the front of a very modernist building, with a semi-circular glass front, topped with a smaller second floor of white, offset partial cylinders. It looked like an architect's mushroom hallucination to me.

"That's the Theater Hof. There was a conference going on yesterday." A glance at the time stamp showed me that this had, in fact, been recorded the day before. "Not sure what it was about, but there were dignitaries from Berlin, Hamburg, Strasbourg, Paris, and Nuremberg in there. I think they were trying to sort out some kind of agreement between the Bavarians and the rest of Germany. I don't know. Point is, they were all inside when this happened."

He pointed to the screen, as two VW semis pulled up in front of the building, turning suddenly to block the street in both directions. The trailers opened and men in black, armed with shorty G36Ks, raced out and sprinted toward the building. Several more got out of the cabs and took a knee behind them, holding security on the surrounding streets, while the rest, about thirty of them, ran inside. Flashes blinked inside the darkened glass, and one of the panes suddenly clouded, probably as a bullet passed through it.

The recording suddenly froze, then ended. "They shut down the CCTV coverage right then. Not sure how, since the controls aren't in the theater." Hartrick laid down a printout of an overhead photo of the Theater Hof, extensively marked up with red map pen. "They brought other vehicles in at the back before they hit the front. Nobody got out. We have confirmation that at least one man is dead, tentatively identified as Dieter Hennig, one of the delegates from Nuremberg." He tapped another icon, and a still photo came up. "That's from the 'manifesto' video they dropped on the internet a few hours ago. It doesn't actually say anything. They aren't making any demands except to keep all security forces and drones well away from the Theater and the Hotel Central Hof." He nodded grimly. "Yeah, they took that, too. At least the ground floor and the roof. Nobody's getting out."

I looked at the photo. A masked man with a rifle and what looked like an old Blackhawk tactical vest filled most of the image, but there was clearly a body on the floor behind him, and the shot had just as clearly been set up to make sure anyone watching saw the body. "That's Hennig?"

"According to facial recognition, it's ninety percent certain that's Hennig."

I glanced at Tucker, who shrugged. He was as mystified as I was. "Okay, I give up. What exactly is going on, and why are we needed here?"

"Because every armed force with any claim on legitimacy in Germany is heading this way right now. At least, the units that can be spared. That means US Army, *Bundeswehr*, *Bundespolizei*..."

"And OWHSC." Tucker got it before I did.

"And the ChiComs." Hartrick glanced at Tierce, but the big officer shook his head slightly. He didn't have anything else to add. "Hof is about to turn into a powder keg. None of those units are cooperating, and the anti-American rhetoric has been getting turned up to eleven in the German press. Not only that, but the *Bundespolizei* and OWHSC have already started setting up checkpoints throughout the city—in spite of the local *Polizei*, most of whom either are *Verteidiger in Bayern* or sympathetic— and are strictly controlling movement through large parts of the city. Including vital infrastructure that's nowhere near the Theater or the Hotel."

"It's a power play," Tucker mused.

"It's a power play. The same people who backed the EDC, and now have direct Chinese support, haven't pushed into Bavaria yet. They haven't been welcome, and Bavaria's been generally secure enough—thanks in large part to the *Verteidiger in Bayern*—that they haven't had an excuse." He pointed to the dead body on the floor in the photo.

"Now they have an excuse." He looked from me to Tucker. "Burkhart's got the Theater under surveillance, and he's looking for a way to get in and end this fast. I might pull you boys in for that on short notice, so keep your comms open. But I've got something else in mind for both of your teams."

He handed us a pair of manila envelopes. "The *Bundespolizei* and OWHSC moved too fast, and they grabbed too much real estate for this to have caught them by surprise. I want them under surveillance yesterday. Find me the link. And be ready to follow that killchain if you have to."

Chapter 21

Finding a place to start wasn't all that hard. The *Bundespolizei* had an office in the Hof train station. It stood to reason that their operations center would be there, so that was where we'd try to set up surveillance.

Getting eyes on was a lot more difficult. There wasn't a lot of high ground, there were a lot of trees, and there was far too much of a security presence to just park a van on the side of the street and watch. We were going to have to either get inventive, or get really sneaky.

Or both.

It didn't take long to see that trying to loiter or simply move singleton operators or buddy teams through the area on foot to maintain eyes on was going to be a non-starter. There were checkpoints on every street for almost half a mile in every direction, mostly manned by a couple of *Bundespolizei* cops and half a dozen OWHSC shooters, each. Anyone getting too close was going to be stopped and questioned, possibly searched.

That wasn't in itself an insurmountable obstacle. We could stay sterile while on recon, especially if we had a couple guys with guns a couple blocks away, just in case. It was a risk, but it was manageable.

However, given what we'd already seen, we suspected that Americans would get much closer scrutiny than Germans. We still had those missing sections that had gotten rolled up, and while one section had been released, with insincere apologies from the Army commander who had detained them, at least two—including Bradshaw's—were still missing.

Walking past an OWHSC checkpoint—and we were sure that was really what they were; the *Bundespolizei* were just there to lend the ChiCom operators some legitimacy—was not going to be a good idea. Especially not if we tried to do it more than once, and we simply didn't have the numbers to keep a constantly changing constellation of faces on recon, not for the length of time we'd probably need. Surveillance isn't a quick thing, and it takes time.

Even though I suspected it was time that we didn't have, considering the growing siege around the Theater Hof.

So, while Lucas and David broke into the multi-story old people's care center across the Banhofstraße, Steve and I did a little breaking and entering of our own just outside the container yard on the south side of the tracks.

Steve held security while I found our way in. We'd moved in from the east, keeping under the trees that lined the south side of the tracks. Fortunately, there was plenty of shadow, even though the container yard was still lit up by streetlights and spots. We'd been able to find a way through without catching the attention of the nearest checkpoint, mainly by slipping between the apartment buildings and across a couple of back yards.

Neither one of us had night vision on. We *had* our PS-31s with us, but they were in the go bags slung over our shoulders, along with spotting scopes, comms, extra ammo, and the concealment kit we'd put together. We were probably going to need all of it—hopefully not the extra ammo—but right then we had to look as normal and non-threatening as possible, just in case somebody looked out their window.

I'd made it to the fence. I could cut my way in, but we wanted this to be as traceless as possible. Instead, I pulled out my T-phone and pressed a single button.

The T-phones had been designed so that we could use them without breaking blackout, which meant certain functions could be programmed to certain buttons—the phone had some actual buttons, unlike most smart phones recently—so that it could be used without lighting up the screen. That particular button was essentially a "speed dial" for a pre-written text.

In position. Need disruption now.

Rolling blackouts weren't anything new in Germany. The war had made things worse, but retarded energy policy had meant they had been semi-regular for a long time. Granted, American energy policy hadn't been much better. But Germany had been in rough shape for a while.

That meant that when one of our contacts in the local power company made sure the next blackout covered the train station, it shouldn't surprise people too much.

The lights went out for blocks around, and we were shrouded in utter blackness.

I looked around, but still left my NVGs in my go bag. It might be dark, but we still wanted to stay as low-profile as possible, and it wasn't quite late enough to ensure that nobody was going to be looking out their windows. Our friend had managed to shut off the power, but not the cell network.

Plus, we didn't want to be hanging out by the fence any longer than we absolutely had to.

While Steve held security, his hand on the PR-15 in his belt, under his shirt, I started climbing the fence.

I'd had to climb brick and cinderblock walls with full gear before. It's a nightmare. Climbing with no body armor and only pistol ammo is a lot easier, but the nightmare part of getting over a cyclone fence is that it's far from quiet.

The fence rattled as I clambered up, but no one came out to investigate. Fortunately, there was no barbed wire on top, which *was* somewhat surprising, given the rising crime rates in Germany, not to mention all the terrorism and guerrilla warfare. It was a welcome oversight, though, since it meant I just had to throw my leg over, careful not to snag my trousers on the tips of the wire, and jump down.

Then I covered Steve while he followed suit.

We were still under the trees, still in deep shadow. We stayed put for a few minutes, doing our SLLS—Stop, Look, Listen, Smell—to make sure we hadn't been compromised. If we had been, some security guard was probably going to be along, if not OWHSC when somebody called the cops.

Nothing. A siren whooped somewhere in the distance. A dog barked. No vehicles came screaming toward the truck yard, no security guards came nosing around to check out the noise of a rattling fence. I hoped they were watching a movie on a tablet, had looked up as the lights went out, cursed, and gone back to their diversion.

I checked my watch, pulling back the cuff I'd slipped over it to disguise the tritium face. We might have ten or fifteen minutes of blackout left. We needed to move.

The line of trees continued along the fence, taking us behind lined up box trucks almost right to the wall of the one-story building at the east end of the big warehouse that was our chosen perch. We stayed in the dark the whole way.

Getting up onto the roof wasn't exactly child's play. We had a couple of options, though. If worse came to worst, we had climbing ropes and lightweight grappling hooks. Neither of us particularly wanted to go that way, if only because we didn't entirely trust the hooks. There was also the risk that we'd make even more noise climbing up the wall. The building was brick, but it was still a risk.

Fortunately, it wasn't a risk we needed to take. Not at this stage.

There was, indeed, a back door, and a quick check didn't reveal any powered locks. Just an old-fashioned key lock that was quickly opened with a bump key. The door opened almost soundlessly, and we slipped inside, careful to shut the door and lock it behind us.

While we didn't have a good idea of the building's interior layout, it wasn't that big, and it didn't take long to find the stairs leading to the roof access. None of the doors were locked, fortunately, and we quickly made our way up onto the roof.

Time was flying. We didn't have eyes on the *Bundespolizei* station from that roof, so we had to get up top.

That took a little bit more effort. I braced my back against the wall, my legs bent, and Steve clambered up onto my knee, pushing off and grabbing hold of the edge of the warehouse roof. From there, I stood up, my hands cupped under his boot, propelling him up until he could get his upper body onto the roof and crawl the rest of the way over.

It took him a moment to get situated, then he came back over the edge and held his hand out for me.

I jumped, fortunately high enough that I could grab his wrist. He clamped his grip down on mine, and then, as I climbed and he pulled, I got up on the roof.

It wasn't completely flat, but the low peaks were plenty shallow, and there was a low parapet all the way around. We moved quickly but carefully to the edge, staying as low as we could, even as the lights came back on all around us. Our blackout was over.

Getting out was going to be somewhat more interesting, since it would be difficult to time another blackout perfectly without it seeming suspicious, but we'd tackle that when the time came.

As I got set up, finding a good window where we could prop ourselves up just far enough to see over the parapet without exposing much, Steve started to get our overhead cover out. As thin as a mylar survival blanket, the edges and corners stiffened with wire, it unfolded to roughly the size of a poncho, with short legs at each corner. It stretched completely taut, presenting its gray, black, and white, random, slightly pixelated pattern to the sky above us. It looked an awful lot like the Army's old ACU "couch-camo," but it had been picked to blend into an asphalt roof as much as possible. This wasn't an asphalt roof, but the coloration was close enough that hopefully a drone wouldn't notice us, at least not without a very close inspection.

With the cover set up, Steve low-crawled under it, and we began our vigil.

***

For all the physical obstacles we'd had to overcome to set up the two OPs, another effort, that was more likely to pick up something actionable, was even harder, in its own way. That was Greg's job. He was sitting in a van about three blocks away from the *Bundespolizei* station, with a Scorpion, a repeater, and several other tech toys at his disposal. He was trying to break into their comms, either the *Bundespolizei*, OWHSC, or both. Given the fact that neither organization was exactly what you might call a bunch of amateurish terrorists, that was going to be tough. He was going to have to not only find the right places to try to tap in, but he was also going to have to get past encryption, possibly VPNs, and all sorts of active countermeasures.

I didn't envy him the task. I'm no tech guy, myself, anyway.

Our view was limited, and Steve and I took turns watching the target area. All we could really see was the south side of the building, facing the tracks, and the main entrance was definitely not there. Lucas and David—who had made it into position without trouble; I'd confirmed that via a comms check once I dared to open the T-phone's screen—had a much better view, looking over the traffic circle in the middle of the front parking lot. But we needed to maintain eyes on the entire building, just in case, so here we were.

Frankly, I didn't expect to see anything useful. The *Bundespolizei*, think what we might about their leadership's decision making, were pros. The ChiComs who were pulling their strings at the moment were, too. The likelihood that they'd do anything out in the open was slim. It would all be electronic, somewhere in the ether of the parts of the internet that most people never see.

I was equally doubtful that Greg was going to find much, at least not on the timeline we were working with. There were too many variables, and while Greg was good, he was no wizard. Scott would have had a better chance, and even he would have struggled.

That hurt, thinking about Scott. I usually managed to keep our losses compartmentalized, but when you're lying on a roof under a glorified poncho, with nothing to do but either watch the objective or rest between your shifts on glass, your mind has time to go all sorts of places you don't want it to.

I was grateful when it was my turn to observe again. It gave me something to focus on aside from suppressed grief and worries about the future.

Time crawled by. The trains weren't running as frequently as they had been before. Some companies and agencies were working hard to get things back to normal, but the German economy, none-too-robust after the last few years—or couple decades, depending on who you ask—had taken one hell of a blow with the collapse of the EDC. There simply weren't as many trains running.

The train that pulled in half an hour into my shift on glass wasn't big. There was nothing in particular about it that made it stand out. I observed it and noted the people getting off because that's what you do when you're on observation.

Then I saw a face that made me sit up and take notice, so to speak.

We had decks of cards that displayed the faces of most the known EDC senior officers still at large. It was a time-honored way of disseminating a most wanted list, dating back to World War II playing cards with the silhouettes of enemy aircraft on the backs. I'd never been much of a card player, but I'd let Reuben talk me into playing endless rounds of Spades during some of our off time, if only to better memorize our targets. Not everyone on the deck was EDC. We'd added quite a few jihadis, DDSB communists, and a few Fourth Reich neo-Nazis to the deck. But the majority of the cards still bore the faces of the leadership of what remained of the EDC, which still controlled the southern half of what had once been East Germany, though Berlin was largely trying to ignore it.

I'd seen that face often enough on the back of a Three of Spades. Chretien Travere was a true believer and a stone-cold killer. He'd been in Slovakia. We'd gotten some reports from our Nationalist friends, who'd gotten word across the border into Poland, about some of what that man had done in Nationalist-majority towns.

Of course, he'd justified it all, since the Nationalists were all would-be Nazis, and therefore *had* to be crushed, before they committed Nazi war crimes.

Yeah, we'd read some of his statements, too.

I didn't have time to nudge Steve. I *did* have time to capture two photos. They were a little blurry, especially the first one, but Travere was still recognizable.

"I think we just got our link between the EDC, OWHSC, and the *Bundespolizei*," I whispered. I was wishing I'd had my OBR with me right then. I could have dropped the Three of Spades easily. And he'd have deserved it.

"What have you got?" Steve was still down on his back, staring up at the daylight playing on the camouflage cover over our heads.

"Chretien Travere just walked into the *Bundespolizei* station. And the guy who opened the door and let him in didn't look like he was arresting a war criminal who was turning himself in." I was already setting up to transmit the photos over the mesh network. Maybe, if we moved fast enough, we could get a team in place to intercept him, since we couldn't simply storm the *Bundespolizei* station, not with the numbers we had.

Either way, one thing was sure. The EDC *hadn't* gone away, and if they still had their hand on the steering wheel in Berlin—and were allied with the ChiComs—then we were in a much more precarious position than we'd thought.

Chapter 22

I didn't see Travere leave the *Bundespolizei* station. Nor did we have the chance to move in to interdict him.

The explosion came first. Not at the train station, but up north. I couldn't see from my angle, but something told me that whatever had blown up had been at or near the Theater Hof.

The rolling thunder of the detonation was followed by the rattle of small arms fire, then several heavier *thud*s, that sounded almost more like anti-tank rockets or rocket propelled grenades than bombs or IEDs. More gunfire followed.

My T-phone lit up. *Can you get out of your OP without being observed?*

I looked around. I couldn't see enough of the lot below us to tell, but I doubted it. *Unlikely before dark.*

Three of Spades presence acknowledged. Higher priority taskings are in the works. Hold what you've got until we can get an exfil platform to you.

That was ominous.

The chain of explosions and almost frantic gunfire to the north was even more so.

Something had just changed, and not for the better. Steve and I traded a look, then hunkered down to wait, while all hell kept breaking loose up north.

***

Things sounded like they'd calmed down, though smoke was thick on the air and sirens kept wailing and whooping across the city, when I got another message over the T-phone. *Your ride has arrived. Get below and don't worry about being spotted. You're covered.*

I frowned. I wasn't sure what that meant, but it was obvious that Hartrick wanted us back at the COC, fast. He never would have told me to get out of an OP in broad daylight and not worry about getting spotted, otherwise. The correct course of action would have been to stay in place until dark, stage another blackout, and slip away in the darkness.

Judging by the noise up north, though, things in Hof had just gone sideways, and we needed to move quickly to adapt to a changing situation. So quickly that we had to abandon good tradecraft.

We broke down the OP fast, stuffing the folded cover back in Steve's go bag, and then we were moving back to the edge of the roof. I went first, easing myself over, lowering myself until I was hanging by my fingertips from the edge, then dropping lightly to the roof below.

It was a lot easier than if I'd been wearing body armor, a combat load, and carrying a rifle, never mind the rest of an OP kit.

Steve followed, then we moved quickly across the roof to the stairs. The roof access was still unlocked, and we hustled downstairs, getting wide-eyed stares from the people working in the building, though they kept their mouths shut as there were two *Polizei* in vests and helmets waiting for us.

I tensed a little at that. Both of us were carrying only pistols, though at that range, it was hardly a game-stopper. But a second glance showed me that neither of these men were *Bundespolizei.* They were Hof cops, half of whom were *Verteidiger in Bayern,* and one of them was wearing a Bavarian flag pin on his lapel, as if to identify himself as such and reassure us.

"Deacon?" The big man's accent was pretty thick. "Are you ready?"

There was no way the *Bundespolizei* would have my callsign. "Yeah."

"We are ready." I wasn't sure if the guy just wasn't particularly voluble, or if his English was just that bad. He pointed outside, where I could see a Hof *Polizei* van parked in the lot.

I nodded and waved at him to lead the way. We were getting a lot of looks, but nobody said anything.

"They seemed awfully cool with two dudes they'd never seen before climbing down off their roof." Steve kept his tone casual as we climbed into the van, but the question was pretty plain.

"I told them you were part of the *Bundespolizei*'s outer security cordon." Turned out old boy really could speak English well, accent or no. He grinned as he pulled his door shut. "Can't be too careful, with terrorists in the city." He flashed us the little Bavarian badge on his uniform lapel. "You are among friends, Deacon." He held out a hand. "I am Lars."

I shook it. He had a decently firm handshake. "What happened?" I wanted to get as much info as I could as we pulled out of the parking lot, past a guard shack with a bored-looking security guard inside who didn't even bother to look up.

"I should probably let your commander brief you." Lars turned back forward. "Things went bad at the Theater Hof. He probably has much more detailed information for you, though."

I couldn't help but notice that he'd used my callsign, but not Hartrick's. I couldn't see Hartrick telling some rando German cop that his callsign was "Happy," after all.

The smoke continued to billow, black, ugly, and threatening, over the skyline as we drove away from the train station, heading for our temporary camp outside the city.

***

Security on our combat outpost was *tight*. Far tighter than even OWHSC was managing in the city. Triple-strand

217

concertina wire surrounded the tents, and earthworks had already been put up, with more concertina on top of them. Bulldozers were hard at work even as we spoke, still expanding the defenses. Most of the machines looked civilian, with *Verteidiger in Bayern* guys operating them.

The gate wouldn't stop a determined vehicular assault, but the men dug in to either side had Mk 48s and AT-4s. Anybody trying to rush that gate was going to get lit up.

The fighting positions flanked an opening in the wire that had been partially blocked off by 55-gallon drums. I didn't doubt that there were some nasty surprises in those drums, since they couldn't have been filled with concrete to the point that they'd be impossible to move. Two Triarii infantry, their M5E1 rifles slung in front of them, waited behind two of the drums as we pulled up.

"We'll walk in from here, Lars." It was entirely possible that the *Polizei* would get through without any difficulty, but we were in a hurry, and I could walk to the command tent without needing one of those drums to get pulled out of the way.

"Okay." He nodded. "We need to get back to patrol, anyway."

Shaking hands with the two German cops again, Steve and I piled out and headed in, though not without having to show the two infantry Triarii our creds. Things had to be tense, when even we had to get cleared through.

"Hartrick's waiting for you." The guy looked young as hell, as young as a lot of those kids we'd fought across Slovakia with. I hadn't realized we were recruiting from the general population already. It had always been talked about, but most of us had been drawn from the ranks of the military and the contracting world, so most of the Triarii I'd gotten used to seeing were generally older dudes, in their thirties or forties. I guessed that things really had gotten that bad. "Said to send you right in."

I nodded to the kid, and Steve and I stepped it out for the command tent.

We weren't quite the last ones there. David and Lucas were still en route. The rest of the team, along with Burkhart's and Tucker's, were already assembled. Hartrick was talking with Tucker, and waved me over as I came in.

I was tired, hungry, thirsty, and still had my go bag on my shoulder. But I headed over anyway.

"How much did you see on the way in?" Hartrick asked.

"Smoke. Not much else." My voice was a bit of a dry rasp, and Bobby Burkhart tossed me a bottle of water. I cracked it open and sucked half of it down in one pull. "What happened?"

"I'll go into details in the main brief. But the *Bundespolizei* tried to storm the Theater Hof and got blown to pieces. Whoever's in there has some serious hardware, and they were well-prepared for an assault. They took out multiple Fuchs armored vehicles and a helicopter with ATGMs and well-placed mines. Not IEDs, either. From what we've been able to ascertain, they actually used anti-tank mines.

"We haven't been able to get casualty numbers from the *Bundespolizei*." Hartrick sneered. "To absolutely no one's surprise, they're in full CYA mode."

"Well, given what I saw, I wonder." When Hartrick gave me a raised eyebrow, in part because he was probably wondering where I was going with this, in part because I was interrupting his warning order, I pushed ahead. "We just watched the Three of Spades walk into a *Bundespolizei* station that's crawling with OWHSC operators. I wonder if the guys who got tapped for that assault weren't *very* carefully selected."

Tucker could see it. He was nodding, if somewhat reluctantly. "Put all the anti-EDC guys on the assault force, knowing it's a suicide mission? That's cold, but I don't guess it's beneath these people."

"I don't put anything beneath these people." Hartrick was thinking it over. "It's certainly possible. I'm not sure how it fits in with the fact that Berlin just formally requested US Army assistance with ending the Theater Hof siege."

My eyes narrowed. "That is weird." Something wasn't quite right. "That just blew up, what? An hour ago?"

"About that." He nodded. "Yeah. It's fast. *Real* fast. Given the recent rhetoric, a lot faster than any of us expected the Germans to turn to the Ugly Americans. Gutierrez is suspicious as fuck about it, too."

"So, what's the play?" I knew there was something. Hartrick wouldn't have pulled us if there wasn't something in the works. I saw movement out of the corner of my eye, and saw Lucas and David come in, similarly still in their civvies and go bags, looking around at the gathered teams.

Hartrick saw them, too. "Okay, everybody's here, which means the warning order's shelved. Let's get to it." He moved to the main map board, which had a photomosaic overhead of Hof, put together by our own drones in the last day or so. "So, as you may or may not have already heard, the *Bundespolizei* just tried to storm the Theater Hof and got their teeth kicked in. Two Fuchs armored cars destroyed, a helo shot down, a lot of dead Federal cops, and from what we can tell, none of the bad guys so much as scratched. Berlin has formally asked for US Army intervention."

"Wait. They're asking for the US Army ahead of the *Bundeswehr*?" That was Powell, one of Burkhart's guys.

"Yeah, they are. And yeah, it's suspicious as hell." Hartrick turned to the map. "That's not the only thing that's sketchy as fuck, either." He used a laser pointer to indicate each location as he was talking. "Drones have spotted unusual movement through the checkpoints here, here, and here." He pointed out several main routes and side streets leading into Hof from the northeast. I frowned. Some pieces were coming together. Travere shows up at the *Bundespolizei* station, all hell breaks loose at the siege while we're watching him, potentially set up deliberately to purge undesirables from the local *Bundespolizei*, and meanwhile, reinforcements, supplies, or both come in from EDC-controlled territory.

"What we have are multiple vans and trucks being let through the checkpoints without searches. They park not far away, usually somewhere that has some overhead cover, and then we lose track." He looked around at us. "We have set these checkpoints and the last known positions of the trucks—well, two of them we still have eyes on—as your NAIs. Find out, if you can, what just came in here. Preferably *before* the boys and girls with Joint Force Germany walk into a meat grinder."

"Can we get the Army to hold off?" Tucker didn't sound optimistic, and Hartrick immediately shook his head.

"The commander's one of those who doesn't even want to talk to us. I've tried. Gutierrez has tried, from Poland. We keep getting the runaround. *Their* overhead hasn't seen anything suspicious, and the US Army is invincible, anyway. Didn't they drive clear to Berlin in a few days?"

I snorted. "When it was only supposed to take one? They're not *really* trying to hold that fiasco up as a success, are they?"

Hartrick smirked. "Of course they are. They might be admitting failure if they do anything else, and then their careers are sunk. You can't expect them to sacrifice their careers for something like integrity, can you?"

He looked around at all of us. "Because they're not talking to us, we don't know when go-time is. So, get your planning done as fast as you can, get jocked up—low profile, for now, but have the heavy stuff ready to go if you need it—and get out there. We're up against the clock, and it's moving quick."

Chapter 23

Getting to our objective was the hard part. It was on the far side of the city, north of the besieged Theater Hof, and we had to go around easily a dozen checkpoints to get there. We knew we didn't want to cross any of them, not after what we had observed over the last few hours. Something bad was brewing in Hof, and it looked increasingly like the Germans themselves, and their OWHSC allies, were the ones stirring the pot.

I didn't know what the endgame was. That wasn't something I could see, even putting the pieces together like I was. Why start a siege and then try—unsuccessfully—to break it? It didn't make any sense to me, unless there was something else going on that we hadn't figured out yet.

That was almost certain. I just hoped we could track down this truck and get ahead of whatever it was before everything blew up in our faces.

Should have just pulled back to Poland and run ops with the GROM guys. Left Germany and France to fend for themselves after we knocked off the EDC. It was a nice thought, but I knew it wasn't practical. As long as that EDC remnant was still sitting there, the war wasn't over.

A war's over when both sides agree that it is. If only one side still figures that it's game on, then the war ain't over.

It didn't help that it was becoming increasingly obvious that we might have decapitated the EDC in Brussels and the raids immediately after, but we hadn't really killed it. That hydra was still there, quiescent in Berlin, Paris, and a hundred other governmental and elite institutions throughout central Europe. And it was gathering itself to hit back.

Crammed into a VW van, we circled far around to the north, almost going into Köditz before turning back toward Hof. There were a lot of patrols out and a lot of helicopters and drones in the air. It took a lot longer to get back into Hof than we'd hoped.

It looked an awful lot like the majority of the armed forces in the country were converging on Hof. That was bad for any number of reasons, not least of which how much chaos could be sowed elsewhere in the country while everybody was focused on Hof. I at least *hoped* that the Army hadn't been so foolish as to strip every other area of operation in Germany for this one incident, but given the numbers I was seeing out in the fields and on the roads outside of Hof, they'd brought in a *lot*.

Maybe somebody thought that a full-court press might make for a moral victory and confirm the wisdom of Berlin's faith in the American fighting man—or woman—to protect them from the big, bad terrorists. I just had a rising feeling of dread, looking at it all.

Somebody was missing something, and I didn't think it was the bad guys.

Our first target was parked under the overhang of a loading dock on the end of a local brewery's warehouse. We staged the vehicles several blocks away, dismounted with our SBRs in backpacks and pistols concealed in waistbands, and started moving in.

There wasn't a lot of cover or concealment on this route. That's always an issue when operating in cities. But we were also short on time, and while we were inside the OWHSC cordon, we hadn't seen any of the men in gray in a while. It was almost as if they'd cleared out to let whatever was happening take its course.

That was plenty ominous in its own right.

A quiet, thunderstorm tension seemed to have settled over Hof. As if everyone knew something was coming, and no one was quite sure what, only that it was going to be bad.

We spread out, keeping contact in twos and threes, sweeping in on the brewery and the attached warehouse in a sort of pincer movement, as well as we could within the limits of the streets, buildings, and trees. No one came out to stop us. The street and the parking lots were deserted. The windows of the surrounding buildings were dark and still. It was morning, but it may as well have been the middle of the night.

I paused at the corner, watching the parking lot, while Chris watched my six. David and Greg weren't far behind. Jordan took up rear security. Across the way, I saw movement in the trees that lined the street as Tony, Lucas, Jim, Reuben, and Steve moved up.

I made eye contact with Jim and nodded. Time to go.

None of us had drawn a weapon yet. We hadn't seen any targets, and as long as we could stay soft, we might still have an advantage. We had pistols at hand if things got sketchy, but if there was anyone on the truck, I hoped to get the drop on them and take them alive. I wanted some answers.

Stepping into the parking lot, I closed rapidly on the loading dock, the rest of the Alpha element spreading out behind me while Tony and the Bravo element closed from the northeast.

The truck was a new-looking Mercedes, the cab blue, the trailer white. It was backed up against the dock as if it was just another beer truck, parked for loading or unloading. We only knew that it wasn't because the drones had picked it up when it had passed through the checkpoint to the north without a search.

The windows were dark, but I couldn't see anyone inside the cab. That didn't mean there wasn't a driver or passenger in there, just that I couldn't see past the glare of the sun and the shadow under the overhang. I closed quickly but carefully, every nerve thrumming, my hand ready to snatch my shirt out of the way and draw.

I reached the cab and decided that caution trumped stealth for the moment. While I was somewhat concealed from view by the shadow of the overhang and the cab itself, just below the passenger side door, I drew my PR-15, held it ready at my sternum, and stepped up to look in the window, lifting the pistol so that I could engage through the glass if I had to.

I came up over the top of the door and peered inside. Both the passenger and driver seats were empty. I couldn't see anyone back in the sleeper compartment behind, even as I leaned toward the front, angling so that my muzzle went where my eyes did. It looked empty, the bed folded up.

Dropping down to the ground, I turned toward the back. Nobody in the cab. Time to check the trailer.

Jordan, Tony, and Jim were already up there, and already had the trailer open. It hadn't been locked. I clambered up onto the dock and joined them.

The trailer stood empty, completely cleared out. A couple of metal packing strips lay on the floor, but that was it. Whatever they'd brought in was gone.

Without a word, I dropped back down and headed toward the cab again. I inspected the door *very* carefully before I tried to open it. I'd been in too many places where there could very well have been an IED wired into the door.

I didn't see anything. I still broke the window with my pistol and swept the glass out of the way before I stuck my head in and checked even more carefully.

No wires. No visible explosives. That didn't mean they weren't there. If they'd wanted to be really thorough, the bomb might well be inside the door itself, and the initiation system wired into the latch. I needed to take the risk, anyway. With a deep breath—I hate IEDs more than just about any other threat out there—I unlocked the door and opened it.

It didn't go boom. I wasn't turned into pink mist. Progress.

A quick search of the cab turned up nothing. I double checked, but this was our target. It just wasn't particularly useful anymore.

With a grimace, I got out and got down. Pulling my T-phone out, I called Hartrick.

"What have you got?" Things were far too tense and dangerous for any kind of preamble.

"Nothing. It's the right vehicle, but it's been cleared out and there's no evidence left in the cab, either. No notes, no maps, no comms, nothing. Completely sterile." I couldn't keep some of the frustration out of my voice, even as I scanned our surroundings. The rest of the team had already spread out, more than one down on a knee with an open go bag at his feet, ready to snatch out a rifle and go to work. This felt a little too much like an ambush.

Hartrick's angry sigh rasped in the speaker against my ear. "Same thing everywhere. They were thorough, I'll give 'em that." He paused, and I waited for the next frag-o, while I scanned our surroundings, including the skies above the parking lot, looking for the attack we hadn't seen coming.

This was all a little too pat. We'd spotted the trucks easily—the lack of a search had been a dead giveaway—and tracked them down just as easily. I would have expected somebody to be waiting to hit the teams that moved in to check them out.

It's what I would have done.

Still, there was no movement, no attack. Not even the kamikaze drones that I'd dreaded since Nitra.

"Get back here." Hartrick's voice brooked no argument. "Make it quick, but don't get rolled up at a checkpoint."

I just acknowledged and hung up. If Hartrick was going to give reasons over comms, he would have. We needed to get back and hear it from him. I circled my hand above my head and pointed back toward where we'd staged the van.

As unobtrusively as we could—considering we'd just smashed a window and searched a vehicle in broad daylight—we faded and headed back the way we'd come.

***

It took almost an hour to get back. One of our S70s was on the LZ just outside the main camp when we pulled up, and there was a lot of activity. The shooters at the gate stopped us anyway, and I had to confirm our bona fides.

The kid at the gate still looked young as hell. "Mr. Hartrick wants to see you in the COC, Mr. Bowen. He said to have the rest of your team get jocked up for an overt op." The kid was clearly reciting from memory, but he also spoke as if he knew what he was talking about, and wasn't just parroting what he'd been told. Given his apparent age, I had to assume that training had expanded to pick up the slack where experience was lacking.

"Good copy." We didn't wear nametapes, so I didn't know the kid's name, but he must have been told to expect us and generally what we looked like. I drove the van inside the wire while the gate guards moved the drums back into position behind us.

Tony got everyone moving back to our tent while I headed for the COC, my go bag still over my shoulder. Whatever was on the docket, I didn't expect to have much time to shuffle stuff around.

Hartrick was on comms with somebody when I walked in, and he looked up, held up a hand, and I waited. I scanned the busy COC as I did so, my eyes narrowing as I saw an awful lot of pins getting moved around the map, most of them converging on the Theater Hof. Was the next move going down now?

Hartrick finished and turned to me, waving me over. "The push is happening in the next half hour. We actually got warning from Tierce; Colonel Brice wasn't going to tell us. Two columns of Strykers are heading in as we speak. We're seeing movement all over the place. We suspect that the bad guys aren't just in the Theater and the hotel, and that the Army's not ready for what's coming. Get changed over, grab your rifle, and get on the bird that's on the LZ right now. I want you overhead, ready to run aerial interdiction on whatever's coming."

I stayed put just long enough to get an intel update—it wasn't much; none of the other teams had come up with any more than we had—and then I was running out of the tent, heading for my greens, my body armor, and my OBR.

Things were getting interesting. Not that they'd ever stopped.

Chapter 24

I was buckled in, my OBR across my knees, right behind the door gunner as we rose into the sky. I didn't have a drone feed or any other kind of real-time intel stream, but I did have my Peltors plugged into the bird, so I could hear the updates that the COC was pushing out to all hands.

"Lead elements are five minutes out." The Strykers had started moving about half an hour before, but they were advancing on the Theater carefully, though from what I'd been able to ascertain, they were moving slowly mainly because the command wanted them to encircle the Theater all at once, before presumably sweeping in and saving the day.

I wasn't sure what it was about their plan that the *Bundespolizei* hadn't already tried, but unless they had a way to neutralize anti-tank rockets and IEDs, they were proceeding in much the same way.

Our pilot—another guy I didn't recognize, but there were more Triarii in Europe than I could keep track of at that point—took us north, staying about a hundred feet above the rooftops. I scanned the city below, watching as the door gunner pivoted his MAG-58 from side to side, searching for threats.

Hof looked deceptively peaceful at the moment. The smoke that had blanketed the city after the *Bundespolizei*'s abortive raid had dispersed, and the sunshine was dappled on the roofs and waving green treetops by the broken clouds high above us.

That peace and quiet was an illusion, and I knew it better than most.

We passed over Kulmbacher Straße as a platoon of Strykers rolled toward the Theater Hof, their CROWS turrets alternating left and right, but none of them were traversing much. My eyes narrowed as we passed over, watching them for a few more moments. They were acting as if the only threat in the city was the terrorists in the theater.

Maybe that was what they'd been briefed. It didn't bode well, though. Good tactical habits are good tactical habits, and bad tactics get you killed when you least expect it.

After all, the intel's *never* complete. Some of us had learned that the easy way, from veterans who knew and gave a damn. Some had to learn it the hard way.

Pride goeth before a fall.

We hadn't gotten far past the convoy when there was a flash behind us, and then the *boom* of an explosion. I craned my head out the side door of the bird, looking past the tail, to see an ugly black mushroom cloud rising above the Kulmbacher Straße. I couldn't see the street itself over the roofs, but if I was judging the landmarks right, that had gone off right about even with the rear vehicle.

I frowned. Usually, you target the lead vehicle to halt the column, then the rear.

Unless you *want* them to come deeper, but not get out. My blood ran a little cold.

A trio of explosions went up around the city in the next few moments. The Strykers hadn't quite managed to all swoop in at the same time, but they were close. And their slow pace had given the enemy plenty of time to prepare.

We maintained our wide circle, though the door gunner, a heavyset older guy named Coris, was leaning more heavily into his weapon, scanning the ground below us. The game was on. Now we just had to find the bad guys.

"Golf Lima Charlie, Golf Lima Ten-Six." I had a double PTT switch on my plate carrier, and I hit the one for my radio instead of the helo's intercom.

"Send it." Hartrick was terse and short. He was watching a dozen things at once.

"Do we need to set down and move to support any of these columns? Thinks are looking a little hot down there."

"Negative." He sounded more pissed than usual. "The Army's insisting everything's under control. I've been explicitly told to keep Triarii assets away from the assault and the Theater."

I didn't bother to say anything. Politics. It gets more people killed than bullets.

We continued to circle, as the situation on the ground continued to unravel.

All four columns of Strykers had stopped as they got hit, and as we flew over, we narrowly avoided getting shot at, one of the turrets rising toward our bird before the pilot got on the horn and frantically identified us as friendlies. The Strykers were armed almost exclusively with M2 .50 cals or 40mm HK GMGs, unlike the Powells with their 35mm cannons, but a .50 can still do a number on an aircraft.

With the advancing columns of armored vehicles halted, the infantry piled out and started to secure the area while they tried to rescue any of their brothers and sisters in the stricken vehicles. They were still halted in the middle of the street. They were sitting ducks. Just as the bad guys had planned.

If I'd had any doubt that the EDC and OWHSC were behind this, it was dispelled by the first wave of the counterattack.

The EDC had used drones extensively in the past, not least in the battle against the Slovak Nationalists for the city of Nitra. Those had been aerial suicide drones, though. These were different.

They weren't a design I recognized, but the little, six-wheeled vehicles were clearly unmanned, and just as clearly armed to the teeth. Several of them had mounted machineguns and 40mm grenade launchers, but two mounted twin quadruple stacks of what looked a lot like MBDA Enforcer missiles in their boxy launchers.

They came out of the parking lot behind the Hotel Central Hof, moving fast from where they'd been nestled in between vehicles, close enough that they'd evaded drone surveillance. At least, they'd evaded *our* drone surveillance. I suspected that most of the drones above Hof at that moment had different priorities.

Or at least their operators did.

The drones opened fire almost all at once. The two lead Strykers were hit by Enforcer missiles at such close range that there was almost no pause between the backblast from the squared-off tubes and the brief flash and puff of smoke and sublimated metal of the hits. The drones were far too close to miss, even without the Enforcers' guidance systems. They'd appeared only about a hundred fifty yards from their targets.

The first Stryker rocked under the impacts, and as the smoke and dust from the first hits cleared, it started to burn fiercely, flames erupting from every hatch.

Nobody got out.

Half a dozen soldiers had either thrown themselves flat in the street or been knocked there by the concussions of the AT missile strikes. The drones with machineguns opened fire then, and Nailaer Straße turned into an abattoir.

Coris and I were leaning out as the pilot brought the bird around sharply, trying to get a shot at the drones. Any of them. Those kids were getting murdered down there, and unless we stepped in, they didn't have much of a chance. The Stryker was now belching black smoke that was being blown back into their faces, making it even harder for any of them to target the drones that were trundling toward them, spitting death. We had a much better angle.

Coris leaned into his MAG-58 and sent a chattering stream of bullets down at the street, the red tracers stitching a zigzag of destruction across the street and into the trees. I squeezed off a shot as my reticle passed over one of the drones, my weapon braced against the door, the sling taut across my shoulders. I wasn't entirely sure if I'd hit it, or even how much damage a single 7.62 round was going to do to a drone, but it was better than nothing.

Then we were past, and we suddenly had other problems to worry about.

Without warning, our pilot suddenly dropped us toward the railroad tracks like a rock, twisting away from the firefight on the street, as a sextet of dark arrowhead shapes flashed past overhead.

"Somebody get some fire on those drones before they knock us out of the sky!" He banked back sharply in the opposite direction, and the port side gunner opened up, though how well he was going to be able to hit something that small, moving that fast, while we were twisting all over the sky, I didn't know.

I could tell we were taking fire as we roared low over the railroad tracks, practically skimming the rooftops, but only because a few of the rounds actually hit the bird. A hole suddenly appeared in the door, three inches from my hand, with a *bang* that I could hear even over the snarl of the rotors.

Coris was pivoting, bringing the MAG back toward the tail. "Drones are still on us!" I leaned back to make damn good and sure I was out of his line of fire, while I silently prayed that we'd at least get a chance to set down and get off the bird before all hell broke loose.

The muzzle blast hammered at me, and I fought to keep from flinching, dropping my head to keep the burning shockwaves out of my eyes. Hot brass and links cascaded across the floor of the helo, and then Coris had to cease fire as the pilot set us into a twisting bank to port again.

Our pilot was hot shit. He got even lower, if that was possible, following the railroad tracks as he set us racing away from the Theater. But the bad guys weren't just in the Theater.

I didn't see the SAM launch from the Jahnsporthalle. I heard the pilot curse over the intercom, a moment before we swerved again, the *thump*s of the helo's flare launchers reverberating through the fuselage.

The concussion as the SAM hit one of the flares and detonated was still close enough that the entire bird shuddered. I got on the intercom.

"Find a place to set us down before we get shot out of the sky!" Perhaps not the most politic thing to demand of a shit-hot helicopter pilot, but we couldn't engage for crap up there, particularly not with the maneuvers he was making. Good on him for keeping us alive, but we weren't doing the boys and girls down there a bit of good as it was, and that was the whole reason we were up there in the first place.

He didn't reply, but we banked sharply to the east again, racing away from the hot zone, just barely a few dozen feet above the rooftops. I understood the decision, as much as I didn't like it, but a moment later, I understood it even better. There were no LZs nearby. As he turned north, I suspected that he was probably heading for another park or soccer field.

Either way, we were going to be a long way from the fight, and on foot. I turned and looked around at the rest of the team, who'd really had nothing more to do than hang on and try not to get sick as we roller-coastered across the sky.

"We're heading for a soccer field about half a mile northeast of the target zone." The pilot was talking to me, I realized. "You'll have to do a bit of a Mogadishu Mile to get in there, but hopefully we don't get shot down beforehand."

He'd barely gotten the words out before something hit us with a staccato series of *bang*s and the entire bird started to shudder and shake. The tang of smoke hit my nostrils as the noise got worse. The helo was starting to shake itself apart.

"Hold on! Fifteen seconds!" I could hear the strain in the pilot's voice as he fought to keep the bird in the air a little longer. It wasn't entirely for our sakes, either. While we'd all die if this thing went down hard enough, so would a lot of civilians if we hit a building, or even one of the streets where a few brave souls were still trying to move around and go about their business.

I could feel the bird shudder and shimmy. The tail rotor must have been hit, or else some of the controls to the tail surfaces had been damaged. The smoke was getting thicker, and I could see as well as smell the black plume starting to belch from behind us.

We almost clipped a rooftop, and I got a glimpse of the truck we'd checked out earlier, still parked at the loading dock, the window still smashed, just before we came down, hard.

Chapter 25

I might have blacked out for a moment, but only for a moment. We hit hard, but our pilot was good enough that he'd just barely managed to flare before dropping us right in the center of the soccer pitch.

Trying to ignore the pain in my head—and the rest of me—I looked around the compartment. Everyone had been strapped in, and the pilot had managed a better crash landing than I'd feared. It looked like everyone was intact, and even conscious.

Coric was shaking off the shock of the impact. We had zero time, though. I could smell aviation fuel *and* fire.

Popping the seatbelt, I heaved myself to my feet, just about gave myself whiplash as the intercom cable tried to pull my head off, yanked the cable out of my Peltors, grabbed Coric, and unclipped his harness. "Grab the gun and as much ammo as you can and get out!"

Tony was already on his feet, though he hadn't beaten Lucas, who was already out the door and on a knee just outside, scanning for bad guys. The rest staggered out, spilling out both doors. The pilot had set us down flat enough that we could do that.

The crew chief was on his feet and getting the pilot and copilot out. I checked my guys as they got out, but nobody seemed to be seriously injured.

239

I thanked God for that. We were in a bad enough situation as it was.

As we cleared the bird and got away before the fire got worse, I could hear a hell of a lot of gunfire off to the west. The survivors of the Stryker platoons were putting up a fight, but it sounded like they were getting hammered. Smoke billowed, black and ugly, above the trees. It wasn't just from the vehicles, either, I didn't think.

"Get clear of the wreck! Consolidate in the trees!" The smoke stung my throat as I bellowed the order. We needed to get some distance.

Not only because of the fire, either. I didn't doubt there were bad guys on their way, and at that point I fully expected them to be wearing OWHSC storm gray.

We hustled away as the bird began to burn in earnest, belching more black smoke toward the sunny sky. The pilot, copilot, and the crew chief were staggering a bit, and it looked like the copilot's leg was broken. Coric seemed fine, and he was carrying that big MAG-58 like it was one of our rifles. He was a big dude, and he didn't seem to mind having been in a helicopter crash, except for the fact that now he was stuck on the ground.

We got to the trees, spreading out to cover both directions, up and down the street. I got on my radio. "Golf Lima Charlie, Golf Lima Ten. We are down approximately half a mile from the theater. Everyone's alive, but I have two injured crew. Bird's a total loss."

"Copy all. Stand by." That wasn't Hartrick, but another one of the watchstanders. Things were probably really hectic at the moment.

That thought was punctuated by the unmistakable sound of a missile launch from above. Everyone dropped flat, but the *boom* was some distance away. The bad guys were probably still concentrating mostly on the Army.

"Golf Lima Ten, I can't get any assets to you. If you can proceed on foot, you should be able to link up with an Army unit, callsign Primal Six Two, at the intersection just north of St. Konrad's Church. Advise you stay off the main roads."

"Copy." I eyed the copilot. He was looking more than a little pale. He wasn't going to get far on that leg, at least not at any kind of good pace. But the only other option was to try to strongpoint the wreck, and it was fully engulfed in flames at that point, belching yet more black, oily smoke into the sky.

I told Tony first. He didn't say much, but his look at the injured copilot said enough. He didn't think the guy was good to go any more than I did.

I shrugged as I turned to talk to the crew. What other choice did we have?

The pilot looked at his copilot as I filled them in. "I don't think Styles can walk that far."

"Screw that, Tommy." Styles was a big dude, though not as big or as hard as Coric, and he was obviously in a lot of pain, but he was equally obviously unwilling to be dead weight. "I'll fucking crawl if I have to."

Tommy looked almost helplessly from Styles to me, then his crew chief grabbed his arm and spoke quietly and urgently. He seemed to steady then and looked down at Styles, then at me. "We'll help Styles. We won't move very fast, but it'll be faster than if he tried to walk on his own."

"I've got the gun." Coric was on his sector, still down behind the MAG-58. That dude had to have some prior infantry experience. He was older and stockier, and he'd probably picked helicopters because he didn't have to run, but he had fight in him.

"All right. David, you're on point. Tommy, you and your boys stay in the middle. We're going to move fast, so keep up as best you can." I looked down at Styles. "Do we need to splint that first?" I begrudged the time, but it wouldn't do anyone any good if we got bogged down halfway there because he couldn't handle the pain.

Styles shook his head. "I'll be all right." He was obviously biting back a lot of pain, and I almost overruled him

241

right then and there, but Tommy and the crew chief were already picking him up and getting ready to move, one man under each arm.

We headed west along the south side of the brewery, following the same route the Alpha Element and I had taken to get from our staging point to the brewery a short time before. It felt wrong, retracing our steps that way, but right at the moment, we didn't have a lot of options, especially since we couldn't afford to go too far out of our way to avoid the fight raging off to the west, not when we had a man with a broken leg.

I wondered where all the numbers were coming from. The bad guys had drones, obviously, and those could be a hell of a force multiplier, but drones aren't invincible, and they have certain limitations that mean you can't conduct an entire assault with them. No, there were definitely shooters on the ground, too.

We didn't stay on the street for long. As soon as possible, we ducked into the trees, not only to stay away from the linear danger area that is every street in an urban environment, but also to get at least some overhead concealment from the drones. I was having flashbacks to Nitra all of a sudden.

The fight was intensifying. Gunfire crackled almost constantly, punctuated by the heavier reports of heavy machineguns, cannon, grenade launchers, IEDs, and rockets. The smoke was getting thicker as we got closer to the railroad tracks. Fortunately, we still hadn't taken contact yet.

David turned northwest to parallel the tracks while keeping us under the trees. As that little patch of woods thinned, I signaled David to hold up a moment, switching my radio to the Army's net. "Primal Six Two, Primal Six Two, this is Golf Lima Ten."

For a moment, I worried that we'd been shut out to the point that the Army wasn't going to answer. But a few seconds later, a harried voice crackled across the radio, almost shouting in order to be heard above the rattle of gunfire and the all-too-close *thud* of another explosion.

"Golf Lima Ten, this is Primal Six Two. Send your traffic."

"I have a ten-man team and a busted-up helo crew, two hundred yards to your east. We are coming in. Watch your fires."

There was another pause, I hoped because whoever was commanding Primal Six Two was telling their security not to shoot the guys in green who were about to come out of the trees. I hoped. "Roger that, Golf Lima Ten, come ahead. Be advised, we have air inbound, so make it fast."

I didn't have to pass that along. David must have switched his radio freq over as soon as I'd told him to hold. He looked back at me, nodded, and then he was on his feet and moving.

We threaded through the trees, David and I pausing to hold security on the tracks as Greg, Steve, and Jordan got the helo crew across, then Tony and Lucas bumped us, and we moved to join them.

Nailaer Straße was a nightmare of wreckage, fires and dead bodies. We could only see the tail end of it, beyond the two surviving Strykers that had managed to back up past the still-burning wreck of the first one that had been destroyed by an IED. But it was a glimpse of the floor of hell. Torn and charred bodies lay amid smoking wreckage, fragments of blackened metal and pulverized asphalt scattered across the street under a drifting pall of smoke, whipped into whorls by bullets as the American soldiers continued to trade fire with the terrorists.

"Friendlies coming in!" We halted in the trees to conduct final deconfliction before running into their perimeter. Only when the two soldiers stationed on the corner of one of St. Konrad's outbuildings waved at us to come ahead did we move.

We made sure to get the helo crew across first, then the team followed. Tony barked, "Last man!" as he passed the two guys on perimeter security, both of them looking awfully bulked up with all the gear and armor they were wearing. All the old lessons learned had been brain-dumped, again, and the Army was back to Operation Up-Armor.

Primal Six Two appeared to be a leg infantry platoon, at least until I noticed an MP patch on a shoulder guard. Great. We just linked up with the epitome of the term "Blue Falcon."

Ignoring that unpleasantness, I started looking for their commanding officer. A military police officer was likely to be even more insufferable than your average MP, but this was what we had to work with.

The unit had four JLTVs, herringboned along the sides of the street, just on the south side of the railroad tracks. The CO, a fresh-faced 2nd lieutenant who looked about twelve to me, was on the radio next to the second vehicle back.

"Lieutenant?" I held out my gloved hand. He shook it, surprisingly not insisting on a salute. Maybe he'd survive. "Matt Bowen, Golf Lima Ten Six."

"Lieutenant Guistozzi." He seemed a little distracted and harried. He flinched as another burst of machinegun fire ripped overhead with a crackle. Several of the other soldiers did too, one of them diving for the dirt as if she was about to take cover under the vehicle.

It said something about what we'd been through that none of us so much as blinked.

"We've dealt with most of the drones, but we're taking concentrated fire from what appears to be prepared positions *around* the hotel and the hospital." The kid knew how to sound professional, at least, though his eyes were wide, and he was clearly about one close call away from a complete freak-out. It almost seemed as if he was feeling a little steadier since we'd arrived. Maybe he was just relieved that clear combat professionals had just showed up, even if we were in Triarii greens.

It's amazing what life or death threats can do to a man's thinking.

"They were dug in and ready to defend this place, and they had spread a lot farther out than the Theater." Guistozzi seemed somewhat surprised at that, almost offended. As if the terrorists should have stayed where they were.

244

Or maybe he was starting to figure out that the "terrorists" had plenty of friends on the outside, and that some of those friends wore uniforms and were supposed to be containing the situation.

Before I could say much of anything, though, what sounded like half a dozen rapid missile strikes hit somewhere just about a block away to the southwest. They came in one after another, dopplered shrieks punctuated by heavy *boom*s that I could *feel* through the ground, as smoke, dirt, and far less wholesome debris fountained skyward.

The MPs that hadn't hit the dirt hugged their vehicles. It wasn't an unreasonable reaction. Bits of shrapnel and fragments of pavement and trees whickered by overhead with deceptively soft whispers. If we could hear them, they were probably big enough to kill if they hit a man.

Guistozzi started to get up, then heard something on his radio and put the handset to his ear. He blanched, then barked, "Everybody take cover! Danger close, thirty seconds!"

I cursed, looking around to make sure the rest of my team was getting to cover before throwing myself flat and trying to get under the same JLTV where Guistozzi was currently taking cover. A moment later, the airstrike hit.

I don't know who authorized a fixed-wing strike on what was supposed to be a hostage situation. It was possible that they were taking so much fire from the hotel that they decided they simply needed to drop something to force a pause, at least.

That's not what happened.

The first bomb hit right at the entrance to the Freiheitshalle Hof, the indoor amphitheater attached to the Hotel Central Hof. I don't know if the JTAC controlling the bird had eyes on drone launchers or mortars, or whatever, or not. Whatever the case, they dropped, and all hell broke loose.

The hotel blew up. Not just the entryway. A rippling series of explosions tore the Freiheitshalle Hof's roof off and reduced most of the hotel to rubble. More explosions thundered through the neighborhood, clouds of smoke and dust rising as the earthshaking thunderclaps blended together into a world-ending blast of noise that hammered us all into the road as the shockwaves washed over us, shaking the trees, stripping leaves off the branches, and even making the armored JLTVs rock.

The noise faded, leaving only ringing in my ears and a brutal headache. I felt like I'd just been hit by a truck. I might have actually blacked out again there for a second. I was going to be hurting for a while, after two such impacts in a day.

Hof was strangely quiet all of a sudden. I crawled out from under the JLTV and onto the ground floor of hell.

Dirt and debris rained down from a rising mushroom cloud billowing above the wreckage of four city blocks. Stripped and shattered trees lifted their smashed and broken limbs into the clouded sky above the burning heaps of rubble that had once been buildings.

Chapter 26

"Well, whoever made the call to drop was still an idiot, but it wasn't that JDAM that did it." Chad Easton leaned back in his chair, making it creak under his weight. Not that Easton was all that big a dude; the chair was just cheap. Easton himself was only about five foot seven, and about a hundred thirty-five pounds soaking wet. "That was the first drop, and the Dash Two didn't even get a chance to make a run before everything blew up."

"The usual suspects are already screaming about cluster munitions." The sarcastic contempt in Tucker's voice echoed my own feelings.

Easton snorted. "Right. Because cluster bombs can level entire city blocks. Fucking morons." He swiveled the laptop around so we could see the screen. He had a drone feed up from just before all hell had broken loose. It was still right at the moment, but Easton had several circles highlighted. "See these?"

I leaned in. My headache had gotten worse, but Jordan had checked us all out and was fairly sure none of us were concussed. Beat up, definitely, but everyone was still ticking over right. No blown pupils, no disorientation, no difficulty focusing. There'd been just enough cover between us and the blasts that we'd evaded the worst of it.

"Looks like a box truck."

"That's exactly what it is." Easton flipped to another image, this one more recent. It was blurred by dust and smoke, since that deadly pall was still hanging over the city as we spoke. We were going to be coughing and spitting up dust and worse for a while. "Look where it was parked."

I compared the placement of where I'd seen that box truck with the devastation on the newer photo. It was hard to make direct correlations, the damage was so extensive, but unless I missed my guess, that truck had been right at ground zero of one of the bomb craters that had half flattened the AOK Bayern insurance building, right across from the Freiheitshalle.

"Here's another one." He flicked back to the first image, pointing out what looked like a panel van parked next to an apartment building. Overlaid on the newer photo, sure enough, that van had been parked right at what was now the center of a crater that had blown the building in half.

"It was a fucking setup." Burkhart's voice was a harsh rasp. He'd been even closer to the blast, and he'd been coughing almost nonstop since we'd gotten back to the camp. "Drew everybody in then blew everything up." He coughed again. "How many of the Army boys did they get?"

"Too many. They're still working up the casualty counts. That's not all, though." Easton pointed at the laptop. "There were still a lot of civilians in there. Most of them are dead or maimed. The death toll keeps going up, but it's in the hundreds, at least. Probably going to top a thousand in the next couple hours." He leaned over and switched to a video. "But if these bastards think they've gotten away with it, they've got another think coming."

The video was short, but it was telling. While it wasn't specifically focused on the van—in fact, it wasn't focused on that part of the neighborhood at all, but rather on the Freiheitshalle—there was a clear view of the van, as a man parked it, fiddled with something under the dash, then got out and got into a green sedan and drove away.

Tucker was watching the screen closely. "Have we got a license plate number on that car?"

"We do." Easton grimaced then. "Finding it's still going to be a bitch, especially in all the confusion since the big boom."

"Maybe not." I was thinking as I watched the video repeat. "Have the checkpoints lifted?"

I saw the faint frown on Easton's face as he went completely still. "No. No, they haven't." He sat up and grabbed the laptop again. "Which means they've still got the city cordoned off. Maybe the car's still in Hof."

Tucker snorted. "Aren't y'all missing something?" All eyes turned to him as he raised his eyebrows. "Seriously? Who here doubts that anybody who was involved got sent right out through those checkpoints before the first shots were even fired?"

"He's got a point." Burkhart coughed again. "If the ChiComs wanted this to happen, then they would have made sure the perps got out of Dodge before anyone could figure it out and go after them." He frowned. "But what's the endgame? What do they gain by killing a bunch of civvies along with some patsy terrorists and a bunch of US Army soldiers?"

Hartrick had just heard that as he stepped inside the tent. "I'll tell you what they gain. The potential to get the US kicked out of Germany." He stalked across the tent, found the laptop that was hooked up to the local cell network—that computer was as sterile and isolated as we could get it—found a news feed, and swiveled it toward us.

The German spokeswoman was slight, blond, and speaking English, even if it was more than a little stilted. "...with horror. The loss of life due to such negligent overuse of firepower cannot go unremarked or be dismissed. The American forces in Germany have already recklessly caused the unnecessary deaths of many, but today's events have gone beyond what could be explained away as accidents and individual actions. This was a war crime, perpetrated by those who justified their assault on the European way of life by

249

blaming us for crimes committed in Slovakia, most likely by Russian proxies among the Slovak Nationalists."

"Boy, she's laying it on thick, ain't she?" Tucker spat.

"It gets worse." Hartrick sounded even more pissed than usual. It was a quiet sort of pissed, though. That was when Brian Hartrick got *really* dangerous. Most of us had learned to deal with his permanent snarling, growling bad temper. None of us wanted to be too close when he got this way. "Keep listening."

"The American Army is now the greatest source of violence and instability in Germany. The *Bundestag* officially calls on all American forces to be withdrawn, effective immediately, and the commanders and all other personnel responsible for this atrocity to be publicly punished. This is not warfare. This is terrorism."

Hartrick turned it off. "On the one hand, they're not picking on us, for once. On the other, I doubt that's going to really matter. Americans are being blamed for this, and Americans are therefore persona non grata, time now." He slapped the laptop closed, looking like he'd much rather throw it across the tent. "Furthermore, General Sellar is already bringing Colonel Brice up on charges, along with anyone else she might be able to hit in his chain of command." The general murmur of disgust and swear words only made Hartrick nod. "She's throwing everyone she can reach under the bus to appease the Germans, without even investigating what happened."

"Well, that just sounds typical of the last half century." Tucker was surprisingly laid back about all of this. He probably just wasn't surprised. If I thought about it, I wasn't really, either. It fit with everything we'd seen since we'd started dealing with Big Army once we'd gotten to Poland. Reeves had learned. Sellar wasn't the type to learn. She was above learning. She already knew everything, despite the fact that, from her bio, she'd never heard a shot fired in anger before reaching Poland back in the spring.

She probably hadn't heard an actual shot fired in anger since. That wasn't what generals did. They briefed politicians and occasionally darkened the doors of a TOC somewhere.

"So, what's the plan for us?" Burkhart knew as well as the rest of us that Hartrick wasn't just telling us this for our situational awareness. He did that sometimes, but there was something about this entire situation that had my hackles up, and Hartrick wasn't given to inaction under these circumstances. We didn't have to wait on orders from higher. Even the infantry sections were roving in Germany, without being tied down to particular AOs like they often were Stateside. We could follow the intel, or the situation, where we needed to.

"Nothing's turned our way yet. The Army's locked down. It's worse than Slovakia before Matt and his boys hit the ground there." Hartrick nodded to me. "Everybody's back on their FOBs and nobody's moving. Word on the street is that Berlin has requested more personnel and equipment from OWHSC, and that there are two more ships already en route, heading for Hamburg."

"Where have I heard that song before?" Tucker wasn't looking for an answer. We'd all seen the reports from the West Coast just after the cyber attack. Ships loaded with "humanitarian" aid and security personnel had arrived in every major Pacific port with an alacrity that could only be described as "suspicious." The subsequent takeover of those ports, along with the trafficking of weapons to cartels and terrorist organizations throughout the Southwest, had confirmed those suspicions, and the Chinese "PMCs" been beaten back with significant casualties.

It had almost worked, though, and Beijing apparently had a much cozier relationship with Berlin than they'd had with San Diego, LA, San Francisco, and Seattle.

"Yeah. Looks like the power play is in full swing. Nobody's said it yet, but I fully expect General Metzger and the remaining EDC 2nd, 3rd, and 4th Divisions will be brought back into the fold in the next few days." Hartrick sighed angrily. "This is what happens when you pat yourself on the back for winning a war that's far from fucking over." He gathered himself, looking around at all of us. "Get your teams ready to move. Airspace is locked down, so we can't get birds in. We got the last of the ones we had on station, that didn't get shot down..." He looked at me and I shrugged. *I* hadn't been flying it. I hadn't even directed Tommy where to fly. I'd just been aboard. "We got them away from here before the lockdown happened."

"How the fuck are the conquered going to lock down airspace?" Burkhart wasn't buying it.

Hartrick only laughed bitterly. "Who said they were fucking *conquered*? They're not, which is why we're in the fucking shit-show we're wading through right now. I'm pretty sure only about half the *Luftwaffe* got put out of action before everybody decided the fighting was over. And the Army sure as shit ain't gonna back *us* up."

Burkhart looked even more sour at that, but he didn't have an answer.

"So, it's going to be ground transport." Hartrick leaned on the table. "We had some Growlers, but I sent them south a while ago, too. Anything that looks like American military is going to be a target." Even as he spoke, a couple of the young-looking Triarii infantrymen came in, and Easton started quietly directing them to tear the TOC down and get everything either ready for transport or destroyed. "We don't know how much time we've got, so I'm not going to dawdle around here. The tents and the security perimeter are a lost cause. The bad guys will get them. I don't give a fuck. Get your guys, get your gear, get on the low-pro vehicles you came in on, and get the fuck out." He glared around at all of us. "Just don't fucking convoy down the autobahn. I want a bombshell out of here. Don't make it easy on them."

The chuckles that went around the tent as we all got up were dry and humorless. "Because we've been making it *so* easy for them so far." Tucker got a patented Hartrick glare for that one, but he just let it slide off his back. We had too much to do.

Hustling out of the tent, I headed straight for our own, small as it was, next to our Atlases. Fortunately, we still had them, so we weren't going to have to shove ten not-small dudes into one of the support VW minibuses again.

I burst in through the flap, to see that I didn't have to do much more than give the situation. Everybody was already packed up and ready to move. Sure, it *was* kind of our SOP, especially when we'd been moving around as much as we had been the last couple months. We only took what we needed out of our rucks, and whatever it was went right back in when we were done with it. "Time to roll. We need to be away from here, soonest." I grabbed my ruck as I spoke, heaving it onto my shoulder and turning toward the flap. "We don't know who's coming or when, but Americans are officially PNG, and we can expect exactly zero help from the Army. Mount up; I'll brief on the way."

Nobody needed any more prompting. Weapons, gear, and rucks were close at hand, and we were loaded and ready to roll in less than two minutes. Less than a minute after that, we were heading out the gate. The infantry Triarii on gate guard duty had pulled the drums out of the way and weren't even trying to put them back between vehicles.

Even as we raced down the rutted dirt farm road that led toward the airport, we saw the OWHSC vehicles coming, the boxy armored trucks all mounting up guns. Chris took the turn toward Krötenbruck almost without slowing down, and we disappeared into the trees a moment later, the number two truck following. Tony had taken a more northerly route. He was on his own. Reuben's truck—or ours—needed to break off soon, but right at the moment, we only had so many routes to pick from.

"We're gonna run into a checkpoint going this way, Matt." I hadn't told Chris to make the turn, and he wasn't blaming me. He was asking which way I wanted to go now.

"I know." Unfortunately, I didn't have many good answers. I'd hoped to get out before the ChiComs or the *Bundespolizei* could close in on us. "We need to find a backroad." I was already head down, letting Chris, David, and Greg hold security while I tried to find a route.

"We're heading straight for the autobahn, both east and south." We all knew the area well enough to know that. "They're *going* to have checkpoints up." He craned his neck to look up through the windshield. "If they don't already have a drone or a helo on us."

If they did, we were in for a fight. But when I glanced up, the sky seemed clear.

The map wasn't showing me a perfect escape route. But that wasn't the nature of tradecraft, anyway. If it was obvious, it wouldn't be a good escape route.

"Turn north."

"What?" Chris was already doing what I told him, even as he asked the question. "There are a lot of bad guys up there, Matt."

"I know. But they can't be everywhere, and if we can get in through the back side of Krötenbruck, we can get across the autobahn and down through another side route."

I hoped I was right, as we sped into the tree-shrouded residential neighborhood of Krötenbruck. We'd stand out a little bit, but not as badly as we would have in some places I'd been, especially since our truck looked like a whole lot of other civilian vehicles out there. We might be able to disappear, if we'd broken contact thoroughly enough.

I hoped it would work. The same way I hoped that the OWHSC goons had just rolled up to an empty, abandoned patrol base.

Chapter 27

Oscar Gutierrez looked tired.

I couldn't blame him. Things were unraveling, if not quite so badly as they had a year before.

"Okay, gents, here's the picture as best we can figure it out." Gutierrez was standing by a smartboard, a rare such piece of technology in one of our TOCs, but this was also a *Verteidiger in Bayern* operation, so we were using some of their hardware and facilities at the moment, in this case a school gym in Bayreuth. "We no longer have GROM support. With the Army hunkered down and playing turtle on their FOBs, things have deteriorated between the Germans and the Poles to the point that it's no longer feasible for them to try to maintain a presence. The Russians are pushing out of Kaliningrad and toward Elblag, too, so they're needed out there."

That sucked. We'd worked with the GROM guys off and on, and while some of them could be pretty shady, they were good dudes on the whole, and I'd gotten attached enough to the Poles that I wasn't thrilled with the idea of staying in Germany without our Polish friends.

"Attacks are up across the board, though they seem to be primarily concentrated where the *Bundespolizei* have only a light presence, especially where they're not being backstopped by OWHSC. We have reports that the *Bundespolizei* have been ordered not to intervene in certain areas, most notably in Bavaria and parts of the east where Berlin's gotten the most pushback."

"That sounds familiar." Carlos Ramirez was one of the infantry section leaders, an older man with salt and pepper hair and a badger-striped beard. "Domestic violence as political tool. Where have we seen that before?"

It was a rhetorical question that we all knew the answer to, from bitter personal experience. It was, in many cases, why most of us were Triarii instead of cops or soldiers.

"There have been three bombings here in Bavaria in the last twelve hours, all aimed at infrastructure rather than government buildings. The German government seems to have hunkered down, leaving the *Verteidiger in Bayern* and us to try to deal with the violence. To that end, we're going to be spreading out to try to cover most of the major threatened areas." Gutierrez pointed to the map on the smartboard, which shifted to divide Bavaria into about a dozen zones. "It's going to look a lot like our operations Stateside. Infantry and armor sections will be assigned to particular AOs, and will work with the locals as much as possible to ensure security." He looked around at us all. "It's not going to be that easy, though it'll probably be no worse than some of the places you've worked. We will make sure that there's at least one *Verteidiger in Bayern* liaison with each section. I hope you boys have brushed up on your German."

He searched the crowd, picking out the Grex Luporum team leaders. "My GL guys...you're going to be doing what you do. Nobody's going to be tied down to a particular AO. If an infantry section gets actionable intel on a cell of bad guys, you're going to fly in—where the airspace allows—to deal with it. It's going to be a rough op-tempo. I'm not going to bullshit you. Bavaria is our sole semi-safe haven in Western Europe at the moment, which means the bad guys are going to be doing whatever they can to crush this place. Expect a lot of work. They're trying to ratchet up the chaos so that the people beg for the *Bundespolizei* and OWHSC to come in and restore order. We're going to do what we can to head that off. Make OWHSC the invaders they are. So, get what rest you can between ops, and be ready to go at all times."

He looked around the room once more. "This doesn't look good, gents. We'll hang in there and support the *Verteidiger in Bayern* for as long as we can, essentially creating a Bavarian Fortress Doctrine, but that's only because giving up goes against the grain for all of us, and we don't want to abandon our friends. If we'd had the chance to handle this our way, we might not be in this pass. But Washington wanted a quick fix, so here we are." He took a deep breath. "We'll stick with it as long as we can, try to give the Bavarians, at least, a fighting chance. Nobody here wants to see a second Afghanistan fiasco."

There were more muttered curses at that. Some of our guys had been involved in that rout that had been called a "withdrawal."

"We've got a lot of work to do. Dismissed." Everyone stood. We didn't technically have rank in the Triarii, we had billets. But Oscar Gutierrez was a man who commanded respect by who he was, not the silver eagles that he had once worn on his collar.

The room started to clear out, but I suddenly found Hartrick at my elbow. "You guys stay here. We've got an op for you."

I just nodded. We'd had a few hours to rest since getting to Regensburg. Probably about the best we could expect going forward.

It wasn't as if the rest of the war had been overflowing with opportunities to sleep and recharge, anyway.

He led the way up toward the smartboard, where Gutierrez was reading another report on his tablet. He had to be getting a constant stream of bad news, but when he looked up as we approached, he managed a wan smile.

"Matt. Tony." He nodded to the rest of the team. "Been a while. Sorry about that. I've been a little swamped." He shook hands around the team, then straightened and shook off the weariness that seemed to weigh him down. "I've got some good news with this brief. We found Bradshaw's section."

Everybody seemed to stand a little straighter. No, that wasn't it. More like we were all leaning forward a bit more, that predatory readiness quivering in every muscle.

He flipped the smartboard into a mission brief mode. "It turns out they're not being held in either a *Bundespolizei* or *Bundeswehr* facility. The German government handed Schloß Dieskau over to OWHSC, and they're using it as a black site for our missing Triarii infantry sections. It seems we've attracted the ChiComs' particular attention."

"Where'd we get the intel?" I wasn't going to look a gift horse in the mouth, but it was an important question. The source of intel could validate or invalidate it. If it was vetted and trustworthy, it might offer a way forward. If it turned out to be suspect, it might just lead us on a wild goose chase, or it might have been planted to draw us into an ambush.

"A high-ranking *Bundespolizei* officer who's not happy with the way things are going." Gutierrez raised his hands to head off the objections. "I know. That alone is suspect. *However*, he's already known to us." He looked straight at me. "He stayed out of Vogt's coup attempt, but he could see the writing on the wall. He fed us a lot of information in the lead up to the strikes on the EDC, including the locations of two of the council members who weren't in Brussels when we hit the council building. He hasn't led us astray so far."

"Okay." Tucker folded his arms. "So, the real masters are interrogating our boys in an old German castle. What kind of security do they have? And are we going to have to carry them out?" It was a valid question. The Chinese were not known for their sterling human rights record, to say the least.

"Those we don't know. You're going to have to conduct your own reconnaissance prior to the raid." That elicited shrugs. We were kind of used to that by then.

"That said, these are ChiComs we're dealing with. We don't know how much time you'll have if you get compromised. Be ready to go loud fast."

"As always."

***

Kabelsketal was a municipality formed out of three villages south of Halle. It wasn't that far from the city, but it was far enough that we had some fields and patches of woods to work with, making our infiltration a little bit easier. It's never a good idea to stage your insert platform too close to the objective, but often urban environments kind of required it. We got to do a proper greenside infil this time, at least on the reconnaissance.

We got dropped off in the trees near the Hallescher Canoe Club at about 0100, and headed into the trees. I'd considered trying to go low-pro gray man, in civilian hiking clothes and with all our gear and weapons in our packs, but it was one in the morning, and we needed our NVGs up. No civilian hikers were going to be out in Dieskauer Park after midnight, let along strolling along with PS-31s in front of their faces. So we committed, staying in greens, geared up, though we were carrying the SBR Tactical .300 Blackouts loaded with subsonic rounds instead of our OBRs. If this went hot, we still wanted to stay as quiet as possible.

It was nice to have enough support that we had options.

The park was dark and quiet, as we'd both expected and hoped it would be during wartime. I was still a little concerned that OWHSC might have drones or other sensors out, but there was only so much we could do about that.

Our own drone overflight had gone relatively smoothly. We'd been careful to avoid directly overflying the old castle, keeping high enough and far enough away that the drone shouldn't have been noticed at all. We had decent imagery of all four sides, as well as what security they had out. Most of the latter was guesswork. The OWHSC operators were keeping a lower profile here. There were no CS/VN3s on the roads or men standing out in the open in gray fatigues, plate carriers, helmets, and carrying rifles. There *were*, however, several vehicles parked in places where anyone inside them could watch the approaches to the Schloß Dieskau, and presumably engage quickly. It had been hard to see through the drone feed, but at least one of them appeared to be occupied.

David, Lucas, and I were on the ground tonight to confirm that. The rest of the team was staged a little less than a mile to the northwest, the vehicles hidden in the trees, ready to roll on my call. Under different circumstances, we might have slipped in, set up surveillance, and stayed in place for a day or two, building a pattern of life and confirming every little detail for the raid force.

We didn't have that kind of time. Given how many days had already passed since they'd gotten rolled up, none of us thought that Bradshaw and his boys had that kind of time, either.

Because we had a very short infiltration and were planning on moving right into the raid if it looked feasible, we'd all packed light. Weapons, ammo, water, and what optics and comms we might need, and that was about it. Considering we were wearing body armor, since this was about to turn into a CQC fight, the lower weight was an important consideration.

It also helped us stay quiet as we moved from tree to tree, slowing even more as we got closer and closer to the castle.

The trees thinned the closer we got, and I dropped to a knee behind a big oak, barely a hundred fifty or so yards from the Schloß. It looked almost more like a big house than what I though of when I heard the term "castle," but it was what it was. Three stories from ground to gables, and at least another story and a half of peaked roof above that, the building was shaped more like a "G" than anything else I could compare it to.

Clearing that with ten guys was going to be a bastard. I was hoping that at least some of the infantry guys were in halfway decent shape, so we could hand them guns and keep pushing.

A Mercedes ECQ was parked on the road just ahead. I'd been watching it through the trees, noticing that the windows were rolled up, which meant they had to be relying entirely on either NVGs or any sensors that they had planted out in the woods. Thermals are neat, but they can't see through glass, so if those clowns had the windows up, they either weren't using thermals, or they were sitting there wondering why they weren't seeing shit.

Or they were napping. It was entirely possible that the screwups got put out on security, especially if they thought they had this place locked down and quiet.

I watched the vehicle for a while. No movement, no sign that they'd seen anything. I'd been careful to keep trees between me and the vehicle since I'd spotted it, but nothing's perfect, especially in what boiled down to a German woods park. The grass was pretty tall, but there was otherwise very little concealment under the trees.

We were going to have to deal with that vehicle sooner or later, though.

I didn't see any other security besides the vehicle, at least not on that side of the Schloß. They were really trying to keep this low-key. I didn't even see cameras on the corners, and while those were getting awfully small and unobtrusive, I still should have been able to spot them.

I sent two clicks over my radio, not daring to make any other sound that close to the bad guys. That should get the rest of the team moving, aside from Reuben and Jordan, who were staying with the vehicles for rapid exfil.

Then I got up and started moving toward the Mercedes, Lucas and David right behind me.

Chapter 28

There was no sign that I'd been noticed as I sidled closer, keeping as many tree trunks between me and the vehicle as I could. Granted, the Mercedes was facing away from me, down the road that I hadn't followed, but if they were serious about security, they should be watching their six, too.

I was going to make them pay for their complacency.

We spread out as we moved. In moments, I was just behind the passenger side door, my weapon trained on the window. Lucas was covering our six, while David was ready to step out behind the SUV.

We were right on them, but we waited. Still no sign we'd been spotted yet. And the rest of the team was going to need a little time to close the distance.

I got two clicks in my earpiece. Tony and the others were within two hundred yards of the objective. I leaned out from behind the tree and got a good look in the passenger compartment.

The two security guys were watching a movie on a tablet. Even as I moved, one of them lifted his head, putting his flat PRC NVGs to his eye, and scanned around them.

He turned toward me just as my trigger broke.

If it hadn't been wartime, it would have been murder. The kid had no chance. But he was clearly not just some rando sitting next to the road, since he was using PLA issued NVGs, and had a QBZ-03 thrust between his seat and the center console next to him.

I shot him through the NVGs, twice, just to make sure the glass didn't divert my rounds far enough to make me miss. He slumped immediately, and I followed up with two rounds to the blinded driver, who was staring uncomprehendingly at the blood and brains spattered across the screen in front of him. The window was no longer an obstacle, but I double tapped him through the temple, anyway, blowing more blood, hair, and brains against the driver's side window, which cracked as the bullets punched through and hit it.

The only sound besides the glass breaking had been my rifle's action cycling. I was glad it hadn't been an armored vehicle. I would have had to get a lot louder in that case.

Lucas let out a faint click of his tongue. I looked back, lifting my muzzle, to see the dim silhouettes of the rest of the team moving through the trees behind us. We'd had to work on signals since everybody on the other side had NVGs, too, so flashing a lot of IR around, like we'd been trained to way back in the mil—even after most of the bad guys in the world had started using night vision, too—was out.

Tony was in the TL spot, just behind Chris. He moved up to me and took a knee, the rest of the team getting into a tight perimeter behind the tree and the now neutralized vehicle.

Letting Steve take security off the front of the vehicle, I ducked back to quickly brief everybody. "It looks like they're holding security with the guys in the vehicles. No signs of foot patrols. No visible cameras, either. Looks like they're trying to keep this as low-profile as possible. If we circle south and come up through the trees, we should have plenty of darkness and concealment right up to that back door. We'll breach there."

Tony nodded. "Sounds like a plan."

There wasn't much need to go into detail. We'd chalk-talked the whole thing from the drone footage already. It's not necessarily the same thing as getting eyes on the ground, which was why we'd done a leader's recon in the first place. But when time is short, it's better than nothing.

With David taking point again, we headed away from the vehicle and the castle, heading for where the trees overhung the road, providing at least some deep shadow to hide us as we crossed the road and turned back up.

That plan didn't last more than about ten yards, though.

A voice was raised behind us, shouting in Mandarin. I couldn't make out the words, but the tone was unmistakable. *Hey, dumbasses, we're here.*

Relief had just showed up for the dead guys in the vehicle. We were moving in right at shift change.

The shout got a response, all right. Lucas pivoted, snapped his SBR up, and double-tapped both men in less time than it takes to blink. The hissing *snap*s of the shots barely traveled, and both men dropped like puppets with their strings cut, the second hit so fast that he hadn't even had time to register that his buddy was already falling next to him.

They were in the middle of the open, right on the road. Cameras or no, there was no way we were hiding that. It was time to go loud.

"Move on the door!" I didn't yell. There was no need, and it might have only told the bad guys more about what was happening than they already knew. Instead, I just pivoted and ran toward the door.

I didn't have any breaching tools, but Tony was right on my heels with the Halligan.

We hit the door a few seconds later. It opened inward, rather than outward, and so Tony slammed the duckbill between the door and the jamb, throwing his considerable weight on the Halligan as he shoved toward the hinges.

The jamb cracked, the door started to open, and Tony acted quickly, stopping himself with one foot before backstepping, putting his back to the wall, and donkey-kicking the door inward.

I went in past him as he flattened himself against the wall, Lucas right behind me, his suppressor dropping past my shoulder.

There had been a restaurant in the Schloß, but it had been closed for a while, at least since the beginning of the war. I half expected to come into the kitchen, but the door opened onto a darkened hallway.

Intel said that the parts of the castle that hadn't been used by the restaurant or the AirBnB that rented out rooms on the ground floor weren't in good shape. I hoped that meant that OWHSC had left the upper floors alone. It would save us a lot of time on the X.

Unfortunately, we had to clear every single room that was remotely viable, so I moved to the first door on the left, while Lucas covered the long hall. David moved to the door on the right, and we both paused just long enough to get a squeeze to the upper arm before going through the door.

I hooked through the opening, weapon up and searching for targets, but found myself in a completely empty, abandoned room, pale moonlight shining through the window and onto the bare floor. Without a word, I turned back and fell in behind Chris as he flowed back out into the hallway.

David and Greg were already coming out of the opposite door. No gunfire. Lucas and Tony were on the corner, and Steve and Jim were coming out of the next room past us. The ChiComs weren't using this wing.

So far, everything was quiet. There were probably only a couple watchstanders and the security team awake at the moment. There was a reason we'd inserted just past one in the morning.

Light flickered in my NVGs, a glow coming from down the long leg of the main hallway. Nobody was in that intersection except for Lucas and Tony covering, and they'd both eased back as the flashlight flickered down the hall. A voice called out in what sounded to my admittedly unschooled ears like Mandarin.

It was less a challenge than a query, though. Somebody had heard the door get cracked open and was coming to investigate.

These people were awfully confident that they were secure, and that nobody was going to come kick in their door. They were acting like they were in a mostly permissive environment, instead of a war zone where there were very dangerous men entirely willing to slaughter them to a man to take their prisoners back.

Lucas waited until the flashlight was casting a bright circle on the wall before he stepped out and shot the man twice.

He did it so quickly that I wondered if he'd really identified a weapon or not. There were stories about Lucas Edwards.

But when I pushed out into the hall, trying to keep away from the cone of light still splashed across the wall, I saw immediately that I needn't have worried. The man had been armed. A Type 92 pistol lay on the floor, fallen from suddenly nerveless fingers.

We moved past the body, down the hall, each step as silent as we could make it. That pair of shots had been about as noisy as a door latch.

I'd moved up to cover the hallway, as Lucas and Chris got ready to make entry on the next room to my right, and Tony and Jim on my left. I didn't think it had been much more than a minute since we'd breached. We were flowing well.

Of course, Murphy always has to throw his oar in.

A voice echoed down the hallway. It sounded like somebody was asking the dead guy behind us what was taking so long. A moment later, another man in OWHSC gray fatigues, another Type 92 in one hand and a flashlight in the other, stepped out into the hall.

The three of us facing him, shoulder to shoulder across the hallway, all shot him at the same moment. He dropped limply to the floor, leaking a lot of blood all over the stones from a perforated skull.

Unfortunately, there was another guy inside the room, and he saw it happen.

A yell sounded, followed by a harsh electronic siren. We were made.

Just on the other side of the door the dead man had come out of, another door flew open and three men ran out into the hall, weapons in hand but without their gear. Well, except for one who had a plate carrier in one hand.

It was like shooting fish in a barrel.

Three SBRs spat, the *snap-hiss* of the shots drowned out by the yells from inside that room while the bodies dropped. One got a single shot off as he took three rounds to the chest, cranking off a single 5.8mm round into the floor as his knees buckled.

Then Tony and Jim went into the first door while I swept past with Lucas and Chris, heading for that team room door.

I heard the watchstander yelling into the radio just before Tony silenced him. Then I was coming up to the doorway.

If there were hostages in there, the only way to tackle it would be simply to rush in, flood the room, and hope we could overwhelm them before we took too many hits.

This was a little different sort of situation. That was a team room with an unknown number of hostiles, all presumably armed.

I couldn't just frag the room, though, not without knowing for *certain* that none of our guys were in there.

So, I started pieing the door off, moving faster than I might have if the shooting hadn't already started. A silhouette appeared, a man with a rifle, and I shot him through barely three inches of door opening. He crumpled and I kept moving, but I cleared the entire corner of the room without spotting another target. Anyone who was left in there was gathered at the far end, probably aimed in at the fatal funnel just inside the door.

I had gotten a better picture of the room's layout, though. This front end was mostly the team room sort of stuff, lined with weapon racks, gear trees, and a whiteboard with what looked like it might have been a duty roster in Mandarin on it. Bunks were stacked against the wall on the far side, disappearing back into the part of the room I hadn't quite been able to see. There were more on the near side, too. That gave me my opening.

Even as I dropped to the floor, still without having broken the threshold, Lucas and Tony had pushed ahead and found a second door to the team room. They breached at the same time I shoved myself into the room on my side, my pack dragging on the floor and slowing me down even as I moved.

Four more OWHSC operators were crouched behind the bunks at the far end, and just as I'd expected, they were all aimed in at the fatal funnel, fully expecting us to storm in and try to clear the room from the doorway. I shot one of them under the first bunk, getting just enough of an angle to hit him in the guts, beneath his plate, from underneath the bed. He screamed as he crumpled, red soaking his gray fatigues, at the same time the door next to the four of them was kicked open, hard enough to dislodge the stuff they'd stacked against it as a barricade, and a hail of suppressed 200-grain bullets cut down the other three.

I was already getting back on my feet. The room was clear, no sign of our grunts. We moved back out into the hallway and kept going.

The next door was reinforced and locked, and Jim was already working on it, while Chris, Greg, and Steve held on the hallway. Generally speaking, this kind of assault required constant movement, flowing through as fast and as smoothly as possible, staying well ahead of the enemy's OODA loop. But when we didn't know how many bad guys were on site or where our packages were, we had to be a little bit more deliberate.

The lock opened with a loud *click*, and then Chris and Jim were going in fast. Chris had barely broken the threshold when I heard a croaked, "Friendlies!" from inside.

The room stank. The OWHSC guys had crammed twenty-two men into what had once been a bedroom. They were mostly lying on the floor or sitting against the wall, shoulder to shoulder and feet to feet. It smelled like none of them had had a chance to clean up since they'd been taken. In short, it smelled like feet and ass.

Tyler Bradshaw was struggling to his feet. He looked like he'd been through hell. His face was bruised and swollen, one eye almost entirely shut. He was in the worst shape, but most of the rest, seen under PS-31s and IR illuminators, looked like they'd been worked over.

"Can you boys move?" It was a necessary question. "More importantly, can you fight?" Words about the missing would have to wait. I already knew what had happened to them.

There'd been no way Bradshaw would have surrendered without a fight.

"Everybody should be able to walk." Bradshaw looked around the room. "And we'll fight with fists, feet, and teeth if we have to."

"Shouldn't need to." I jerked a thumb at the team room behind us. The rest of the team had moved out into the hallway again, either holding security or working on another locked door across the hall. "There's a team room back there, with QBZ-03s and ammo. Some of 'em might have some blood on 'em, but they should still function."

Even as I spoke, we heard the rattle of more suppressed gunfire out in the hallway, punctuated by another high-pitched scream of agony. We weren't done yet.

"All right, you monkeys, on your feet!" Bradshaw had never been much of a shouter, but under the circumstances, I could see him shifting tactics. "Stark, Grillo, Boudreau, you're in the best shape, so you'll be on point with me. Let's get some guns and get to work."

As he passed me on the way out into the hallway, Bradshaw just gripped my shoulder, briefly but firmly. That said all that needed to be said.

We got to work.

***

The rest of the clear went even more quickly. As battered and malnourished as they were, Bradshaw's boys were pros and they were *pissed*, and they fell in with us fast once they were armed up. The fifteen of Thomas's boys who had survived were in worse shape, but there weren't guns for them, anyway. OWHSC seemed to have kept a fairly small guard force on site, presumably leaning on firepower to keep the prisoners in line, as well as a combination of stealth and German government backing to keep any raids like ours from disrupting their operation.

I didn't doubt that there was a QRF en route. The longer we were on the X, the more likely we were going to get rolled up. So, we didn't waste time. As soon as we confirmed that the ground floor was clear and that the upper floors were indeed unused, we headed out, back the way we'd come.

Two helicopters roared overhead as we hustled through the woods toward the staging point. We didn't have a lot of time.

Reuben and Jordan already had the vans out on the road. It was going to be a tight fit, but we'd get everyone in, one way or another.

Fortunately, our Triarii infantry brethren didn't need any cajoling or motivating. They piled into the stripped-out vans as fast as they could, the guys without guns on the inside, the guys with guns on the outside, just in case. The rest of us boarded last, pulling the doors shut quickly, almost at the same time Jordan and Reuben started us rolling, heading away and into the dark.

Chapter 29

"Good to have you boys back." Hartrick wasn't given to display, and he wasn't really deviating from that now, but he still shook Thomas's and Bradshaw's hands firmly. "We're probably going to need every gun we can get."

"We didn't get any of the gear back." Bradshaw sounded almost apologetic. "We checked, but they weren't storing it in the castle."

"No great surprise. We'll get you kitted out. It might be a bit hodge-podge, and you might not be able to share mags, but we'll make sure everybody gets at least the tools they need to work with." He jerked his head at me. "A word, Matt?"

I nodded, giving Bradshaw a clap on the shoulder, letting him know in as many words as he'd used that I was glad to have him back, and in one piece. Then I followed Hartrick toward the TOC.

"We've got a would-be visitor." Hartrick kept his voice low. "She's not here yet. In fact, she contacted us from up in Erfurt. She wants to speak to the Triarii and *Verteidiger in Bayern* specifically, and she wants us to go meet her up there and escort her down here to Bayreuth."

"Who is it? Do we know?" It had to be somebody important if we were being asked for an escort. Either a source or a VIP.

"Greta Blomberg." He said the name as if it meant something, which meant she was a VIP rather than a source, but I still couldn't place the name.

I shrugged. "You're going to have to enlighten me."

Hartrick ushered me into the TOC first. It was bigger than what we'd been working with before, mainly because this was the nerve center for all Triarii operations in northern Bavaria. Three tables set up in a U-shape were stacked with radios, laptops, notebooks, and maps, while three big map boards stood off to one side, across from the briefing area. All the watchstanders had headphones on, so unless things were cracking off and more people needed to hear what was going on, the TOC was actually pretty quiet.

He led me to the briefing area and picked up a printout. The photo on the first page appeared to be from a news site, of a pretty blonde in her early to mid-forties, standing at a podium with a forest of microphones in front of her. "She's been a member of the *Bundestag* for about ten years now. She's CDU, but she's always leaned pretty far left for that party. At least, until now."

My frown got deeper. "So, what's changed?"

"We don't know. She wasn't getting into specifics over the phone, presumably because she's worried—rightfully so—that somebody might be listening in. She just wants to meet, and she wants an escort to a secure meeting place here in Bavaria." Hartrick's expression was as unreadable as his tone. He wasn't sure what to make of this, either.

"Think it's a setup?" Paranoia was not an unreasonable reaction, given what had already happened. At least, I didn't think it was.

"It's possible. Doesn't make a huge amount of sense, though. They *might* get some more Triarii to parade in front of the cameras, at the cost of a whole lot of their own dead." There was no question there. I hadn't gotten details from Bradshaw, but it had taken overwhelming firepower to get the infantry Triarii to put down their weapons. And that was after they'd taken some

274

serious losses. "No, this seems to be something else. From the way she talked over the phone, she's definitely upset about something. We don't know what, but given her position in the Berlin government, Gutierrez and Pascal both agree that it's worth talking to her." Pascal was the nominal leader of the *Verteidiger in Bayern.* I'd met him—surreptitiously—before the push, but I hadn't seen hide nor hair of him since. Considering how busy everyone had been, that was no great surprise.

"Do we have exact coordinates?" I didn't bother to ask who was getting the tasking. Hartrick wouldn't have wasted time telling me about it if my team wasn't getting tapped.

"Close enough." He pointed to the printout. "There's a café across from the Erfurt Cathedral where she wants to make contact." He smirked. "That made your team the perfect one, Matt. You being such a big Catholic, and all."

I ignored the jab. It was old hat with Hartrick, though he hadn't pulled it out in a while. "Does she have a PSD?"

"She didn't say, but being an MP, you should probably expect that she does." I nodded absently, studying the layout. The *Wirtshaus ad Dom* was right on a large, open square in front of the cathedral.

"Lot of open ground." That could be good and bad at the same time. Long sightlines meant if there was somebody set up with a long gun, we'd never spot them in time. Open areas were also shooting galleries for drones. On the other hand, if Blomberg was on the up-and-up, it meant both she and we could see anyone coming who didn't belong there.

"I'd give you some suggestions for overwatch, but I'm pretty sure I trained you well enough that I shouldn't have to." I gave Hartrick a wry look at that. He might have been chief cadre when I'd gone through Grex Luporum Selection, and my first team leader, but I had enough experience under my belt that "training" was now a long time ago and far, far away.

He just smirked.

There wasn't much more. I hefted the printout. "Does this need to stay here, or can I bring it back to the team room?"

He waved. "Take it. I don't think you'll be letting any outsiders into your team room to read it."

I tucked it into a cargo pocket and turned to leave the TOC. We had a lot of prep to do, and not a lot of time to do it in.

***

Here she comes. The message lit up my T-phone. Fortunately, the device looked enough like most other smart phones, at least from a distance, that it didn't look out of place that I was sitting in the back of the Wirtshaus looking at it. *Just parked around the corner, and she's walking toward the meet with one other dude.*

A moment later, a photo popped up. There was Blomberg, all right, wearing a blue pantsuit, her hair perfectly done up. She looked like she was going on a date, not a covert meeting in a warzone. The man walking next to her, however, didn't. He was wearing Euro skinny jeans and a collarless button-up shirt, and he had a bag over his shoulder, but the man was a little too jacked, a little too alert to be a simple bit of arm candy for a feminist German politician. My guess was either GSG-9 or KSK. Though KSK was very much out of favor since the Vogt coup, and our reporting indicated that the unit had been gutted, and really only existed on paper anymore.

There was something familiar about this dude, though. He wore his blond hair long, had an operator beard, and was wearing sunglasses, but I could have sworn I'd seen his picture before.

I avoided staring at the picture too long. They were going to be out front of the Wirtshaus any second.

The meet time was in two minutes. I'd gotten there about twenty minutes before, just to watch the place and look for any surveillance. So far, I hadn't seen any.

Getting across the *officially* non-existent, but very real, line of demarcation between Bavaria and Thuringia had been easier than we'd expected. The *Verteidiger in Bayern* had more friends elsewhere in the country than Berlin wanted to admit, and we had official German government documents to get us through those checkpoints we hadn't been able to avoid. None of us were tac-ed out, either, and we'd driven in low-profile vehicles, two electric SUVs and a couple of sedans. Most of those vehicles were now carefully staged around the Domplatz, while most of the team wandered around and played tourist.

Erfurt was weirdly normal, given everything else going on. Thuringia hadn't been a major target zone for the jihadis or their sponsors, and we knew of exactly one attack in Erfurt itself within the last couple of months, and it was still up in the air as to whether that had been terrorism or just violent crime. People were still going about their business, though I expected, given what I'd seen already, that that would change fast once something clacked off.

This was Germany, not the Middle East. Or Africa.

Blomberg and her escort came in through the door, and I watched them out of the corner of my eye, still looking at the phone, or close enough to it that it appeared that was what I was doing. I wouldn't stand out that much. I was back in the shadows, near the rear of the café, dressed in uncomfortably skinny jeans, a v-neck t-shirt, and a blazer. I looked like a hipster, and I hated it, but I wasn't broadcasting *meat eater* the way old boy next to Blomberg was.

Of course, the blazer hid my PR-15, several spare magazines, a tourniquet, a low-profile dagger, a small blowout kit, and several other smaller tools that I hoped I wasn't ever going to need. Ideally, I wouldn't need any of them, but it pays to be prepared.

I waited, apparently engrossed in my phone, as the two of them entered, the meat eater scanning the room. *These German operators have a few things to learn about tradecraft.* The message wasn't really meant to communicate anything. I was just killing a little bit more time and making it look like I was engrossed in my smartphone instead of watching the room.

Blomberg and the blond man settled down at a table, looking around the room. They had no way of knowing what I looked like, so they were looking for the signal. I just wasn't giving it yet.

Despite the logic of the situation, I still wasn't convinced this wasn't a setup. I had a few minutes to play with. I wanted to be sure they hadn't been followed.

Blomberg was obviously nervous, but she was trying to put a brave face on it. She kept looking around, not nearly as subtly as her companion, though he was still broadcasting his alertness a little too much.

Finally, I checked my watch and saw that I was getting awfully close to the end of the time window for the meet. It was time to either commit or fade.

I coughed, and several pairs of eyes turned toward me. Blomberg and Beard turned toward me first, and I saw the flicker in both their eyes as they saw the glass upside down on the table with a napkin thrown over it. It wasn't the greatest signal, or the most subtle, but it was what had been prearranged. Beard had already set up the same thing.

This wasn't a place where I wanted to sit down and have a discussion. That could wait until we were in the car and moving. So, instead of waiting for them to join me, I got up and walked out, right past their table.

I kept going toward the Domplatz, my hands in the pockets of my blazer, studiously avoiding looking back. As far as any outside observer should be able to tell, I hadn't noticed Blomberg or Beard at all. I was just going about my business.

I reached the green Mercedes ECQ that Lucas and I had driven into the city. Lucas himself wasn't in it, but I had the spare key, and let myself in. I didn't drive away, because as I shut the door, I saw Blomberg and Beard come out of the Wirtshaus.

Pulling my phone out again, I sent an All Hands. *Hook is set. Reeling them in.*

Lucas reached the car as they crossed the trolley tracks that ran through the brick road outside the Wirtshaus and started across the narrow street between the brick and the Domplatz to where we were parked. Without a word, the two of them got into the back, I started the vehicle—which was almost silent—and pulled away.

Lucas turned in his seat, and I saw he already had his PR-15 in his hand, under his own blazer. He wasn't taking chances, and I couldn't blame him.

"Ma'am." He stared at Beard, who handed over his bag and put hands on the back of my seat without being asked, or even saying a word. Lucas glanced at me, shrugged a little, then shoved the pistol between the seats and proceeded to search Beard. Then he turned to the bag. Looking up at Beard, he chuckled. "You know that off-body carry's less than ideal, right?" I glanced over as he showed me the inside of the bag, where old boy had a placard installed with a USP P12, four extra mags, a blowout kit, and several other pieces of gear. He'd come strapped, but had handed it over to Lucas without being asked.

"I know, but if you'd found a pistol on my body when searching me, it might have made things…awkward." Beard had a deep voice and good English. He held out a hand to Lucas. "Joerg Oursler."

"KSK? Or GSG-9?" Lucas asked as he turned forward a little more, tapping out the all-clear message on his T-phone for the rest of the team.

"Joerg was one of the KSK officers arrested after the Vogt coup." Blomberg's voice was soft, her accent thicker than Oursler's but still understandable.

"If you don't mind my asking, ma'am, what we have on your profile doesn't suggest that you'd be all that friendly with someone like that." I watched her in the rear-view mirror as I put that forward. I needed to watch the road and maintain security, but I also needed to feel this situation out.

Blomberg didn't look like she was all that eager to talk to us, probably figuring that we were just the knuckle-dragging functionaries sent to pick her up. It was Oursler who answered. "Things have changed."

"For her?" Lucas looked back at him. "Or for you?" That was an important question, and Lucas had thought of it faster than I had.

"For me." Blomberg's eyes were moving from one to the other of us. "You are Americans."

"Yes." Apparently, she hadn't been sure if she was going to be meeting with us or with the *Verteidiger in Bayern*. "Ma'am, in case we run into trouble, I need to know exactly what this is about. If we have to let you out early, I don't want this meet to go to waste."

She thought about it. Clearly, she'd been expecting a formal meeting somewhere secure, where she could talk at length. But Oursler nodded to her, saying something in German that sounded like he was telling her that an explanation, even if brief, was a good idea.

"Have you seen the news lately?" she asked.

"No, ma'am, we've been pretty busy." That was an understatement. Most of the news sites and channels were little more than conduits for information operations and less-subtle propaganda anymore, anyway.

She hesitated again. She clearly wasn't entirely comfortable with all of this. "There was an... information leak. Quite extensive. It included video and documentary evidence of a plot to trigger the destruction in Hof and make it appear that the Americans were responsible. There were elements within the German government who were... complicit."

Her voice hardened, and when I glanced in the rear-view mirror, her expression was brittle, but there was rage in her eyes. She wasn't just upset. She was *angry*. "There are German politicians who now have civilian blood on their hands, just to advance a political agenda." Her nostrils flared. "This cannot be allowed to stand."

I glanced at Lucas. He raised an eyebrow and shrugged. We'd find out when we got back.

***

"Damn. This is all over Germany?" Gutierrez was scrolling through the data dump, posted not only to Wikileaks but at least half a dozen other sites, some of which seemed to have been set up purely to host it. Several major news sites had been hacked just to host this document leak. Someone with some serious cyber chops did *not* want this getting ignored.

And it was going to be hard to ignore. Not only were we looking at video of the truck bombs being emplaced—in a couple of cases well before the theater siege had started—but also at HD images of identified EDC operatives on site, memos and emails between EDC officers and several individuals at all levels of the German government, including at least two members of the *Bundestag* itself.

"Berlin is trying very hard to stifle it, but it is now all over social media." Blomberg sounded like she wasn't entirely sure what to think of that. It had to go against the grain, at least a little, from what we knew about her. She'd been opposed to the American presence in Europe since the first peacekeepers had landed in Slovakia. "New cloud folders are being set up with all the files as fast as they can be taken down."

"Is that why they made their little announcement today?" When I looked over at Hartrick with a frown, noting the dead sort of angry tone in his voice, he elaborated. "Berlin announced this morning that the *Bundeswehr* and *Bundespolizei* will no longer be cooperating with the US Army, giving a one-week deadline for all American forces to be out of Germany, and formally inviting the remnant of the 2nd, 3rd, and 4th EDC Divisions to rejoin the *Bundeswehr* and help restore order."

There was a stony silence after that. Eyes were on Blomberg and Oursler.

"So, if that's the case, why come to us?" Gutierrez straightened up, turning away from the laptop, and faced the two Germans.

Oursler looked at Blomberg, who nodded, apparently giving him permission to take over the conversation. "Those members of the *Bundestag* named in the emails all have close ties to Beijing, not only through investments and NGOs, but also through One World Holistic Security Concepts." He took a deep breath. "This is a power play for control of Germany by the Chinese Communist Party, working with and through the EDC. We cooperated with the EDC in the past because it was believed to be necessary, not only to avoid the war that has come anyway, but to keep Europe under European control, instead of falling to Russian or even Chinese influence. And yet…"

"And yet, the ChiComs probably already had their claws in the apparatus before it even got off the ground." Gutierrez wasn't especially sympathetic.

"Probably." Blomberg took over again, holding out a thumb drive. "We are working on establishing which elements of the *Bundeswehr* and *Bundespolizei* are not compromised. Once we have accomplished that, we will deal with those elements in Berlin that have perpetuated this atrocity. That will not stop the 'European Defense Corps,' however."

Gutierrez took the thumb drive. "And this will?"

Blomberg took a deep, shuddering breath. "That is all the information that the BND and the *Bundespolizei* have on the EDC, their leadership, and their dispositions. If you move quickly enough, you might be able to stop them."

"Gonna have to move fast, then." Hartrick lifted a plastic bottle to his lips and jetted a wad of dip spit into it. "We just got a report ten minutes ago that the lead elements of the EDC 2nd Division just passed Plauen, headed for Hof. They're already on their way."

Chapter 30

"They're awfully confident, aren't they?"

I had to agree with Jordan. The EDC hadn't operated this openly since the final offensive had pushed into Germany and we'd flown in and hit the Council building in Brussels.

I didn't see any tanks—it appeared that most of those had been knocked out in the major fighting or the "mopping up" airstrikes afterward—but they probably didn't figure they needed them so much, in what was effectively a "police action." The lead vehicles we were watching as they rolled down the autobahn from Hof toward Bayreuth were all Pumas and Boxers.

Those were still going to be a big enough pain to deal with, since the Army was still locked in its FOBs while Sellar groveled in front of the *Bundestag*, pointedly ignoring the fact that a growing number of the MPs had seen the data dump and were increasingly convinced that the slaughter in Hof had, in fact, been a setup.

Sellar wasn't the type to stand on the truth, though. The impression we'd always gotten was that she'd always resented having to fight "enlightened" Euros instead of Russians or other Slavs. She was still rolling with the narrative, never mind the fact that it had been invalidated over two days before.

We didn't have the time or the inclination to give a damn about Sellar's misplaced scruples, though. We weren't in her chain of command—especially at this point; nobody had said as much, but the general sense was that while the Triarii might still ostensibly be American auxiliary forces, it would probably not be a good idea to roll up to an American FOB and expect support—and so we were going to do what needed to be done.

"They've got plenty of reason to be. Everybody's just as confused and at each other's throats as they intended." I keyed my radio. "Tango India Seven Six Three, this is Golf Lima Ten. We have eyes on a mech column, approximately company strength, moving south on the Alpha Nine, passing the solar farm at nine-four-six, five-five-two, time now. Be advised, we're seeing mostly Pumas and Boxers, with some up-armored ENOKs in between."

"Good copy, Golf Lima Ten." I didn't know Chalmers well, but he had a decent rep, and Bradshaw had vouched for him. He sounded a little flustered at the moment, though. "Do you think you can buy us a few extra minutes?"

I grimaced as Jordan sighed angrily. "What the fuck does he think we're packing, here?" Jim was up on the Mk 48 mounted in the Growler's turret. "Magic bullets that can stop a fucking IFV?"

While I fully agreed with the sentiment, Jim was exaggerating our situation a little. No, we weren't in any position to go head-to-head with a mechanized infantry company, but we had a few tricks up our sleeves. Not the least being the two kamikaze drones we had in the backs of the Growlers.

Still, our role was reconnaissance at the moment, and once you engage, you're not doing reconnaissance anymore. We *could* knock at least one of those vehicles out, slowing the column, but then our own freedom of movement—and therefore our ability to report more thoroughly on enemy strength, position, and movement—were going to be severely curtailed.

"Tango India Seven Six Three, Golf Lima Ten. We could, but we'd be compromised shortly thereafter." I sighed as I took my thumb off the push-to-talk, then keyed the mic again. "How much time do you need?"

There was a pause. "We're having some coordination issues between the *Verteidiger* and the *Bundeswehr* units that have come down to join us. I don't think any of them entirely trust each other. Not everyone's in position yet." Another break. "We need another hour."

"Hell." Jordan's curse from behind the Growler's wheel was far more venomous than mine.

"What, they want breakfast in bed, too?" Greg was behind me in the back seat. It said something about how far things had deteriorated when *Greg* was getting bitterly sarcastic.

I glanced over at the other Growler. We were set in just under the edge of the trees on a farm up the hill and north of Witzleshofen. The farmer hadn't really objected to our presence, though he also hadn't been happy. Few people are when men with guns and tactical vehicles announce that they're going to be using their property for a while, and then take steps to cut off all communications out of the area. There were probably ways that the farmer *could* still get a call out, but it would be difficult, and he seemed more worried about his home and barns becoming targets than the fact that we were Americans.

Not many of the folks out in the countryside, particularly in Bavaria, were especially sympathetic to the EDC's stated ideology, or its big-city enablers.

That didn't necessarily mean they embraced Americans with open arms, either. We had a reputation in Germany that wasn't necessarily all that accurate, but had been beaten into most people's heads, nevertheless. I saw it a lot more in the cities, but some of it had leaked out into the country, too.

Still, what worried me most wasn't the farmer giving us away, or even the fact that we were going to have to shoot and scoot if we hit the column. No, it was the fact that we'd barely started our reconnaissance. We knew there was close to a division reinforced—if not two entire divisions—moving toward Bavaria. So far, we'd only gotten eyes on this lead element.

I'd much rather stay clandestine longer, and get a better picture to pass on to the Triarii infantry, *Verteidiger* militia, and vetted *Bundeswehr* units.

It was a weird war. We'd been killing the *Bundeswehr* only months before. Now, we were still going to be killing some of them, while fighting side-by-side with others.

Welcome to the brave new world.

I eyeballed the column. They weren't moving fast, rolling at about thirty or thirty-five miles per hour. We had a short window, but we *did* have a window.

"Get the Maul up." Designed from the ground up as a vehicle-killer, the Maul had a lot in common with the older Israeli Hero-30 drones. Less of a loitering munition or hunter-killer than the EDC's drones that they'd fielded in Nitra and elsewhere, it was heavier and somewhat cruder, with less flexibility and flight time, but it still packed a warhead that could turn a Puma into a funeral pyre.

We had two of them. I only wanted to use one, and what I had in mind was going to stretch its capabilities.

Greg and Chris got out without a word and started pulling the case out of the back of the Growler, where it was piled up with our rucks. We still had almost everything we owned in Europe in those rucks, and they went with us everywhere when we could swing it.

Living out of rucks for survival's sake while being hunted across an entire country tends to ingrain certain habits that are hard to get out of.

The Maul was designed to launch from the case, so all they had to do was open it up, setting it on the ground a few yards behind the Growler, where there was just enough open space between the trees to keep it from getting caught up in the branches, then power on the remote and bring it back to the vehicle.

Chris handed me the controller, then held security on the outside of the vehicle. Just in case.

I powered it on, watching the screen as the drone went through its startup sequence. It was longer than it needed to be, largely because the software had been built from off-the-shelf systems that had a lot of bells and whistles that were completely unnecessary for a drone that was going to spend itself in a fury of frag and shaped-charge plasma in a few minutes. But I finally got the "Ready" screen, and with the press of a button, I launched it.

The Maul was propelled by a pusher propeller behind the X-shaped wings, but it was launched out of the case by a compressed air cylinder that popped it about ten feet in the air before the prop really engaged. There had been some interesting accidents in development, or so I'd heard, but that was why the warhead didn't arm immediately.

The prop bit the air before the drone started to fall back toward the case, and a moment later it was climbing, getting above the trees while I steered it using the little controller in my lap.

It would be simplest to just guide the drone into an arc that would terminate on the top deck of the lead Puma, which was almost out of sight already, passing behind the trees west of Wirtzleshofen, but that was going to be about as subtle as tracer fire, and tracers work both ways. I wanted to keep our position as obfuscated as possible, at least for a while.

So, I steered the drone north, trying to keep it as low to the trees as possible. It wasn't easy. This wasn't a quad-rotor copter, that could hover and loiter for a long time. It was a strike package, and I was really starting to wish that whoever had designed it had made it a little more stable at lower speeds and flatter trajectories. I was still able to fly it generally along the wide loop that I'd had in mind, however.

I had two objectives in mind with that flight path. On the one hand, provided the drone wasn't immediately spotted, I'd be able to bring it in from a direction that wouldn't immediately point back to our position. On the other, I might get a better view of the rest of the landscape, including the other routes between

Hof and Bayreuth. If our recon was going to get cut short, I was going to make the best of the situation.

What I saw was not confidence-boosting.

The company-sized mech unit we were watching *was* only the vanguard. In the brief glimpse I got as I sent the drone winging over the wooded hills and the resort hotel just to our north, I spotted at least three spread-out columns of up-gunned ENOKs, Boxers, and a few Pumas. They didn't appear to have much air cover at the moment—most of that really *had* been blown out of the sky—but they had numbers and firepower aplenty.

This was not going to be a good day.

Still, the mission was the mission, and so far it didn't look like they'd spotted the drone. So, I brought it winging around from due north, got the lead Puma right in the targeting box, and gave the Maul its head. Then I pointed to the southeast, though Jordan was already pulling the Growler out of the trees and turning us away from the autobahn without needing any prompting from me.

The road wasn't that smooth, and Jordan was moving fast. Rueben was driving the other Growler, with Tony in the right seat and Steve up on the gun, and they were right behind us as we got moving. I could hear Jim swearing from the turret as he tried to hold on.

I was watching the screen as best I could as we bounced and rattled down the path. I got a bird's eye—or drone's eye— view of the strike as the Maul tipped over and dove on the lead Puma.

There was no sign that they'd spotted it, not that there was much they could do except pop smoke and try to evade at that point. They kept trundling along the autobahn, still going far slower than the road had been designed for. Not that it had been designed for tracked vehicles like the Pumas, anyway.

That lead vehicle grew in the screen until it blotted out everything else then the screen went black. Down below, though out of sight since we were moving and already on the other side of the hill, the Maul hit with a flash and a puff of smoke and debris, the *boom* reaching us a moment later. As we cleared the trees, we could already see the column of black smoke billowing into the sky above the stricken infantry fighting vehicle.

Things were just getting started.

Chapter 31

I didn't see much of what happened next. We were too busy moving and getting around on the EDC's flank. But we got thoroughly briefed after, including drone footage.

The EDC's lead element was halted on the A9, the point vehicle burning fiercely after our Maul slammed through the roof just behind the remote turret. The rest of the vehicles hastily herringboned to either side, dismounts pushing out and into the trees, looking for the IED trigger or the drone operator. They were a bit too far away—and on the wrong side of a terrain feature—to find us, unless they got drones of their own up.

We were still trying to get off to one flank of the multiple advancing columns of mech infantry, which seemed to form the bulk of the assaulting force heading toward Bayreuth. There were columns on just about every road that could handle their vehicles between Schwarzenbach am Wald and Marktredwitz.

While we were moving, though, the EDC wasn't standing still.

These guys had training that most of the European militaries had long since abandoned. The Euro Defense Corps had been put together after the Western European militaries' disastrous showing in Kosovo during the Fourth Balkan War. Largely trained by former French Foreign Legion—the Legion itself had furled its colors rather than be absorbed—they were hard, aggressive, and they were good at what they did.

So, they didn't dawdle on the road. They got any survivors out of the burning Puma while the dismounts spread out through the trees to either side, clearing the sides of the autobahn for IEDs, and then they mounted up and kept moving, getting off the X as fast as they could. They weren't even close to being stopped.

They'd been delayed by a few minutes, but that was it.

In the meantime, Chalmers had gotten fed up with the bickering between his German allies, and had put his foot down, using my report to galvanize the defenders to quit mistrusting each other and get into position. They were set in along the tree-swathed heights to either side of the A9 as the diminished column came into the cleft in the hills just outside of Himmelkron, more alert than they had been.

The EDC *had* made a tactical mistake in using the A9. They were trying to move fast, and the autobahn ostensibly provided that speed, but with tracked vehicles they may as well have used some of the side routes. Routes that didn't go through what was as close to a ravine as you could find in central Germany.

Chalmers waited until the company, all remaining twenty-five vehicles, were in the ravine before he triggered the ambush.

The easiest and cheapest way would probably have been to set in a daisy-chain of IEDs, but there hadn't been time. The Triarii had a handful of Javelins that we'd wheeled out of the Poles, and the Germans had a mix of Panzerfaust-3s, Matadors, and MBDA Enforcer missiles.

With a rippling series of *bang*s, anti-armor missiles slammed out of the woods on both sides, and in seconds, half the column was smashed and burning.

The reaction was almost immediate. With the southbound lanes blocked by the blazing wreckage of the rear vehicle—lead and rear had been the first vehicles targeted—the rest of the survivors quickly raked the surrounding hillsides with machinegun and cannon fire as they bulled their way across the median and into the northbound lanes, heading out of the kill zone as fast as they could manage. They almost high-centered a few of the vehicles on the mounded, grass-covered median, designed to stop just such a crossing, but the surviving Pumas crushed the mounds down far enough to get the ENOKs over.

The storm of fire kept any more anti-tank missiles at bay, at least for a little while. Another Javelin popped out of the trees, soaring skyward before plunging back down toward one of the Pumas. It hit with a catastrophic impact, slamming into the armored vehicle's roof and sending a chunk of the remote turret flying skyward in a blast of black smoke and whickering debris.

The survivors didn't even pause. Holding in the kill zone was death, and they knew it. They kept moving, sending sporadic bursts of fire back at the wooded hills even while they blasted out radio warnings to the other elements moving down the A9 and their flankers on the surrounding main roads.

The main column behind them slowed its advance as the warning went out. The overall commander looked at the terrain and realized he'd screwed up, sending his point element into that slot. Terrain still matters, tech or no.

The entire offensive slowed at that, then turned north, toward the gap in the hills and woods near Wirsberg. The northern elements were already there, but it took time to get the others shifted. Military units don't shift on a dime.

The southeastern flank column didn't get the message quite in time, and the lead elements were nearly at the outskirts of Bad Berneck by that time, already well into a narrow slot in the hills even tighter than the ravine that the A9 had passed through.

The *Verteidiger* had already prepared Bad Berneck in case the EDC came through it. They'd had time to set in IEDs.

The lead ENOK was hit by a charge big enough that it threw the vehicle on its side, shattering the armored glass and blowing a ragged hole through the driver's side door. When the dust faded, flames were licking at the side of the vehicle and a few of the EDC soldiers from inside were climbing out as dismounts from behind moved up to cover them.

They got the wounded out and back to the next vehicle behind it, and then began to withdraw. There wasn't room to turn around, at least not with any rapidity, so they just tried to reverse out.

They backed right into a daisy-chain of a dozen more IEDs buried on the side of the road. Four vehicles disappeared in the black cloud with a resounding *boom* that echoed across the hills. The rest didn't stick around this time, but dropped back to Hohenknoden and set up a herringbone defensive formation before sending foot-mobiles back in to get the wounded out.

The Bad Berneck column had stalled, but after about an hour, half of the brigade behind the smashed lead element had turned north to catch up with the rest on their end run around the hills.

***

Trying to stop the entire offensive cold with what we had wasn't going to work. But the *Bundeswehr* unit assigned to the north of Bayreuth, an ad hoc mishmash of two *Panzergrenadier* battalions and several smaller units of *Gebirsjägers* and *Fallschirmjägers*, was willing to give it a go. After all, they'd all seen the data dump. That was why they were there. They knew that the people commanding the force heading their way had ordered the mass murder of German civilians to further their political goals, and they were *pissed*.

Unfortunately, those disaffected *Bundeswehr* units didn't have everything in the way of gear that they might have had. I didn't know details about all the wrangling behind the scenes, but from what we'd heard, there had already been some falling out along "nationalist" versus "pro-EDC" lines, and the EDC still had enough pull in the German government that the "nationalists" had been under suspicion and therefore measures had been taken to make them as ineffective as possible.

So, they had a few Marders, Pumas, and Boxers, and not nearly enough MBDA Enforcers, or enough ammunition. But they were still determined to make the oncoming EDC forces bleed.

They had set in a massive L-shape, mostly concentrated on the Wilhelm Kneitz textile factory up in Wirsberg and the railyard in Neuenmarkt. They'd done their damnedest to get as many of the civilians out of Neuenmarkt as possible before things kicked off, and now they had small teams scattered throughout the town, armed with what anti-armor weapons they had and backed up by their armored vehicles. They had a handful of drones, too, which their commander, an older *Oberst* by the name of Weisman, was hoping to leverage to their full advantage.

Those drones launched from the textile factory as the lead elements, mostly Pumas again, roared out of the trees and fields and across the road just south of Wirsberg. The drones weren't too different from our Mauls, though they were fixed wing models with smaller warheads. The first two smashed a pair of Puma turrets, but otherwise didn't do much. The drone operators in the textile factory quickly adjusted, and the remaining drones started going for mobility kills.

Three blew tracks off the advancing infantry fighting vehicles. One hit an engine, blowing it apart and halting the Puma in a belching cloud of smoke.

One popped up and came down just behind a remote turret, hitting the ammunition. That vehicle brewed up fast, crackling flames shooting out of the blowout panels. It probably didn't hurt too many of the men inside, but the vehicle halted anyway, and the dismounts piled out to avoid the fire.

The vehicles that hadn't been hit turned north and started to close on the factory. The drone operators beat feet while several of the limited MBDA Enforcer teams started to engage.

Three more Pumas died, and as many Boxers. The survivors popped smoke, adding white obscurant to the ugly black clouds billowing from burning vehicles across the valley while they backtracked to better cover and began to disgorge infantry near the road, out of line of sight from the factory.

Not out of sight of the houses at the edge of Neuenmarkt, though.

Machinegun fire and more Enforcer missiles reached out across the fields, hammering into what was now the enemy flank. Nearly a squad of EDC infantry was ripped apart, thrown into the ditch in a welter of blood, and two more Boxers blew up, burning fiercely in the aftermath of the missile strikes.

The remaining infantry took cover in the ditch as the armor began to redeploy, and more infantry dismounted to the north, heading into Wirsberg to clear out the textile factory. They were immediately brought under fire by more *Fallschirmjäger*s set into the resort at the top of the hill.

More of the EDC brigade descended on Wirsberg and Neuenmarkt, setting up a perimeter around the two towns while infantry dismounted and prepared to move in with armor and drone support, clearing both towns house-to-house. The EDC commander began calling for artillery, but with the new arrangement with Berlin, artillery support on civilian targets was a bridge too far. He couldn't get authorization, yet.

The battle of Bayreuth had begun.

Chapter 32

While the *Bundeswehr* nationalists stalled out the EDC thunder run on Bayreuth, we were maneuvering on the EDC's rear area.

Our recon mission was effectively over as contact was made and battle was joined. I was all about hitting the EDC's flank, but as soon as I brought the subject up with Hartrick, I got a solid "No."

I know you can do a lot of damage, but you can do more by tearing the guts out of their command, control, and logistics. The infantry and the Germans will slow them down and make them bleed. Let them find out that they've got no support coming, and this will be over faster. Get on your target deck.

I wanted to argue. Those boys were bleeding and dying out there, and we could see the smoke rising and even hear some of the small arms fire and explosions from our new rally point above Burg Stein.

Yet we had our own mission, and despite my feelings, I knew that we were probably going to do a lot more good for them by wreaking havoc in the EDC's rear area, where they thought they were secure. At the very least, we'd hamper their logistics and reduce their combat power that way, cutting their supplies of fuel and ammunition. We might also draw more of their forces away.

So I simply acknowledged and got down to route planning.

We were heading into Saxony, while the infantry sections, the *Verteidiger*, and the *Bundeswehr* fought and died to hold the line.

***

If we'd taken main roads and autobahns, we could have been in Stollberg in an hour and a half. Given the current situation, that hardly seemed like a good idea, so it took us more like five or six hours to get into position, staging the Growlers in the woods, as deep into the pines and firs as we could get them, about two and a half miles from the objective.

We'd be on foot from there.

The EDC had taken control of the Logistikpark Stollberg, and from what we'd been able to determine via reporting and drone overflights, they'd turned it into a staging point for materiel heading for Bavaria. That made it our first target.

I would have welcomed Tucker's or Burkhart's backup, but there were enough targets in and around Chemnitz, where General Metzger had set up his headquarters, that we each had our own tasking. We had to make do with ten men, or else it wouldn't get done.

We finished camouflaging the Growlers as the sun went down. "Since we don't have a drone that won't give the game away, I'm going to take David and do a quick leader's recon." I wanted to get eyes on, really *see* what we were up against, before making a concrete plan. An open assault was out of the question. We were going to have to find a weak point, infiltrate, set charges—or just start fires—and get out.

That was doable, especially if we could find a hole in their security. That was what David and I were about to go tackle.

"We'll be off comms for the most part, but I'll try to check in on regular comm windows, every two hours." I was at the hood of my Growler with David, Tony, and Jordan, giving the brief in the deepening dark. "We'll use T-phones unless we lose the network, then we'll go to radios." I looked around at the others. "Drop dead time is an hour before sunrise. If we can't make it back here before then, I'll send a message. If there's no comms and we're still not back, consider us dead or captured, and fall back, link up with Hartrick, and plan from there." I stared at Tony, even though it was getting too dark to see facial expressions without NVGs. "Do not try to mount a half-baked rescue mission with only eight dudes."

Tony might have chuckled. Truth be told, I would probably have been the one who needed to be told that, not him.

I looked at David. We were all geared up, assault packs and chest rigs over lightweight plates, helmets, NVGs, and OBRs. "Ready to roll?"

"Let's do it." Without another word, he nodded to Tony and Jordan, and turned into the woods, already heading north, toward Stollberg.

"We'll be here. Just don't get caught, or have all the fun before we can come catch up." Jordan punched me on the shoulder. I returned it.

We'd come a long way, Jordan and I. He'd been a bit of a sore spot in the team for a long time, carrying that two-ton racial chip on his shoulder, always the first to take offense and start a fight. After the last year, though, while I couldn't necessarily say that he'd mellowed all that much—combat soldiers don't tend to be "mellow"—he'd dropped a lot of his defensiveness, at least with the team. We were brothers, finally.

Then I turned and followed David into the dark under the trees, silently saying a prayer before combat, one I'd found in an old World War II prayerbook long ago.

Lord, at any moment we may find ourselves in battle. However rigorous the task that awaits us, may we fulfill our duty with courage. If death should overtake us tonight, may we die at peace with You.

***

Getting to a position where we could get eyes on the Logistikpark was a chore in and of itself.

The woods we were working our way through stretched all the way to the Bahnhofstraße, which we then had to parallel. And even the woods were more park than forest. This was Germany. There wasn't exactly any real wilderness left in most places. This country had been settled for centuries.

Fortunately, the Bahnhofstraße itself was mostly raised and lined with trees, giving us plenty of shadow and concealment as we moved in. Things got a little dicier as we passed a large, artificial lake, or reservoir, and had to walk near a residential house. I hoped and prayed that the owner didn't keep dogs, and fortunately, they either had no dogs, or else the dogs were just too tired to bark at the quiet figures with packs and rifles moving through the shadows under the trees.

That house was right next to the Bahnhofstraße itself, and we had to divert south to find a spot to cross the street that was still in shadow. Darkness isn't perfect concealment, but even with NVGs, it's hard to spot someone in deep shade at night. So, we stuck to the dark as best we could, as we moved quickly across the road, David covering one direction, me the other, and plunged back into the trees along the bank of the reservoir.

It only got worse from there.

We had to go through a small farm, and while we were mostly able to stay under the trees, there was still a lot of open ground to cross. Fortunately, it was already past midnight by then, and while a single dog started barking somewhere off to our left, it didn't trigger every other animal in the neighborhood. We got across the small fields and were almost to the next road we had to cross, a major tributary off the Bahnhofstraße, when a car appeared from beyond the gas station right in front of us and turned down that same road.

David was about two yards ahead of me, and he dropped flat just as he saw the beginning of the headlights' glow. I followed suit quickly, painfully aware as I got as low as possible that we were far too close, and there was next to no undergrowth to hide in. We were going to have to bank on the darkness and the hope that the driver hadn't seen movement as we'd gone prone.

The headlights swept over us as we lay in the slightly damp grass, hardly daring to breathe, trying to stay absolutely still. I suddenly hoped that the headlights hadn't glinted off my scope's objective lens.

But the vehicle kept going, rolling quickly past us, the red brake lights dwindling to the south. The driver didn't slow, gave no indication that he or she had seen anything out of the ordinary at all.

I breathed a little easier, but we both stayed put for a few minutes before finally carefully getting to our feet and moving to the edge of the road.

There were trees right across the way, leading to a thicker strip of woods behind the gas station and what looked like an auto repair shop on imagery. We hustled across the shortest gap to that strip and started working our way around.

The field to our left was empty and dark. A few lights in Mitteldorf flickered through the trees to our south, but there shouldn't be a good line of sight on us for a long way.

Then we were moving into the last bit of forest before we got eyes on our target.

***

This was going to be easier than I'd thought. Either that, or this was a dry hole, and we were wasting our time. And the lives of those who were trying to keep the EDC out of Bavaria, off to the southwest.

Getting eyes on the Logistikpark had been somewhat more difficult than we'd planned, mainly because it and the factory next to it were on raised ground, standing about fifty feet above the Bahnhofstraße, which precluded getting eyes on from across the road. We'd had to wait until we were pretty sure there was no traffic, rush across the road, and then crawl up the slope, working our way slowly and painfully through the empty lot next to the factory to the strip of trees standing between the massive warehouse and the factory.

From there, though, it became obvious that the EDC was relying a lot more on stealth than heavy security. Again, *if* this was the logistics hub that we believed it was.

No fortifications, no HESCO barriers, concertina wire, or sandbagged bunkers and guard towers. The warehouse was fenced in, sure, with an eight-foot cyclone fence topped with barbed wire, but that was barely going to slow us down. In fact, we'd already climbed it easily on the way in.

Drones are useful for surveillance and early warning, but they make noise. They're hard to hide, no matter how small you make them. And the smaller they are, the less dwell time they have. That means that they don't make great sentries. If you're going to use them in that capacity, then you have to have continuous patrols, with enough units available that you can swap them out when they need to be recharged. Swarms of drones circling an installation are also a good indicator that there's something of interest there.

I hadn't heard any yet. That didn't mean they weren't there, but so far, so good.

There were cameras on the corners of the warehouse, of course. That was going to be a problem, because after the trees and bushes we were currently hiding in, there was zero cover or concealment between us and the warehouse. It was a small wonder that we hadn't been spotted already, given some of the open ground we'd had to cover.

That we *hadn't* been spotted, though, I was pretty sure. If only because the ENOK that was occasionally orbiting the warehouse hadn't stopped, and no one had come to investigate our position.

That also assured me that there weren't any pressure sensors on the ground or the fence. Otherwise, we'd have already been in a fight.

Carefully shielding the screen after the ENOK—the presence of a German military up-armor was the first real confirmation that we'd had that we were in the right place—glided past, I pulled out the T-phone and started to call the rest of the team in, giving precise directions so they could avoid contact. They were going to have to move in in twos and threes, but we'd all trained to do that.

The truth was, we'd penetrated a lot deeper than I'd intended. We were right on the bad guys' doorstep. Sometimes that was unavoidable in urban reconnaissance, but I hadn't planned on getting this close, this soon. Unfortunately, the realities of the terrain had forced my hand.

So, once I got an acknowledgement from Tony that the rest of the team was on the way, I put the T-phone away and resumed my examination of the target building. We had about an hour to build a plan of attack that would allow us to get in and still get out.

**

The trees were the only covered and concealed position we had to work with, so that was where we were, spread out along the entire one-hundred-fifty-yard strip. David and I had worked our way to the northern end, and I was already aimed in on one of the cameras.

In the end, it was the only way to disable the surveillance. We didn't have a good way to jam them or otherwise bypass them, and cutting the power would have meant another substation strike, like we'd run in the lead-up to the assaults on the EDC's Division headquarters. We didn't have the time or the resources at the moment. Not when our guys were fighting and dying down in Bad Berneck and Neuenmarkt. Possibly in Bayreuth itself by then.

We'd pinpointed six cameras on the east side of the warehouse. Each one currently had a weapon already aimed in on it. All we were waiting for was the right moment.

The ENOK passed by again, following the same circuit it had since David and I had gotten into position. Those guys had to be bored out of their minds, and it showed. They hadn't varied their routine at all from what I could see, and I just about had the patrol timed down to the second. They wouldn't come back around for at least another fifteen minutes.

We were about to make them regret that.

I'd considered bringing the SBR Tacticals on this mission. They were still in the Growlers, but I'd decided to stick with the OBRs. They were bigger and bulkier, but we could reach out farther with the 7.62x51 than we could with the .300 Blackout, provided we were using full-power loads.

We weren't right at the moment. We'd loaded subsonic for tonight, and so when I squeezed the trigger, the suppressor gave little more than a *pop*, as the 200-grain bullet smacked into the camera's casing and stilled it.

A ragged fusillade of similar *pop*s sounded down the length of the strip of trees a moment after that, and just like that, all six cameras were out of commission.

I had no way of knowing just how their system was set up, so I didn't know how likely it was that a technical fault might drop all surveillance on one side of the building. We weren't going to wait around to find out.

As soon as the faint echoes of the gunshots had faded, we were up on our feet and rushing the two loading docks in the rear of the warehouse.

The rollup doors were down, and it would be just as difficult to breach those as a regular pedestrian door. Fortunately, there were those sorts of doors to one side of each rollup door. And they were secured, but not secure enough.

Halligan tools were pried into the joints between door and jamb, and with sudden heaves, cracked the doors open. Then we were going in fast, rifles leveled and NVGs down.

The warehouse was stacked nearly to the ceiling with pallets and crates. It looked like the Logistikpark's original inventory had just been shoved to one side and the EDC's supplies moved into the center.

Stacks of munitions, parts, clothing, gear, rations, and batteries stood next to more ENOKs and CS/VN3s, mortar tubes, and what looked like mobile rocket launchers that could be mounted to the ENOKs, the CS/VN3s, or even a pickup truck.

We'd found our jackpot, all right.

Footsteps rapped on the concrete floor, somewhere out amid the stacks. Someone had heard the *crack* as we'd broken through the door, and in addition to the cameras going out on the east side, that had alerted them that something was going on.

We were already spreading out, moving in twos and threes, and I angled toward the far wall and a larger stack of what looked like auto parts, still palletized and wrapped in plastic, as the first of the guards appeared, the bright cone of his flashlight beam probing ahead of him, a pistol already in his hand.

That pistol was his death warrant. Even as he swung the flashlight toward me, I put my offset red dot on his chest and double-tapped him.

He crashed backward onto the floor with hardly another sound. The subsonic 7.62 rounds had still made noise, and it had echoed in the warehouse. And that had been enough.

Voices were raised on the other side of the warehouse, both unaided and over the radio. I heard the next man behind the guard I'd just shot a moment later, responding to the radio as he pied off the gap between pallets.

Unfortunately for him, he wasn't on NVGs, and was still using a flashlight. David shot him before he came all the way around. We weren't showing light, and we were staying in the shadows.

More suppressed gunshots *pop*ped loudly, and a strident voice barked in German over a loudspeaker. "Fall back to the guard shack!"

I glanced to my left. No one was coming after us. Good. We weren't there to kill the guard force. We were there to destroy the warehouse.

"Start with the munitions." I moved up to cover David as he took a knee next to a stack of what looked like cases of mortar rounds and started pulling charges out of his pack.

We had to move fast, but we had plenty to work with.

***

The Alpha Element had everything set and ready to go within five minutes. The guards tried to push on Bravo, near the south end of the warehouse, but Tony and Reuben killed three of them in as many seconds and ended that.

"All fuses burning." Tony sounded downright bored. Which was no great surprise with him. "Falling back."

"Affirm. On our way." I was still watching the front as Chris pulled the igniter on the last of our charges. That one was going to really make some sparks fly. It was attached to a pallet of lithium batteries.

There was plenty of stuff in that warehouse that was going to burn or blow up when those fuses burned down. I didn't expect there would be a lot left over once the smoke cleared. Which was exactly what we were after.

Chris gave me the thumbs up and turned toward the back. I covered him as he bounded back toward the door we'd come in, but right then, it didn't look like the guards were coming for us. They were probably huddled in the guard shack, screaming for support.

That was the main reason we needed to make tracks. If a mech infantry platoon showed up, even if they didn't have anything heavier than machineguns on ENOKs, we were going to be in a world of hurt.

"Turn and go!" Chris, David, Jim, and Greg were already at the door, David and Chris watching the inside and covering my movement, while Jim and Greg covered the outside.

I plunged out through the door, pivoting to cover the nearest corner. Just in time, too, because the ENOK we'd watched circle the warehouse for hours was right there.

A man with a rifle was watching over the hood, but he must not have been expecting me to come out quite the way I did, because his first shot missed. The bullet went over my head with a harsh *snap*, and then I was throwing myself flat, returning fire as I moved. My first rounds blew the tire and smashed into the fiberglass hood, then I got lucky and put a bullet into the guard's shin.

He collapsed to the ground, screaming in agony, but he still had his rifle in his hands, so I shot him again, under the vehicle, and silenced him. His head bounced a little at the impact and he went limp.

Then Chris was hauling me to my feet as the rest of the team ran for the fence. David sprinted to the corner and covered our retreat while we got across the back road and into the trees.

I dropped to a knee behind a tree and yelled at David to turn and go. We had precisely no time left.

He sprinted toward the trees as the first of the charges went off inside. The *boom* echoed from the open door we'd exited, followed by a rippling series of explosions, several of which were heavy enough to blow sections of the roof skyward as the warehouse started to burn.

Flames leaped toward the sky, lighting up the night as we went over the fence and headed back the way we'd come, moving fast to get clear of the target area before the EDC's QRF showed up.

One target down. On to the next.

Chapter 33

Marienberg was a switch from the Stollberg operation.

We'd had to leave the Growlers outside the city again, camouflaged deep in the woods closer to the Czech border. Under different circumstances, I might have tried to get some support from our Czech friends. They'd already helped us infiltrate Germany months before, when we'd first made contact with the *Verteidiger in Bayern*, hoping to slowly erode the EDC from within.

I didn't know if that would have worked better than what we'd ended up trying to do, but it sure as hell couldn't be much worse.

We'd gotten some reporting on events near Bayreuth while en route. The fighting for Bad Berneck, Wisberg, and Neuenmarkt was over, the surviving friendly forces falling back toward Bayreuth. They'd bled the EDC, though not without taking some serious losses, themselves. Especially once the EDC commander had finally prevailed, and gotten artillery called in on Wisberg.

That was not a good sign. It meant that the politicians in Berlin were folding fast when the EDC put pressure on them. Maybe OWHSC, too, but at the moment we couldn't be sure what role they were taking in all this.

I suspected, but I still couldn't be sure.

We had no idea what kind of atmospherics to expect in Marienberg, but we couldn't just swoop in and grab our target without advance reconnaissance on the ground, and trying to sneak around the city in greens, plates, helmets, and rifles wasn't going to work. So, we had to go back to the gray man strategy that we'd adopted in Erfurt.

As much as we could.

We had *some* intel on our target's habits, but tracking him down still wasn't going to be easy or quick. In the meantime, we had to avoid getting rolled up.

Drifting into town, dressed as hikers, we came from several different directions. I'd been skeptical that this would work, but Steve had insisted that there were still enough rich retards playing tourist in Europe that it would be a workable cover.

We were in the heart of EDC Remnant territory, but close enough to Czechia that maybe he wasn't wrong. We'd have to see.

I was walking up across the fields from the south, about an hour before sunset, my go bag on my back, carrying my SBR Tactical inside it, wearing essentially the same clothes I'd worn in Erfurt, except that I'd exchanged the hipster blazer for a more outdoorsy jacket.

We hadn't seen any checkpoints from a distance, but there were definitely uniformed troops on the streets. We'd seen at least one black G-Wagen parked next to the road on the way in, with several men standing nearby in black fatigues, plate carriers, and high-cut helmets and carrying HK433s.

While the *Bundeswehr* had managed to get some for units like the *Fallschirmjäger*s and the KSK after the EDC had formally been destroyed, for the most part, the HK433s had all gone to the European Defense Corps, leaving the *Bundeswehr* with older G36s. There'd been more than a little bitterness about that, I understood.

We'd been much too far away to see any insignia when we'd observed that vehicle, but the odds that the EDC was openly wearing such insignia at this point were pretty long, anyway. And given where we were, I seriously doubted that those guys were regular *Bundeswehr*.

Nobody else thought any differently.

Fortunately, I didn't see any patrols as I walked across the fields and into the trees along the south edge of Marienberg. The residential neighborhood that I entered seemed sleepy and quiet. I guessed that there wasn't much reason to patrol it, at least not at the moment.

It paid sometimes to remember that the bad guys didn't necessarily have bottomless numbers, either.

Still, I was alert as I worked my way toward my target area, trying to look as much as possible like a clueless hipster. While jumping at every shadow tends to make you stand out on an infiltration, getting complacent is worse.

As I got deeper into the city, though, I started to spot the enemy. They weren't on the street in great numbers, but they were definitely there. There were EDC shooters in black and OWHSC in gray, both.

If there'd been any question about who was pushing all of this, the sight of those two uniforms hanging out on the street together would have immediately answered it.

I steered clear. The trick was doing that without making it *look* like that was what I was doing. The best bet is usually to disappear into a crowd, but there weren't many crowds out on the streets in Marienberg at the moment.

In fact, the longer I walked, the fewer people I saw. Marienberg wasn't a huge metropolis, but right at the moment, it looked like a bad day short of a ghost town.

That was going to make this difficult. Without people to blend in with, we were going to stand out. I was already adjusting the plan. We were going to have to try to do this a little bit sneakier, and by that I meant relying more on physical stealth, staying out of sight.

Risky enough, even without being in the middle of an urban area where someone might just spot you acting furtively and report it.

I didn't immediately abandon the plan, though. Crossing the railroad tracks, I headed north into the more built-up part of the town, most of it old-school, gabled German architecture, the kind of thing that puts you in mind of beer steins and good German food.

The streets weren't *as* empty, but they weren't crowded, either. And everyone who was out and about, and wasn't wearing a uniform and carrying a rifle, looked about as furtive as I felt.

I tried not to look too much like I was casing the joint as I moved toward the Döner Eck Soraya, a kebab shop on the corner just down the street from the target building. I was supposed to be a hiker and a tourist, a hipster who was too oblivious to realize that walking into the middle of EDC territory during a civil war was a bad idea.

All the same, I didn't want to walk into the middle of a situation that I couldn't walk out of.

Now, a kebab shop in Germany was not necessarily connected with the jihadis who effectively ruled the Islamic enclaves. There are plenty of Muslims who just want to live their lives. There are also people who just like kebabs. I still had to be careful.

I needn't have worried. This was still much the same shop that Angela Merkel had visited, back before things had really started to fall apart—yeah, we'd found the pictures while doing mission planning—and everything was still neat, clean, and welcoming, with the menu and the signs all in German, instead of Turkish or Arabic. They didn't just serve kebabs, either, but also pizza and regular German food.

I took all of this in as I glanced through the window as I approach the corner and the front door. Once I entered, I was committed.

The young man behind the counter didn't seem all that nervous, though he gave me a pretty good look over as he greeted me when I walked in.

I wasn't the only one in the place, but the other three or four people didn't look like outsiders. They looked like locals who'd just walked maybe a block to get there. I wondered if that was why the staff was watching me a little more closely, or if I'd let something slip. None of them tried to get me to leave, though, and none of them immediately pulled out a cell phone, so I might be okay for the moment.

Fortunately, I was able to pick my own seat, so it didn't take too much doing to find a small table next to the window, where I had a view down the street toward the Hotel Weißes Roß Marienberg. We didn't have solid confirmation that our target was there, but he was known to take his latest conquests there a lot.

Unfortunately, finding a vantage point on the hotel meant that I had my back to the door. I didn't like that, but I could sort of slump in the chair with my back mostly toward the wall between the door and the window, so that I only had to turn my head slightly to see anyone coming in behind me.

Singleton operations are always a collection of compromises. That's what makes them so dangerous.

With my go bag at my feet, I dug my T-phone out of my pocket while I looked at the menu. *In position. Eyes on target building*.

Another young man, who looked about in his early teens to me, though he was probably closer to twenty, came to take my order. I went with a doner kebab, sort of a wrap or Middle Eastern burrito. The young man was friendly enough, though he seemed nervous, especially since my German was unavoidably accented. There was no disguising the fact that I was a foreigner, and probably an American.

Still, while I had to maintain my surveillance of the staff through the corner of my eye, I didn't see any restless activity that might have indicated they were calling anyone in. I was probably about as safe as I was going to get for the moment.

That all changed about two minutes later.

The three men who entered weren't all that special at first glance. One was noticeably overweight, the other was cadaverously skinny, and the third just looked pasty and soft. They were all dressed in dark clothing, but none wore any insignia or even had any visible tats, though doughboy had his ears gaged.

It was the attitude that made me give them a closer look. Of course, I didn't stare at them. That's asking to be made. I'd learned a long time before how to kind of let my eyes go unfocused, staring at nothing and letting my peripheral vision pick up more detail. It's a useful skill when you want to keep an eye on your surroundings without *looking* like that's what you're doing. You'd be amazed what you can see that way, all without anyone noticing.

These characters looked around the inside of the kebab shop with visible contempt, most notably aimed at the young men and one young woman running the place. I'd seen that attitude before, most notably among the Fourth Reich. I remembered that they and their splinter groups had their heaviest presence in Germany right here, in the areas around Chemnitz.

Why would they come in a place like this, though?

I got my answer a moment later.

Ludovico Keller's money was the only explanation I could think of for his constant, and very public, string of nubile young hookups. There was nothing physically appealing about the man. Balding, short, and probably pushing three hundred fifty pounds, there was something about the way he carried himself and looked at other people that was even more repulsive than his physical appearance. This man was a predator who viewed people as things to use for his advantage or amusement, nothing more.

Yeah, I got all of that as he walked in past me, glanced at me appraisingly—with a look that made me feel like I needed a shower a lot more than just the last few days in the field would have accounted for—and moved to join the three neo-Nazis at the table closer to the middle of the restaurant. He was a mouth breather, too.

Target just walked in here. I didn't see a lot of security, but Keller had his fingers in so many pies that he probably figured he didn't need it, especially not this close to EDC headquarters. It couldn't be this easy. But if Keller was here, we might be able to snatch him as he left the restaurant, instead of trying to hit the hotel.

I got acknowledgements from the rest of the team. We'd known all along that we'd probably have to flex on this, but none of us had figured we'd be shifting to endgame this fast.

Of course, it wasn't that simple.

I recognized the next guy who came in, though the two goons to either side of him were unknowns. Kiril Sergeyevich Morozov wasn't what I'd call high on our target deck, but he was there. A major *vor* in the *Bratski Krug*, the Brother's Circle, one of the largest networks of the Russian *Mafiya* in Europe. Intel suggested that he had been instrumental in getting weapons, explosives, and materiel to the DDSB and several other anarchist groups in Germany, France, and Czechia over the last couple of years, and with the uptick in violence, he was on everybody's BOLO list. Nobody could say for sure just how extensive the network was—in fact, a lot of people denied that the *Bratski Krug* even really existed—but he'd been seen in the company of enough others on the most wanted list that it was becoming a little hard to ignore.

And while I studiously tried to look as unconcerned and oblivious as possible, this Russian gangster walked over to the table in the center of the restaurant, embraced Keller, and sat down.

Holy hell.

The surprises didn't stop there, though. Keller barked at the staff and soon they were dragging several of the other tables toward the middle. It looked like there was a major meeting going on, here.

My OP had just become the target site.

I could hear their conversation if I strained my ears, but I knew that I wasn't going to be able to memorize it all. Tapping through the T-phone's apps, I found the audio recorder and turned it on.

Over the next fifteen minutes, more people filtered in, few of them recognizable at first glance. I managed to get a few pictures taken surreptitiously and uploaded over the mesh network to the TOC back in Bayreuth. They had a lot of other things to worry about, but this could be big.

We'd targeted Keller because his name had come up a lot in the digging that our intel guys had done after the fall of the European Defense Council. Half the captured Councilors had had close dealings with him, mostly of a financial nature, though there was plenty of evidence that he'd also facilitated plenty of illegal stuff, too, up to and including human and drug trafficking. He was a billionaire financier, with his fingers in multiple international hedge funds, and he also appeared to have plenty of connections in the global underworld. Most people in a position to know knew about those connections, too, but his money made him untouchable. We were still getting to the bottom of it, but his funds seemed to have gone a long way toward financing the creation of the European Defense Corps itself.

It didn't look like he was out of the game, either.

The phone vibrated in my hand. Looking down at the screen, I saw a photo of the small, dark-haired man who'd just come in. *Corwin Mayr. Former Austrian* Bundesheer, *now primary liaison officer between OWHSC and the* Bundespolizei. *Works for OWHSC.*

The next photo came almost immediately after. This time it displayed the hatchet-faced man with a buzzed head who had joined the group last. *Matheo Richard. Believed to be current commander of 1st Special Group, 3rd EDC Division.*

There was a pause, then a new message came up. *Matt, I'm not going to tell you to stick your neck out any farther than necessary, but if you can kill or capture everyone at that table, it's going to throw a hell of a monkey wrench into things for the bad guys. Again, it's your call. You're the man on the ground. If it's not feasible, don't do it.*

That was a hell of a thing to drop in my lap, and I knew that Hartrick knew it. He wouldn't have been nearly that apologetic otherwise. He'd been there, though. We'd had a similar situation pop up in Detroit.

He'd made the call to back off, that time. We'd have been dogpiled and slaughtered before we could have gotten clear.

The question was, could we do this and still get out in one piece?

More situation and position reports were still streaming in from the rest of the team. About two thirds of us had closed in on the block and were within thirty seconds of my position. In fact, even as I thought it over, Lucas walked into the restaurant, looking even more like a hipster hobo than I did, looked around, and joined me at my table.

He'd almost completely transformed his attitude and even his appearance. Lucas wasn't a big dude, but he always seemed bigger than he was, simply because of the swagger he never seemed to quite get rid of, the compact hardness of his build, and the set of his jaw. He was a meat-eater, a killer, and anyone who had an ounce of situational awareness could look at him and pick up on it.

Except now he was...well, I won't say he was *simpering*, but he'd changed the way he walked, the set of his shoulders, and something about his facial expression. No, it wasn't his facial expression as such. It was the thick-framed Birth Control Glasses and the scarf he was wearing. *Where the hell did he get those?* The hard-as-nails Lucas had been replaced by somebody else. Somebody soft, oblivious, and harmless.

He wasn't quite harmless enough for Morozov's goons, though.

I was turned the wrong direction to see them get up, but I definitely saw them when they loomed over our table. I looked up, widening my eyes to look as innocent and naïve as possible, flipping my phone over to disguise the message I'd just sent.

Wildfire.

Chapter 34

The Fourth Reich guys might have looked far less intimidating than they thought they did, but these guys weren't them. They weren't bodybuilders, but there was something about them. One was pretty big, but they were both kinda chubby, and the smaller one had a barely-there scruff of beard on his chin that was just pathetic.

But it was pretty clear that both of these guys were well-versed in violence. The scars on the big guy's knuckles were all too obvious, and the smaller guy had an ugly look in his eye that told me that he'd ended some people, many of them without any reason besides the fact that he'd taken a dislike to their continued existence.

I didn't think they'd come over to have a friendly talk. Especially since I could see the P99 behind the big guy's crossed hands in his waistband.

"What are you doing here?" The big guy was speaking German, which made sense, but there was something in the tone of his voice that told me he didn't actually give a damn about an answer to the question. He was there to get rid of us. Either he or his boss had noticed us when Lucas had come in, and they had decided that even if we were harmless hipsters, we'd seen too much.

Too bad for them.

319

I saw Lucas move out of the corner of my eye while I stared up at the big guy, blinking like I wasn't sure what he'd just said. His German was heavily accented, so there was that. "What?"

The big guy didn't seem bothered by my attempt at saying I didn't understand him. He was going to kill us, but he thought he was just tying up loose ends. I could see it in his eyes.

Then Lucas shot the smaller one.

He'd shifted in his seat as if he was trying to get some distance from the *brodyagi*, shrinking away from the threat inherent in their presence. I'd never imagined that Lucas Edwards could have disguised himself as such an easily-frightened rabbit, but he pulled it off just long enough.

That movement had put him facing the smaller guy, his hand within easy reach of the pistol he was carrying in an appendix inside-the-waistband holster.

His draw was lightning quick, his off hand snatching his shirt away from the weapon barely a fraction of a second before his gun hand closed on the grip and snatched the pistol out. We were so close that he was already shooting as soon as the gun came level, his first bullet punching into the little guy's gut just above his folded hands, the next three shots walking up his chest and into his throat.

The necessities of concealment meant none of us had a suppressed pistol, and the 9mm's bark was deafeningly loud in the confines of the restaurant. There was no disguising what had just happened.

The big guy's eyes turned from me in shock as Lucas dumped his buddy, and that gave me the fraction of a second I needed. Big Guy was pulling just as my own muzzle came level and I blew a hole up under his ribcage and through his lung just before I double-tapped him in the sternum. He was already starting to fall as I put a fourth shot through his chin and out the top of his skull, blood and brains painting the ceiling.

Lucas had already pivoted without leaving his seat, and dumped the rest of his magazine into the two men who'd come in with Richard. As fast as those shots cracked across the restaurant, every one hit a vital zone, punching into chests and skulls.

The men at the table scrambled for the floor at the gunfire, though one of the Fourth Reich assholes snatched a pistol out of his waistband. He was far too slow, though, and I shot him through the teeth before he could even clear his beltline.

Another one of the neo-Nazis had dropped below the table, but there wasn't more than a couple of chair legs between him and me, and I blasted two rounds through his chest and collarbone. He screamed, the noise rapidly turning into a sick gurgle. Richard got the next pair as he yanked his service pistol out from under his jacket, though he actually got a shot off. He'd have blown the top of my skull all over the wall behind me if I hadn't thrown myself out of my seat and into a side prone on the floor at almost the same moment that he squeezed the trigger. The bullet smacked into the plaster where I'd just been, showering me with grit, and then I shattered his knee with my own, the second round going into his pelvis.

The Fourth Reich guy's gurgling screams were nothing compared to the shrieks of agony that Richard let out a moment later, as the shock of what had just happened sank in.

Pelvis shots are a bitch.

Shifting targets, I caught the third Fourth Reich type, the pasty doughboy, pulling an old Skorpion machine pistol out of his jacket. It must have gotten hung up, which was a good thing for me and anyone else in that restaurant, since I didn't have a very high estimation of old boy's potential fire discipline or target discrimination. I shot him through the throat, and the next two shots were little more than insurance as I blew his eyeball out and spattered blood, brains, and bone across the floor behind him.

Then my slide locked back on an empty mag. I frantically dropped it and reached for a reload. Lucas had already opened fire again, dumping the rest of Richard's security detail.

Keller was crawling desperately for the back, and Mayr wasn't far behind him. Morozov and two of the other unknowns had knocked the second table over and taken cover behind it, but that only works in movies. I hammered half the magazine through the veneered particle board tabletop, and one collapsed with a scream. The other just dropped. I saw no sign of Morozov from where I was, but nobody was shooting anymore.

Then Chris, Greg, Tony, and David were coming through the door, their SBRs up and ready.

I pointed toward the rear, where the last two targets were almost to the kitchen. "Get Keller and that Mayr bastard!" I picked myself up off the floor as the four of them swept toward the rear, Chris and Tony moving to pop around behind the corner, where the staff was presumably huddled behind the counter and hoping that they didn't accidentally get shot.

Greg and David descended on our targets, Greg stopping Keller with a gentle muzzle tap on the back of his skull and a cheerful, "Hello, friend." David was a little rougher, dropping a knee in the middle of Mayr's back before lifting his muzzle toward the ceiling and quickly searching him.

The rest of the team had gotten inside by then, and I was hauling my own SBR and plate carrier out of my go bag, quickly donning the armor before looping the sling around my neck. From where I stood, I could see that Morozov didn't have long for this world, shaking as he bled out on the floor, one hand to his ruined throat.

David had a wheezing, shell-shocked Mayr on his feet, his hands already flex cuffed. Greg was having a bit more trouble with Keller, not so much because the man was struggling, but because he was grossly fat, shaking, and babbling in near panic. Tony moved over and helped haul the financier to his feet.

"How's the street look?" I slung my go bag on my back again, getting ready to move.

"We've got some company coming." Jim was watching the street to the southwest, toward the hotel. "About five or six guys in black and a few more in gray."

"Got what looks like a police vehicle pulling up to the corner to the north," Steve reported.

"Okay, we're going to have to shoot our way out of here." Less than ideal, but it had become inevitable as soon as those two Russians had stood up. "Cover right, move left. Go."

There wasn't time for a lot more planning than that. This was time to move fast, hit hard, and break contact.

Steve and Reuben opened fire from the corner, shattering the windows and showering glass on the sidewalk outside as they hammered rounds at the vehicle on the corner. Jim, Lucas, Tony, and I burst out onto the street a moment later.

We stayed on our side of the street, but Jim and I were offset just enough that we could both bring the oncoming EDC MPs and OWHSC "contractors" under fire almost immediately. The bad guys had the disadvantage of not knowing exactly who was who or what was happening, while we could engage anyone with a weapon.

My first round took one of the black-clad EDC shooters high in the chest, but he was clearly wearing plates, and he only staggered. I followed up with a fast quartet of shots, low to high, and while two more hit the plate, one went into his groin and the last one hit him in the side of the head. It wasn't fatal, but the groin shot was already going to stop him, as his leg collapsed underneath him.

Jim had simply raked the other three on our side of the street with half a mag. Two were down, and the last one had just ducked into the alcove of a door to get out of the line of fire.

Too bad for him that was the way we were going.

Tony and Lucas had sprinted across the street, and I could hear their suppressors spitting as they took the OWHSC contractors on that side under fire where they'd taken cover behind a couple of cars at the end of the street. Glass shattered, unsuppressed 5.56 and 5.8 fire *crack*ed down the street, and sirens—both car alarms and Polizei sirens—wailed and whooped. We might have snuck in, but we sure weren't sneaking out.

We kept moving, pushing down the street at a fast glide, guns up and looking for trouble. If we hadn't had known bad guys right in front of us, we might have just gone for it and sprinted to the corner, but right then, the last EDC shooter tried to lean out of the doorway, and my hasty shot spat fragments of plaster and stone into his face. Then Jim blew his knee to a bloody pulp, and he collapsed onto the sidewalk.

We both shot him a split-second later, then we were running.

I slowed before we got to the intersection. Trees shadowed the streets and the traffic circle immediately to the south, but I was more concerned with those OWHSC shooters who had taken cover behind a couple of smart cars parked on the brick sidewalk just outside the hotel's attached restaurant. Tony and Lucas had them effectively pinned down, but we were about to hit an angle where they'd be able to shoot at us without exposing themselves to our teammates' fire.

There. One of them leaned out behind his QBZ-03, but he'd miscalculated just how far he could move and still stay behind the car. My first shot skipped along the rifle's receiver and clipped his ear. He reared back and I shot him three more times, dumping him on his back on the cobblestones, thrashing in pain as he bled out.

Then I was at the corner. The last man had scooted back even farther behind the car, apparently unwilling to risk his own neck any farther. The three gray-clad bodies sprawled in the street, not to mention the one still writhing in pain next to the car, were ample evidence that trying to take us all on by himself was just going to get him killed.

I was sure he had reinforcements coming. The sirens were getting louder. We had to make tracks.

Jim and I held on the corner as the rest flowed past me, ducking under the trees and heading for the railroad tracks. Mayr and Keller weren't being all that cooperative, but they weren't really resisting, either. We were just moving faster than they were prepared for, or possibly capable of.

Tough. We had to move, and they were coming with us, whether they liked it or not.

"Last man!" Reuben slapped me on the shoulder as he ran past. I didn't pause for long, but turned and followed him as soon as I was sure Jim was already moving. Jim was still hobbling a little after getting shot in Aachen, but he was moving.

Ideally, when you run a break contact drill, you bound to cover each other. Sometimes, though, you've just got to run for it. Speed is security, and when we'd just gotten inside the enemy's OODA loop as hard as we had, we just needed to move. No one was currently shooting at us, so we had to make tracks before they got someone out in front of us.

That was still going to be dicey. I wished that we'd brought civilian vehicles in on this instead of the Growlers. We might have rolled right into town, done our dirty work, and gotten out before they'd managed to figure out what was happening.

We hadn't, though. So now we were on foot, just over a mile from our ground transport, with two less-than-speedy detainees.

So, we ran.

Staying under the trees on the south side of the railroad tracks, we turned east, hopefully moving in a direction they wouldn't expect while simultaneously taking advantage of what minor concealment that strip of woods provided. Sirens were still whooping, but as I ran, I tried to figure out exactly where they might have been coming from. The more I listened, the more I started to suspect that I was only hearing two or three vehicles, and that they were still gathered around the kebab shop.

They really didn't know exactly what had just gone down, and the longer it stayed that way, the happier I'd be.

Of course, if the restaurant had had security cameras, it probably wouldn't take long to figure it out, but we'd take full advantage of every minute.

We got past the sports arena and turned south. Pushing through more trees, we burst out onto the street again, and then we just had to run for it. There were too many fences to go across the residential yards. We'd slow down too much, and there was no way we were getting Keller up and over more than once or maybe twice.

Keller was already staggering with fatigue. It was doubtful that he'd run more than a couple of paces—if that—in years. Greg wasn't letting him slow down, though, even though he and Jordan were practically dragging the corpulent financier by the time we got to the woods at the edge of town.

That was when the bad guys caught up with us.

A black G-Wagen came screaming around the corner and barreled down the Waldstraße toward us. Tony and Reuben had fallen back to the rear, and now they turned and opened fire, mag-dumping as fast as they could shoot at the oncoming vehicle. The windshield starred and clouded, but didn't break. The vehicle was armored.

Tony shifted his fire to the grill, but while he might do some damage to the radiator—engine compartments are rarely armored, even on the heaviest up-armors—the .300 Blackout is no .50 caliber RAUFOSS.

Everyone else was in the trees, and I got behind a big oak and added my fire over Tony's shoulder. "Turn and go!" That G-Wagen wasn't going to be able to follow us into the woods.

Both men turned, though they both remembered to look first so that they didn't run across my muzzle, and then they both sprinted past me and into the woods.

The G-Wagen had stopped, still about a hundred yards away. The windshield was a mess, a cracked, bullet-pocked layer of shattered laminate. It had held—it was rated for a lot heavier than .300 Blackout subsonic—but it had to be next to impossible to see out of it. And while I kept dumping the last of my mag at it, the guys inside didn't look like they were all that eager to get out.

An up-armored vehicle without a mounted gun doesn't work all that well on offense unless you think things through a little more.

I reloaded as I turned and followed the rest into the trees.

***

We made it across the highway and into the woods and fields to the south before the first helicopters showed up.

They were EDC birds, NH90s, recognizable as EDC instead of *Bundeswehr* because they were painted dark green and still sported the Europe-star-and-sword logo on their tails. We went to ground as the first ones roared over, but we were deep in the woods, and it was still late summer, so we had plenty of overhead concealment.

"We need to keep going." It was entirely possible that we were going to have to go to ground in the woods until nightfall, but I'd rather be at the vehicles, and have the firepower of the Mk 48s at our disposal, not to mention our OBRs.

Keller was still shaking. Mayr had gotten over his shock, but his first attempt at slowing down had been met by David's knife point, and he'd cooperated ever since.

As the helos growled overhead once more, we got back on the move, heading south through the woods, keeping to the thickest trees and out of the clearings.

If we were fast, and lucky, we might manage to get the hell out of dodge before they widened their search enough to spot us.

Chapter 35

Hartrick walked into the TOC with his eyes a little wide and one sardonic eyebrow raised. "Well, I guess I should congratulate you guys. You hit a fucking gold mine."

The fight for Bayreuth had settled down to a stalemate. The EDC's thunder run had gotten bogged down in the hills and woods above the city, and while they'd managed to get through the *Bundeswehr*'s initial defense, they hadn't managed to get far into the city itself. Sporadic skirmishes were about it for the moment, though that could change at any time.

"Is Keller talking, then?" I didn't expect the fat money man to be particularly tough under interrogation.

"Oh, Keller's singing like a fucking canary." Hartrick chuckled in that humorless way of his. It's a sound with a lot more mockery in it than enjoyment. "Mayr's clammed up, but he's cracking. But neither of them is nearly as useful as that recording you made, Matt. Of course, the audio quality kind of goes to shit there at the end, when Lucas starts shooting, but beggars can't be choosers, I guess."

I rubbed my eyes. We'd gotten outside the EDC's search pattern before the helos had managed to spot us, but it had still been a grueling trip back into Bavaria, sticking to back roads and trails, hiding during the day and moving when we could at night, driving on NVGs. It had taken two days to make a trek that would have taken an hour and a half under peacetime conditions.

We hadn't had much time to sleep since turning our prisoners over. "Will you get to the point, Brian?"

He sat down at the table. "We're already getting it out through the same information ops channels that put out the leaks about Hof. Most of it's in German, but we've included helpful transcripts and subtitles in English, French, Spanish, Czech, and Polish. Working on more. It's also led to some of our hacker nerds digging even deeper, and they've found some interesting stuff based on the threads they started pulling."

"What were they talking about, Brian?" He was enjoying this far too much.

He grinned, the expression downright feral. "It seems like the Hof massacre didn't quite have the effect they'd been hoping. That document dump kind of killed their narrative in the cradle. Even their friends in Berlin couldn't get ahead of it. Nobody knows who dropped it, but right now the running theory is that it was the Russians."

"Really?" Tucker's frown kind of screwed up his whole face. "Why would the Russkies do something like that?"

Hartrick shrugged. "Chaos? The Russians don't want Western Europe to settle down. They don't really give a fuck who wins. If we'd been coming out on top, they'd have dumped info that helped the EDC. They still might, if we manage to get ahead of this. *If* we take too long to do it."

"So, Hof didn't work out the way they'd hoped. Their buddies in the *Bundestag* are running scared and trying to cover their asses and point fingers everywhere else." I sighed. "What else?"

"One of those unknowns was a staffer for Adele Hoefler, who, it turns out, has been one of the quieter EDC sympathizers in the *Bundestag*. Well, she's been quiet *publicly*." He shrugged. "Turns out she's got a *lot* of money moving around, in both directions. There's *just* enough of a veneer of respectability over her political contributions to keep the authorities from looking too closely—assuming that they really give a shit in the first place—but it's looking more and more like the majority of them are coming from Chinese-linked companies. She's then been 'investing' in front companies that are helping fund the EDC while she profits handsomely off the whole thing. She's not the only one, either.

"Anyway, this staffer kind of kicked things off. Heofler and her compatriots—the staffer doesn't say who they are, just calls them 'associates'—are concerned that things are turning against them. The Americans aren't stirring out of their FOBs at the moment, but more and more *Bundeswehr* units are moving to oppose the EDC's push into Bavaria. The exposure of the Hof operation destroyed their cassis belli for the push, and the voices calling for it to be ended and for the EDC to be investigated on terrorism charges are getting louder.

"So, they need something new. Something bigger, that shifts things their way. That was where the conversation got really interesting."

Hartrick rubbed his hands together. "We always suspected that the war started because the EDC was getting desperate. Crime was up, terror attacks by the 'immigrants' were up, their economies were tanking, and they needed to do *something* before it all slipped out of their hands. The Slovak Nationalists were getting too uppity, most of the rest of Eastern Europe had already told them to pound sand, Italy and Spain had cut away for all intents and purposes. People get stupid when their dreams start to fall apart, and it looks like the same thing happened here.

"Which is why the options being bandied around the table weren't exactly what you'd call 'subtle.'"

He pulled a map across the table and started pointing to cities as he talked. "Richard suggested the broad strokes of the plan. You guys broke things up before they finished, so we might be out ahead of it, but I suspect that they'll find another way to get things moving, though not having Keller to coordinate the money side might slow it down.

"First, there were going to be a series of attacks in *OWHSC* controlled areas. These were then going to be connected to statements made by those members of the Berlin government who have had the guts to come out against the EDC. Exactly how they were going to do this was a little hazy, but it looks like not everyone is completely clean, and the *Mafiya* might have made some inroads into their finances. If not, then Hoefler's rep said that they had plenty of 'opposition research' they can use, if they can get it out fast enough and thick enough."

That was common enough. We'd seen it over the years in the States, too. It largely didn't matter whether your information was true or not. A lot of times it wasn't. It was either formed by jumping to conclusions before all the intel was in, or just built out of outright lies. What mattered was getting it out first and spreading it the widest. By the time the truth came out, months or even years later, the damage was done, and nobody cared anymore.

It's a part of warfare that often goes unremarked, but it can be every bit as vital as the kinetic part that we've gotten so good at.

The Chinese call it "political warfare."

"That was only going to be the first phase. With that done, then OWHSC would have to arrest the offending politicians and officers, calling in the EDC to assist in putting them down. The Fourth Reich and the jihadis would keep the Americans bottled up in the meantime."

There was a pause as he finished talking and looked around at the three of us. I was frowning as I stared at the map. When I looked up at Tucker and Burkhart, I saw similar expressions.

"Didn't they essentially try that before?" Burkhart sounded downright insulted. "I mean, do they *really* think that'll work after their Hof false flag failed?"

"Ah, that's where they're optimistic." Hartrick laughed, a bitter and sarcastic sound. "See, they're hoping they can discredit the data dump with the *Mafiya*'s help, make it all go away as nothing more than disinformation by disreputable hackers. That's probably wishful thinking at this point, but there's a lot of that going around. They're also hoping that if they deliver a big enough shock, people will forget about Hof anyway."

"What do they have in mind that they think will make that bloodbath go away?" Tucker asked.

Hartrick shrugged. "Your guess is as good as mine, at this point." He looked at me and smirked. "Matt and Lucas shot the place to shit before they got that far."

I shook my head. "So, what are we doing to head this off?"

"That's already started with the data dump that the cyber guys are pushing out right now. Not only the recording, with subtitles and transcripts, but video of Keller's interrogation is supposed to go on every news stream and website we can get our grubby fingers into. We also have people setting up meetings with a number of American, German, French, and Austrian politicians who have signaled that they're back on the fence after Hof. We're turning the pressure up." He stabbed a finger at the map. "That's only the first part, though."

Leaning forward, he got serious. Hartrick had taken a sadistic glee in the way we'd just *potentially* thrown a monkey wrench in the bad guys' plans, but our job involved killing people and breaking things, too, and we were facing desperate people who still had a lot of firepower at their disposal.

"We might be able to politically isolate the EDC, but they're still going to have a lot of combat power and connections with just about every bad guy in Europe. With the Russians still pushing in the east and things getting *really* sporty in the Pacific, we might not have the time or the resources to settle down to a long-term 'hybrid' war with them in Germany."

The team leaders traded glances. "You make that sound like the Pacific's gotten hotter," Tucker said slowly. "We've heard about the fights in the South China Sea, but it sounded like that was going well. What's changed?"

Hartrick hesitated. The sense of foreboding only deepened at that. Brian Hartrick had never been the kind of leader who kept things from his guys unless he absolutely had to.

Finally, he sighed. "I wasn't going to get into it, since we've got bigger fish to fry here right now. We haven't been told in as many words that we might have to redirect, but the PRC has not reacted well to getting their shorts pulled up over their heads in the Spratlys.

"They've started the invasion of Taiwan, they're getting more aggressive with Japan in the Senkakus, and the Norks are getting even more restless. We've got elements helping the Taiwanese, but it's starting to look touch and go."

"*Are* we going to get pulled?" Burkhart's question wasn't an idle one, and it made more than a little sense. After all, we were increasingly persona non grata in Europe, with both the Army and the locals generally wishing we weren't around.

It worried me, in a way, though. If we headed for the Pacific, there was no guarantee we were ever going to come back to Europe. No guarantee that I was ever going to see Klara again. I didn't have any illusions that our own State Department would be remotely interested in helping a Polish Catholic girl get to the States so she could marry a Triarius.

Maybe that was me being selfish. After all, I was there to fight a war, not to get married. All the same, though, a man can only put his family and loved ones behind him for so long. Especially when the war appeared to be more and more of a quagmire that we wouldn't be able to truly win.

"Not yet." Hartrick snarled a little, returning to his usual state of simmering anger. "This is why I wasn't going to say anything." He jabbed a finger at the map on the table. "*This* is our mission right now. *This* needs to be the focus, not worrying about whether we're going to go halfway around the world next month." He glared around at all of us. Nobody really wanted to meet that stare. We'd all seen it before, and it rarely boded well. "Focus. Or you're going to get your dumb asses killed, along with your teammates."

When he was sure that we were all focused on Europe instead of the Pacific, at least for now, he got back to business. "There are some moving parts on the political and information side that need to get into position first, but we're going to start planning and getting prepped now." His finger landed on Chemnitz.

"While most of our conventional forces—what we have, including the handful of Army units that will work with us—deal with the remaining EDC forces here in Bayreuth, you and your teams are going to be moving into Chemnitz to disrupt their command and control, and then kill or capture their central command when the time comes.

"We might have a limited amount of time left in this part of the war, but we're going to take the EDC off the board permanently before we leave."

Chapter 36

It took a few days before we were ready to move. Not that we necessarily needed the time. We were packed up and ready to go, running rehearsals and chalk-talking multiple courses of action in the meantime, within about five or six hours after the brief with Hartrick ended. But we needed those other moving parts to get in place, first.

The data dump from our mission in Marienberg hit the already-shaky *Bundestag* like a bomb. Hoelfer was in hiding. There were arrest warrants out for a dozen members on both sides. Berlin was in chaos.

In the absence of orders, most of the *Bundespolizei* and the *Bundeswehr* had simply gone to ground. That hadn't had the desired effect, because the disorder had only spread from there, with the Fourth Reich staging bombings from Leipzig to Lübeck, jihadis rioting—again—in Mainz, Bremen, Berlin, and Dresden, and the DDSB staging even more bombings, riots, and kidnapping attempts. There was a hostage situation currently ongoing in Hamburg.

The real icing on the cake, though, had been in Bonn.

The attempted capture of three ostensibly neutral *Bundestag* members had gone very badly. One was dead, one other was in the hospital, and the third had been successfully rescued by his security detail. Every politician, technocrat, and

VIP in Germany had a security detail these days. All but three of the attackers had been killed.

Just like in Ukraine, about a year and a half before, the EDC's Special Group had botched a hit and screwed their own plan in the process.

Every hitter's face was all over the news and the internet, complete with identification that confirmed that they'd been EDC Special Group. The same thing had happened in Kiev, and the resulting backlash had delivered Ukraine—even the western half—right into Russian hands. Signed, sealed, and delivered.

The mad scramble after that would have been entertaining as hell if it hadn't been deadly serious. The Usual Suspects claimed the whole thing was fake, only to have even more photographic and video evidence put out by the *Bundespolizei*, of all people, complete with biometric data. There was no getting around it after that, though there were *still* German and French politicians claiming it was a false flag. They were outnumbered, though, and the damage control efforts went into high gear.

A spokesman for OWHSC went public with a denial that the company had had *any* contact with the EDC, backed up by the Chinese consulate, which claimed that the EDC remnant no longer held any official capacity whatsoever, so *of course* the Chinese had not had any meetings or communications with them. It was a hell of a circular argument, but what else could you expect from the ChiComs? Nothing was ever their fault. They never did *anything* wrong.

After all, the attempted takeover of the West Coast ports back home had only been because certain *rogue* PMCs had gotten *over-enthusiastic* and *misinterpreted their orders*.

The EDC hadn't waited around in the hopes that the winds were going to turn back their way. Those elements of the 2nd and 3rd EDC Divisions around Bayreuth abandoned their positions in the wee hours of the morning, retreating back toward Saxony in decent order, calling in drone and rocket strikes on our guys' positions as they went. They fell back in discreet elements, spread out across the countryside to avoid getting knocked out as a whole by any one strike or attack.

They'd learned a lot. And they hadn't exactly been slouches at the warfighting business before.

This was going to get interesting, fast.

***

Now, right at about 0240, we were skimming the treetops in an S70, watching the flashes and flickering flames off to the south as another skirmish between *Verteidiger* advance units and an EDC column raged outside Hohenstein-Ernstthal. Those elements of the *Bundeswehr* that were getting involved were advancing in slow but good order, and the *Verteidiger* and Triarii were engaged in most of the advance work, pushing ahead of the official "front line."

The Army had, finally, officially thrown in with the assault, mainly because they couldn't save any more face if they continued to oppose the push against the EDC. After all, the EDC had been the big bad guys from the get-go, and had been behind the attacks on US FOBs in Slovakia and American forces alongside the Poles afterward. There was still only so far that US government hypocrisy could stretch.

Even so, only about a battalion of US Army troops had been committed, in an "advise and assist" capacity with the *Bundeswehr*. Which meant that most all of the Army assets were far behind us, spread out to the south and west, staying in the rear of the *Bundeswehr* advance.

If things continued to unfold the way they were, the EDC was going to be dug into Chemnitz like a tick by the time the really heavy lead elements got anywhere near the city. This was going to get ugly.

Which was why we were in the air, circling around toward the northeast.

There was still a chance that the bad guys had radar up, though the electronic environment was just about as confused as the political and threat environment on the ground. That was why Jon Breckenridge was flying nap of the earth, and doing a good enough job that he was making me a little queasy. And I don't get motion sickness.

Still, as I watched the trees and the landscape fly past in shades of gray through my PS-31s, no SAMs came arrowing up out of the dark to blow us to pieces, no cannon or C-RAM fire came slithering up to swat us out of the sky. Hopefully, all eyes were on the fight outside Hohenstein-Ernstthal.

After all, while the EDC remnant had largely been left alone for the last several months—yes, that was as baffling to me as it was to all the rest of us—they had lost enough assets to raids, airstrikes, and interdiction that their capabilities had to have been seriously eroded from what they'd been only six months before. Despite indicators that they were still getting official backing under the table, they didn't have the entirety of Western Europe to fund them and funnel them arms and materiel anymore.

"Thirty seconds!" Breckenridge called over the intercom. I gave the crew chief a thumbs up, held up my thumb and forefinger, about half an inch apart, to pass the word to the rest of the team, then unplugged from the bird's intercom. We were going to have to move fast once we hit the LZ. Breckenridge was *not* going to be sticking around long.

Breckenridge flared the bird hard and dropped us to the LZ, a clearing in the forest only about two miles from our objective. The doors were already open, and as soon as the wheels touched, I was throwing myself out onto the ground.

It wasn't so much a meadow as it was a hay field surrounded by trees. Fortunately, the hay had already been cut, and was rolled and stacked along the northern tree line, but the field was still tilled, which made for difficult footing, especially with rucks on.

We were all out in seconds, taking a knee in a wide circle, just beyond the rotors, and it was only a heartbeat later that Breckenridge pulled for the sky again, the rotor wash blasting us with dirt and bits of cut hay, trying to hammer us onto our faces as the ferocious wind battered our backs. But the bird was gone in the next few seconds, nose down and roaring away over the treetops, leaving us in darkness and relative quiet.

I was pretty sure Breckenridge had missed one of those treetops by inches.

Struggling to my feet, weighed down by my pack, which was loaded with explosives, extra ammo, backup comms, sustainment for four days, batteries, and a few other toys that might come in handy, I turned toward the trees. Staying out in the open after a helicopter had just touched down was *not* a good idea.

We'd already done three touch-and-gos on other fields on the way in, and Breckenridge was going to do a few more on the way out, but it's never a good idea to get lazy in the field, especially when all hell's breaking loose only a few miles away.

And it was, too. As we moved into the shadows of the woods, forming a tight perimeter and settling down to do our long security halt, I heard a rolling *boom* from the south, and the echoes of small arms and cannon fire got even more intense. That skirmish was turning into a major battle.

Sucked to be the guys down there, but so much the better for us. It made it far more likely that our insert would go unremarked, and that we'd be able to move in on our objective undetected.

That didn't mean we were going to cut corners. Even as another rippling series of explosions lit up the southern sky and their thunder rumbled across the fields and the city to our south, we stayed in place, silent and still, watching, listening, and waiting for any sign that we'd been compromised and were about to get in a fight.

Ten minutes later, we finally got up and headed out.

***

The movement was only about two and a half miles, and the first mile and a half went relatively quickly. We had woods to cover our movement, except for the one road crossing, and that had gone fast and smooth, since nobody in their right mind was out and about at that hour, not with the blowup happening out by Hohenstein-Ernstthal.

Now, as we got closer to our target and the considerably riskier part of the movement, we slowed down. We had another task to perform before we started hitting targets.

Greg was glad as hell to stop and put his ruck down. He was carrying the majority of these little surprises, and as anyone who's ever rucked in a war zone can tell you, ounces equal pounds and pounds equal pain.

We set up a perimeter, staying well back inside the woods. We were right at the southern end of that particular patch of trees, and while there weren't as many lights on as there might have been six months ago, we could see the little village immediately to our east and south clearly enough through the darkened boles of the trees. We were getting into an increasing risk of compromise, which made this next step all the more vital.

It didn't take long. Greg dropped his ruck as soon as our initial pause to listen and look for threats was over, unbuckled the top flap, and pulled out a little box topped by half a dozen short antennas, immediately closing the ruck back up.

He peered at the little box under his NVGs. As useful as night vision is, focus at short range can get difficult. But Greg was just looking for where exactly the switch was, and once he found it, he turned it on, then set to burying the box under leaves at the base of a tree.

That took seconds, and then he was shouldering into his ruck again and giving me a thumbs up. We were good to go.

Every cell tower within about three quarters of a mile would now be disrupted. Even if we were spotted, and whoever saw us wanted to alert the EDC, they'd have a hard time calling it in. And we had at least twelve more of those little boxes, which we hoped would mess with the EDC's local comms at least enough to disrupt any response to our movement and the subsequent destruction we intended to wreak.

We kept moving.

***

Getting through the village, across the road, and into the strip of trees that paralleled a narrow country road leading toward the southeast was easier than I'd feared. The battle to the south meant that most people were staying indoors and desperately trying not to draw attention to themselves.

From there, we stepped it out, a creek to our left and the fields to our right as we moved in toward our target.

The compound was now clearly visible in the fields to our west, surrounded by concrete T-walls, each corner sporting an armored guard tower, a single coil of concertina wire across the tops of the T-walls. Antennas rose into the sky from somewhere around the center of the compound.

Intel had fingered this spot as the EDC remnant's new field headquarters. This was supposedly where General Metzger was holed up, coordinating his remaining forces. This was our primary objective for the night.

And it looked completely dead.

There were no lights on inside, which should have stood to reason, given the havoc going on to the south. Military bases go to black out conditions in combat situations all the time. We'd all seen it ourselves many times. The darkness alone wasn't a make-or-break indicator.

I couldn't see any movement in the towers, though. Nor could I see anyone at the gate, which was just barely visible from our position.

I frowned as I watched the target. The plan had been to set in with some standoff and call in the Broadswords to bomb the hell out of the place, then move in to conduct the bomb damage assessment and mop up anything that the planes had missed. But I wasn't going to call air on an empty compound.

As I shouldered out of my ruck, I leaned over to Tony. "I'm going to take David and move in to get a better look. Something's weird here."

He just squeezed my shoulder to indicate he'd heard.

There's a reason we called Tony, "Chatty."

343

Leaving our rucks behind, taking only weapons and on-body gear, David and slipped out of the trees, heading for the low line of bushes between fields, overshadowed by a high-tension power transmission tower. I could hear the wires buzzing overhead as we moved, and I briefly thought about going back for some of the explosives we'd brought. Dropping that tower wouldn't knock out the power to all of Chemnitz, I was sure, but it would do a number on a good chunk of the city.

Just putting the lights out would do wonders for our freedom of movement.

Primary objective first.

Skirting the bushes, we worked our way toward the tower and then got down on our bellies and started to crawl.

A lot of modern tactical gear really isn't set up for this kind of movement. Chest rigs are great when you're carrying a ruck or sitting in a vehicle, but there's no way to low-crawl without the mags and pouches digging into the dirt. Helmets aren't usually designed to make it easy to lift your head and look up while you're crawling on your belly, either.

We made it work.

It was a rough hundred yards to the next tower, especially since we needed to cross another dirt road. That took a little more finesse, since we'd been able to use some microterrain as cover as we'd crossed the field, but there was no cover or concealment on the road. Finally, after taking a few moments to watch the towers closely, I decided that a quick dash was probably a better bet than trying to crawl.

Shortly after that, I started to consider just getting up and patrolling toward the place. I'd gotten a couple more looks through the windows of the guard towers, and so far, they looked empty as hell. There weren't even any IR spots sweeping the open ground around it. There were zero signs of life. I couldn't even hear any movement.

Granted, I'd lost some hearing over the years, and the fight down by Hohenstein-Ernstthal was still pretty loud, but I should have been able to hear *something*. Particularly if this was a division-plus-sized headquarters.

I had to make a decision. We were running out of darkness, and if this *wasn't* our target, then we had to know. I got to my feet and started moving in.

David hissed at me, but I was already a good distance toward the gate. He got up, sweeping our six as he did so, and closed in with me. He was a good head shorter than me, so that took a little doing. If he'd been less of a pro in the bush, he'd probably have been cussing me under his breath the whole way.

I'm sure he was doing it silently, anyway.

Reaching the wall, I slowed slightly, but not by much. I was already sure. The fact that I'd gotten to the T-walls without somebody up in one of those guard towers taking me under fire had already told me everything I needed to know. The compound was abandoned.

It might have been a headquarters at some point. But we'd already seen the EDC successfully use decoy installations to get their enemies looking in the wrong direction. My team had spotted one of those decoys not all that far from here the year before, just before the EDC launched its initial assault on Gdansk. Now, it seemed they'd done it again.

Reaching the gate, I peered inside. Sure enough, there were several plywood structures and some tents in there. A couple of vehicles were parked outside, but even in the dark, they didn't look like they'd run in a very long time. That was it. No people, no traffic. The place was a decoy.

Turning back, I circled my hand above my head and pointed back toward the trees. We had to find a place to go to ground for the day.

It was almost a good thing that the *Bundeswehr* were taking their time.

Almost.

Chapter 37

We worked our way north of Draisdorf, hustling across the fields to find ourselves a hide in the thick stand of woods along the west side of the A4. That was somewhat more easily said than done. The Glösaer Wald, like most German woodlands, was almost more park than forest. There wasn't a whole lot of undergrowth or fallen trees. The whole place was a wide-open fairytale playground of birches, firs, and aspens, the leaf-carpeted forest floor all too clear.

I was about to double back and try to find a barn to take over for the day, when David found a spot. It wasn't perfect, but two trees had fallen against some rocks, creating a little debris shelter that we could all probably get into.

It was a tight fit, but we got everyone inside and the opening covered up before it started to get light.

***

Sitting in a hide site all day is not fun. It's bad enough when you have an objective to watch, where there is rarely anything interesting happening. When you're just hiding because you can't afford to be out and about in daylight, with ten dudes crammed under a pair of fallen trees, practically on top of each other, unable to move or talk much for fear of attracting attention, it's particularly miserable.

Pain sets in quick, and all you can do is shift your position by a few inches to relieve it for a few moments, before the next ache announces itself. And with nothing to focus on but security—and that's limited, since you might have to rely almost entirely on sound—time *drags*.

I was able to keep my mind focused on something other than the aches and pains, the needles and branches jabbing their way past my fatigues, and the crushing boredom of sitting in a pile of nine other dudes and their gear and weapons for hours on end. I had to get comms with Hartrick and readjust our plans.

Getting a poncho out of my ruck to hide the glow of my T-phone screen was an exercise and a half. I managed to do it, though, without displacing the entire forest in the process.

Primary target is a no-go. Decoy site. If it was ever a HQ, it's nothing but empty shacks and abandoned T-walls now. Currently set in a lay-up site until dark. Three cell jammers in place. Planning to proceed to secondary targets at nightfall. Any updates?

The T-phones wouldn't be affected by the cell jammers. They were on a completely different network, with completely different frequencies, and those freqs had been picked precisely to keep them out of normal cell traffic. That made them far more useful than regular commercial phones.

Hartrick's reply took about an hour. That told me that there was a lot going on. Ordinarily, he was right on top of things when he had teams out.

Good copy. Drone RF triangulation suggests that new HQ is located in industrial district at north end of Chemnitz. A nav pin dropped, and I followed it to the imagery, which pointed out the business park almost immediately south of us. Hell, if I was reading the map right, we were barely a half mile from what appeared to be the northern defensive line.

The imagery that came down the pipe a moment later was low-angle drone footage, showing that there were indeed what appeared to be defensive positions around the business park, including sandbagged armored vehicles posted up on most of the streets that connected to the park. The angle was low enough that the window was too narrow to see everything, and the resolution was too low to pick out the really nasty surprises that they probably had hidden. Drones were going to be the least of our worries, going into that.

Confirmation of multiple SAM sites in the vicinity and at least one Wiesel 2 has been spotted within the compound. Those will have to be cleared out before you can get air.

I swore silently as I stared at the screen. We didn't have the firepower to clear out multiple SAM sites *and* destroy the minimum of four to six Wiesel 2 armored vehicles that I expected to find in there. This was already putting a monkey wrench in the plan to decapitate what was left of the EDC via airstrike.

Yes, I was well aware that a decapitation strike wouldn't end things outright. Hell, the allies had already tried that in Brussels, and look where we were now. But when you're up against a mostly conventional military unit, it *can* put just enough of a wrench in the gears that you might be able break their formations and scatter them to be dealt with as separate, smaller threats later.

If you keep the pressure up and don't just declare victory as soon as you got the head shed.

We do not have the capability to neutralize that many defensive positions. I had to say it, even though I was pretty sure that Hartrick already knew.

Understood. Of course he did. *GL IX and XI are going to move in from the west to join you. Godine's going to lead a spearhead along the A4 toward the headquarters, with enough* Bundeswehr *and Army support to present a credible threat. The fighting outside Hohenstein-Ernstthal tore open a gap, so it will appear that they are under threat. Hopefully, that will draw enough of their defenses out.*

I could see where this was going. I wasn't entirely opposed, either. It was going to be risky, but it wasn't anything we hadn't done before.

After all, we'd walked right into the middle of an EDC Division headquarters before, thrown frags into their ops center, and waltzed out. And that had been at the height of the EDC's power.

This wasn't necessarily going to be as easy. After all, they were cornered rats, now. But it *was* doable, if we were careful enough.

Of course, if we could even the odds a little beforehand, that would help, too. While the SAM threat might have grounded the Broadswords and Vipers for the moment, they weren't the only tricks up our sleeves. *Drone support?*

We'll have some at your disposal. We'd gotten a new update for the T-phones before insert, which made it possible, if we had the right codes, to control one of the Kestrel drones that we'd gotten in-country after Brussels. While their primary purpose was reconnaissance and surveillance, the Kestrels could also be used as kamikazes, and they carried a charge about the size of claymore mine. It wasn't much, but it could be enough in the right place. *Codes to follow.*

Roger. I looked at the imagery again. This was not going to be easy, but fortunately, we'd had to do some interesting stuff already, so it didn't look like an insurmountable problem. *We'll contact GL IX and XI and start planning.*

Good copy. More intel to follow as we get it.

***

I would have preferred to sit down with Tucker and Burkhart and plan things out in person, with a map in front of us. But that would mean moving openly in broad daylight, less than a mile from our target. Not a great idea.

So, we were going to have to do this over the T-phone mesh network.

It wasn't something I would have considered doing before, as a Triarius. We tended to avoid the technological solution when we could. Some of that was simple prudence. There were a *lot* of security issues with tech, especially the stuff that we could get over the counter, before we had put together our own tech shops. The T-phones had been built from the ground up in the States, and they were even powered by alkaline batteries instead of lithium, because we could build alkaline batteries Stateside, without sourcing rare-earth minerals. They were relatively crude, compared to some of the smart phones out there, but they were secure, and they were ours.

Of course, part of the reason we'd been borderline Luddites was the fact that most of us were older guys, most of us were vets, and we'd seen fancy gadget after fancy gadget shit the bed when it was needed, and we'd also seen the loss of a lot of basic tactical skill thanks to over-reliance on the tech. Granted, I hadn't seen that so much as I'd learned about it after joining.

The tendency of higher headquarters to use that tech to micromanage only made things worse.

So, it was with a certain degree of discomfort that I opened up a group messaging window next to the tac-nav app and started talking with Tucker and Burkhart.

There's a lot that goes into planning an assault, under ordinary circumstances. Coordination, fire support, logistics, intel updates, phase lines, stuff like that. It *can* be done relatively quickly. While I'd been a regular grunt in the Marine Corps, most of the guys who had put the Grex Luporum teams together had been either Recon or Rangers. They'd cut their teeth on the six-hour planning cycle. At least, the Recon guys had. The Maritime Special Purpose Force had set the planning loop in stone back in the '90s.

The MSPF planning cycle had also been built around the creation of a full five-paragraph order and briefing it to higher as well as the team. We just had our teams, and this was a Frag-O. We didn't have to worry about the fancy stuff. Hartrick wouldn't be demanding PowerPoint slides. We'd still have to send him the high points of what we were doing, but we were pretty much out here on our own, and that meant we had as much freedom of action as we needed.

We didn't have all the options that we might have, planning in the rear, though. We had our teams, our organic weapons, what intel updates Hartrick was sending trickling our way, and potentially up to six Kestrel drones. That wasn't much, and there was only so much we could do with them.

Fortunately, we all had some ideas, and we all had the same imagery to work with.

We had about six more hours before sunset. We could chalk talk quite a few courses of action in six hours.

I glanced up as a helicopter went by overhead, but we were under the branches and out of sight. *Ours or theirs?* No way to tell at the moment.

Back to work.

Chapter 38

Godine moved faster than we'd expected. The sun was just about to set when all hell broke loose out to the southwest.

We heard it first. There was still a bit too much light out to risk coming out of our hide yet. And I'd heard movement in the woods several times during the last few hours. But the thunder of 35mm cannon fire and the *thud*s of explosions were hard to miss.

I could only lie there and listen, feeling a growing urgency to get out and get moving, before Godine blew our diversion and our window to get in from the north while the EDC was looking down the A4 closed.

Patience is a necessity in this sort of operational environment. Rushing makes you sloppy, and when you're seriously outnumbered and relying on stealth and surprise, that just gets you and your team killed and your objective unreached. So, we had to stay still, stay quiet, and wait for darkness.

As time went on, however, that fight out there showed no sign of quieting down. I didn't know Godine very well, but it sounded he was hitting the EDC with a *lot*, and he was holding his own. The battle didn't seem to be moving much, though the noise ebbed and flowed, even as a couple of louder, rolling *boom*s that I could *feel* through the ground thundered through the evening.

I started to hope that the longer the fight went on, the more attention—and assets—would be drawn that way. There were no guarantees, of course. The EDC were pros, some of the most dangerous professional soldiers Europe had fielded since the Cold War. It was probably too much to ask that they'd leave their six uncovered just because there was a major fight going on right on their doorstep.

My head came up slightly. Was that a new series of rumbles off to the south? Farther away? I couldn't tell, not over the noise of the fight on the A4. Maybe there was more happening, which would be a good thing for our infiltration and assault, but I didn't know. The Kestrels weren't on station yet, and I didn't have a link to one of the bigger Stalker recon drones.

Hartrick was on it, though. *Lead* Bundeswehr *elements have made contact with two battalions of EDC 4th Division infantry with Puma and Boxer support. Currently engaged around the A72 cloverleaf and the southern edge of Markersdorf. Stalkers are picking up movement to the north and east, as other elements are moving to reinforce and attempt to flank.*

True to his style, Hartrick didn't tell us we needed to go right then. He'd had some particularly bitter curses for the commanders who had pushed tactically unsound actions just because of timing, commanders who had almost always done so from a TOC well removed from the actual situation on the ground. No, Hartrick was going to give us the information and let us make the call.

Another message came up from Tucker. *Go time?*

I peered out through the tree limbs. The sun was setting, though it would still be just above the treetops to the west. The broken clouds, barely visible through tiny gaps in the leaves overhead, were starting to turn pink as the light died. We wouldn't be really into EENT—End of Evening Nautical Twilight—for another twenty or thirty minutes.

It would probably take almost that long to get out of the hide, get prepped, and step off, though. I hastily typed my reply.

Go time.

The smoke was getting thicker as the fighting down the A4 got even more ferocious. Tracers spat lines of fire across the darkening sky, and billows of black smoke rose toward the clouds, lit from below by red flames as vehicles burned, their crews turning to cinders inside their blackened steel coffins.

We'd halted beneath the bridge where the A4 crossed over the Chemnitz River, staging our rucks beneath the highway. They'd only be in the way with what we had to do next. Jim, Steve, and Chris donned assault packs stuffed with explosives, and the rest of us carried the initiation systems. It's generally a bad idea to carry the two of them together. Tony got everyone ready to move while I ducked my head under a poncho to keep the T-phone's screen from giving our position away.

The Kestrel linked easily. It took me a second to orient myself to the view on the screen. There were a lot of lights, a lot of smoke, and a lot of fire and tracers flickering in the video feed. It was chaotic and confusing, but after a moment I spotted the interchange just to our east, and I knew what I was looking at.

The fighting on the A4 was moving our way slowly, but the EDC forces were still holding near the cloverleaf and the Chemnitz Center mall. I could see a couple of our M1200 Armored Knight vehicles burning, along with older Fuchs and Marder armored vehicles that the *Verteidiger* had gotten their hands on, but they were matched by a *lot* of smashed ENOK and Boxer armored vehicles. There were no *Bundeswehr* on this spearhead, so that made target identification easier.

As I steered the Kestrel toward our target, I spotted another column of three Boxers getting on the A4 and heading toward the fight. They made for a tempting target, but I didn't think the Kestrel had a big enough charge to knock out one of those eight-wheeled armored fighting vehicles, and we had more pressing targets and a limited number of drones anyway.

I steered the drone north, trying to avoid the Boxers. It was *possible* that they might spot the drone. It was even more of a risk that any sensors or security on the target site that might be overwatching their movement might pick the drone up.

Banking south again, I started looking for just that. The business park *had* been hardened, but they'd tried to be somewhat sneaky about it. The sandbagged armored vehicles had been covered with tarps meant to mimic the roofs of the buildings nearby, and most of the other defenses were similarly camouflaged. That was a large part of why the place had been missed in favor of the compound to the north. That had been what we were *supposed* to look at.

That meant, however, that they hadn't surrounded the compound with T-walls or HESCO barriers. Which meant there weren't many physical barriers we had to get through. That didn't make me more confident, though. I'd walked into some villages in Africa that hadn't *looked* fortified, but had turned out to be death traps once we got in deep enough. And given what we knew about the EDC, we had to assume that they'd planned this just that way.

There. We didn't have to worry about the Wiesel 2 with the boxy Stinger missile mounts that stood over the bank of the river. It mounted an MG5, but it wasn't currently manned. The boxy guard post next to it, though, was my target.

The Stalker feeds had pinpointed several phone-booth sized boxes that were probably the low-profile security perimeter posts around the outside of the business park. Those were the places we needed to either neutralize or bypass. And bypassing them was going to require some careful movement and misdirection.

The Kestrels weren't intended to blast an opening for us, though. They were just another layer of diversion.

Seconds later, I sent the drone arrowing down toward that guard post, on the south side of the Bornaer Straße bridge.

We were too far away to see the flash. There were too many buildings and trees in the way. But I'd been sure of the hit. I stashed the T-phone, got out from under the poncho, and got ready to move.

We didn't need to cross the river, fortunately. There were still plenty of trees along the bank to give us some concealment. It wasn't going to be easy, but this kind of infil never was.

Spreading out, the team crawled up toward the northern edge of the business park and the parking lot at the tree line, where there were enough civilian vehicles parked to make it look like it was still just a business park. They had a couple of ENOK gun trucks under shelter on that side, but they hadn't cleared fields of fire, which meant they didn't have eyes on much of any of the approaches except the cleared gravel yard that ran under the A4 to the north.

The need for stealth had overridden good tactical practice, and now we were right on their doorstep with a concealed approach practically all the way in. If they'd been really smart, they would have used the helipads and open courtyards to the north of the Zollamt Chemnitz customs office as a killing ground, setting their outer security cordon back by the main buildings. But they were here, at the tree line, instead.

I had to resist the urge to put some charges on the ENOKs and blow them sky high. That would only draw eyes our direction, and we weren't trying to make this a frontal assault. That would be suicide, especially with only thirty of us total. Even more so if anyone on the vehicles saw us while we were doing it.

While Tony took the Bravo element to the east, I led the way south, staying close to the riverbank, crawling along the strip of woods toward the row of warehouses along the west side of the business park. One of the outbuildings went clear to the edge of the trees, and wasn't well lit.

Once again, the need to disguise this place was going to work to our advantage.

It was a grueling crawl, made worse by the fact that I could still hear the fight going on, and hear some of the EDC response to the drone strikes on the south side. In fact, one of those ENOKs we'd seen up at the north end passed us, roaring down the road between us and the helipads, moving to reinforce the south end. They knew they were under attack, and it appeared they had taken the bait and were expecting the assault to hit from the south.

After all, that was where the *Bundeswehr* spearheads were coming from, too. It made sense.

The outbuildings now stood between us and the road, and I came up on a knee, my suppressed OBR across my thigh, checking for shooters. There were cameras mounted on the corner of the building, but there wasn't much we could do about that. If this went according to plan, it wouldn't matter. If it didn't…well, it probably wouldn't matter then, either, because we'd all be dead or captured.

We moved fast, getting up to the wall beneath the cameras, possibly fast enough to avoid being spotted. We didn't pause for long there, either, but kept moving, staying in the shadow of the building.

I did hold up at the corner, peering around it briefly to take in what I could see of the road and the yard beyond. Everything looked pretty empty. The sounds of gunfire from the south explained that. Tucker had split off his Bravo Element to start sniping at the react forces from the trees on the south bank of the river. I hoped they kept moving. If the react forces got across the bridge, those boys could find themselves in a world of hurt.

That was their mission, though. Ours was a little different.

Slipping around the corner, I started jogging out of the little alleyway and toward the old customs office, doing my best to make it look like I was just another one of the react force guys, rushing to secure vital areas as all hell broke loose. I didn't know what the base defense plan looked like, but sometimes, if there's enough chaos and confusion, you can slip in somewhere you're not supposed to be, if you just look like you belong there and you know what you're doing.

Hartrick had taught us that, on more than one occasion.

The street was all but deserted, the only movement I could see down on the south end, as the security force moved in response to the attack from that direction. Somebody had to be panicking, hard. From what we'd seen through the Stalker feeds, almost all of the EDC's regular forces were now committed, trying to hold the southern and western approaches against the *Bundeswehr*, US Army, Triarii, and *Verteidiger*. That had left an estimated company minus on the compound. And now they were under attack when they'd thought that their enemy was still several miles away.

We needed to move fast if we were going to take full advantage of the confusion.

Coming around the corner of the northernmost warehouse, I jogged out across the street, heading for the three-story concrete block of a building with "ZOLLAMT" painted in giant letters on the north wall. Intel didn't know for sure that the EDC's COC was in there, but after a day's Stalker surveillance, it was considered the most likely candidate.

Three stories tall, there would be quite a few rooms to clear. *And* the building was connected to a much larger, sprawling warehouse/business complex. The COC might be in there, too, or if it wasn't, the bad guys might escape into that warren.

Speed, surprise, and violence of action were going to be absolutely paramount.

There was no one outside the building as we jogged up, but the door was locked. That made sense. Good thing we had explosives.

Chris started setting the breach while the rest of us tried to look like we were just another part of the base defense plan.

He was almost done when figures appeared at the corner of the outbuilding behind us. A quick circle of an IR laser on the ground identified the Bravo Element.

I returned the signal, and they moved up to join us, while Chris stepped back from the door, the breaching charge ready to rock.

At almost the same moment, the door opened.

The man inside was in full battle rattle, plate carrier, helmet, and HK433, and he looked around at us for a second before demanding, "Was macht du hier draußen?"

He never got a chance to figure out his mistake. Chris had dived for the dirt as the door swung open, and when the breach charge went off, it shattered the door and threw frag everywhere.

The rest of the team had already backed off, so while I felt a stinging impact in my shoulder, we were far enough away that none of us got much of the frag. Old boy in the doorway, however, took the brunt of the blast in the face.

He fell backward as we scrambled to get in the door before it closed. The breaching charge should have smashed up the latch badly enough that it couldn't close all the way, but that was no guarantee.

David got a boot inside the door, but he needn't have bothered, since the wounded man, who was now screaming his lungs out on the floor, had fallen right in the doorway in his pain-wracked writhing, his legs holding the bent and twisted door open. We went over him, Chris crouching down just long enough to take his HK433 and sling it as we passed, just to be on the safe side.

Others might have just finished him off. I half expected Lucas to suggest it. But nobody went for the "insurance round." The man's face was a mask of blood, and I was pretty sure he'd never see again.

Flowing into the ground floor hallway, we faced the task in front of us.

The place looked like it had been built any time between the '50s and the '70s. Yellow plaster walls, cheap wood doors, and the standard industrial government signs in German tacked on the walls next to each door. There were more signs on the doors themselves, mostly printed on paper and taped up, mostly in English. Weirdly enough, the EDC had gone with English as their official language, even though the UK had not been a part of the Council.

How much they spoke it amongst themselves was anyone's guess, given the fact that the man still moaning in pain behind us had used German. Not that it mattered at this stage.

So far, no one else was in the hallway. The sign on the door in front of me said, "4th Platoon Comms."

If they were going to post where we needed to go on the doors, I wasn't going to look a gift horse in the mouth.

"Incendiaries here. Tony, pick two to hold the door. The rest of us are going to move in and find the COC." Until we had a credible threat, there was no need to clear each and every room, as long as they were all labeled.

If the enemy was going to help us out, I'd take it.

With Reuben and Steve holding the door, the rest of us started moving quickly along the hallway, reading each sign as we went.

The place was quiet, almost as if no one had noticed the explosion at the door. Maybe they hadn't. Maybe things had gone so far sideways for them that they were completely focused on the fight down south.

Maybe we were in the wrong building. We still had to clear it to make sure.

We hit the stairwell a moment later and got our answer.

As I turned the corner, I found myself face to face with two more shooters in EDC fatigues, body armor, and helmets, HK433s in their hands, waiting on the landing. I don't think they'd quite been expecting us. The *bang* of the breaching charge apparently hadn't been quite enough warning. But they were both facing me, both armed, and barely eight feet away.

Chapter 39

I already had my weapon up, the sights barely an inch beneath my eye. While those two were alert, they still had their muzzles pointed at the floor. I snapped the OBR up, putting the offset red dot on the first man and slamming a round into his front plate as I kept pushing across the stairwell, knowing that the moment I stopped, I was dead.

The bullet hit hard, knocking him back in his seat—I'd only noticed after the fact that both of them had been set up on folding chairs on the landing—as I pushed under the next flight, and then David popped the corner and dropped both of them with headshots before I could get a follow up shot in.

Both of them slumped in their chairs, blood dripping from under one man's helmet as his lifeless head hung over to one side. The man on the left actually slid out of his seat to the landing, his rifle clattering slightly on the concrete.

So, they *did* have base defense set in.

Fortunately, the whole thing had happened so fast that there hadn't been time for them to get a radio call out. That I *was* sure of, since I would have heard it, especially since we were running the subsonic 7.62 NATO for this op.

Every advantage we could get. The longer we could go without giving away the game, the better.

David didn't even pause after shooting the two EDC soldiers, but immediately mounted the steps, already twisting around to cover the landing above us as he moved toward the two corpses. I hadn't heard any yelling or radio traffic yet, so presumably there wasn't another pair up there backing these two up, but there was no way we were going to assume that.

Greg was right behind David, since I'd pushed to the far side, and Jordan was covering the door to the warehouse beyond me, so I fell in behind Greg and started up.

The landing was clear, and David was already holding on the flight above, leading to the third floor, as I came to a stop next to him and saw why he'd paused.

The door in front of us was cipher locked. It was still a commercial cipher lock, not one of the advanced ones that requires a keycard and mag-locks the door otherwise. But it looked out of place in that cheap, '70s industrial government building.

We might have the time to search the upper floor and then come back to the cipher lock, particularly if I stationed two of the team to watch this landing. Maybe. Something told me that this door was far enough out of place that it was *probably* our target.

A moment later, the entire building shook as an explosion *boom*ed far too close outside. Either Tucker or Burkhart had gotten busy. That sounded like a munitions dump going up. The building hadn't stopped shuddering when the dead men's radios just below us started going nuts.

There was no more time to dawdle after that. Jordan moved first, yanking his cipher lock breaker—essentially a small but extremely powerful rare earth magnet—out of his pocket and slapping it against the side of the lock housing.

With a *click*, the cipher lock disengaged, and then Greg yanked the door open, backing up to let us flow through. Lucas went first, and I was right at his elbow.

We found ourselves in a hallway, practically identical to the one below, right next to the restrooms. The lights were on, but only about every other one, casting the yellow walls and brown carpet in a dim sort of glow that made the place look that much more run down. Right at the moment, there was no one in the hallway but us. Open doors lined both sides, though the last door at the near end was closed. There was a *lot* of yelling and radio chatter going up and down that hallway, though. We'd hit the jackpot.

I'd half expected them to have gutted the entire floor to turn the whole place into a single, big TOC, but it looked like they'd gone the cheap route. Cables were taped down along the floor, connecting several of the various offices with strands of red and blue. That would make this somewhat easier.

Somewhat. Even as I murmured, "On me," ready to move to that first door with a jumble of blue and red cables disappearing into it, a man came out of one of the far doors on the left, dressed in EDC fatigues and carrying a P99 on his hip.

He saw us. He couldn't exactly help it, as he was hustling down the hallway toward us. But it took a second to register that we weren't friendlies.

I saw his eyes widen as his hand dipped for the pistol at his side, his mouth opening to yell an alarm. I've got to give him credit. He didn't freeze, didn't panic, didn't run. He was ready to fight. He was just way too slow.

My suppressor coughed with the sound of a heavy book being slammed shut, and his head snapped back, red droplets spattering the wall behind him, as his knees buckled and he hit the floor with a muted *thump*.

Then all hell broke loose.

I was already moving to that door I'd previously pinpointed as my target, as a head and an MP7 appeared at the short corner just beyond the restrooms and the utility closet. The guy was hasty, and his first burst punched into the plaster just behind me, scattering fragments and dust on the carpet. He didn't get a second, as Jim and I both fired in the next second, one bullet smashing the PDW's optic and receiver before tearing into the side of his head, the other punching right through his other eye. There hadn't been much of a target there, but aim small, miss small.

Jim stepped out by my shoulder to cover the hallway ahead as Greg gave my tricep a squeeze and called, "With you." I went in the door, following the cables.

I found myself in a small anteroom with an empty desk and a couple of chairs. Another closed door faced us, opposite the main entry. There wasn't a lot of room to maneuver, but Greg and I managed to quickly move to that door, following the cables as they disappeared underneath, getting out of the fatal funnel and still covering down on the opening.

Greg reached around me, grasped the doorknob, and tested it. Locked. Too bad for whoever was in there that it was a simple hollow-core commercial door. I pointed my muzzle at the ceiling, put my back to the wall, knowing that the longer this took the more likely somebody was going to get desperate and start shooting through the door or the wall—though the wall itself should be pretty solid—and donkey-kicked the door just beneath the knob.

If it had been reinforced, this might not work. But my boot hit the door, the jamb cracked with a *bang*, and the door juddered open, Greg already rushing past me, shouldering the door itself aside while I pivoted and dropped my muzzle past his shoulder to follow him in.

Greg had moved too fast for the two men crouched behind the desk, which was covered with maps, laptops, a radio, and a couple of secure phones, but I was right in the fatal funnel when one of them leaned out and dumped a burst of 4.6mm fire at the door. He wasn't in the best position, but he was still accurate enough.

Ever been kicked in the chest by a horse? That's probably about the best way to describe what it felt like to take four 4.6mm bullets to the front plate. It knocked the wind out of me, and I staggered, even as I tried to press forward and kill him before he followed up with that headshot that was going to spatter my brains all over the doorframe.

Greg beat me to it, though. The two of them had taken cover behind the desk, which put them both in a small space with

366

no real escape route. And the one who'd shot me was still pointed at the door.

Survival in a gunfight can sometimes come down to margins of a fraction of a second. And Greg had gone through that door fast enough that he was just that far ahead of them.

He didn't bother with precise aiming. He just put his red dot on the two huddled forms in EDC uniforms and dumped half his mag into them.

Neither one was wearing body armor. The bullets that punched through the first man's body and skull kept going right into the second. They collapsed in a bloody heap on the cheap carpet.

"Clear." Greg turned to me as I staggered into position on the door, still struggling to breathe. "Holy shit, Matt, are you all right?"

"Just took a couple rounds to the plate." It hurt to breathe, I was pretty sure my front plate was cracked—meaning it was now close to useless if I got hit again—and I might have cracked a rib. Greg was checking me for bleeds, anyway.

I shook him off. The best medicine is lead downrange, and if one of us got hit and killed because we had two guns out of the fight before the fight was over, I'd probably wish that I'd bled out. "Let's keep moving." It was getting a little easier to breathe, and I couldn't feel anything wet, aside from the sting where a fragment had hit my lat earlier.

Gunfire continued to hammer through the second floor. The EDC COC staff were putting up a fight. We flowed back out into the hallway, to find most of the team posted up on the short corner just beyond the stairs and the comms room. Tony, Lucas, and Chris had pushed across the hall and into the office behind the utility room, and were now barricaded on that doorway.

Three or four shooters down at the end of the hall were keeping us bottled up. We didn't have time for this.

I wasn't the only one thinking that, either. Even as I came up behind Jim and Jordan, while Greg covered our six,

Tony yanked a frag out of his chest rig, pulled the pin, and let the spoon fly.

He probably held onto that sucker longer than I would have. He counted to three before hooking it around the corner and down toward the end of the hallway as hard as he could.

We all ducked back as the *thud* of the grenade blast shook the building and set my ears ringing. Frag tore into the plaster on the walls and the acoustic tiles overhead, shredded a few of them and added their floating debris to the cloud of dust and smoke billowing down the hall.

There was no hesitation. That frag had just bought us a few seconds, and we needed to use them.

Jim and Tony were already out in the hallway, pushing into the cloud of smoke. The rest of us moved in behind them, though I paused just long enough to tap Greg. "Last man!"

Tony buttonhooked into another of the offices on the right, with Lucas on his heels, and then Jordan and Jim took another door on the left. I'd pushed out into the center of the hall to cover the end of the hall.

I drove past the side rooms as suppressed gunfire in multiple calibers hammered from inside them, the smoke dissipating as it roiled against the ceiling, and then I found myself faced with a T-intersection. Door to my left, door to my right. Both open.

Shading to the right, I covered down on as much of the left side as I could see. A figure in EDC cammies appeared with a pistol and got a double-tap to center mass. He fell on his face just in front of the bathroom door.

Then, having cleared as much of the left as I could, I went right.

Rifle up, searching for targets, I found myself in an actual office. This wasn't like the rest of the COC. There were a couple of maps and a laptop on the desk, but no radios, no watchstanders, none of the other tech that went into a modern tactical operations center. Judging by the EDC flags behind the massive desk and the wide I Love Me wall to the right, I'd just stormed into General Metzger's inner sanctum.

At first, it looked like the room was empty. I could hear more gunfire behind me, as somebody moved into the rooms opposite this one, past the man I'd shot, but I didn't dare turn my back on this place until I'd cleared it. And that desk left a *lot* of dead space behind it.

Chris had come in behind me, and we had just paused, shoulder to shoulder, in our point of domination just inside the door. I could move around the desk to the north, which risked exposure to the windows, or the south, which would put me back in the fatal funnel of the door.

I went with the windows. The EDC shooters were professional enough that I doubted they'd open fire indiscriminately on their own building with their own guys inside.

Angling around the corner of the massive oak desk, I saw a figure down on the floor, dressed in an EDC uniform. As I leveled my rifle at the man with short-cropped, salt-and-pepper hair, he looked up at me, his fingers already intertwined behind his head. His pistol lay six feet away, against the wall, unloaded and with the slide locked back.

General Metzger wasn't going to put up a fight, it seemed.

"Cover me." I waited for Chris to move to join me at the corner of the desk, where he could both shoot Metzger if necessary and hit anyone coming in the door after us, then I slung my rifle to my back and moved to secure Metzger.

He hadn't said a word, and his eyes were cold. He didn't resist as I put a knee in his back and pulled his hands down to flex-cuff them behind him. Only when I hauled him to his feet did he finally speak.

"I have one request." His English was probably better than mine.

"You're not in any position to make demands, General." As much as I doubted how much capturing him was going to put

369

an end to things—he was only one of a *lot* of elements fueling this nightmare—I wasn't inclined to give him an inch. This man had been responsible for prolonging the agony of the war in Europe, and he was going to pay for it.

At least, I hoped he was. Deep down, the cynical part of me sincerely doubted it.

"I have no demands." Despite his position, and the fact that he had been the instrument of a whole hell of a lot of death and destruction in the name of what amounted to a grift by the rich and powerful to get all of Europe under their thumb, Metzger was more aloof and dignified than I'd expect the likes of any of our generals would be under the same circumstances. I could only imagine Sellar's reaction if we'd stormed her office and zip-tied her at gunpoint. "I wish to contact my men and order them to stand down." He seemed to sigh, and a little bit of the stiffness went out of him, his shoulders slumping slightly. "You must understand, they have fought for each other and for the pay we have been able to give them. They saw no other alternative, given the propaganda your country has put out about us."

Chris snorted at that. *Propaganda. Right.* We'd seen the truth of that "propaganda" up close and personal.

"Please. They will stand down if I give the order. No one else needs to die tonight."

I glanced at Chris. This was almost too good to be true. But it did make some sense. The EDC was an ideological project on its face, but it ultimately boiled down to rule by money and raw power. What we'd seen of the EDC's soldiers weren't fanatics. They were professionals, if generally unscrupulous professionals.

And if this worked, we might save the lives of a *lot* of *Bundeswehr* soldiers. The EDC had been created after the *Bundeswehr*'s abysmal showing in Kosovo. Those boys and girls were outclassed in the training and motivation categories.

Chris shrugged. "It's worth a shot." Chris *was* a preacher, of sorts. He wasn't nearly as bloodthirsty as some of my guys.

I try, but even I'm more bloodthirsty than Chris, sometimes.

I propelled Metzger toward the door. "Fine. We'll give it a shot. But we understand enough German that we'll know if you try to pull a fast one, in which case you're a dead man."

I might have been bluffing. He was unarmed and his hands were tied behind his back. But I couldn't let him think he could do whatever he felt like without consequences.

"Coming out!" The gunfire had died down outside. The floor was probably clear.

"Come ahead." Tony had moved to cover the stairs. The rest of the team was barricaded on doorways with most of the rest of the hallway covered. Four men in EDC cammies knelt against the wall, their hands flex-cuffed behind them.

"Is there a radio still working?" There'd been an awful lot of shooting, not to mention that frag. I expected that a lot of the tech in this place wasn't in the greatest of working order anymore.

Tony jerked a thumb toward the left-hand door that I'd bypassed. The corpse of the man I'd shot still lay on its face in the doorway. "That looks like the main ops center. It didn't get too shot up."

I started pushing Metzger toward the door, even as a storm of gunfire erupted below us. Some part of the react force was trying to get past Reuben and Steve and retake the building.

Tony was already moving, grabbing Lucas and Jordan and heading for the stairs. I let them handle it. If Metzger could end this, that had to take priority.

Chris came with us. He'd cover me while I held the handset for Metzger. We were taking no chances.

The urgency of the thing clawed at me while we moved to the bank of radios against one wall, stepping over another body on the way. These guys might not have been fanatics, but they were fighters. They hadn't just given up. And these were the TOC commandos.

More gunfire thundered beneath our feet. I prayed that Reuben and Steve had managed to fall back to the stairs without getting gunned down in the hallway as I picked up the handset. "What's the channel?"

"Seven. That is the Corps net."

I twisted the dial and then held the handset to his head. I looked him in the eye. "Don't make me regret this."

Metzger nodded slightly. I keyed the handset.

"All European Defense Corps units, this is Command Six. I am issuing the order to cease fire, stand down, and surrender to German forces." He sighed, but I kept the radio keyed. He was doing okay, so far. I hoped there weren't programmed duress words in there, though it was a possibility. "We have done all that we were asked. Even when those who sent us to war surrendered or hid, we still fought for each other. But there is nowhere else to go, now. Our allies have abandoned us."

That raised my eyebrow. As if we'd needed any further confirmation that the EDC had been working with the German government and OWHSC.

"Lay down your weapons. It is over. Save your lives. There is nothing else left for us." He stepped back from the handset and I lowered it.

Metzger looked me in the eye, then. I saw a man who still thought he was going to get out of this, but who had just enough integrity to hope that he'd saved some of the men who'd fought for him. He was tired, but there was still a spark of anger there. Anger that he'd been reduced to this, anger that he'd lost. This was a proud man, who still thought he should be in charge. Yet he'd surrendered to save his men.

I could respect that, while still recognizing that this man was my deadly enemy.

Slowly, the sound of gunfire and explosions died down outside. The fight below ended first. Tony's voice came over our net. "Deacon, Chatty. These guys just stopped shooting and tossed their weapons out into the hallway. Whatever you did, it looks like it worked."

"Roger that." Metzger nodded a little then.

It was over.

Epilogue

The mopping up operation took the better part of the next week. Most of the remaining European Defense Corps units might have stopped fighting, but only about a third of their estimated strength actually surrendered. The rest dumped their weapons, vehicles, and gear, and disappeared into the population.

I expected there was going to be one hell of an uptick in organized crime in Germany in the near future.

We turned Metzger over to the *Bundeswehr* commander, an *Oberst* named Zellweger, who looked like he'd last passed a PT test fifteen years before. Metzger couldn't have held the man in much more contempt than we did, after we saw the simpering look on his face and the condescending sneer he couldn't quite disguise when he looked at the Triarii escorting a handcuffed Metzger. He hadn't risked a hair on his own head for this win, but he was going to look down on those who had, just because we were Americans.

I had a bit of a sour taste in my mouth as we headed back to Bayreuth.

None of my teammates had been killed this time. We'd all made it through. Burkhart had lost Charlie, mostly due to dumb luck. When that ammo dump had gone up, a fragment of an artillery shell—no doubt intended for employment as an IED, since the EDC hadn't had any tube artillery left—had come spinning out of the night and taken him in the head.

Godine's force was down by half. The Triarii infantry had taken some losses, too. I hated myself a little bit for thinking it, but I was glad to hear that no more of Bradshaw's guys had gotten hit this time. They'd taken a beating over the last year, especially in the course of the fight for Nitra.

The European Defense Corps was officially no more. Arrests were happening in Berlin, as several of the German politicians who had lied and facilitated the attacks and crimes intended to get the EDC back into control of Germany's security apparatus were rounded up.

Somehow, I expected they were only going to prison because they had been dumb enough to make a play and get caught. Just like Metzger, they were now the sacrificial lambs.

My suspicions were backed up by the sheer number of OWHSC vehicles we saw on the way back to Bayreuth. More and more of their contractors, it appeared, were Germans, but the officers were all still Chinese. I didn't doubt that this was far from over. It had just entered a new phase.

We wouldn't necessarily see that next phase through, though.

***

About a week later, in our team room in Bayreuth, we were getting ready for another meeting with our *Verteidiger* counterparts when Hartrick walked in, his scowl even blacker than normal.

"Pack it up, gents." He looked around at the maps, the comms, and the packets of intel printouts and other planning materials, not to mention the weapons and gear that we always kept close at hand. "We have to be across the border and back in Poland within the next twelve hours."

"What?" Burkhart looked like he wasn't sure he'd just heard what he'd just heard.

"What happened?" I'd seen that look before.

Hartrick looked like he was grinding the words out through his teeth. "Our Letter of Marque and Reprisal was specifically targeting the EDC."

"Oh, fuck." Burkhart had just figured it out. Tucker looked like he was ready to flip tables.

"Now that the EDC is no more, Sellar has decided there is no longer any reason for Triarii presence in Germany, or cooperation between us and the US Army. And I've already heard whispers that OWHSC might move on us soon, based on 'terrorism' charges stemming from the action in the Pacific." He clapped his hands loudly. "So get ready to roll, gents. Germany just turned entirely non-permissive.

"We won the battle, but we're still losing the war."

***

If OWHSC was coming for us in Bavaria, they were too slow. The Bavarians didn't want them in their territory, anyway, and the *Verteidiger in Bayern* made life a living hell for any of them who tried to move in and take over policing. Local *Polizei* units were not exactly cooperative, and by the time any of them had made it to Bayreuth, we were long gone.

The Poles weren't unhappy to have us back. We moved right back into our previous headquarters in the old Fort Grodzisco without much trouble or fanfare.

Gutierrez had a full brief for us as soon as we got settled in. Things weren't looking all that great.

The Russians had slowed their push in the east, though they now controlled a strip of territory nearly twenty miles deep, running from Belarus to Kaliningrad. The Poles wanted it back, but the Russkies weren't likely to give it up without a fight. We might have a task there.

The former EDC countries weren't in good shape. Gutierrez had been accompanied by a former *Bundestag* member named Wiegand. He was relatively young, probably not even forty yet, but the look in his eye had been that of a much, much older man.

"Almost the entirety of German security and control of infrastructure has now been turned over to OWHSC. And I do not need to tell you who they answer to." His shoulders were slumped in defeat.

No, he didn't.

We'd beaten the EDC on the battlefield, but a whole lot of the same people who'd been behind it were still there, behind the scenes, pulling things their way. And our own government was helping them out.

Heading home and putting all of our efforts into strengthening the Fortress Doctrine states was starting to look better and better.

***

Being back in Poland wasn't all darkness and gloom, though. While the Russians remained a formidable threat in the east, and Germany was now effectively every bit as hostile as it had been a year ago, without the EDC, the Germans simply didn't have the combat power to push Poland the way they had before. We—and I mean both Triarii and Poles—had some breathing room, at least for the moment.

I had some time for personal matters, too. Klara and I powered through marriage prep, and about a month after the fight in Chemnitz, we got married in St. Barbara's. We even had three days to ourselves for our honeymoon.

It was the last note of happiness I was going to see for a while.

***

"Pack it up." Hartrick didn't sound like his ordinary self. There was a note of dread in his voice that I'd never heard before.

"What's up?" I looked up from the latest intel dump. "Are the Russians moving again?"

"No. Worse." He actually looked *pale*.

"Brian. What the fuck is going on?"

377

He took a deep breath. "A nuclear weapon just detonated in or over downtown Taipei. Option Zulu on the PRC has just been called in.

"We're heading for Japan."

THE STORY CONCLUDES IN:

OPTION ZULU

MAELSTROM RISING BOOK 9

From the Author

I hope you've enjoyed this eighth chapter in the *Maelstrom Rising* series. While *Thunder Run* depicted the triumph of maneuver warfare, this one dealt with something that many of us who are veterans of the GWOT have faced for many years. A war is over when both sides agree that it's over, and cutting the head off the snake doesn't always necessarily kill it.

Sometimes that snake turns out to be a hydra.

The next book, *Option Zulu*, will bring all the threads together. If you've been paying attention, you might know where this is going. To keep up-to-date, I hope that you'll sign up for my newsletter—you get a free American Praetorians novella, *Drawing the Line*, when you do.

If you've enjoyed this novel, I hope that you'll go leave a review on Amazon or Goodreads. Reviews matter a lot to independent authors, so I appreciate the effort.

If you'd like to connect, I have a Facebook page at https://www.facebook.com/PeteNealenAuthor. For those who have departed FB, I'm also on MeWe at www.mewe.com/i/peternealen. You can also contact me, or just read my musings and occasional samples on the blog, at https://www.americanpraetorians.com. I look forward to hearing from you.

Also By Peter Nealen

The Maelstrom Rising Series
Escalation
Holding Action
Crimson Star
Strategic Assets
Fortress Doctrine
Thunder Run
Area Denial
Power Vacuum
Option Zulu
SPOTREPS – A Maelstrom Rising Anthology

The Brannigan's Blackhearts Universe
Kill Yuan
The Colonel Has A Plan (Online Short)
Fury in the Gulf
Burmese Crossfire
Enemy Unidentified
Frozen Conflict
High Desert Vengeance
Doctors of Death
Kill or Capture
Enemy of My Enemy
War to the Knife
Blood Debt

The Unity Wars Series
The Fall of Valdek
The Defense of Provenia
The Alliance Rises

The Lost Series
Ice and Monsters
Shadows and Crows

The American Praetorians Series

The Jed Horn Supernatural Thriller Series

CPSIA information can be obtained
at www.ICGtesting.com
Printed in the USA
LVHW010806140222
711064LV00004B/242